W.J. Burley lived near Newquay in Cornwall, and was a schoolmaster until he retired to concentrate on his writing. He died in 2002.

By W.J. Burley

A Taste of Power
Wycliffe and the Three-Toed Pussy
Death in Willow Pattern
Wycliffe and How to Kill a Cat
Wycliffe and the Guilt Edged Alibi
Death in a Salubrious Place
Death in Stanley Street
Wycliffe and the Pea-Green Boat
Wycliffe and the Schoolgirls
The Schoolmaster
Wycliffe and the Scapegoat
The Sixth Day
Charles and Elizabeth
Wycliffe in Paul's Court
The House of Care
Wycliffe's Wild Goose Chase
Wycliffe and the Beales
Wycliffe and the Four Jacks
Wycliffe and the Quiet Virgin
Wycliffe and the Winsor Blue
Wycliffe and the Tangled Web
Wycliffe and the Cycle of Death
Wycliffe and the Dead Flautist
Wycliffe and the Last Rites
Wycliffe and the Dunes Mystery
Wycliffe and the Redhead
Wycliffe and the House of Fear
Wycliffe and the Guild of Nine

Wycliffe and the
Last Rites

Wycliffe and the
House of Fear

W.J.BURLEY

Wycliffe and the Last Rites
First published in Great Britain by Victor Gollancz Ltd in 1992

Wycliffe and the House of Fear
First published in Great Britain by Victor Gollancz Ltd in 1995

This omnibus edition published in 2008
by Orion Books Ltd
Orion House, 5 Upper St Martin's Lane
London WC2H 9EA

A CIP catalogue record for this book is available from the British Library.

ISBN 978-1-4072-1711-6

Printed and bound in Great Britain by
Clays Ltd, St Ives plc

The Orion Publishing Group's policy is to use papers that are natural,
renewable and recyclable products and made from wood grown in sustainable
forests. The logging and manufacturing processes are expected to conform to
the environmental regulations of the country of origin.

www.orionbooks.co.uk

Wycliffe and the Last Rites

W.J.BURLEY

Chapter One

Wednesday

He came in from the bathroom, still naked, and reached for his briefs. Katherine, sitting up in bed, watched him dress. Geach was a big man – not tall, but powerfully built, rough hewn; his body surfaces seemed to consist of intersecting planes rather than curves. The tangle of hair on his chest was turning grey but his head was thatched with dark, tight little curls. He put on his shirt, socks and trousers and came to bend over her.

'All right?'

'I expect I'll live.'

He kissed her on the lips, then on her breasts. His features, like the rest of him, were on a generous scale; the skin of his face, free from any blemish, was coarse, lightly pitted like the skin of an orange. He was smiling, a little smile of self-content.

He went to the door, paused, and looked back. 'See you later!'

'I'll be down.'

'Don't bother; have a lie-in. Elsa will look after me.'

It was as though he had patted her on the head and said, 'You've done your bit.'

She remained in bed, motionless, staring at nothing. After sex with Abe she seemed to exist only by proxy, a reflection in a mirror. She was nothing, she felt nothing, she had nothing – not even a body that was hers.

Of course this was nonsense! Abe was no monster, and she was better off than most; she had a daughter; she had a home – an old house which she loved; a car for her own use . . . money, which she could spend without question . . . True, these things were contingent upon her being and remaining Mrs Abe Geach, but hadn't she settled for that?

'You don't know when you're well off!' Others would have told her, but there was no need. She told herself. But that was logic and she had never found much consolation in logic.

From the bed she could see herself in the mirror of the dressing table: one of Abe's contrived titillations. I am thirty-nine. Do I look it? Her hair was dark and lustrous; no sign of grey yet. Later she would go through that iron-grey phase which is supposed to make men look distinguished but delivers women to the sorcery of hairdressers. Well, she would have none of that. If it turned out that there was life after the menopause she had no intention of making herself ridiculous, fighting a rearguard action.

The pallor of her skin was accentuated by her dark hair and eyes. Johnny Glynn had said once, 'Your eyes are like minefields, Kathy – still, yet menacing.' Vintage Johnny Glynn, master of the slick phrase and the slicker lay. God! I mustn't start thinking of all that.

Watching herself in the mirror she ran her hands slowly through her hair, lifting its weight from her head and letting it slip back through her fingers.

Her twin sister, Jessica, had gone about things differently . . . She wondered about Jessica. Was she happier? Silly question. Was she content rather than resigned? Against all the odds it might be so. Two women, a man, and a teenage boy, trying to scrape a living out of a few acres with little real know-how between them.

In a sudden burst of restlessness Katherine got out of

bed and drew back the curtains. There it was, the scene that had become part of her: the lawn and the shrubbery, then the low, crumbling bank, a stretch of muddy shingle, and the creek. There were primroses in the hedge which separated them from the churchyard. Across the creek the little boatyard, with its shed and thicket of masts, stood out against the rising ground of Trennick Wood. The rusty iron roof of the old shed glowed red and orange in the sunlight. It was half-tide and gulls padded about the muddy margins. Perhaps it was the house she had married.

She put on her dressing gown and slippers, spent a few minutes in the bathroom, then went downstairs to the kitchen. They always breakfasted in the big, old-fashioned kitchen. Abe was finishing his second egg and there was a yellow smear on his chin. He had eaten two soft-boiled eggs for breakfast every morning since the age of thirteen, when his mother decided that male adolescents required special nourishment. Now, at forty-one, regardless of hazards from cholesterol and listeria, he clung to his eggs as an addict to his regular shot.

The wall clock showed ten minutes to eight. Kathy said, 'Julie not down yet? She'll be late for school.'

Abe looked at her in mild reproach. 'It's Wednesday; from today she's off school for the Easter holidays. You did know, Kath.'

Black mark. She should have remembered.

Elsa came in from the yard. 'Oh, you're down, Kathy. There's plenty of coffee in the pot.'

Elsa's position in the family was ambivalent, a sort of cousin who was also a sort of housekeeper. She was three years younger than Kathy, unmarried and childless, yet, in Kathy's eyes, she was the real woman of the two. One could hardly look at Elsa without being conscious of her plump body, her pink skin, and her freckled fairness. Did

7

Abe ever . . . ? Very likely; but Kathy had decided early on that there would be no friction on that score.

Kathy poured herself a cup of coffee; no sugar, but a dash of semi-skimmed.

Abe finished his second egg, drank his coffee, and said, 'I shall be in the site office for most of the day if you want me . . .'

Abe looked what he was, a prosperous builder, and he followed tradition in carrying on the family firm.

'Try to keep Julie away from the farm, and the Vinter boy.'

Kathy was irritated. 'I can't choose her friends for her and neither can you; she's seventeen.'

'You could try.'

As he spoke, Julie came in wearing a jade-green dressing gown over her nightdress. A slim, dark girl, her hair was tousled, her eyes puffed with sleep. She yawned, bracing her shoulders and stretching her arms. 'Any coffee going?'

Abe, briefcase in hand, was ready to go. 'Ah, there you are!' He pecked at his daughter's cheek, ruffled her hair, and said, 'Bye, kid! Have a good day, and keep away from young Vinter, he's a poof!'

'He's not a poof, Dad.' Julie's protest was mild.

'Well, if he isn't he's in training to be one.'

Julie produced a handkerchief from the pocket of her dressing gown, moistened it with her saliva, and wiped the egg from his chin. 'You are a mucky pup, Dad!'

She went with him out into the yard, to his car.

Elsa said, 'They make a good pair. She knows how to handle him, which is more than can be said for her mother. I bet she'll come back with a nice crisp tenner tucked in the pocket of her dressing gown.'

They heard Abe's car drive out of the yard and a moment or two later Julie came in with a handful of mail which she dropped beside Kathy's plate.

8

'I met the postman.' She stood, hesitating, then, 'I think I'll go up and get dressed. Then I'm going out – is that all right?'

'It's your holiday.'

The two women sat on, nibbling cold toast and sipping coffee. Elsa lit a cigarette.

Although Abe built houses with designer-everything, fingertip central heating and a proliferation of elegant plumbing, Trigg House itself was, in all these things, at least forty years behind the times. But that was how Kathy liked it. Above all there was this archaic kitchen with a great square table in the middle, reminding her of the farmhouse in which she had been brought up.

Julie came down dressed for the street: jeans and a T-shirt with an unreadable slogan. 'All right; I'm off. Don't worry if I'm not in for lunch . . . Bye!' She was gone.

Katherine's eyes followed her daughter. 'She's changed. I seem to be losing contact and it worries me sometimes.'

'She's growing up, Kath; she's a young woman.'

Katherine reached for another piece of toast, changed her mind, and pushed her plate away. 'Abe is right about young Vinter; I wish she would find somebody else.'

Elsa mumbled with her mouth full, 'You don't know when you're well off. At least he's safe. She's not going to turn up pregnant one day – not by him, anyway.'

Elsa cleared her mouth and reached for her coffee cup. 'By the way, I suppose you know that Jessica is working part-time for Arnold Paul?'

Kathy paused, her cup to her lips. 'What on earth is she doing there?'

'Housework, I suppose – what else? I gather things have got too much for the old housekeeper biddy now that Arnold has his brother there. I heard it in the shop yesterday but I thought you must know.'

Kathy put down her cup. 'I can't believe it!'

'I don't know why not; she's done the church cleaning for years.'

Kathy was tense. 'That's different. I wish to God she'd agree to sell the bloody farm. Abe's syndicate would pay through the nose and it's not as though she'll ever make a decent living from it.'

Elsa blew out a cloud of pale-grey smoke. 'Not with the hangers-on she's got there now, she won't. At least Jess is willing to work, I'll say that for her; I don't know how she fits it all in.'

Kathy was on her feet. 'I'm going upstairs to change. I shall have a word with Jessica.'

A quarter of an hour later Kathy came down, transformed; she wore a fine checked skirt, a silk blouse, suede jacket and shoes, all in matching shades of grey, set off by a jade necklace and earrings mounted in gold – Abe's Christmas present.

Elsa was appraising. 'You're taking the car?'

'No.'

'You're never walking along the river bank in those shoes?'

'I'm going round by the road.'

'I see. We want to bolster our courage. Anyway, don't blow your top when you get there; it won't do any good.'

The village square, junction of three roads, merged with the foreshore where boats were drawn up on the shingle. At spring tides, when the wind was right, there was sometimes flooding and none of the houses around the square was without its stock of sandbags, ready filled. Across from Trigg, the garage with its petrol pumps adjoined the boatyard, while pub, post office, general store, café and a few houses completed the square.

'Morning, Kathy!' Tommy Noall, at the garage, his head under the bonnet of a car. They had been at the

10

village school together until the age of eleven. Henry Clemens, who kept the general store and post office, was washing down his shop front. 'Nice morning, Mrs Geach! Makes you think the good Lord has given us spring at last.' Henry was the churchwarden.

Kathy usually enjoyed walking through her village, knowing, and being known. She was still one of the Dobell twins but she was also Mrs Abe Geach, wife of the contractor who built quality housing, government offices and schools. At such moments it pleased her to be both, but the news about Jessica had put her off-balance.

She turned up Church Lane, which followed the Trigg boundary until it reached the churchyard. The trees, their leaves breaking out of bud, were misty green against the sky and, opposite the church, in the gardens of detached villas, there were camellias and magnolias in flower.

Another two or three hundred yards, and she was in open country, out of sight of the village. Only the church tower, with its four pinnacles and flag-pole, rose out of green fields to mark where the village lay. A ramshackle gate labelled 'Minions' gave on to a rutted track which ran through an area of scrub where tethered goats were browsing. The track dropped steeply between high hedges, to end at another gate and the farmyard where hens strutted and pecked over the cobbles. A house backed on the yard and there were outbuildings on two other sides. As always, the yard, the hens and the smells brought back her childhood with disturbing poignancy. Nothing had changed.

Minions had belonged to her parents, both killed in a coach crash in the early years of her marriage. Jessica had insisted on keeping the farm going, first with the help of paid labour, later with the doubtful assistance of a succession of lame ducks needing a roof over their heads. The latest and, so far, the most enduring of these, was a

11

family of three: Laurence and Stephanie Vinter, and their son, Giles.

As Kathy unhooked the gate Jessica's collie came bounding out of the house, barking, but changed to tail wagging when he saw Kathy. The door led directly into the kitchen and Kathy went in without knocking. The boy, Giles, was seated at the kitchen table, his school books spread out in front of him. He was the same age as Julie and they were in the same form at school. Slim, and small and fair, with the delicate features and colouring of a girl, his eyes were an intense blue, accentuated by the powerful lenses of his spectacles.

'Oh, Mrs Geach!' His manner was precise and distant.

'Working in the holidays, Giles? I wish Julie would. What subjects are you doing for your A-levels? Physics, chemistry and biology – the same as Julie, isn't it?'

'I'm doing mathematics instead of biology.' Giles glanced down at his books and back again. 'You want to see Miss Jessica? I think she's mucking out the goat house.' The blue eyes blinked at her and she realized that she was being dismissed.

She found Jessica manhandling a bale of bedding-straw into the goat house.

'Kathy! Let me dump this and we'll go indoors.'

They were twins, but no more alike than most sisters. Jessica was more sturdily built; her hair and eyes were less dark, her skin was lightly tanned, and her expression more open. She had a ready smile. In her denim blouse and jeans, her hair caught back with a clip, she seemed to typify the modern working woman in a way that Kathy had no desire to emulate but envied all the same.

The bale disposed of, Jessica came out of the goat house brushing herself off. She surveyed her sister. 'You look like an advertisement in *Country Life*, Kath! Those shoes haven't been along the river bank. Where's the car?'

'I walked round by the road.' Katherine was terse.

'Oh, I see; giving the peasants a treat.'

In the kitchen Jessica spoke sharply to the boy, 'There's straw in the goat house that needs spreading, Giles. Don't use it all; there's enough for tomorrow as well.'

Giles got up without a word and went out into the yard. 'That boy would never get off his backside unless I chivvied him . . . Gets it from his mother. Come into the sitting room . . .'

Kathy said, 'I thought Julie might have been here.'

'She was, but it seems his highness wasn't in the mood for dalliance. They chatted for a few minutes then she was dismissed. Everybody to their taste but I don't know what she sees in him.'

The house fronted on an inlet from the river overhung by trees, and the tiny window of the sitting room let in a dim and sombre light. Little had changed here over the years except by wear and tear; the black leather sofa, the armchairs, his and hers, the coloured prints in gilded frames, the upright piano against one wall – all had been there when the girls were born in the room above. So had the roll-topped desk and the wooden filing box which successive Dobells had used for their farm records and accounts.

'Take the weight off your feet, Kath. Feel like a sherry? To be precise, do you feel like risking my fortified wine which I now buy in five-litre plastic containers? I serve it from a sherry bottle but it might taste better from an old boot.'

The two sisters sat, side-by-side on the sofa, sipping fortified wine. 'Where are Laurence and Stephanie?'

'Laurence is out digging potatoes. As for Stephanie, it's the first day of the curse so she won't put in an appearance till mid-morning.' Jessica sighed. 'And lately she's taken to having afternoons off. Where she goes, God knows, but

13

I notice she's having more baths than she used to.'

'But if they're no use, why do you put up with them, Jess?'

Jessica poured herself a little more wine. 'Top you up? . . . No? . . . Oh, I don't know! I can't get anybody else and though Laurence isn't God's gift as a farm labourer, he works hard at whatever you tell him to do.' Jessica grinned. 'And he's got other attributes – of a sort.'

Katherine looked at her sister. 'I hope you don't mean what I think you do.'

Jessica's laugh had in it a strain of bitterness. 'You're an old prude, Kath! Sometimes I think you've turned being a woman into a career – like you took a course or read it in a textbook.'

Katherine was piqued. 'And what have you done?'

Jessica emptied her glass. 'Me? I don't know – what comes naturally, I suppose.' She was suddenly serious. 'If I've done nothing else I've plucked the feathers from a few cockerels and put a stop to their crowing – and I'm not dependent on any one of the bastards.'

'And I am? You might as well say it. But don't let's get into an argument. If you agreed, we could sell this place to the syndicate. You'd get a good price for your share and you could insist on a stake in whatever they made of it. You'd be well off, and still your own woman.'

But Jessica was indignant. 'Not on your life! If you've come here to push Abe's barrow, you're wasting your precious time. If I give up here it won't be for what I can get. Billy Eva would like to add it to his holding; then, at least, it would stay as a farm. As it is, I sell all I can grow, there's a steady demand for the goats' milk, and Billy is going to rent Five-acre for his store cattle . . . All that, with what I get from the church, and now from Arnold Paul—'

'That's another thing, Jess – I've just heard about it.'

14

'So? It's only two afternoons a week and the money's good.'

'But it's charring, Jess!'

'So what? I've been keeping the church clean for years.'

'But that's different . . .'

'Why? Because people might be daft enough to think I do it for love? Really, Kath!'

As always, in her encounters with her sister, Kathy was outmanoeuvred and made to feel naive and snobbish. It was she who changed the subject.

'I was saying to Elsa, I'm a bit worried about Julie; she's been seeing a lot of Giles lately.'

Jessica's reaction was similar to Elsa's. 'At least she's safe with him – no drugs, and not much sex either if I'm any judge.'

'What do they do when she comes here?'

'Sometimes they go out bird-watching but mostly they stay up in his room. For God's sake, Kath; they're seventeen! All the same, I wouldn't be surprised if they spend the time doing their homework.'

Jessica broke off and became solemn again. It was as though she had waited for a chance to turn the conversation her way. 'Kath, did you see in the local rag that Mrs Ruse – Derek's mother, is dead?'

'Ruse? The mother of the boy killed in the hit-and-run – yes, I saw an account of her funeral. What about it?'

'She was only fifty-five and they say she never got over Derek's death. After sixteen years she was still grieving . . .'

'So?'

Jessica was silent for a while, then she said, 'I was going around with Johnny Glynn at that time.'

'Everybody thought you would marry him – me included.'

'It was all fixed, and it was what happened that night which put an end to it.'

'But Johnny satisfied the police he wasn't involved. Of course, not everybody believed him.'

'I know they didn't, but he was telling the truth.'

Katherine looked at her sister. 'If Johnny wasn't there, who was?' Her manner became more intense. 'Jess, were you with him, whoever he was?'

Jessica made a sudden movement. 'I'm being morbid, Kath. Forget it! Let's talk about you. I hear Abe's got the contract for the new school up Liskeard way . . . I hope he's going to live long enough to enjoy it all – not like his father.'

Good Friday

'Almighty God, we beseech thee graciously to behold this thy family, for which our Lord Jesus Christ was contented to be betrayed . . .'

The Reverend Michael Jordan, Vicar of Moresk, in his high-pitched, boyish voice, recited the first collect for the day to a congregation that filled his church.

By some quirk of tradition the Good Friday morning service had acquired a significance for many villagers who were unlikely to be seen in church at any other time. The occasion was signalled, shortly before half past nine in the morning, by a stroke on the tenor bell to be repeated at one-minute intervals until the service began at ten. Each stroke marked a year in the thirty-three years of Christ's life on earth.

The morning was fine and sunlight streamed through a south window to fall dramatically on a larger-than-life statue of the Christ, set at the top of the chancel steps.

It was a family occasion; the Geaches were there,

16

occupying a pew halfway down the central aisle. Abe, out of his element, was flushed, as though he had fortified himself beforehand. He fumbled the responses and was unsure when to sit or stand. Even Jessica, who rarely attended a service, sat next to Julie on the inside. Kathy, in a hat that she kept for funerals, looked about her and realized that hers was one of less than a score of hats in the congregation, and those were largely confined to women whom she regarded as church hens.

'We will sing the hymn, "O sacred head, sore wounded, Defiled and put to scorn . . ." Verses three and four will be taken as a solo.'

Arnold Paul, at the organ, reached his high point in a composition of his own: 'Chorale Prelude by Arnold Paul, in the manner of J. S. Bach'; a lengthy introduction to the hymn based on Hassler's melody.

Kathy was watching her daughter who seemed to have eyes only for Giles Vinter. The boy sat with his parents in the pew in front; he faced straight ahead, as though unaware of anyone else in the church, and followed precisely the requirements of the ritual. She asked herself again, what did Julie see in him? Surely it was natural for a young girl to be attracted by masculinity? But there was nothing macho about Giles. On the contrary he was half a head shorter than Julie, his appearance was effeminate, and his short-sightedness caused him to peer like a cartoon professor. Of course he had more than his ration of brains, but when had brains stirred the hormones of youth?

Paul's prelude came to an end and a chord brought the congregation to its feet. For no obvious reason Kathy felt vaguely depressed and apprehensive. Her sensations were similar to those she often experienced at the approach of a thunderstorm, when the atmosphere itself seemed permeated by some undefined menace. She wondered if she might be on the brink of an illness.

17

To her surprise the solo was taken by Stephanie Vinter from her place in the congregation. Kathy was impressed. Stephanie's unaccompanied soprano had a bell-like sweetness, a magical quality which suspended normality and, when the organ brought in the congregation for the final verse, it was as though everyone drew breath again. During her solo Giles had watched his mother with total absorption and seemed to live with her through every moment of the experience.

The congregation knelt. 'Almighty and everlasting God, by whose Spirit the whole body of the Church is governed . . .'

Laurence Vinter, his head bowed low, studied the grain of the bookrest. For weeks he had lived with a growing sense of unease and tension. He could point to no significant change in the daily life of the farm, nor in their relationships, yet he was conscious of an impending crisis.

As each day passed it seemed that their words became overloaded with meaning, that their simplest actions might be fraught with sinister implications. At times he felt that he was picking his way along a crumbling traverse, and his concern was not lessened by his inability to decide whether the crisis was real or, as he often suspected, a creation of his own disordered mind.

Another hymn, and towards the end of it the vicar ascended the steps to his pulpit.

'My text is taken from Isaiah, chapter 53, verse 3: "He was despised, and we esteemed him not."'

On those occasions, as now, when Jessica attended a service, she felt a little like an actor on the wrong side of the footlights, detached and inclined to be cynical. It was she who had dusted the altar, polished the lectern, swept and hoovered, cleaned and tidied. It was she who, when the Eucharist was to be celebrated, prepared the elements. But, by one of those curious psychological quirks, she retained an almost superstitious regard for the statue of Christ which dominated the approach to the chancel. The statue was a loose 3-D rendering of Holman Hunt's excruciating painting, *The Light of the World*, differing mainly in that the statue held the lantern aloft.

Jessica always dusted the Christ figure with a feather duster, never allowing contact with her hands or her clothing and, in doing so, she avoided the eyes.

Now, while the vicar developed his theme, she found herself gazing at those eyes, though she could not see them distinctly, and she was disturbed; they seemed to be accusing, and she was filled with a sense of guilt.

'Now to God the Father, God the Son, and God the Holy Ghost . . .' A final hymn, the benediction, and the service drew to its end. With the church clock striking eleven the congregation trooped out into the sunshine.

Kathy said: 'Will you be in for lunch?'

Abe glanced at his watch. 'Christ, no! I've got a site meeting in St Austell and I'm late already.'

'It's Good Friday.'

'So what? It's easier without a lot of blokes around pretending to work. I'll collect the car and be off.'

Julie was hanging back. 'Aren't you coming home, kid?'

'I want a word with Giles.'

Geach muttered, 'That young wimp! She's hooked on him.'

Kathy turned to her sister. 'Why not stay and take pot luck with us, Jess?'

Jessica looked across to the porch where Stephanie Vinter was the centre of a congratulatory group, while her husband and son waited on the fringe. 'Thanks all the same, Kath, but it doesn't look as though anybody else intends to do any work this morning, so I'd better.'

She set off up Church Lane.

The Vinters got away at last and started walking up the

hill. Giles saw Julie waiting and joined her; his parents walked on.

Stephanie said, 'Are you ill, Laurence?'

'No.'

'There's something the matter with you.'

'Doesn't that apply to each of us?'

'Don't fence. You're cutting yourself off. Sometimes I wonder if . . .'

'What do you wonder?'

'Nothing. Here's Giles. What did Julie want?'

'She wanted me to go out with her this afternoon.'

'Are you going?'

'No.'

'What's the matter between you and Julie?'

'Nothing.'

Easter Saturday

On Saturday evening Jessica went as usual to do one of her stints at the church. She entered by the south door in her stockinged feet, having kicked off her half-wellies in the porch. No point in getting river mud on the nice carpet; she would only have to clean it up. It was overcast and raining and, though it was light enough outside, inside the light was dim; the lantern held aloft by the Christ figure glowed like a maleficent eye and she looked away. The altar and chancel were barely visible in the gloom.

Following an unconscious routine, she dropped the padlock on a little table next to the visitors' book and walked down the carpeted aisle. The chancel tiles were cold to her feet. After the severities of Lent there were flowers everywhere – lilies and tulips, ready for Sunday – Easter Sunday. The flower ladies had been and there would be a mess in the vestry toilet where they got their water.

Cleaning up messes was work for the peasantry.

She was on her way to the vestry; the self-closing door from the chancel was wedged open – the ladies again. She tried to shut it but it wouldn't budge. In the vestry she removed her mac and hood, and put on an old pair of slippers which she kept in a cupboard with her cleaning gear.

First things first: the Lenten hangings which had been in place through Passion-tide had been taken down but they must be brushed and folded away with their mothballs.

Jessica worked with seemingly effortless ease, but her thoughts were elsewhere; she was thinking of her sister. Kathy has everything a woman could want; she doesn't have to do a hand's turn if she doesn't want to. And if she took the trouble to understand him, she could twist Abe around her little finger.

While I . . . What do I do? I work like a slave for little more than subsistence, and I play the whore for nothing. Yet we are twins, two peas from the same pod. Why do I do it? To stop myself thinking? . . . As a punishment? . . . And what about him? Does he have nights when he forces himself to lie awake for fear of nightmares? . . . Always the same: the boy's white face, and his eyes staring up through the spokes of the cycle wheel. As I move away, those eyes seem to follow me . . .

She had brushed and folded away the hangings; now she was dealing with the vestry door. The flower arrangers had forced the wooden wedge in too far and she couldn't shift it. A hammer: there were a few tools in a cupboard in the tower, a hammer amongst them. She went to fetch it and while she was there the church clock went through its groans, grunts and clatter, preparatory to striking seven. She found the hammer and returned with it to the wedged door. Stooping, she swung it very gently, nudging the wedge.

'Practising your croquet, Jessica, or is it golf?'

She was startled. It was Arnold Paul, the organist, for whom she now worked a couple of afternoons a week. Plump, amiable, and a trifle smug, he was standing in the aisle, watching her.

'It's jammed. One of the women on flowers this week doesn't know her own strength.'

'I came in to collect some music.' He crossed to the organ console and was hidden by the curtain.

The wedge was freed and the door to the vestry closed. The organ played softly, an odd little tune. Jessica had no ear for music. Next on her schedule: cleaning the vestry toilet. The floor was swimming with water mixed with leaves, flower stalks, and wrapping tissue; five or six unwanted vases had not been put away.

When she returned to the church the organ was silent and there was no sign of Arnold. Odd. He usually called out when he was going. Perhaps he had. She crossed to the console, there was no-one there and the lid was down over the keys. She was being foolish, yet she was tempted to wedge the south door shut. But that would be too absurd.

Saturday evening routine dictated two more jobs: a whisk round with a feather duster on the altar and chancel, and a bit of elbow grease on the lectern to bring up the shine. It was while she was dusting that she thought she heard a movement somewhere in the body of the church.

'Is anyone there?'

She was unusually nervous. Why am I so jumpy? She followed the same routine in the depth of winter on nights when, without a torch, it would have been impossible to find her way through the churchyard. She called again with no reply and she went on with her work. Then there was someone – the vicar. She was polishing the lectern.

'Good evening, Jessica. I hope I didn't startle you? I came across to fetch my nice new service book.'

She was glad he had come.

Apart from anything else she liked the vicar, and it was not given to many to be liked by Jessica. She believed that he was a good man, and innocent; the sort who could touch filth without being soiled, perhaps without even knowing.

'I'm almost through.'

'It all looks splendid, Jessica, but then, it always does. I really don't know what we would do without you.'

Easter Sunday

The following morning at seven-fifteen, Michael Jordan, Vicar of Moresk, crossed the road from the vicarage to his church. At thirty-eight, he was unmarried, and his sister, Celia, several years older, kept house for him. It was a balmy spring morning but whatever the weather, in winter darkness or in the brash light of high summer, he took pleasure in so beginning his day. He felt part of the great Christian tradition which, probably on this very site, reached back to the missionary work of St Sulien, patron saint of his church, among the heathen Celts.

He passed through the sixteenth-century lich-gate, followed the gravelled walk among the gravestones, glimpsed the river between the trees, and arrived at the south porch. To his astonishment he heard the sound of the organ, a sustained chord of discordant notes. He had in his hand the key to a padlock by which the church was supposedly secured against latter-day Vandals but the padlock was missing and the heavy oaken door with its wrought-iron latch and ring stood open.

He experienced a tremor of disquiet; an awareness, as he interpreted it, of the proximity of Evil. Michael saw himself and the rest of mankind doing daily battle with

Evil which, for him, was a positive and potent force. He pushed the door wide and was somewhat reassured to see the padlock on the table just inside the door, next to the visitors' book and offertory box. But the vibrant dissonance of the organ chord filled the church, setting his teeth and his nerves on edge. He looked across at the console but the curtain hid anyone who might have been there. Somebody playing the fool?

He entered the nave, genuflected towards the altar and, in the act, caught sight of a figure sprawled across the chancel steps. His fears intensified. Summoning his courage he walked down the aisle and approached the steps. Jessica Dobell lay on her back, diagonally across the steps, and she was certainly dead. Her head was turned slightly to the right and her skull had been smashed, just forward of the crown. Her hair around the injury was a mass of clotted blood, while something more viscous than blood had oozed on to the tiled step. Her blue denim shirt had been ripped open, exposing her breasts; and her jeans, unzipped, had been dragged part-way down her thighs along with her briefs.

Adding to his horror and sense of desecration, she was lying at the very feet of the statue of Christ; Christ with his lantern held aloft – *Lux Mundi* – *The Light of the World*.

Jessica's hair was spread out so that it reached, and partly covered, the bare feet of the statue, and Michael was irresistibly reminded of Mary Magdalene who anointed the feet of Jesus with her perfume and 'wiped them with her hair till the house was filled with the fragrance'. Always a little disturbed by the image which that passage conjured up, he was deeply distressed that his mind should seize upon it at such a moment. Instinctively he crossed himself and murmured an incoherent prayer.

Only last night . . . Had she been there ever since?

Although he was filled with revulsion he could not keep

24

his eyes from her body. He was astonished to see that, away from her injury, her features were composed; she looked in death as she had been in life, a very attractive woman. If only her breasts and thighs were covered . . . He stooped, with the foolish intention of drawing her shirt-front together, but stopped himself in time. The police would take a poor view of such interference and there was no possible doubt that they must be involved.

The continuing, droning chord on the organ made it impossible to think. He could hear the muffled purr of the electric blower and, as he approached the console, he saw that five notes, apparently chosen at random in the 'great', were permanently depressed by little wedges of paper, folded to the appropriate thickness and inserted between the keys. Once more he was on the point of committing a blunder – by removing the wedges; instead, he switched off the blower and silence descended like a benediction.

What he had to do was clear: he must lock the church, go back to the vicarage and telephone the police. But he really could not persuade himself to leave the poor woman so obscenely exposed. He went to the vestry and returned with a surplice which, with great gentleness, he arranged to his satisfaction.

Then he prayed briefly, genuflected, and left.

Eight o'clock Holy Communion was celebrated at St Sulien's each Sunday but, on this special Sunday which commemorated the risen Lord, those who came would find their church locked against them.

Forty odd miles away, as crows are said to fly, on the estuary of the Tamar, Detective Chief Superintendent Charles Wycliffe was in his garden accompanied by the cat, Macavity. The pond had recently been cleaned and refurbished so that now, its ecological equanimity disturbed, it had produced inordinate quantities of blanket weed. Wycliffe, armed with a trident-like weapon, had lifted out a mass of the green, filamentous, slimy stuff and from it he now rescued trapped newts, tadpoles, young frogs, and nymphs of dragonflies, all to be returned to the pond.

But not snails. Helen was adamant. There were too many snails, so those that were found must be banished into the outer darkness. He disliked such a god-like decisive role but the task was otherwise agreeable; contemplative, and on balance constructive, ideally suited to his middle-aged psyche.

Macavity, more virile in his pursuits and aspirations, put on his mouse-hunting act. Watching some phantom rodent, whiskers a-tremble and tail rigid, he would stalk the imagined quarry and, insinuating his plump body through the herbage with infinite care, the mighty hunter would crouch, ready for the spring – then pounce.

All this despite the fact that the sight of a can of Whiskas, preferably open, was necessary to induce in Macavity any sign of a salivary reflex.

The Wycliffes would never see fifty again; they were on the slope – definitely. For twenty years they had lived in the Watch House, a former coastguard station converted to a dwelling house, and their half-acre of garden sloped to the narrows where the estuary met the sea. Were they happy? Wycliffe told himself that happiness is a peak experience that comes in small doses – a few seconds at a time; at most a few hours. But they were content; content with each other and with their lot.

After rearing their two children they were mostly alone again. The boy, David, was married and more or less settled in Kenya with his wife and child; while their daughter, Ruth, lived with her former boss in a nebulous relationship so far unproductive of offspring.

Easter Sunday: the church bells of St Juliot, their nearest village, were pealing in celebration and their sound rose and fell, carried on a fitful breeze. The air was soft and warm. Wycliffe knew that it was going to be one of those idyllic days, always to be remembered. For a few hours at least the Watch House and its garden would become an exclusion zone within which he, Helen, and Macavity would pursue their separate illusions in blissful relaxation.

He was wrong.

Helen's voice came from the terrace. 'Telephone!' And, as he reached her, she said, 'It's Lucy Lane.'

Detective Sergeant Lucy Lane was the day's duty officer in CID. 'Sorry to disturb your Sunday, sir, but there's a report from C Division, logged at 09.33. At about 07.30 this morning, Jessica Dobell, a woman in her late thirties, was found dead in St Sulien's Church, in the village of Moresk, near Truro. She appears to have died from a depressed fracture of the skull caused by a powerful blow. DI Rowse from sub-division, attending, says it's murder.'

'You did say Moresk?'

'I did, sir.'

'That's only a few miles from the Duloe place.'*

'A bit nearer Truro, and on the other side of the river.'

'What on earth's happening down there?'

'I've no idea, sir; perhaps they get bored in the off season.' Lucy Lane had little time for rhetorical questions.

Wycliffe sighed as he replaced the telephone. A well established routine made detailed instructions unnecessary. DI Kersey, on call, would gather together a small headquarters team while the local inspector would call in the police surgeon, inform relatives, arrange formal

*Wycliffe and the Dead Flautist

27

identification, and notify the coroner. But Wycliffe must visit the scene and, according to what he saw and heard, decide whether or not to become personally involved.

'A murder, apparently, at Moresk, near Truro.'

'I'll make some coffee.'

Helen was by no means indifferent to tragedy but when crime and violence are woven into the fabric of daily life an extra skin is part of the survival kit.

'Are you likely to be home this evening?'

'Possibly, it's only fifty-odd miles.'

Helen grinned. 'Some of them very odd, as I remember. Anyhow, I'll put your weekend bag in the car. Go and make yourself respectable.'

So much for his Easter Sunday.

Helen was right; getting on to the spine road from the complex of creeks and streams which is the Tamar valley, and off it, to that not dissimilar complex which is the valley of the Fal, makes an interesting experience. Wycliffe was not a good driver; in fact he had no rapport with any mechanical device more complex than a can opener, and the journey took him longer than it should have done. 'Turn off left in Tresillian', he told himself. He did, then got lost in a bewildering maze of lanes, narrow and tortuous, and peopled by stolid men in large cars who simply stopped and waited with patronizing patience for him to extricate himself from every impasse.

He finally arrived in the village as the church clock was striking twelve.

Chapter Two

Easter Sunday (continued)

Moresk village and a patch of woodland on the other side of Truro are almost all that survive to perpetuate the name of that great forest of Morrois where Tristan fled with Iseult, only to be discovered by King Mark. Although the village is quite close to Truro it was Wycliffe's first visit, and he was surprised to find such a populous little place tucked away in one of the creeks. He stopped in the square which, on one side, was bounded by the foreshore and the waters of the creek. Small boats were stranded on the shingle, lying at odd angles, and a pair of swans waddled around the garage forecourt among the petrol pumps. He decided at once that he liked the place.

He could see the church through trees away to his left but separated from the square by a substantial house in its own grounds. He left his car, found Church Lane, and a minute or two later arrived at the lich-gate where a small crowd had gathered under the eye of a uniformed policeman.

'DI Reed is in the church, sir.'

Wycliffe found the south porch and entered the church. Coming in out of the sunlight, the nave seemed to be in near darkness though the chancel and altar were floodlit like a stage set. Three men were in conversation near the chancel steps and one of them came to greet him. It was DI Reed.

Reed and Wycliffe had worked together several times. He was a large man with a high colour, fleshy features, and a neck which bulged over his collar. A fringe of red hair surrounded a bald patch. 'Welcome aboard, sir.'

Reed led him to the chancel steps. Tread boards were in place to protect whatever evidence there might be until scenes-of-crime had finished. The body was sprawled across the steps, at the very feet of a statue of Christ. The head to one side exposed a ghastly wound to the parietal region of the skull.

Wycliffe stood gazing down at this woman whose concerns in life had now, by reason of her death, become his. What shocked him most about violent death was the ease with which the thread is snapped; but here was something more, something bizarre, and he was troubled.

'She wasn't killed here, like that – the body has been arranged.' A banal observation but something was expected of him and it was all he could find to say.

Reed, at ease, comfortable, said, 'No, she was dragged from over by the pulpit. There's blood on the tiles there, and traces in between.'

Wycliffe could scarcely take his eyes from the body. Never before had he been confronted with a murder which made such a profound first impression; yet he found difficulty in putting that impression into words.

Ripping open the victim's blouse to expose the breasts is a common enough feature of sexual assault on a woman, but jeans and briefs had been pulled down just far enough to uncover the pubic triangle – and no further. Her body had been arranged in an abandoned pose across the chancel steps and her abundant hair, dark and lustrous, had been ordered so that it reached and spread over the sandalled feet of Christ.

What he was seeing was a set piece such as a surrealist sculptor might devise in order to shock, and so to make a point. But to prepare this set piece and make whatever point was intended, a woman had been murdered.

Belatedly he noticed that she was wearing bedroom slippers, an old pair that had seen better days.

Reed said, 'That's how she was found, sir; nothing has been disturbed except that a surplice, used by the vicar to cover her, was taken away. No sign of any footwear other than those slippers, and she didn't walk here in those.'

'Doesn't it strike you as . . . as grotesque?'

Reed puffed out his cheeks. 'Kinky is the word that comes to mind. If it was a sexual assault it didn't achieve a climax.' Reed smoothed his bald patch with an enormous, freckled paw. 'My guess is that it was never intended to, but what was intended, God only knows.'

'What was she doing in the church?'

'She was a sort of caretaker-cum-verger and she looked in on Saturday evenings to make sure everything was ready for Sunday.'

'Next of kin?'

'There's only a sister and she's been told. Deceased wasn't married. There's a smallholding just up-river from here which she ran with the help of a couple living in. They've been notified. The sister lives in Trigg House, adjoining the churchyard, and she's married to Abe Geach, the contractor.' A quick look. 'Does that mean anything to you, sir?'

'Should it?'

Reed shrugged. 'Money. He's got contracts all over the two counties and he's one of those who manages to keep warm and dry whatever the financial climate. I mention it because he carries quite a bit of weight around here.'

'She has no parents living?'

'Both killed in a coach crash several years back.'

DS Fox, Wycliffe's scenes-of-crime officer, had completed his first series of photographs of the body but more would be taken when the pathologist arrived and it could be disturbed. Now Fox turned his attention to the immediate setting.

Wycliffe, as always, was fascinated by Fox; it was an experience to see him go to work. He would arrive, unburdened, followed by his assistant, the long-suffering Collis, laden like a Spaniard's donkey. A room, a river bank, an alley, a night-club, or a church, it was all the same to Fox. He seemed to show not the slightest interest in his surroundings in general but concentrated on each item or aspect as it presented itself to him on some mental list. A wizard with molehills, he was apt to miss the occasional mountain.

Brooding, Wycliffe turned once more to the inspector. 'The weapon?'

Reed pointed. Lying at some distance from the body, near the pulpit, and barely visible in its shadow, was a long-handled hammer with a smallish head. 'It's an unusual sort, sir – like they used to use for wheel-tapping on the railway.'

Stooping, Wycliffe could see that the head was encrusted with dried blood and there was blood on the tiles.

Wycliffe returned to the chancel steps and the body. 'Presumably she's been here all night. What was the weather like yesterday evening?'

'Wet. It rained all the evening, sir; I checked.'

'So it's unlikely that she came here dressed like this.'

'She didn't; there's a heavy mac with a hood in the vestry but, as I said, no footwear. I understand she usually came to work along the river bank and that must have been pretty muddy. What she wore on her feet is a bit of a puzzle at the moment.'

Wycliffe was soaking up all the detail of which he was capable. His questions were curt and there were intervals during which he stood, staring down at the dead woman or watching Fox's antics with the camera.

'Who found her?'

'The vicar: the Reverend Michael Jordan. There he is . . .' Reed indicated a youngish man in clerical garb, seated in one of the pews, head bent, eyes closed, as though in prayer.

Now that Wycliffe had become accustomed to the uneven lighting he could see that the church must have the support of dedicated and well-heeled parishioners. There was an impressive tapestry above the altar and the altar cloth was elaborately embroidered; the aisles and the pews were carpeted and many of the pews sported embroidered hass-ocks on which the knees of the devout might rest at ease. Flowers were everywhere and the air was heavy with their scent, blending with the lingering tangy odour of incense.

'What did the doctor have to say?'

'He's still here. That's him, talking to my sergeant – Dr Sparrow. I think he's loath to go; he's not often in the limelight and I suppose it's a change from sore throats and backaches.'

The doctor was in his early sixties, short, stocky and weather-beaten. Dressed in shabby tweeds he was almost a caricature of the traditional country doctor.

'You don't need me to tell you what she died of but you might want my view on when. My guess would be, sometime last evening, between eight or nine and mid-night. I can't do better than that but I imagine you will have Franks to do the clever stuff.'

'And the sexual aspect?'

The doctor pouted. 'What about it? The chap obviously didn't really get around to it. I imagine the situation was a bit off-putting.'

'One more question, Dr Sparrow – not a professional one – are you acquainted with the vicar?'

33

'I know him, naturally, but I'm no churchgoer.'

'An unbiased view, then. What sort of man is he?'

Sparrow chuckled. 'So that's how you blokes go about it! Well, I'd say he was a sincere, hardworking chap; always on call – like me.' A sly grin.

'Popular?'

'I think so; he's pushed up church attendance, so they tell me, and despite his Holy-Joe appearance and manner, he's accepted by the young. They call him Michael, or even Mike. He didn't go down well with the diehards at first, but they seem to have come round. Why don't you have a chat with him?'

'I'm going to.' Wycliffe thanked the doctor.

Jordan got up from his seat as Wycliffe approached. His blond hair clipped short and his smooth, pink, unblemished skin gave him an unused look, reminiscent of a young baby. Wycliffe had the uncomfortable feeling that he might be dealing with a postulant for sainthood.

The preliminaries over, Jordan said, 'This morning I was due to celebrate Holy Communion at eight, and matins at eleven . . . Now, I suppose, it will be some time before I can conduct any services here at all . . . Apart from anything else there is the question of desecration. The bishop will have to decide what is to be done . . .' The blue eyes were troubled.

'How long have you been in Moresk, Vicar?'

'Four years at Michaelmas.'

'So you must know the people. This woman, Jessica Dobell . . . I understand she kept the church clean.'

'That is an understatement; Jessica saw to everything, from cleaning, to preparations for the different services. I don't know what we shall do without her.'

'You've seen the weapon?'

The vicar nodded. 'It comes from a cupboard in the tower where we keep all sorts of things which might be

34

handy about the church – from flower vases to drawing pins. It's horrible to think . . .'

'I gather that the dead woman didn't live with any relative.'

'No, Jessica had certain views about marriage and family life . . .' His eyes sought Wycliffe's and seemed to beg for understanding. 'You will hear rumours . . . gossip.'

Reed and the vicar between them were opening up vistas, giving Wycliffe his first glimpse of the people whose intimate lives would be his concern in the days or weeks ahead. It was his job to invite their confidence and probe their deceptions until a rather special kind of truth was established – that arcane variety which is recognized in the Courts.

As always, he felt a stirring of excitement at the prospect; an excitement tinged with the guilt of a voyeur.

'If I might suggest, Mr Wycliffe . . .' The vicar was nervous but resolved to make his point. 'If I might suggest, it could be a mistake to approach this young woman with a prejudice. After all, a certain laxness in sexual matters does not necessarily mean that those concerned are not caring and hard-working people.'

Verily, a saint! But Wycliffe was mildly snubbing. 'I try not to prejudge anybody, Mr Jordan.

'Now, you must have noticed that the dead woman is wearing slippers—'

The vicar smiled. 'Jessica always wore slippers when she was working, and always the same old pair. She kept them in a cupboard in the vestry. You see, she walked to work by way of the river bank, which is always muddy, wearing short wellingtons which she left in the porch.'

'Show me.'

He was conducted to the south porch with its slatted seats and notice boards but there were no boots.

Jordan was puzzled. 'That is strange.'

Back in the church Wycliffe said, 'One more question, Mr Jordan, and I want you to think carefully before you answer. Apart from the south door being unlocked and the body on the chancel steps, was there anything else, however trivial, which struck you as unusual when you arrived this morning?'

The vicar put his hand to his forehead. 'Of course! The organ! It's hard to believe, but that went entirely from my mind . . . Anyway, I'll show you.'

Wycliffe followed him to the organ console.

'An instrument of this quality – it's a two-manual Willis – may strike you as a little out of place in a country church like ours, but Arnold Paul, our unpaid organist, rescued it from a disused London church, had it dismantled, renovated, and rebuilt here – all at his own expense.'

'What about it?'

'Yes, of course! I digress. If I switch on the blower you will understand.'

The vicar threw a switch and the church was once more filled with a nagging discordance.

'You see that certain notes in the "great" are wedged down with folded bits of paper and when I arrived this morning this rather distressing sound greeted me along with the rest.'

'Does it mean anything to you?'

The vicar looked blank. 'Nothing at all!'

'Anyway, switch it off.' Wycliffe waited until peace was restored, then: 'This organist . . .'

'Mr Arnold Paul – he lives almost opposite the church; a man of independent means, a keen and able musician. I would have expected him to be here but he was probably prevented by your man at the gate.'

'I'll send for him. Just one more question, Mr Jordan.

Would you have expected to find Jessica here when you arrived this morning?'

'Oh, no. She was only concerned with the preparations, not with the actual services.'

'And yesterday evening?'

'Yes, she usually comes – came in on Saturday evenings. She liked to have everything spick and span for Sunday.'

Crossing over by the chancel steps Wycliffe asked Fox, 'Anything to tell me? What about the weapon – any prints?'

'The weapon has been wiped clean; in fact there are no significant prints anywhere that I've examined so far.'

'All right. When you've finished here, take a look at the organ console – you'll see why when you get there. I shall want photographs. Pay special attention to the paper or card used to wedge the keys but don't disturb anything until the organist has seen it.'

He left the church and walked in the churchyard. Unlike Fox, he felt a compelling need to fit the crime and the scene of the crime into a broader context.

The church was built on sloping ground between the creek and the river; a fringe of pines and a scattering of ash and lime trees offered shelter in winter and shade in summer. Through the trees he could see the grey roofs of a substantial old house, presumably Trigg, where the dead woman's sister lived with her affluent husband. Beyond the house he glimpsed the silvery waters of the creek.

The earliest tombstones he could find dated from the sixteen-nineties and there were not many later than the nineteen-sixties when, with the dead making increasing demands on the land of the living, cremation became necessary as well as fashionable. He was interested in the names: Angove, Geach, Carveth, Noall, Dobell . . .

One of the newer stones caught his eye: 'In loving memory of our dear parents, John and Katherine Dobell, killed in a coach accident, 23rd September 1975. This stone is erected by their twin daughters: Katherine and Jessica.'

The churchyard was well but not obsessively cared for so that primroses flourished and bluebells were sprouting.

'Nice place!'

It was Doug Kersey, his principal assistant and colleague for twenty years.

'So you've arrived.'

'I brought Shaw and Potter; Lucy Lane is following on with Dixon.'

'Have you been inside?'

'I had a look and a word with Reed. What is it? Some sort of ritual killing – or what?'

'Or what, I should think.'

'It's bloody queer, anyway.'

A relief not to have to spell everything out.

'There's a guy in there, says he's the organist and that you want to speak to him.'

'Have you heard anything of Franks?' Franks was the pathologist.

'They couldn't find him at first but they've run him to earth. He's down here, spending Easter with friends in St Mawes. He should be along at any minute but he won't be pleased, that's for sure.'

It would have been easy to write Kersey off as a hardfaced cop. He looked the part and, to some extent, it was the image he cultivated. But, early in their association, Wycliffe had discovered behind the mask a moral and compassionate man.

Wycliffe found the organist sitting in a pew at the back of the church. As it happened, the sun was striking down through a stained-glass window in the south wall suffusing the man's face with a rosy pink glow. Paul was in his late fifties but his hair was white; he was plump, smooth-skinned, meticulously groomed, and soberly dressed. Wycliffe recalled Mr Polly's 'portly capon' and smiled secretly.

Wycliffe held out his hand. 'Mr Paul? Have they shown you your organ?'

'I've been shown nothing. I was told to sit here and wait.'

Evidently a man not accustomed to being instructed, but he was not slow to thaw. He stood, looking down at the wedged keys. 'How very odd!'

'Do you make anything of it?'

Paul fingered his smooth chin. 'I hesitate to answer that because the notion seems so utterly absurd. On the other hand, those notes could hardly have been chosen by chance.'

'Tell me.'

'Doesn't that combination mean anything to you?'

'I'm afraid not.'

'Well, the depressed notes are A,B,E,G, and a second G, an octave higher: the notes used by Schumann in his Variations to flatter Meta von Abegg, his girlfriend of that time.'

Wycliffe, despite Helen's efforts, knew little about music but he thought he knew the keyboard. He said, with diffidence, 'But isn't the second note, the black one, B flat?'

The organist was impatient. 'Of course it is, in our notation; but the Germans call it B, which is what Schumann did. That fact, if nothing else, makes it certain that these notes were not chosen at random.'

'Can you suggest any reason why someone might want to draw attention to this piece of music in such dramatic circumstances?'

Paul looked at him with puzzled eyes. 'It means nothing to me. I can't understand it.'

'The dead woman was employed to clean the church so, presumably, you knew her?'

The abrupt change of subject was too much for Paul's precisely ordered mind but he made the effort. 'Knew her? Of course I knew her; and not only through her work here. A few weeks ago I persuaded her to work for me part-time in the house. She came two days a week – Tuesdays and Fridays – for three hours each afternoon. She was very good and, surprisingly, she hit it off with my old housekeeper who is not the easiest of women to get along with.'

'Was she interested in music?'

'Not as far as I am aware.'

'Would you say that anyone setting up this charade needed to be knowledgeable about music?'

Paul hesitated. 'It depends what you mean by knowledgeable. I am sure that a great many people who would not think of themselves as particularly musical would know of the Abegg Variations and of the differences between our notation and the German.'

'Just one more question, Mr Paul – one that will be asked of everyone in any way involved – where were you between, say, seven-thirty and midnight last night?'

'I was at home.'

'Anyone to substantiate that?'

Paul hesitated. 'My housekeeper, I suppose, but she is very deaf and, as we were not in the same room, her evidence may not be reliable.'

There would be more questions for the organist but now Wycliffe wanted to broaden his approach, to get some idea of the probable scope of his inquiry. And Dr Franks had arrived.

Wycliffe joined the pathologist as he stood, taking in the disturbing spectacle of the obscenely exposed body of a murdered woman sprawled at the feet of a holy statue.

Franks was short, not really fat, but a roly-poly of a man. He was cynical, as most pathologists are, but good humoured, as many are not. More to the point, Wycliffe respected his judgement.

Franks said, 'I suppose you realize you've spoilt my holiday?'

'It's a habit I have. What do you make of it?'

Franks, unusually sombre, admitted, 'I thought I'd lost the capacity for surprise, Charles. On the face of it I shan't be much use to you; the forensic aspects seem plain enough. But my guess is you'll be up to your neck in trick cyclists if it ever comes to court. Anyway, let's get on. If Fox is ready to take his pictures . . .'

When Franks had made his preliminary examination, he said, 'Well, it all seems consistent with a nasty knock on the head and I shall be surprised if I have much more to tell you after the autopsy.'

'Nothing on the relative positions of attacker and attacked?'

Franks shrugged. 'If you think it would help, I don't mind doing your job for you. The cranium was fractured in the region of the left parietal, not far from the sagittal suture – in other words, near the top of the head. My guess is that she was stooping or crouching at the time, that her attacker was to her left, and that she raised her head to look up at him as the blow fell. How's that?'

'The power behind the blow?'

Pause for thought. 'The long handle, with a good swing, would generate plenty of momentum without much muscle power behind it. The hammer head isn't very heavy but it didn't need to be.'

'So it could have been a man or a woman?'

Franks nodded. 'Yes, sex doesn't enter the picture from that angle but there seems to be plenty of it about otherwise.'

'Time of death?'

A chubby grimace. 'She seems to have been what the books call "a sound muscular subject" and she was doing moderately energetic things before she got clobbered. On the other hand the temperature in this place in the late evening and night can't be anything to write home about.' He was bending over the body once more, attempting to flex an arm. 'Now, as you see, rigor is on the way out . . . Taken with the body temperature . . .'

Wycliffe said, 'Well? Do I have to do my own sums?'

'I'd give it between seventeen and twenty hours. What is it now – about three? . . . Say between seven and ten last night. If I had to be more precise I'd go for mid-way between the two, but don't put much on that.'

Kathy was in the garden, standing by the steep bank which was almost a wall, the boundary separating Trigg from the churchyard. There were clumps of primroses and the hawthorn bushes which surmounted the bank were coming into leaf. Through the screen of twigs she could see the graves, and the church itself, mellow, lichen-encrusted stones which looked as old as time.

And Jessica was lying dead, just that little distance away. At some time during the evening or night Jessica, in some ways her yardstick, her touchstone, had been viciously murdered. She tried but failed to grasp what it would mean to her. The little policewoman in her trim uniform – a girl in her twenties – had tried to cover her feeling of inadequacy with a professional gloss. 'Your sister would have known almost nothing, Mrs Geach. The doctor says death was instantaneous.'

She had never imagined life without Jessica and she could not now. It was strange, for in recent years they had not been close. Not since . . . Since when? . . . Her marriage to Abe? No, their intimacy had survived that. It

42

dated from Jessica's break with Johnny Glynn. Something to do with the death of the Ruse boy? That seemed to be what Jess was hinting at on Wednesday at the farm. She had been on the point of confiding something, but had changed her mind. At any rate it was sixteen years since they had ceased being twins and had become merely sisters.

Now Katherine felt that she wanted to weep for Jessica, for herself, and for the might-have-been.

'I think you should come indoors; it's clouding over and getting chilly out here.' Abe had arrived, ponderously solicitous.

'I'm not cold.'

'Vinter has been on the phone.'

'What does he want?'

'Well, it's only natural he should want to make contact.'

She was venomous. 'All they're worrying about is being kicked out of the farm, but they've got some explaining to do.'

'Explaining? You don't think they had anything to do with it?'

'Why wasn't I told – why wasn't anybody told – that Jess didn't come home last night? It was the police who went to them, not the other way round.'

He put his arm around her. 'Come in and have a hot drink – a toddy is the thing for you, my girl!'

For some reason Katherine was incensed by his attention and broke away. 'Lay off, Abe, for God's sake! You think everything can be cured by sex or alcohol – or both.'

Chapter Three

Easter Sunday afternoon

The headquarters team mustered by Kersey had arrived:
Detective Sergeants Lucy Lane and Shaw; and Detective
Constables Dixon and Potter – known, because of their
respective physiques, as Pole and Pot. With help from the
local police, Sergeant Shaw, the squad's Pooh-Bah,
wearing his administrative hat, was involved in arranging
accommodation for the team and finding a hall or other
building which could be used as an Incident Room. The
two DCs, again with local support, would be concerned
with interviews and inquiries under Kersey's direction.

All of which left Wycliffe free to assume his preferred
role, a roving commission, getting to know everybody who
was, or might be, involved – in particular, the victim. He
considered whether to begin with the sister and brother-
in-law at Trigg, but decided on the farm because that was
where the victim had lived her life.

He conscripted Lucy Lane – Detective Sergeant Lucy
Lane, in her thirties, dark, warm-skinned and eligible, but
still single. 'I wouldn't inflict this world on a child of
mine. I see too much of it.'

A sentiment which shocked Wycliffe to whom hope was
an ultimate resource.

'Shall I get the car?'

'No, let's walk.'

It was characteristic that he should walk rather than

drive or be driven; he refused to allow his days to become crowded with events in a frenetic succession of images like a television screen, lacking even commercial breaks to aid digestion.

The immediate countryside about Moresk is one of low, rounded hills and gentle slopes, moist lanes and trickling water. Standing by the ramshackle gate which led to the farm they could follow the course of the river as it narrowed and was lost between the slopes. No more than a quarter of a mile away a rambling old house in a hotch-potch of styles, not unlike Trigg but larger, fronted on the river. It was backed by a plantation of larches and, on the rising ground behind, a tower dominated the Lilli-putian landscape.

Wycliffe said, 'What is it? It looks like a lighthouse.'

It had the proportions of a factory chimney, but it had lancet windows and, at the top, a domed structure slightly greater in diameter than the tower.

Lucy, who had relatives in the county and knew about such things, said, 'I suppose it's a folly. Anyway, it belongs to the Carey family who live in the big house – what's left of them – and it.'

Wycliffe had a weakness for follies and promised himself closer acquaintance with the tower but he had no intimation then of the circumstances which would bring this about.

They passed through the farm gate, and between tethered goats, down the slope to the farmyard which vividly recalled Wycliffe's own childhood. In the yard a man in bib-and-brace overalls was scattering handfuls of grain for the chickens. It was like being in a time warp of fifty years.

'Mr Vinter?'

The man was very tall; thin, and bony, with that stoop which is sometimes habitual to the tall. He seemed to study Wycliffe for a while before speaking, his blue eyes expressionless, then, 'Laurence Vinter – yes. Are you a policeman?'

'Chief Superintendent Wycliffe. This is Detective Sergeant Lane.'

'You'd better come inside.'

They were taken into the sitting room where a woman sat by the window, reading. The light from the window with its tiny panes fell on one side of her face and form, leaving the rest in shadow. She was very fair, with an oval face and perfect features; her straight hair, with its meticulous central parting, precisely framed her face and was caught up in a coil at the back. She wore a blue pinafore frock over a print blouse.

'My wife, Stephanie; Chief Superintendent Wycliffe . . . Detective Sergeant Lane.'

Stephanie Vinter rested her book, still open, on the windowsill, and stood up, eyeing the policewoman. Her little blue eyes were hard.

On the face of it the Vinters were an oddly assorted couple, the woman, small, refined – exquisite; the man, ungainly, angular, and somehow unfinished. But they shared a certain deliberation in speech and manner as though they existed in a world where the pace of life was slower.

The preliminaries over, Wycliffe was seated in a wicker chair which creaked, while Lucy was given a hard kitchen chair which did not. Wycliffe began his questions. 'When did you last see Miss Dobell?'

The two looked at each other and, after a pause, it was the woman who answered, 'Last evening, at about seven. We have our meal at six . . .'

Laurence Vinter said, 'She always goes to the church on Saturday evening to make sure that everything is right for Sunday.'

'But last evening she didn't come back.'

'No.'

Wycliffe was impatient. 'Didn't you expect her back? Weren't you concerned?'

It seemed for a moment that they had no more to say, then Laurence spoke: 'You must understand that our position here is somewhat equivocal. I mean we are not family; we live here in return for helping out on the farm.'

It was Lucy's turn. 'But surely that doesn't mean that you were indifferent to her being out all night with no news?'

Another silence. Laurence Vinter studied his long bony fingers, his wife looked across at him, her gaze expressionless. Wycliffe would have liked to shake them both. 'Well?'

Finally Laurence raised his head. 'It wasn't unusual for Jessica to be away all night.'

'Without warning you?'

'Yes.'

'Have you any idea where she spent those nights?'

'No, and she wouldn't have welcomed any question or comment.'

'How often did this happen?'

Laurence shrugged. 'Three or four times a month? Probably about that.'

'Was it always a Saturday night?' From Lucy Lane.

'On the contrary, it was usually mid-week.'

'Was she ever away for more than one night?'

'A couple of times but then she warned us in advance.'

Wycliffe turned to the woman. 'Presumably, if she intended to be away, she took an overnight bag or something . . .'

'No. She left here the same, whatever her intentions, dressed for the weather as it happened to be.'

'She had a car?'

47

'No, there is a truck, but that is used only for farm work.'

'So she left here yesterday evening, just after seven, to walk to the church. Is that right?'

'After our meal, as my wife said. It was raining, and she put on her heavy mac with a hood, and the short wellingtons she wears about the farm.'

A collie dog padded into the room, looked and sniffed around, then went out disconsolate.

Wycliffe said, 'How long have you lived with Miss Dobell?'

'Three years last month.'

'Before that?'

Vinter, after the customary pause, said, 'I was a lecturer at Bristol; I had a breakdown and had to give it up.' He spoke slowly, as though his words were being dredged up from some deeper layer of consciousness. 'In the process we lost our home and it happened that we spent the winter of eighty-seven in temporary accommodation near here – a winter let. At the start of the holiday season we had to get out, and Jessica offered us accommodation on condition that Stephanie took on the housework and I helped on the farm.'

'You have no outside source of income?'

Stephanie intervened. 'That sounds impertinent, Superintendent, but I suppose you are interested in our bona fides. We have nothing to hide. Laurence receives a small pension from his former employment and he does a certain amount of translation work for a publisher.'

Wycliffe, trying to decide what it was about the woman that impressed him, concluded that above all else it was her serenity; everything about her was calm and cool and he wondered what it might take to ruffle the surface of her composure or raise her emotional temperature to blood heat.

Vinter found it necessary to supplement what his wife had said: 'I was a lecturer and tutor in modern languages, that is why I am able to undertake translation work. We get a small weekly payment and, of course, our living is free.'

It was Lucy who asked, 'What is likely to happen now?'

Vinter replied with a lift of the shoulders.

Wycliffe was looking across at a roll-top desk. 'Is that where Miss Dobell did her accounts?'

'Yes.'

'Miss Lane will go through its contents and I would like one of you to be with her.'

Once more the exchange of glances and Vinter stood up.

Wycliffe said, 'Where do you do your translation work, Mr Vinter?'

Vinter seemed surprised by the question. 'Upstairs; in our room.'

'May I see upstairs? Perhaps while Mr Vinter is occupied here . . . ?'

Stephanie said, 'If you wish.'

As he followed her up the crooked stairs he heard Vinter say, 'Jessica kept her desk locked, but the key is on a little hook in the knee-hole.'

On the landing, at the top of the stairs, three doors opened off. Stephanie pushed open all three. 'Jessica's is the double room at the front, ours is the double room at the back, and my son, Giles, has the box room.'

Both the larger rooms must have been furnished early in the century: the beds had brass rails with elaborate knobs, and in each there was a washstand with a flowered ewer and basin as well as a dressing table, a chest of drawers, and a wardrobe. The Vinters had an additional table – placed tight against the window; it held a few books and a portable typewriter, but books were also stacked against the walls on makeshift shelves and even piled on

49

the floor. A tiny electric fire had its place near the table.

'This is where Laurence works.'

Jessica's room was characterless. Wycliffe opened the wardrobe and pulled out one or two drawers of the chest. The chest was full of bedding, and the clothes in the wardrobe seemed hardly to cater for the minimal needs of ordinary occasions or, indeed, for the succession of seasons.

The box room had space only for a single divan bed and a chest of drawers. Rows of books were lined up on the chest and a violin case lay on the bed.

'Your son plays the violin?'

'I am teaching him.'

'You are a musician?'

A slight shrug.

'Was Jessica musical?'

'Not as far as I know.'

They were on their way back down the stairs. 'There is a bathroom adjoining the kitchen, if you wish to see it.'

She was being ironic but Wycliffe said, politely, 'Thank you.'

There was a great deal that he wanted to ask but very little that he would learn from her answers; he wanted gossip, and she was no gossip. Lucy was still busy at the desk, while Laurence stood by showing little or no interest.

'I understand that recently Miss Dobell has been working at Arnold Paul's house – the church organist.'

Stephanie said, 'Yes.'

'Did she ever mention her work there or discuss the Pauls?'

'I remember her saying that she liked Arnold but not his brother.'

'Did she give any reason?'

'She said they were very different.'

'Do you know the brothers?'

'I know Arnold because I attend church and I belong to the Musical Society but I have never, to my knowledge, seen his brother.'

'One more question, Mrs Vinter: did either of you go out yesterday evening?'

'My husband was out and about on the farm.'

'Apart from that?'

'No, we were at home the whole evening.'

Wycliffe was standing, not tempted by the wicker chair a second time, and now he decided that he had got as far as he was likely to without more ammunition.

He thanked them. 'I shall leave DS Lane here. After she has finished with the desk she will look over Miss Dobell's room and, perhaps, other parts of the house. We are anxious to get some sort of picture of Miss Dobell, the kind of person she was, and the life she led. Obviously you and your husband can be helpful so there may be many more questions.'

Wycliffe was looking out of the window at a romantic water-colourist's dream. It was high tide; the inlet was flooded and the overhanging trees were reflected in still water. The prow of a sizeable craft just obtruded into the picture, painted black with the gunwale lined in white.

'That boat, is it anything to do with the farm?'

'It's a houseboat; a man called Lavin and a boy live on it and pay rent to the farm for the berth. The man is badly disfigured and rarely leaves the boat.'

'Is there a path along the river bank back to the village?'

'If you don't mind mud over your ankles.'

She saw him to the front door and he was about to leave when a slim, blond youth, dressed in jeans and a denim jacket, came up the grassy slope which separated the house from the water. Slung over his shoulder he carried a pair of binoculars in a much-worn leather case. The boy eyed him with a certain hostility and did not acknowledge his casual greeting, but the expression on Stephanie's face answered his unspoken question as to what might ruffle her calm or raise her emotional temperature.

'The path leads off on your right.'

Mother and son went into the house and the door closed behind them.

He walked down the slope which ended in a low bank and a narrow strip of shingle. The path gathered itself together out of the shingle and was lost to sight almost at once as it rounded a bend where the inlet joined the river. He could see the boat now – a houseboat with a super-structure covering most of the deck. Wycliffe prided himself that, after more than twenty years living by the sea, he had learned enough to identify this craft as a former fishing boat of that vaguely defined species called 'luggers' from the sails they are built to carry. She was well maintained, the hull painted black, with a white super-structure, and varnished, hardwood windows.

Smoke came from a cowled stove-pipe; curtains were drawn across the windows, and he saw no-one but, looking back, he glimpsed a man's bearded face peering after him from between the curtains. There was a canoe, hitched by its painter to the stern of the boat.

Along the path the going was muddy and there were brown pools, but nowhere did water or mud reach his ankles. Shortly after leaving the house he had the river on his left and an area of reedy marsh on his right. A great place for birds. Even now there were swans and at least three different sorts of duck on the water. He knew nothing about ducks and decided that he would learn.

It was very quiet. When, close by, some creature plopped into the water it had almost the impact of a shot. Here in this narrow valley, between wooded banks, evening came early and he found himself hurrying as though to overtake the dusk. In the back of his mind he was brooding on the dead woman and on her way of life. He felt sure that the farmhouse had changed hardly at all since that day, many years ago, when her parents set out on their ill-fated coach trip – or for years before that. He asked himself: how many women of Jessica's generation would have shown such apparent indifference to comfort and convenience?

Lucy Lane's verdict would be enlightening.

In a surprisingly short space of time he had arrived where the churchyard bordered the river and there was a kissing-gate. He could continue along the river bank to the village or he could go up through the churchyard. He decided to leave the path and look in at the church.

Lucy Lane found little of interest in the roll-top desk: invoices and receipts and a simple account book recording farming transactions, copies of returns sent to the Ministry, a few letters concerning the farm, nothing personal . . . There were the minimum records which, processed on the cheap by some shrewd, old-fashioned book-keeper, would serve to keep the tax dragon at bay and claim all the subsidies on offer.

In one of the pigeon-holes she came across a chunky, hard-covered, well-thumbed manuscript book labelled 'Farm Diary' and she leafed through it. Jessica had made systematic but telegraphic entries about seed-sowing, planting, spreading fertilizer and goat-kidding – there was not, as far as she could see, a single entry of a personal nature.

She turned to Vinter. 'Now I want to look at Miss Dobell's bedroom and I would like you or Mrs Vinter to come with me.'

Vinter was sullen. 'It's nothing to do with us.'

But Stephanie said, 'I'll come up with you.'

In the bedroom Lucy opened drawers and peered into the wardrobe. She was impressed, as Wycliffe had been, by the characterless nature of the room, and by the fact that in all probability it had been the same for fifty years at least. Stored away in the chest were unused sheets and blankets which must have been new in Jessica's grandmother's day, and when the drawers were opened the stench of mothballs filled the room. The window was small and tightly shut so that one seemed cut off from the river and the world outside.

Jessica's clothes were incidental: several pairs of jeans, a couple of skirts, two or three jumpers, a blouse or two and a random selection of underclothes.

It was depressing. Stephanie, watching from the doorway, was ironic. 'Clothes were hardly Jessica's main interest in life.'

'But didn't she have anything personal? What did interest her other than the farm?'

A faint smile. 'If she had another interest I never discovered it – unless it was men.'

'Didn't she receive any letters other than business ones?'

'I've no idea.'

Lucy was becoming irritated by the woman's smug detachment. 'But you must have seen whatever the postman brought.'

'No. There's a mailbox by the gate which she kept locked. She emptied it herself and handed over whatever concerned us.'

Finally Lucy looked under the bed and was rewarded by a metal deed box which she dragged out. 'Did you know about this?'

Stephanie raised her shoulders but said nothing.

The box was not locked and she spread its contents on the honeycomb quilt: a small, shaggy teddy bear with a squeak; a cheap camera at least twenty years old; a photograph album and a few items of jewellery, wrapped in tissue paper, presumably her mother's. Finally Lucy brought out a small number of envelopes held together by an elastic band.

The envelopes caught Lucy's attention; she sensed a find. There were three; they had been through the mail and carried recent postmarks, the latest, no more than a week ago. They were cheap, business envelopes and were addressed in carefully distorted block capitals, the badge of those who, for some reason, wish to appear illiterate as well as anonymous.

Lucy slipped a single sheet of lined paper from one of them. In the middle of the otherwise blank page was a biblical quotation, written in the same block capitals as the address: 'Thou hast played the harlot with many lovers – Jeremiah: 3:1.'

Lucy was intrigued. It struck her as slightly mad. A daughter of the manse she was nevertheless a child of the sixties and, for her, anonymous admonishment by way of biblical texts belonged to the same epoch as the Salem witch trials. She was tempted, but restrained her curiosity about the other envelopes, knowing that Fox would not welcome her prints being added to any others there might be.

'Did you know she was getting anonymous letters?'

'I knew that she'd had one.'

'Did she tell you?'

'I was there when she opened it. It must have been about a fortnight ago. She had come in with the mail – three or four items, she glanced through them and held up one envelope addressed in pencil and in block capitals. She said, "See this? Somebody who doesn't like me." She slit open the envelope, removed a sheet of paper, glanced at it, showed it to me, and said, "Silly cow!"'

'Did you get the impression she knew who had sent it?'

'I got that impression – yes.'

'She gave you no hint?'

'No.'

Lucy said: 'I must take these – and the photograph album. I'll give you a receipt.'

Family photographs are a good source of background. Everything else went back into the box.

It was downstairs as Lucy was leaving that Stephanie thawed. At the last moment it seemed that she was reluctant to break off contact with another woman. 'You probably think that we are unfeeling, but if you had lived as we have for the past three years . . . You see, neither Laurence nor I had any experience of this kind of life . . . But it wasn't only that.' She paused, then added, 'Jessica was a hard woman. Of course we should never have come here.'

'What did you do before?'

'I was a librarian, I have a degree in English. Of course I made the mistake of giving it up when I married – and lost my independence. Laurence had visions of us doing some literary work together while he carried on with his job, but nothing came of it.' She blinked, and her blue eyes misted over. 'Recently, I've been spending some time at Trecara, helping to catalogue Carey's library . . . Are you married?'

'No.'

'Sensible woman . . . Ah, well, Giles is my future.'

Chapter Four

In the churchyard the rooks were cawing, coming home to roost. Wycliffe entered the church by the south porch. A uniformed policeman stood guard.

'No sightseers?'

'They got tired, sir. But the press have been – and gone. Mr Kersey dealt with them.'

Just inside, on the table where the visitors' book and offertory box were normally kept, Fox and his assistant were logging their treasure trove: little envelopes, each with its tag; the hammer, an ordinary hammer except for its long handle; rolls of film; a clutch of scale diagrams . . .

A grumbling noise from the tower warned that the clock was about to strike and Wycliffe counted the seven strokes almost in disbelief. Fox had taken away his floodlamps, the lighting was dim, the church was returning to normal. Evidence of its desecration had been removed, the flowers were as fragrant as ever, and the statue of Christ looked out across the chancel steps, lantern held high.

'Anything, Fox?'

Fox, excessively lean and lanky, brooded over and fiddled with his hoard like a fastidious stork arranging and rearranging its nest material. Asking him a question was like interrogating a computer, one had to get him into the right mode first. After the necessary lapse of time he said, 'Large numbers of prints, sir, but I've no way of knowing

57

at the moment whose. The weapon was wiped clean, so were the organ keys and the blower switch.'

'You've got the bits of card used to wedge the keys?'

'Pieces of printed paper, sir, neatly cut and folded. They came from a magazine.'

'Any indication which?'

'A religious magazine, but there are several and I shall have to check them out.' Fox produced a block plan of the chancel and the adjacent area including the organ. 'I found a few flakes of mud, sir – river mud, I think, on the carpet of the south aisle. I've marked them with an M on the plan.'

The distribution of the flakes suggested that someone with muddy footwear had walked from the south porch towards the chancel. It was obviously possible that the mud had come from the feet of the killer and that he or she had reached the church by the river bank. The vicar had only to cross the road from his vicarage.

Fox went on, 'I found no actual footprint but one of the flakes carried an impression of the toe of what was probably a rubber boot. It was too fragile to take a cast but I've got photographs.'

'Good. Is Mr Kersey about?'

'I think he must be; I saw him a few minutes ago.'

Wycliffe found Kersey studying an inscribed tablet set in the wall of the chancel. Kersey read aloud: 'Thou shalt not kill, Thou shalt not commit adultery, Thou shalt not steal, Thou shalt not bear false witness . . .' And he added, 'That little lot adds up to our meal ticket.'

Wycliffe grinned. 'I'd be quite willing to take early retirement. Anyway, what's new? I hear you've had the press.'

'A reporter from the Plymouth paper with his cameraman, another from the local, and an agency chap.'

'Did you let them in?'

'Yes. The body had gone and Fox was all but through. I kept 'em up the west end, away from the chancel area, but they got their pictures.'

'Any good news?'

'Shaw has found us a home, an old school building just off the square, only recently vacated. The Central Stores people are fitting it out. Lucy Lane has laid on a house-to-house: the last time anybody saw Jessica; whether anybody was spotted entering or leaving the churchyard last evening . . . Actually, anybody could get in or out almost anywhere along the boundary wall. There's even a footpath and a kissing-gate down by the waterside.'

'I know. What happens here when Fox has finished?'

'The vicar has agreed to us putting seals on the place for the time being. Incidentally, Tom Reed has gone back to his burrow but we know where to find him.'

'I didn't get any lunch; did you?'

'No, and I'm beginning to miss it. Let's look in at the pub, sir, they must do some sort of evening meal. Ted Shaw did a bit of prospecting there earlier and it's got the Shaw Seal of Approval.'

The Hopton Arms was in the square by the post office, on the corner of Church Lane. Its sign carried a colourful portrait of the old royalist general on one side, and his achievement of arms on the other. The windows were diamond paned, there was a bit of fake timbering, and a rustic board, inscribed in Gothic lettering, offered meals and accommodation.

Kersey said, 'It's a bit olde worlde and the food probably comes out of a microwave but if the beer is reasonable I can live with that.'

Inside, the bar was at one end of a long room, cluttered with the usual furniture, tables with plastic tops that looked like marble and shiny wooden chairs that looked like plastic. At the far end, above glass doors, was a sign with the word 'Restaurant' in blue neon light and, beyond the doors, guarded by a couple of rubber plants, tables with blue cloths were laid, ready for the evening meal. Apart from the landlord, and three or four regulars drinking at the bar, the place was empty.

'Chief Superintendent Wycliffe and Inspector Kersey; am I right?' The landlord came from behind the bar, holding out his hand. He was a big man with short, dark curly hair; he wore a Yacht Club jersey and blue denim trousers. 'Johnny Glynn, at your service. Everybody calls me Johnny. Your Mr Shaw, who was here earlier, made provisional bookings for both of you, and for a DS Lane.'

Wycliffe growled and Kersey said, 'What's your draught bitter like?'

'You shall try it, gentlemen – on the house.'

The pints were drawn and the landlord stood watching while they were sampled. 'Well?'

Kersey said, 'It's good bitter, I'll give you that.'

The landlord glanced up at the clock. 'We serve meals from eight on Sundays; seven-thirty on other days; menus on the tables.'

Wycliffe inquired, 'Why Hopton?'

Johnny grinned. 'Royalist general in the Civil War, he met General Fairfax of the parliamentary lot on Tresillian Bridge, not far from here, to agree terms for ending the war in Cornwall. That was March 1646, and legend says he slept here.' Johnny shrugged. 'Could be true, and it might have been good for trade once; now if you said the Virgin Mary slept here they'd want to know "Who's she?" It's the new education.'

Wycliffe picked up his glass, Kersey had his refilled, and they moved away from the bar to seats at one of the little tables. It was dusk, and the lights were switched on.

Kersey said, 'That landlord is a bit of a pain but the

place is all right.' Changing the subject, he went on, 'So you've been to the farm, sir . . . ?'

Wycliffe studied the bottom of his glass but refused a refill. 'The dead woman – Jessica . . . Imagine a girl in her very early twenties, her parents killed in a coach crash . . . She insists on keeping the family farm going and, for seventeen years, she succeeds more or less, sometimes going out to work to make ends meet . . .'

'A determined young woman.'

'You can say that again.'

Wycliffe was still struggling to come to grips with the personality of the victim; trying to assess what he had gleaned from his visit to the farm.

'That little house . . . It's spartan. Either she was indifferent to creature comforts or she had a pretty broad streak of self-denial. The family who lived with her had a bleak time, that's for sure.'

Kersey finished his beer. Knowing from experience what this was all about, he asked the right questions: 'What are they like?'

Wycliffe grimaced. 'The man was a lecturer – Bristol – modern languages, but had a breakdown. Academic . . . Well-intentioned, probably hard working, but there's something . . . A square peg doomed to find himself in round holes, and resenting it.'

'And the woman?'

'Ornamental, probably well educated . . . musical. I'd guess not much of a clue when it comes to things like earning a living or organizing anything more complicated than tea and biscuits for the vicar.'

Wycliffe twisted his empty glass on a beer mat. 'Anyway, we should have the Lane version shortly. I left her there to snoop around and arrange for their statements. By the way, I want you to make inquiries about Vinter – why, precisely, did he give up his job? It shouldn't be difficult, it was only three or four years ago. And, while you're about it, you might check him out with CRO.'

Kersey lit a cigarette. 'You think he might have form?'

'How should I know? I'm simply trying to size him up; he made me feel uncomfortable.'

Kersey waited, but no more came. Time to prime the pump: 'And our Jessie got herself murdered, so there must have been emotional dynamite around somewhere.'

'Exactly. Presumably a man. Jessica was sometimes away all night; on two occasions, two nights running.'

'No explanation offered?'

'None.'

Kersey said, 'All the same, it's difficult to square the staging and the props with any kind of sex killing I've ever come across.'

Wycliffe nodded. 'It's hard to square any sort of killing, sexual or otherwise, with that theatrical set-up in the church. I've never met anything quite like it. Killing somebody against that background to the accompaniment of five notes which Schumann strung together to flatter his girlfriend – all played at once . . . There's a dangerous dottiness . . .'

People were drifting in, ordering drinks at the bar and taking them through the glass doors to the dining tables in the restaurant. They came mainly in couples but there was one party of five or six. 'You'll have to push the tables together tonight, Johnny; Gemma's got a birthday – her twenty-ninth.'

A wag called, 'Hey up, Gemma! You had that one last year.'

Lucy Lane arrived, an attractive, youngish woman on her own, and a stranger. She was watched, and there was obvious surprise when she joined the two middle-aged men at one of the bar tables. Only the better informed knew they were from the police.

Lucy, taken into the squad as a gesture to sexual equality, had quickly established herself in the hierarchy and she had side-stepped promotion because her next move would have taken her out of CID.

'I hope I did the right thing, sir? I suggested to Ted Shaw that it might be a good idea to make a provisional booking here.'

Wycliffe said, 'I'll tell you in the morning. Do you know what he's doing with the others?'

'They've been fixed up by sub-division: a small, private hotel in Truro; transport has been laid on.'

'I think we'd better find a table.'

But the landlord had already reserved one in a corner by the window.

'Will the hock suit you?'

'What's Chicken à la Marengo?'

'I'm not keen on mushrooms.'

'You'll have to put up with 'em if you have that.'

Meanwhile the party atmosphere was warming up. It seemed that everybody knew everybody else and apparently meaningless sallies raised gusts of laughter and fresh banter from around the tables.

The meal was served by two waitresses from a kitchen, seen through an open door, where a fat woman in a white coat did things with pans on a stove. No microwave in sight. Johnny, the landlord, moved from table to table.

'Everything to your liking, madam, and sirs?'

Wycliffe said, 'Is it always like this?'

'Not every night – this is about usual for Wednesdays and Sundays, they're our busy nights. Perhaps they're a bit more subdued than usual tonight because of Jessica.'

Kersey said, 'Nobody would notice.'

Wycliffe asked, 'Was the dead woman in on these occasions?'

'She didn't come here.'

'And the Geaches?'

The landlord's mobile features were suddenly expressionless. 'No.'

Gemma's health was drunk around the tables and they sang 'Happy Birthday to You', but with the arrival of the cheeseboard and coffee, things began to quieten down.

'Well, what did you make of the farm, Lucy?'

Lucy Lane, as always, took time to consider. 'I don't know about the farm, but the house is a museum piece – as you saw. The dead woman intrigues me: all that scraping and saving and going out to work, just to keep going. Incidentally, she kept a farm diary but there's nothing in it of a personal nature that I can see. I brought it away with me just in case.'

After placing a fragment of cheese on a water biscuit and nibbling it, she went on: 'Jessica was getting anonymous letters – or notes, three in the past two months. I handed them over to Fox, still in their envelopes, but I looked at one. It accused her of being a harlot, in a quotation from the Bible. Fox has promised to have them processed, with copies, by the morning.'

Wycliffe said, 'That's all we need! Anyway, what was your impression of the Vinters?'

A wrinkled brow. 'I think I got her measure, sir, but I'm not so sure about him. Stephanie has a degree in English; she was a librarian before she married, and recently she's been spending two or three afternoons a week at Trecara Manor – that's the house with the folly – helping to catalogue Carey's library. I don't suppose she gets paid for that. She doesn't seem a bad sort and I may sound catty, but I doubt if Stephanie has ever felt under any obligation to earn a living.'

'And Vinter?'

'As I said; he's a different case. Not much of what goes on inside shows. Seven-tenths, or whatever, submerged.'

'A possible killer?'

Some hesitation, then, 'If I asked you that question, sir, I'd get short shrift.'

Wycliffe grinned. 'But?'

'I felt there was something, but I couldn't put my finger on it.'

Wycliffe turned to Kersey. 'We've already agreed, that's one for you, Doug: some background on Vinter. Lecturer to labourer in one jump calls for explanation. He mentioned a breakdown but we need to know what kind. It shouldn't be difficult.'

Kersey emptied his coffee cup and sat back. 'That was a good meal.'

Wycliffe refused more coffee and said, 'I think I'll take a walk.'

Predictable; that was his routine when away from home: after the evening meal, a solitary walk, a telephone call to Helen, then bed.

Outside it was chilly, and he fetched a coat from his car, still parked in the square. It occurred to him that he ought to look in at the newly established Incident Room before indulging his whim. DS Shaw would have worked the usual minor miracle and deserved at least a paternal pat.

He found the former school, tucked away behind the post office in the middle of its asphalt playground: traditional Cornish, circa 1900, a single-storied, twin-gabled building of grey stone with granite coigns. Although small, it had two doors, one with 'Girls and Infants', the other 'Boys' carved in the granite lintels. The girls' door was open, and lit. A board propped on the steps carried a poster: 'Police Incident Room', and a uniformed PC said, 'The room on the left, sir.'

The former classroom, separated from another by the usual glass screen, was clean, well-lit, and would probably be almost cosy when the two bottled-gas heaters were working. Furniture and equipment disgorged by Central Stores was being arranged and installed by police personnel, while British Telecom chalked up Sunday overtime. Boxes of stationery were stacked on the floor and a bevy of VDUs, lined against the wall, yearned blankly for partnership with their electronic keyboards. Shaw looked upon his work and saw that it was not so bad, and getting better.

'There's a lady here, sir – Mrs Geach – sister of the dead woman. She insisted on waiting to see you though I told her it was by no means certain you would be in. I put her in the interview room.'

The 'interview room' turned out to be a former store cupboard with a tiny window. It now had a table and two chairs but such is the power of a name that Wycliffe at once recognized and accepted its role. Even the smell seemed to be right. The woman stood up as Wycliffe came in.

'Katherine Geach – Jessica's sister. I thought you would have come to the house . . .' Her manner was accusing.

'Superintendent Wycliffe.' He mumbled the introduction, sounding apologetic. God knows why except that the woman was strikingly good looking, with restless dark eyes. She was obviously distressed.

He tried sympathy but without effect. Her hands, clasped tightly together, rested on the table top. 'You know that my sister worked part-time for Arnold Paul – the organist at the church?'

'He told me.'

'So you've talked to him! You know that he has his brother living with him?'

'I understand that is fairly recent.'

66

'Yes.'

Suddenly she seemed to have run out of steam; she had been rehearsing what she would say for too long, now she had to stop and think. 'Yesterday morning – Saturday – my sister came to see me . . .'

'Is that unusual?' asked Wycliffe, recalling that he was a policeman.

She was pushed a little further off balance. 'Well, I suppose it is.' She made an irritable gesture. 'I don't know; the fact is that I usually go to see her rather than the other way round. Does it matter?'

'Probably not. So she came to see you?'

Hesitation. 'Well, she was in the village, shopping, and she just dropped in. She wanted to tell me about something odd which had happened at Arnold Paul's place on Friday afternoon.'

'She was worried?'

'I don't think she was worried, just intrigued.'

'Anyway, go on.' He was in the driving seat now. Mean, but necessary.

'She doesn't – didn't think that Philip – the man who came to live there – is Arnold's brother. She thought there was something crooked going on.'

'Can you enlarge on that?'

'Apparently she had heard them quarrelling more than once and sometimes Arnold called the other man "Timmy" instead of "Phil" as he usually did. Anyway, on Friday afternoon the quarrel was worse. The other man was threatening, and Arnold said, "All you'll achieve by that, my boy, is to put us both inside." There was more, but I can't remember it all.'

'They must have been very careless to let your sister overhear this.'

'They didn't know she was there; she was early, and Mabel Tripp, the old housekeeper, let her in.'

'But Mabel, herself—'

'Mabel is as deaf as a post.'

'You think this could have something to do with what happened to your sister?'

She looked down, fiddling with her handbag. 'I thought you should know, just in case.'

'Yes, you are quite right.' He suspected that there was something more, perhaps something that she found more difficult to talk about.

She looked up. 'I was wondering if I ought—'

There was a commotion outside and a man burst into the little room.

'Kathy! What the hell are you doing here? I've looked everywhere—' He broke off, and turned on Wycliffe: 'What do you mean by keeping my wife—?'

Wycliffe stood up. 'I assume that you are Mr Abe Geach. I am Detective Chief Superintendent Wycliffe. Your wife was waiting for me here when I arrived. She volunteered some information and I was about to ask her to make a formal statement. But that can wait until the morning when she has had time to think over what she has told me.'

He turned back to the woman: 'You were about to say . . . ?'

'Oh, nothing, it was of no importance.'

'In the morning, then. At the same time, Mr Geach, there are some questions I shall want to put to you, so I suggest that you are available then.'

Geach stood, rocking on the balls of his feet like a boxer. 'I've got my business to attend to in the morning.'

'No doubt, but this is a murder inquiry. I, or one of my officers, will be at Trigg sometime during the morning – unless you would prefer to come here?'

Wycliffe let his gaze rest on Geach until the silence was observable, then turned to the wife. 'Just one other matter while you are here, Mrs Geach, I understand that the farm belonged to you and your sister jointly – is there a formal agreement?'

'Yes, Jessica insisted on it. The agreement was drawn up by Harry Nicholls of Nicholls and Greet in Truro.'

'Do you know if your sister made a will?'

'We both did, leaving our interest in the farm to each other.'

'Well, thank you for coming along, Mrs Geach. I shall certinly look into what you have told me.'

Geach hesitated, then shrugged. 'Come on, Kathy; let's get out of here.'

Wycliffe was puzzled by Madam Geach. The story about Paul and his brother was probably true and might be significant but people, even the bereaved, do not usually come running to the police in such a hurry. Could Katherine really believe that her sister had been murdered in such an extraordinary way because she had overheard something incriminating from the Pauls? Or was she anxious to divert attention from nearer home?

Wycliffe returned to the square, determined not to be deprived of his walk. The square was reasonably well-lit with lights from the houses as well as a couple of street lamps, but as he walked towards the foreshore he seemed to be approaching a wall of darkness. It was only when he had left the square behind and could feel the shingle beneath his feet that he began to see the gleam of light on the water, to distinguish the shadowy banks of the creek, and the outlines of overhanging trees. Then, turning a little more to his left, he could make out the irregular roof of Trigg against the sky.

The organist, Arnold Paul, and his alleged brother: interesting. It was by no means impossible that a man who had made a good killing in some illicit deals and escaped the law should retire to a village like Moresk and find a respected place in the community. Few villains carry labels, many are neither brutish nor uncultured. Wycliffe well remembered a drugs dealer who had a reputation as a poet, and an armed bank robber who translated philosophical works from the Russian . . . Nor was it unlikely that such a man would be sought out in retirement and latched on to by another crook in need of a hideaway.

Walking along the shore, crunching over the shingle, he came upon a footpath which seemed to follow the line of the shore and to mark the boundary of Trigg land; obviously the other end of the path from the farmhouse by which he had reached the kissing-gate and the churchyard. He ventured along the path for a few yards and was surprised to find that the trees gave out and that there was open ground, across a lawn, to the house. There were lights, both upstairs and down, and Wycliffe wondered what sort of inquest was taking place there. For some reason, which he preferred not to examine, overtly sexual men like Geach stimulated his aggression.

The organist thing nagged like a sore tooth. It could be a lead, but he was dubious. Even assuming that the dead woman had overheard something deeply incriminating, how had they found out and acted with such dramatic despatch? And why the bizarre window dressing? Above all, why draw attention to the organ and, therefore, to the organist?

Wycliffe muttered to himself, out of temper, and gave up the idea of a walk. He returned to the square, collected his bag from the car, and re-entered the Hopton Arms. The tables in the restaurant were deserted and had been cleared. There were three or four people around the bar, a couple playing darts, and others scattered among the little tables nearby. Kersey was there, alone at one of them, nursing a glass of bitter.

70

'Lucy is having an early night. Feel like a nightcap?'

'No, I'm half asleep as it is.' He told Kersey of his interview with Katherine Geach, and of the arrival of her husband. 'One of us must go there in the morning. I shall be interested to see whether they choose to be interviewed separately or together.'

'Do you think there's anything in this business with the Paul brothers?'

'I've no idea; that's for tomorrow.' He stood up. 'Now I'm going to phone Helen, if I can find a phone in this place.'

The landlord had overheard: 'There's a pay-phone in the corridor outside the bedrooms, but if you want privacy, you can use the phone in the office.'

Wycliffe was chastened.

'It's me.'

'I thought it might be. So you're not coming home tonight.'

'No, this looks like being difficult. I'm at the Hopton Arms in Moresk Village – I'll give you the number.'

'Comfortable?'

'Seems so. The food is good.'

Just in time, he stopped himself from asking how the garden was looking, realizing that he had been away only a few hours.

'Have you been for your walk?'

'A short one.'

'Look after yourself.'

'And you. Good night.'

He went to bed, determined to put the case out of his mind, and lay awake thinking about Jessica Dobell. Her character, if anything, would provide the key; he was sure of that. And what did that amount to? Jessica – work and sex. It was like the word-association game played by psychologists. Work and sex which she pursued aggressively, with almost frenzied dedication and no regard for her own comfort or anybody else's.

One looked for an aim – an end in view. Money? Security? There were easier ways. Wycliffe felt instinctively that there was no aim, no vision of a future. But what? Could it be an obsessive concern to obliterate something that was past?

He needed to know more about her.

There was nothing wrong with his bed but he tossed and turned. Once, when he got out to recover his duvet from the floor, he looked out of the window and discovered that it was raining, a soft spring rain which sometimes comes when the wind is southerly, bringing with it the tang of a not too distant sea.

His little clock said five minutes past one. He returned to bed and, resigned to sleeplessness, fell asleep almost at once. When he awoke it was broad daylight.

For the Geaches it was a troubled night. To avoid disturbing one another they separated. Abe slept in the spare room but, shortly after daybreak, he crept into their bedroom and found Katherine wide awake. Clumsily solicitous, he came to sit on the side of the bed and stroked her hair.

'We've got to talk, Kath.'

'What is there to say?'

'The police are coming this morning and they will go on until they find out who did it.'

'Isn't that what we want?' Listless.

'Of course, but we ought to be ready to tell them certain things. I mean, they're outsiders, they didn't even know her.'

'You've got something on your mind; why not say it?'

Abe ran a hand through his dark curls. 'I don't want to upset you but think of how she was found. I mean, you *know* how she was found – you insisted on knowing. What I'm trying to say is that there must have been something in her life which explains her death – and the way of her death. That's how the police will look at it.'

'There was what she found out about Arnold's brother – as I told Wycliffe.'

'That the brother wasn't who he said he was and that they seemed to be mixed up in some shady business. Do you think they would have killed her because she overheard something of that sort? The chances are they didn't even know they'd been overheard, but even if they did, even if they decided to kill her, would they have laid on a bloody peep-show to do it?'

She was silent for a while, her dark eyes staring at the ceiling.

Geach went on: 'She must have been killed by somebody who meant to kill her and who chose to do it in that way – making a show, what they call nowadays a statement.'

'Like: "Here is a whore!" That's what you mean, isn't it? You're saying that whoever did it was warped – perverted!'

Abe said quietly, 'All right. Did she know anybody like that? . . . Do we? Or somebody who might be?'

She turned to look at him and for the first time he thought that he had her whole attention. 'You still haven't said all you want to say, Abe.'

'No, I'll say it now. Have you thought of Lavin?'

'The houseboat man!' She sat up in her astonishment. 'But Jess had nothing to do with Lavin. His boat happened to be berthed on the foreshore belonging to the farm and the rent was their only contact. He's so badly disfigured that, apart from the lad who lives with him, he doesn't see anybody. Jess hardly ever mentioned him.'

73

Geach was solemn. 'What you say is true, up to a point; Lavin is a recluse and most of his contacts are through the boy, but you can take it from me, Kath, Jess knew Lavin very well and she spent a lot of time with him.'

'Are you saying they were having an affair?' Her voice was hard.

Geach held out a hand to rest it on her arm. 'I've no proof that they went to bed together, but Jess and he were pretty close. I know that, and I think I should tell the police.'

'Why?'

'Why?' Geach reasoned patiently, as though with a child. 'How old is he? Forty? Not much more, and from what I've heard it's about seven years since he had his accident. God knows what goes on in the mind of a man like that, living there with only the boy for company. Career gone, family gone, friends . . . I don't know the details, but it must be something like that. Then along comes Jess – a very attractive woman, and she gives him friendship and whatever . . .'

Katherine was frowning. 'But everybody says the pair on the boat are gay.'

'Well, they would, wouldn't they? And they may be, but in Lavin's case it could well be Hobson's choice.'

Katherine tried to come to grips with this further insight into her sister's life. 'But even if what you say is true, why would he want to . . . I mean, why . . . ?' Her voice faltered.

Geach squeezed her arm. 'I know what you mean, kid. But what if, for some reason, Jess wanted to stop seeing him – to break off whatever they had between them? That's one possibility, but there's another. If there was a gay thing going between Lavin and his boyfriend there would be jealousy . . .'

'You mean it could have been the boy . . .'

74

'We just don't know, but we ought to put the police in the picture.'

After a long silence she looked up at him with sudden suspicion. 'How could you possibly know what you've just told me?'

He spoke quietly. 'Let's leave it that I do know it, Kath – just for now.' His manner was pleading.

She said in a toneless voice, 'All right. Just for now.'

'There's something else . . .'

'Go on.'

'About the farm. I know it's too early to talk about the long term but it's got to be kept going for the present, and without Jessica . . .'

'Well?'

'I've got a chap labouring on the Highertown site who rented a smallholding until last year when he went bust. Nothing would please him more than to get back to farming, even on a temporary basis. He could help out there.'

'Who's going to pay him?'

'He can stay on my payroll until things – well, until we know where we stand over the other business.'

Katherine swept back her hair in a tired gesture. 'I don't feel right about the "other business" as you call it, Abe. If it goes ahead now it's like taking advantage of what happened to Jess.'

Geach put his hand on her shoulder. 'Yes, well, there's no hurry to do anything. Just see how you feel as time goes on.'

Katherine looked at her husband, and was thoughtful. 'I wish I knew what was behind all this, Abe. It can wait, but don't take me for a complete fool.'

Chapter Five

Easter Monday

Lucy Lane, first down, said, 'It was the usual bacon, egg and sausage thing, or kedgeree. Johnny was anxious to get on, because of the holiday, so I said kedgeree.'

Kersey, who carried on a more or less clandestine affair with saturated fats, grumbled, 'It's as bad as being home.'

Wycliffe, more Jesuitical, preferred such decisions to be made for him. 'Kedgeree suits me.'

There were only two other tables occupied, one by an elderly, studious-looking couple who were probably touring Cornish churches or looking for ley lines; the other, by two pin-striped salesmen types who must surely have strayed off the spine road and got pixilated.

At a little before half past eight the police party left the pub for the Incident Room around the corner. In the fine, misty rain every surface shone or glistened, and every ledge dripped. Kersey stopped at the post office. 'I want some cigarettes.'

'Get a couple of newspapers at the same time.'

Despite the rain there was activity in the square; a van was unloading at the post office, a couple of cars were filling with petrol at the garage, and a boat was being hauled up the slipway. The Truro bus was about to move off, though without its usual complement of workers and shoppers. Easter Monday was a holiday for most people.

In the Incident Room order had been extracted out of

chaos. As yet it was on a small scale – just three fumble-fingered policemen tapping away on their machines. He was guided to his tiny office, leaving Kersey and Lucy Lane to sort out what was new.

Wycliffe's cubby hole had been carved out of a classroom as an office for a former headteacher. There was just room for a desk, a cupboard and a couple of chairs, and the original furniture was still there. In one of the desk drawers he found a little book recording visits by the school nurse and a pad of forms for reporting damage and dilapidations affecting buildings and equipment.

When Kersey joined him he was standing, staring out of the window at the gleaming wet asphalt of the playground and the boundary wall. He was recapturing that childhood experience of school – utterly cut off from the world, while a clock on the wall doled out some of the longest minutes and hours that he would ever know.

The two of them sat down. 'Mind if I smoke, sir?' A ritual question, but an acknowledgement of their hierarchic relationship which would probably last for the rest of the day. Kersey had the newspapers.

'Anything in them?'

Kersey pushed over the regional paper, the *Morning News*, folded back.

'They weren't in time for the national early editions we get down here, but this chap's done pretty well.'

There were two library pictures of the church: one of the exterior, the other a view of the chancel.

The headlines read: 'Murder in Church', 'Ritual Killing?'. And the text went on: 'When the Reverend Michael Jordan, Vicar of Moresk, arrived to celebrate Holy Communion at his church on the morning of Easter day he found the partly clothed body of Jessica Dobell, sprawled across the chancel steps, at the very feet of a statue of Christ. She had been brutally killed by a blow to the head,

77

believed to have been inflicted by a hammer found close to her body.'

The wedged organ keys were said to provide: 'a distressing, nerve-jangling discord as an accompaniment to this scene of horror which confronted the vicar.

'It is difficult to see this crime as other than a bizarre and senseless ritual murder.'

Wycliffe said, 'That should bring 'em down by the car load. Anything more helpful in our own reports?'

'Nothing factual. Nobody was seen entering or leaving the church on Saturday evening or, if they were, it was so ordinary that the fact didn't register. Of course, we now have formal statements from the vicar and from the Vinters – including the boy.'

'What about gossip?'

'Jessica isn't getting quite the flattering obituary the victim can usually count on. There's some talk of her meanness, more of her sex life. No names, but it won't be difficult to ferret them out when the dust has settled a bit. It seems that the Women's Guild, under the presidency of the vicar's sister, resented Jessica having the church cleaning job – not that anybody else wanted it, but she was regarded as morally tainted.'

'The Vinters?'

Kersey brushed ash from his shirt front. 'Vinter is rarely seen in the village but he often goes to church with his wife on Sunday evenings. It seems he's interested in natural history – especially bats, and he's doing some sort of survey. Stephanie belongs to the Musical Society, run by the vicar and the organist. She's regarded as a kind of phenomenon, not quite real.'

Kersey's lined features contorted into one of his baby-frighteners, registering mirth. 'One woman said she didn't get taken down and dusted often enough. The boy, Giles, belonged to the Musical Society but gave up a month or two back, though he still goes to church with his parents. He's got the name for being a big-head. Seems he's something of a prodigy at school; a sound bet for the Oxbridge scholarship stakes.'

'Anything on the Geaches?'

'Another slice of family life. Geach's father died of a heart attack in his early sixties. Mother Geach is still around; she shares a harbour flat at Falmouth with another widow. Abe carries on where his father left off, a workaholic, and is expected to go the same way as his dad. He's also got a name as a womanizer. His contracts take him all over the two counties and he uses a rather plush motor-caravan as a mobile office and sleeping quarters. Useful for his women too.'

'Any suggestion of local women being involved?'

'One doorstep oracle hinted at Jessica – I suppose that was inevitable; but she backed down when pressed.'

'Paul and his brother?'

'Arnold Paul is well liked but so are most people who give away money. Nobody seems to have seen much of the brother.'

Wycliffe brooded. 'I think I'll see the Pauls while you have a go at the Geaches. Turn the screw a bit if you have to.'

Lucy Lane arrived with a handful of polythene envelopes and Jessica's photograph album. 'The originals of the anonymous notes, sir. The envelopes and the sheets have been kept separate. Fox has given them the treatment; plenty of prints on the envelopes but only the dead woman's on the sheets. Whoever sent them knew enough for that.'

Lucy laid them on the desk in front of Wycliffe. 'They are in order and the dates range over the past seven weeks.'

Wycliffe looked them over with a jaundiced eye, then

began to read them aloud: 'The first one says: "Thou shalt not play the harlot – Hosea 3:3." The second: "Thou hast played the harlot with many lovers – Jeremiah 3:1." And the last: "Thou hast played the harlot with them yet couldest not be satisfied – Ezekiel 16:28." A consistent theme.'

Kersey grinned. 'And spot on. I didn't realize the Bible was up to it.'

Lucy said, 'It's all there if you're prepared to look for it, but I can't imagine why anyone would go to the trouble of sending the things. What did they expect to achieve?'

Kersey shrugged. 'What do Jehovah's Witnesses expect to achieve when they come knocking on my door? Even the sight of me doesn't put 'em off. As to who sent these, I expect there are one or two members of the Women's Guild not averse to brooding on the sex life of an unenlightened sister. A spot of reforming propaganda might seem in order.'

Wycliffe agreed. 'Yes, propaganda is the word – these don't threaten. If the sender intended violence I would expect a more aggressive follow-up to these. Surely anybody playing God would get a kick out of threatening the wrath to come before proceeding to execution.'

Lucy said, 'Perhaps, but the fact remains, Jessica is dead – murdered, and these messages were sent to her.'

There was no answer to that, so Wycliffe shuffled the plastic envelopes together and handed them back. 'All right, stir the pond Lucy, and see what comes to the surface. Now, what's this photo album?'

He turned the pages: the Dobell girls, from nappies to school uniform, on to gangling adolescence and the first flush of maturity. In the earlier photographs parents were much in evidence, in the later ones, girlfriends and boyfriends took their place. At home Helen treasured a similar record of their own twins.

Lucy drew his attention to a snapshot taken on a beach, the sea in the background; the two girls skittish in bikinis, and two boys in trunks. They faced the camera, arms linked in pairs. 'Recognize the boys, sir?'

On close inspection he recognized the one with Katherine, a younger version of Abe Geach, the contractor, lusty, brawny and ready to go. 'I can't place the other.'

Kersey said, 'You should never have been a copper, sir. That's Johnny Glynn, our sneaky landlord. He looks a good deal thinner and a lot less smug.'

The sequence came to an abrupt end with several highly professional photographs of Katherine's wedding, a very up-market occasion. Then no more photographs. The wedding, or something else at about that time, seemed to mark the end of an era for the girls. The last two or three pages of the album had been used to paste in news clippings from the local paper.

Lucy said: 'The last is recent – just a few days ago.'

'Anything particular strike you about them?'

'They're a mixed bag. Of course the report of her sister's wedding is there and an account of the inquest on their parents and the coach crash.'

'Nothing significant? – Odd?'

Lucy was hesitant. 'Not odd exactly but it happens that three of the cuttings, including the most recent one, refer to a family called Ruse from Tresillian. In January seventy-six their fifteen-year-old son was killed in a hit-and-run while cycling home. There is a report of the accident, and of the inquest which recorded a verdict of unlawful killing against a person or persons unknown.'

'A bit unorthodox.'

'Yes. Anyway, the latest cutting is an account of the funeral, last week, of the boy's mother, aged fifty-five. I wondered why that family and the incident had such obvious interest for Jessica.'

Most of police time in any investigation is spent chasing shadows but the Yorkshire Ripper case reminded every CID chief of Sod's law – that it's the shadow you don't chase which turns out to be flesh and blood.

'Find out a bit about it – don't spend too much time. The original case will be in the files so have a word with Inspector Reed; he should be able to brief you.'

He turned to Kersey. 'Now, Doug, you're for the Geaches, and I'm for the Pauls.'

But, left alone, he continued to sit at his desk, assiduously manicuring his nails with a matchstick, a habit Helen deplored.

So. Anonymous messages had been added to the elaborate charade in the church. But he knew better than to be fooled by the decoration on the cake. Underneath he would find the usual drama of jealousy or hatred or greed, or any of them in combination; a drama with a scenario little different from many others. The difference in this case was that the theme had been so overlaid; so decorated and contrived that it was unrecognizable. A hint of madness? Perhaps; but madness allied to the logic of Alice's Wonderland.

He was on the point of leaving when Potter came in: 'The boy wants to see you, sir – the Vinter boy.'

'Send him in.'

Giles Vinter came in, looking about him with apparent interest, head held back because his glasses were halfway down his nose.

'Did you ever go to this school?'

'No. I was fourteen when my parents came here and I went straight to the senior school in Truro.' The blue eyes were solemn but there was no sign of unease as he took the seat Wycliffe offered.

'Can I help you? Or, perhaps, you can help me. I assume this is about Miss Dobell?'

But Giles needed none of the routine treatment for young witnesses. The glasses were pushed up with the middle finger of the left hand, an unconscious movement. 'I didn't like her. I am not upset about her death, but I don't want you to suspect the wrong person.'

'Can you help me to suspect the right one?'

'No, but I can tell you something I didn't tell you at first. On Saturday evening there was a telephone call for her after she left for the church.'

'Any idea of the time?'

He looked thoughtful. 'I was up in my room and my parents were downstairs talking. I think they were quarrelling, and I heard my father go out – he usually goes out between eight and half-past so it must have been about then. I was coming downstairs when the telephone rang; my mother wasn't in the living room so I answered it.'

'Go on.'

'It was a man's voice, he didn't give his name, he just asked to speak to Miss Dobell. I told him she was out and he asked if I knew where he might contact her. I told him she would be at the church. He thanked me and rang off. That was all.'

'You didn't recognize the voice?'

'No.'

'Would you if you heard it again?'

'I don't think so; it was quite ordinary and we were always getting calls for her.'

'Did he give you the impression that he was worried or annoyed?'

'I don't think so.'

'I would like you to put what you have said into a fresh statement.'

'All right.'

83

'Before you do, just one or two more points: you said that you disliked Miss Dobell.'

'Yes; she was cruel, and she treated my mother very badly.'

'What about you and your father?'

'That too, but it was worse for my mother.'

The boy sat opposite Wycliffe, a slight figure, his blond hair cut short with a fringe, his head tilted back slightly to cope with his bifocals. He seemed self-contained and totally at ease. Wycliffe tried to draw him into talk: 'You used to belong to the church Musical Society but you gave it up . . .'

'They didn't want me.'

'I hear that you are working for your A-levels and an Oxbridge scholarship; do you think you'll make it?'

'If I decide to go ahead with it.'

'You think that you may not?'

'I don't know.'

'Do you play any games?'

'Only chess; no field games.'

'You play chess at home with your father?'

'He's no good at it. Mother plays with me sometimes, but it's not a woman's game.'

Wycliffe gave up. 'Well, thank you for coming. If you go into the next room someone will take your statement.'

Wycliffe felt deflated. But what the boy had told him might mean something. Had the killer telephoned to make sure that Jessica would be at the church? It was possible.

Before leaving for the Pauls' he studied the 1/2500 Ordnance map. Wycliffe's attitude to maps was ambivalent, even whimsical; they were a necessary evil but they diminished his world. Unless it was essential, he preferred not to know what was around the next corner or over the next hill. But here, on this single sheet of paper, all the secrets of the neighbourhood were laid bare, the village,

Trigg, the church, the path along the river bank, even the reed bed and the tower . . . No wonder people climb mountains and go to Greenland.

A century ago Moresk had consisted of a few cottages, Trigg House, the church and Trecara. The growth of Truro, the desire of shopkeepers and professional people to move 'out of town', and the fashion for second homes, combined to produce an overgrown village, lacking much coherence, but still a pleasant place to live.

The more prestigious villas were in Church Lane, on the other side from the church, and it was in one of these, behind a tall dry-stone wall topped with flowering shrubs, that Arnold Paul had settled in his retirement. Wycliffe arrived there at about ten; it was still raining but there was a pearly brightness in the sky with a promise of sun.

As he stood on the doorstep he could hear music – one of Wagner's blockbusters – he neither knew nor cared which. After some delay the doorbell was answered by Mabel, lean, angular, and no-nonsense. Because he shouted, or because she read his lips, she understood his purpose.

'You'd better come in.'

He was shown into a large room in which the senses were drowned under a welter of sound.

'You'll have to wait; he's still in the bathroom. You can sit down, but you mustn't touch things; he's fussy.'

Wycliffe traced the source of the music to a space-age, slim-line music centre in one section of which a compact disc spun smoothly, and in deceptive innocence, while feeding its coded barrage of sound to two columnar speakers, strategically placed in the room. Any means of volume control eluded him.

Having met the well-groomed, precise, and rotund

organist, who looked like Trollope's Mr Harding, Wycliffe was surprised by the comfortably relaxed and untidy room. Shelves covering most of one wall were stacked with what seemed to be musical scores; shelves on another wall held a little library of books on musicology, wedged in anyhow. Framed portraits of composers found space where there were no shelves, and any convenient ledge supported its dusty plaster bust of some eminent musician.

The point was made that Arnold Paul was a musician.

Despite the ear-splitting noise Wycliffe had not had time to get bored before Paul came in looking more than ever like a well-heeled clergyman in mufti.

'Ah, Mr Wycliffe! The music is rather loud I'm afraid, but I like to hear it in my bath.' He picked up a remote control device and silence came with the impact of a negative thud.

'There! Now, how can I help you?' He sat in one of the several armchairs, crossed his short legs, and was all attention.

'I had hoped to see your brother also.'

'My brother?' A look of surprise. 'I'm sorry, but that isn't possible; he left early this morning.'

'Left? Where did he go?'

Paul seemed slightly put out by the abruptness of the question but he put a good face on it. 'He took the seven twenty-one train to London. I ran him into Truro while I was still only half awake.'

'A sudden decision?'

'Not really.' Paul uncrossed his legs and went on with exaggerated patience: 'My brother and I do not get on well together and recently there has been increased friction. Last week it reached something of a climax and we agreed that it would be better to revert to the old arrangement under which we lived apart.'

'So, where has he gone?'

Paul was brusque. 'If you are asking me for his address, I don't know it. Probably he has booked in at some hotel while he looks around for a place that will suit him.'

'Presumably he has some sort of business?'

The little man shifted irritably in his chair. 'I know nothing of my brother's business, Mr Wycliffe! And, quite frankly, I do not understand your interest.'

'Perhaps you will give me his former address?'

Paul spread his hands. 'I cannot do that. We were in touch only by telephone until he came here and it was always he who made contact. To be frank, when he wanted something.'

'His first name is Philip?'

Paul's little eyes were alert and guarded. 'Yes, but really—'

'But you sometimes addressed him as "Timmy".'

A slight start of surprise. 'You are well informed, Mr Wycliffe. Timmy was a sort of pet name he picked up as a child. I have no idea of its origin.'

Arnold Paul was not easily put off balance but there had been a significant delay before he offered his explanation. Not that what he said was improbable.

'Your brother is younger than you?'

'By two years.'

'You were overheard to say, during one of your disagreements: "All that would achieve is to put us both inside".'

A faint smile. 'Did I say that? That would have been in connection with his suggestion for a joint business venture – a rather bitter joke on my part, I'm afraid.'

'Your brother's business activities were on the wrong side of the law?'

Another smile, a little more nervous. 'Sometimes, perhaps in a grey area; in any case, not the kind of thing in which I would want to be involved.'

'What is, or was, your business, Mr Paul?'

'I was the financial director of the London and Midlands Credit and Investment Bank.' Distant.

'You retired early?'

'I was just fifty. Music has always been my real interest and I worked hard for thirty years so that I could make it my sole concern. I could, of course, have taken it up as a career, but I knew that my talent was insufficient to earn me, as a professional musician, the kind of money I needed to keep me in comfort and security.' A smile. 'You see, Mr Wycliffe, I have never been one for starving in an attic.'

'When did you last see Jessica Dobell?'

The sudden question brought him up short. He shifted uncomfortably in his chair. 'Oh, dear! I have been rather dreading that question. There is something I should have told you, or someone, earlier. I saw her in the church on Saturday evening. I store quite a lot of music in a cupboard behind the organ and I wanted—'

'You have a key to the church?'

'Certainly! I sometimes go across to play for my own amusement and, of course, there is the Musical—'

'Who else has a key, apart from the vicar?'

'Jessica had one, and Harry Clemens, the church-warden – he owns the post office and general store in the square. Oh, and whoever is in charge of the flowers for the week.'

'What time was it when you saw Jessica?'

'About eight? At any rate between half-past seven and eight.'

'Someone telephoned the farm to speak to Jessica between eight and half-past. Was it you?'

'Why would I telephone her? I told you I have my own key.'

'What was she doing when you arrived?'

88

Paul hesitated as though the next bit would be even more difficult.

'There is a door off the chancel into the vestry which closes on a spring and a wooden wedge keeps it open when required. Someone had wedged it too securely and Jessica was trying to free it by knocking it gently with a hammer.'

'With a hammer.' Wycliffe's voice was bleak.

'I'm afraid so.'

'Who would need to wedge the door?'

'Oh, the women doing the flowers on Saturday afternoon. They get water from the toilet off the vestry. Almost certainly one of them wedged it open and couldn't free it.'

Paul was getting flustered. 'I realize that I have been very remiss in not telling you this before but you can see that it has no special significance.'

'That is for me to judge. You neither saw nor heard anyone in the church, or in the vicinity, when you were going and returning?'

'I saw no-one.' He went on: 'I feel very guilty about this but, of course, I have never been in such a situation before. I was deeply shocked when I heard of Jessica's death and I suppose I was reluctant to involve myself.'

'The fact that your brother has now left, and that his whereabouts are unknown, has nothing to do with your belated decision to speak out?'

Paul's eyes widened. 'That is a most improper suggestion, Mr Wycliffe!'

'It was not a suggestion, it was a question, and when you withhold information from the police in a murder inquiry, it is the sort of question that is asked, and answers are sought. I would like to see the room which your brother occupied while he was here.'

'His room?' Paul seemed on the point of refusing but thought better of it. 'All right. If you will come with me . . .'

Wycliffe was taken to a large room at the back of the house on the first floor. It was a bedroom which had been turned into a bedsitter. Apart from the usual bedroom furniture, which included an unmade bed, there was a desk and, on the desk, a telephone and a rack of stationery. There was also a large ashtray holding a briar pipe. The lingering smell of pipe smoke rekindled a vague longing in Wycliffe.

Paul said: 'He's forgotten his pipe.'

'Nothing has been touched since he left this morning?'

'Everything is as he left it. As you see, even his bedding hasn't been removed.'

Wycliffe slid open the desk drawers; they were empty. On open shelves let into the alcove by the chimney breast there were several paperbacks. Wycliffe looked them over: the brainchildren of John le Carré, led by the inimitable Smiley.

'Are these his?'

'Yes, he has a taste for spy fiction.'

'I would like this room left as it is for the time being, Mr Paul. I'll send someone along to take a look at it.'

'Surely, Mr Wycliffe! . . . Are you implying that he might have a record?'

'You said yourself that his business activities were sometimes in a grey area of the law. From what the dead woman told her sister it is clear that she suspected him of some criminal involvement. She has been murdered, and I have to trace your brother if only to eliminate him from the inquiry.'

Paul was silenced.

'Just one more question, Mr Paul: when you saw her on Saturday evening, was she her usual self?'

The organist seemed dazed, but he made an effort. 'Entirely. She made some typical remark about flower arrangers who didn't know their own strength. I collected my music and when I left, she had already removed the wedge and she was polishing the tiles where it had scratched.'

'Thank you. Now, I must ask you to make a written statement concerning what you have told me. I suggest that you come to the Incident Room in the old school building some time this afternoon.'

Wycliffe left, thinking that it was one thing to take Arnold Paul down a peg or two, but quite another to imagine him or his elusive brother staging a melodramatic killing. But it was not impossible, and Philip or Timmy had made a quick and well-timed get-away.

Kersey crossed the square to the Trigg entrance. There was no gate, just two granite pillars with a much-weathered anonymous ornament on the top of each. Although it was not actually raining the air was saturated with moisture, and the moss, which grew on the gateposts and most of the stonework, was intensely green.

Three vehicles were parked on a freshly gravelled area near the house: a deluxe motor-caravan, a Rover saloon, and a Mini. The house had no particular shape, it seemed to have evolved at the whim of successive owners, all very long dead. The result was a pleasing jumble, mellowed by time, lichen, moss and ivy.

At any rate it pleased Kersey, who knew nothing of architecture but hated ostentation.

He had difficulty in finding the door, but when he did it was answered by a youngish woman, plump, pink, and freckled. 'Mrs Geach?'

'No. I suppose you're the policeman; you'd better go into the breakfast room.'

A room in which it was obvious that nobody ever had breakfast, it was a nondescript parking place for visitors who were not paying a social call.

Kersey sat for a couple of minutes gazing at gilt-framed furnishing landscapes, and an enormous walnut sideboard with a marble top on which there stood a hideously ornate samovar. Geach must have made a habit of collecting the left-overs from country-house sales.

Geach joined him, loose limbed, shambling, ready for anything.

'Mr Geach? . . . Inspector Kersey.'

'I was expecting your boss.'

'We all have our little disappointments, sir.'

Geach gave him a doubtful look and sat himself in one of the armchairs. Kersey was perched on one of the high-backed dining chairs with a leather seat.

'All right. Fire away.'

Kersey said, 'I can see you're not a man to beat about the bush; neither am I, so I'll get down to it. How well did you know your sister-in-law?'

Geach screwed up his lips. 'How well do you know yours? Assuming you've got one. She had the farm to run; my wife and I have our own lives; we didn't live in each other's pockets.'

'I saw the motor-caravan. Nice job.'

Geach became wary. 'So?'

'Handy for site work; handy too, I imagine, for entertaining the odd visitor in private.'

Geach remained cool. 'If you intend to be offensive, I should warn you—'

Kersey cut in with practised skill. 'No, I should warn you, Mr Geach, that this is a murder inquiry and, whatever you think, a lot of dirty linen will be fished out of the clothes basket. Whether it's all washed in public will depend on the people concerned. You, for instance; you can talk to me, man-to-man, or you can put up with us ferreting around for days, weeks – months if necessary. You don't need me to tell you that there aren't any real secrets in a place like this. Then, of course, there are the lads who work on your sites . . .'

Geach took a packet of mini cigars from his pocket and lit one. 'Smoke if you want to. Have one of these?'

'No, thanks, I'll smoke my own.'

Geach was looking at him with something like amusement. 'You're an impudent bastard, but I think we might get on.'

'Good! So you entertain the occasional woman in your van.' Kersey put on his best conspiratorial leer. 'Nothing to do with me unless one of 'em happens to have been Jessica Dobell. Think before you say anything, we've already had a hint along those lines and it wouldn't take much for us to have the forensic boys turn over the van.'

Geach drew deeply on his cigar and blew out a cloud of smoke. 'I don't believe this! I've got a bloody good mind to boot you out and put in a complaint.'

'It's up to you, sir, but I think we each had our reasons for coming to this little chat alone.'

Geach thought about this.

Kersey knew that he was on thin ice but he felt that he understood the contractor. He also understood why Wycliffe had given him the job instead of doing it himself.

Geach squinted at him through the smoke. 'All right; I don't suppose it will do me any harm unless you are a bigger fool than I take you for. Jessica did see the inside of my van a couple of times.'

'She was away from the farm three or four nights a month – two nights running a couple of times.'

'Not with me, she wasn't. Twice, as I said.' He seemed about to continue, but hesitated. Kersey, apparently indifferent, was looking out of the window watching Katherine, hands thrust deeply into the pockets of her mac, walking by the river. Geach went on: 'My sister-in-law, sex-ways, was a woman and a half, Inspector; damn nearly a nympho. She couldn't get enough.'

'You are saying there were others? The chap who lives there – Vinter, perhaps?'

'That's for sure, but she wouldn't want to be away nights for that, would she? All in working hours, so to speak.' Geach brushed ash from his jumper. 'No, the man you should be talking to is Lavin – the houseboat man – that's where she spent those nights away – some of 'em anyway. I intended to tell you that much before we started.'

'How do you know?'

'She told me.' He fixed Kersey with a quiet stare. 'She got some of her kicks that way – talking about it.' He shrugged. 'She pretended that in her book, sex-ways, I didn't rate very high; five out of ten, if that.' A crooked smile, 'While Lavin, if half of what she said was true, should have a medal to show for it. But I reckon that was her ploy, she probably did the same with him.' Geach became thoughtful. 'Jessica was one of those women who hates to take anything from a man. When she did, she couldn't bring herself to admit it.'

'You know Lavin?'

'I've only seen him a few times but he's lived in that boat for a couple of years – he took it over from Shorty Boase, when they put the old man into a home. Anyway, Lavin's very badly disfigured – doesn't show himself much; some sort of accident a few years back. But it didn't put Jessica off. No way.'

'Does he live by himself?'

Geach relit his cigar and spoke between rekindling puffs. 'No, he's got a boy living with him – I say boy, but he could be in his twenties. They call him Jumbo because he's a big chap and a bit ponderous. There's something odd about him, but he's Lavin's lifeline to the outside.'

Kersey was almost affable. 'Now, sir, if you can tell me the last occasion when the deceased visited your van . . .'

'It must have been early March, I could probably work it out.'

'You do that; ready for your statement.'

'You still want a statement?'

Kersey was cheerfully ironic. 'You must be joking! You've been sleeping with the victim of a sex killing and you ask me if we want a statement. You're in the target area, my friend, and I think you know it.' Kersey broke off and stood up. 'So let's say, this afternoon, at the old school, sir.'

Geach too, got to his feet. 'Will my wife have to know about Jessica?'

'Why should she? Unless it turns out you're the man we're looking for, then you'll have other things to worry about.'

'You're going to take a statement from her?'

'On the matter of what she was told by her sister about the situation between the Paul brothers. You don't have to worry. I'll send along a nice friendly DC and they can work it out between 'em here.'

As Geach followed him out into the hall a slim, dark girl flitted away down the passage.

'Your daughter?'

'Yes, damn it! Was that door shut?'

'Not quite.'

On the doorstep, Kersey said, 'What do you think of the Vinters?'

'Off the record?'

'Carried to the grave.'

'All right. Vinter's one of life's also-rans; two left feet. And Stephanie? She looks like a bit of Dresden china but there's a rumour Vinter isn't the boy's father.'

'What about the boy?'

Geach blew out his cheeks. 'He's supposed to be very bright but to my mind he's a poof in the making. Our Julie's got a thing about him and he's been to the house once or twice, but I told him to bugger off.'

Kersey left, pleased with himself; the contractor was no longer cocky.

Chapter Six

'The dead woman's clothes, sir. Just returned from the path lab.'

Each item had been bagged and tagged separately: jeans, denim jacket, torn shirt, briefs, socks and slippers. Lucy Lane was laying them out on a trestle table in the Incident Room in case it became necessary to send them to Forensic.

Wycliffe was aware of a certain tension in her manner. 'What's the problem?'

'There's this; another anonymous.' She held out two polythene covers, one containing the envelope, the other the message.

'Another? Where did it come from?'

'It was found in the pocket of her jeans, sir. It's post-marked last Thursday, two days before she was killed.'

'Why wasn't it reported and dealt with last night?'

'It was missed when the body was stripped at the path lab. The clothes remained in the bins all night and the envelope was only found when they came to be bagged and logged this morning.'

Lucy waited for the obvious question: 'Who was attending?' But it didn't come. Wycliffe knew the virtue of the occasional blind eye. Somebody had boobed, but it wasn't the end of the world and nit-picking, to be effective, must be strictly rationed.

Lucy was still uneasy. 'Fox processed it this morning.'

Panic stations, obviously, and a closing of ranks. Lucy had been talked into being the sacrificial lamb; not in character. She went on, 'When it was found, the envelope hadn't been opened. It seems Jessica didn't attach much importance to these messages; she must have stuffed it into the pocket of her jeans and forgotten all about it.'

'What does it say?'

As with the others, the message was brief: 'These shall hate the whore and shall make her desolate and naked – Revelations 17:16.'

'What do you make of it?'

'It's different – an obvious threat this time.'

'The missing link in the chain?'

Lucy looked vague. 'I suppose it could be, sir, but the writing seems different as well as the aptness of the quotation – as though someone tried to imitate the others, not very successfully. The paper and envelope are the same as the others but anybody can buy them.' She added, abruptly, 'I would like to talk to the vicar's sister about these.'

'You think she sent them?'

'With respect, sir, it's only that she probably knows more of what goes on amongst the women of the village than anybody else – I mean, those connected with the church.'

'And you think a woman wrote these things?'

'I would like the chance to find out.' Lucy had recovered her poise. Obviously she thought the storm cones had been lowered.

'All right; go ahead. Anything else?'

'I had a word with DI Reed about the Ruses . . .' She added, to jog his memory: 'The cuttings in Jessica's photo album about the boy who was killed in the hit-and-run.'

'Well?'

'He remembers the case well. He was a sergeant in Traffic at the time and much involved. The lad was cycling home from Trispen at about half-six in the evening. It was winter, and dark, and he was hit by a motorist. His body and the bike were then pushed over the hedge, presumably to delay an inquiry, and not found until next morning. There were doubts as to whether the boy was dead when his body was pushed over, and local feeling was very strong.'

'The culprit was never found?'

'No. Johnny Glynn was a prime suspect but there was no evidence against him that would stand up in court. The inquiry went on for months and, in theory, the file is still open.'

Wycliffe had a vague recollection of reports concerning the investigation but he had not been directly involved. 'Ring DI Reed and say that I will look in on him tomorrow afternoon to discuss the case.'

It was mid-morning when Lucy arrived at the vicarage; the rain had stopped but it was still wet underfoot. The doorbell was answered by Celia, in person. Lucy introduced herself and showed her warrant card.

'My brother is in Truro for a meeting with the bishop.' Uncompromising. Lucy almost expected the door to be shut in her face.

'It was you I came to see – if you can spare me a few minutes.'

Celia Jordan was grey, her hair, her eyes, her skin, and her frock – the frock reminded Lucy of a nun's habit. And Celia's manner was bleak.

She hesitated, sizing up her visitor. 'All right, I can give you a few minutes. Wipe your feet – I've just hoovered the passage.'

The vicarage was modern, built by the Church Commissioners when they sold off their legacy of old and over-large properties which catered for a more prosperous and fecund clergy. But the Jordans had contrived to give the place an appearance of being steeped in decades of ecclesiastical dreariness and gloom. There was an abundance of varnished woodwork, fawn and brown fabrics, and drab wallpapers relieved only by prints of holy pictures.

She was taken to a room at the back of the house, obviously the Vicar's study. There was a desk, a prie-dieu, and a great many shelves of religious works. It was dimly lit because the window was shielded by a conifer hedge grown close to the house. Celia occupied a swivel chair behind the desk and left Lucy with the choice of two kitchen chairs facing her. The reception of young people arranging weddings and christenings must have been equally grim.

Lucy presented the first three messages, arranging them on the desk. Her manner was ingratiating. 'You probably know the village and the villagers better than most. These are anonymous communications received by the dead woman in the weeks preceding her death and we are anxious to trace their source. I've really come to you for advice.'

Celia put on her spectacles which were secured by a silk cord about her neck. She studied the exhibits in silence. It was difficult to judge her age; her cheeks and forehead were smooth, but her mouth seemed slightly shrunken and her upper lip was corrugated with the finest wrinkles. Her examination of the exhibits was brief and when she looked up she seemed mildly impatient. 'You realize that these are quotations taken out of context? In their proper context they are largely metaphorical, even allegorical.'

Lucy was defensive. 'But they were copied out and sent

to the dead woman so, presumably, they were intended to apply to her.'

She received a bleak look over the top of the spectacles. 'That much is obvious. What more do you expect me to say?'

It was going to be hard going.

'You will know, of course, that Jessica's conduct was the subject of criticism by some in the village?'

'By me, you mean, and by women of the Guild. I make no apology for that; a woman with her reputation was quite unsuited to employment in the church. In this matter I disagreed with my brother.'

'So that you are to some extent in sympathy with the sender of these notes.'

A frown. 'They seem harmless. There can be no crime – certainly no sin, in reminding the wrongdoer of her error.'

'As they stand, they seem rather pointless. What could they be expected to achieve?'

Celia removed her spectacles and chose to be sententious: 'One should never underestimate the power of the word.'

'But a threat might have made it more effective.'

'I see no threat in these at any rate.'

Lucy produced the fourth message and handed it over. 'This was sent two days before Jessica was murdered.'

The glasses were replaced and this time the examination took longer. She brought out a Bible from one of the desk drawers and referred to it briefly.

The woman was obviously intelligent and she had a formidable presence. Lucy was reminded of a university tutor under whom she had suffered; a female dragon who commonly handed out the look she now received, usually with a barbed comment: 'Your essay displays a singular, one might say a perverted, talent for missing the obvious.'

Celia contented herself with: 'Surely you must see that

101

this fourth specimen comes from a different source?'

'What makes you say so?'

'Whoever sent the first three, knew her Bible. She may have used a concordance, but she knew how to use it effectively.' Celia held up her hand when Lucy would have spoken. 'Yes, yes! All right! I said "her", and "she", and that is what I meant. These are the work of a woman; there can be no doubt of that.

'Anyway, my second point is that the first three quotations are both accurate and apt, whereas the fourth is neither. A sentence has been made by inserting a capital letter where there was none, and the context is not only allegorical but ludicrously inept.' She was contemptuous.

She went on, her manner accusing, 'I don't know if you have looked up the source paragraph?' And she quoted, giving Lucy no chance to reply: '"And the ten horns which thou sawest on the beast, these shall hate the whore and shall make her desolate and naked."'

A faint smile. 'One would have to be very much at sea before making use of such a source when there are so many more apt ones to choose from.'

Lucy said, meekly, 'That thought had occurred to me.'

'Really.' Celia was not interested; she was shuffling the exhibits, comparing them. 'Apart from that it seems clear that the fourth envelope and message were written by a different hand. However, that is not my concern.' She gathered the polythene wrappers together and handed them back. 'Now, if that is all . . . ?'

Lucy had only a vague idea of what she expected from her interview with the vicar's sister but this was certainly not it. She felt more than ever like a first-year student being dismissed after a tutorial that had gone badly wrong. On the other hand, the woman had confirmed her own ideas about the fourth message, and she had an argument to put to Wycliffe.

Much of Wycliffe's time during any case was taken up with what he called 'fringe activites' – extended telephone conversations with the chief, and with his own deputy, back at headquarters; receiving and reacting to reports concerning other cases all over the two counties, in fact, with the CID management of the police area as a whole. He was fortunate in that his deputy preferred administration to work on the ground – a case of Jack Spratt would eat no fat and his wife would eat no lean. So it worked, and made it possible for him to commit himself to individual investigations of importance.

But, like any other, the present case had its share of administrative and public relations chores. Even on this Easter Monday morning, Bertram Oldroyd, his chief, wanted to know what was going on; and, more remarkable still, the media were turning up in force for a briefing.

Oldroyd was relaxed and teasing. 'You attract these headline-grabbing cases, Charles. Sometimes I think you work it with the media. Seriously, though, is this a piece of black magic ghoulishness or has it been dressed up to look like one?'

Wycliffe, as always on such occasions, aimed to be both brief and vague. 'I don't know . . . I doubt if it's a cult thing.'

'What, then?'

He resented being forced to condense his vaporous notions and impressions into words which, once spoken, condition one's later thoughts. 'I feel that there is hatred behind this thing, and not only against the murdered woman.'

'You think there could be other killings?'

He said, with a curtness and finality, hardly diplomatic in speaking to the chief, 'I've no idea.'

'If you think we are dealing with some kind of psychopath . . .'

'I don't have any view on that at the moment, sir.'

And the telephone was dropped at the other end, with Oldroyd saying to himself, 'One of these days . . .'

In fact, Oldroyd's questions were little different from those he could expect from the reporters when they arrived.

The media is not easily roused from its weekend lethargy. Even in a normal week an investigation which starts on a Sunday stands some chance of escaping serious attention until halfway through Monday. Then their interest depends on certain 'newsworthy' features. As Wycliffe feared, this one had them all, and when the time arrived for the briefing he faced a whole gaggle of reporters and a couple of TV cameras. The murder of Jessica Dobell was news.

But they were good humoured. 'You don't need my help to embroider this one, it's ready made.' They knew him of old and there was an element of camaraderie. At least three of the older men had worked his patch for twenty years. To give them something he dropped a word about the anonymous notes.

'What did they say, these notes?'

'They were quotations from the Bible. I'm not prepared to quote them at the moment.'

'The Bible can be pretty gruesome. Were they abusive? Threatening?'

'Cautionary, I'd say.'

'Were they sent by the killer?'

'As I don't know the killer or who sent the notes that's a difficult question.'

After ten minutes or so they sheared off to the pub. A few drinks, a scout round the village, a spot of chatting-up the locals, and that would be that for a while.

Back in the office he was joined by Kersey, reporting on the Geach interview. Kersey summed up: 'Geach is no fool and he has his eye to the main chance. It's hard to say whether he would have the knowledge or the inclination to rig the set-up in the church, but if it served his purpose he might be capable of anything.'

Kersey yawned. 'It's obvious he thinks he's in the frame and I encouraged him to go on thinking that way. Incidentally, he's more amenable than he might be because he doesn't want his wife to know he'd been sleeping with her sister.'

Kersey yawned again, this time with total abandon. 'This place makes me sleepy – enervating they call it. Anyway, most of what Geach said is in his statement; what isn't, is in my report. Mainly he was anxious to divert attention from himself, and he chose the houseboat man – Lavin. According to him Lavin had been having it off with the girl on a regular basis.'

Wycliffe turned the pages of his copy of the file. 'Have we got anything on this Lavin, apart from Geach's story?'

Kersey said, 'He crops up in the reports. He bought the houseboat just over two years ago and went there to live with his friend – or whatever the boy is. It seems Lavin is a biochemist; he worked for one of the big drug firms until he was badly injured in a gas explosion. According to gossip he got hefty compensation.'

'Any idea how he spends his time now?'

'He's taken up natural history and he's supposed to be making a study of life in the creeks and streams about here. The boy goes off in a canoe, collecting samples and they say the boat is like a laboratory.'

'So we need to know more about him.' Wycliffe looked up at the clock. 'But it can wait until after lunch.'

They had a snack meal at one of the bar tables where there were too many near neighbours to talk shop, so there was little said. Wycliffe watched a couple at the next table, a man and a young girl who, between mouthfuls of cottage pie, jointly attacked *The Times*' crossword. The man's auburn hair, silvery at the ends, hung to his shoulders and his untrimmed beard reached to his chest. Yet his face, where it could be seen, had a youthful freshness. Wycliffe was reminded of storybook pictures of Rip Van Winkle. The girl, fair, with an English rose complexion, had that demure composure of a young lady from a Victorian drawing room.

Wycliffe was intrigued; they spoke little, there were murmurs and small gestures, and from time to time one of them would pick up the pencil and make an entry on the grid, all with an air of felicity and of total contentment in each other's company.

As he was leaving, Wycliffe had a quiet word with Johnny, the landlord.

Johnny said, 'Hector St John Carey and his niece, Alicia.'

'They come here often?'

'Almost every day.'

Wycliffe remembered the riverside house with a folly like a lighthouse. 'The house with the folly?'

'Trecara, the house with the folly.'

Wycliffe was puzzled by the abrupt change in the landlord's attitude whenever he was asked about someone living in the village. In his professional role he was amiable, even chatty; but a question about any of the villagers brought down the closed sign. His replies became taciturn, his manner suspicious.

When Wycliffe and Kersey returned to the Incident Room, each to his own report, Wycliffe was interrupted by a phone call from Franks, the pathologist.

'Nothing new, old chap! Healthy woman. Fit. Muscles like a navvy; I wouldn't care to have tangled with her except in a friendly.'

'Not pregnant by any chance?'

'Nor by any mischance, though you won't be surprised to learn that she was no virgin. She died, in case you're still interested, as a result of a massive depressed fracture of the skull involving the temporal bone of the left side.'

Wycliffe said, 'Don't tell me, I know: the blow was probably inflicted with a blunt instrument such as a hammer. Thanks.'

Franks chuckled. 'We do our best, but we can't solve all your cases for you, Charles.'

Wycliffe had no sooner dropped the telephone than Fox arrived with his report. Fox's reports were models of their kind: scale diagrams, meticulously drawn, and enlarged photographs, all interspersed with Fox's idiosyncratic prose in pristine type. The man worked like a mole and Wycliffe was expected, not unreasonably, to show appreciation. Having done so, he looked at the formidable wad of paper and asked, 'Anything for special attention?'

'There's the toeprint, sir.' He turned the pages to a blow-up, contrast-intensified, of the mud flake print found on the carpet in the aisle of the church. 'It's from the toe of a left rubber boot, sir. An acquaintance in the trade says it's almost certainly size nine or ten and it might just be possible to identify the boot if we find it.

'At any rate we know that the dead woman wore rubber boots and they are missing but they were fives.'

Wycliffe should have been interested, and tried to sound so. 'It's worth following up. Anything else?'

'The pieces of paper used to wedge the organ keys came from the *Church Quarterly* for September of last year. There are quite good prints on two of the pieces, unidentified at the moment. It's a theological publication and, according to the newsagent, it is ordered specially for the vicar.'

'Good! So that narrows the field. No luck with any of the other prints?'

'Not so far, sir.'

Wycliffe picked up his ballpoint and tried to look politely dismissive. Reluctantly, Fox took the hint and left.

The truth is that whatever the contributions from technical and forensic boffins, the hard core of police investigation still consists in what people can be persuaded to tell them. And persuasion becomes increasingly difficult as the champions of everybody's liberty but the victim's turn the thing into a chess game.

Wycliffe pushed Fox's papers away, sighed, and returned to his work. Ten minutes later when he was settling once more to the business of digesting facts and regurgitating them in the bland porridge of a report, he was interrupted again by a tap at the door: Dixon with a letter.

'Sent on by messenger from the Truro nick, sir.'

The envelope was addressed in a woman's hand, schoolgirl style, to: 'Superintendent Wycliffe, Truro Police Station.' The single sheet it contained was headed: 'Tilly's Cottage, Bell Hill, Moresk, Nr Truro.' The message was brief:

> Dear Mr Wycliffe,
> I can't come to see you but if you come here I might be able to help you. I am at home after six o'clock each evening. It is no good sending someone else and you must treat this as confidential.
> Yours sincerely,
> Grace Trevena (Miss)

Every case entices its ration of nutters out of the woodwork. They write letters, usually anonymous, make phone calls, often in funny voices, and even volunteer fictitious statements. This was probably a sample, but there was something about it, a certain basic simplicity, which struck him as unusual. And Trevena was a good Cornish name. He picked up his telephone.

'Is PC Trice there? . . . Send him in, please.'

Trice was the local Community Policeman, now seconded for duty with the squad. He came in, uneasily diffident. 'Sir?'

'Tilly's Cottage – know where it is?'

A look of relief. 'At the top of Bell Hill where it joins Church Lane, sir.'

'And Grace Trevena, who lives there?'

A slow smile. 'I know her; a youngish woman, probably middle-thirties, lives with her grandmother. She's hooked on astrology and fortune-telling . . . She runs a little shop in the market selling the gear and she writes bits for the local papers, "Your Stars this Week", sort of thing. There's also a society . . . Perhaps she's a bit loony but she's pleasant enough.'

'Thanks; that's what I wanted to know.'

As the door closed behind Trice he added to himself, 'Easier to buy a Ouija board.'

'Disraeli B. *Whigs and Whiggism. Political Writings.* Edited by W. Hutcheon 1913.' Stephanie Vinter stood on the library steps against a section of shelves, the book in her hands. 'Hutcheon is spelt: H-U-T-C-H-E-O-N.'

Seated at the long table, Giles entered the book on a numbered, ruled sheet, while, on the other side of the room, Hector St John Carey stood on another set of steps and called down to his niece, Alicia: 'Halliway J. O. *Rambles in Western Cornwall.* First edition 1861.'

The room, with its barrel roof, had some resemblance to the nave of a church, and there were mullioned Gothic windows at each end, but the walls were lined with bookcases which reached to the springing of the roof.

'I've brought you some tea.' A lean, grey-haired woman with a croaking voice arrived with a tray.

Carey descended the steps and took the tray from her. 'That is very kind of you, Winnie. So thoughtful . . .'

Perhaps books, even on shelves, have a civilizing influence. What sort of deviant feels belligerent in a library?

The four of them gathered at the table. Stephanie poured; Carey passed the biscuits, murmuring pleasant nothings into his beard. They cooed at each other like doves. Then Carey said, 'It's good of you to help us, Giles; I hope that you are not bored. This paperwork is not very stimulating but they tell me that if you have a library, then you must have a catalogue. I don't know precisely why this is, but I am quite sure that your mother could tell you.'

Giles flushed, pushed up his glasses and smiled.

Stephanie thought, how long is it since I've seen him smile?

Alicia, wearing a grey overall, looked supremely beautiful.

Carey went on, 'What could be nicer than tea in the library with an intelligent young man and two women who are beautiful as well as intelligent?'

When second cups had been poured, Carey ventured, 'Are there any developments at the farm?'

Stephanie patted her lips with a handkerchief. 'Laurence is expecting to hear from their solicitor. That, I suppose, will be the end.'

Carey stroked the silkiness of his beard. 'You know that I meant what I said? Nothing would give me greater pleasure than to share this place with you – such as it is. You may wish to come for a time – until some other arrangements are made, or you may favour living with us permanently. Alicia and I lead a rather lonely existence, cut off as we are, and it would be good for both of us to have congenial companions. Is that not so, Alicia?'

'You know that I agree, Uncle.'

'There now!' He reached for another biscuit. 'These are good. Winnie makes them herself . . .' When he had bitten into the biscuit he went on: 'Do you know the meaning of Trecara in Cornish? It means the homestead of Cara and the word cara translates as friend.' He added, his eyes mischievous: 'Or even as love and, of course, Carey comes from the same root.'

Stephanie said, 'You are more than kind, Hector, but Laurence would find it difficult to accept such one-sided hospitality.'

Carey spread his hands. 'I do not see it as one-sided, but talk it over. I think that it would be a good arrangement for all of us.'

Giles looked at his mother. 'Is Mr Carey suggesting that we might come here to live?'

Carey said, 'Does the idea distress you, Giles?'

Giles flushed but did not reply.

On the houseboat not far away a man sat reading. The light fell upon the right side of his head and face, on his sandy hair and beard, in both of which there were streaks of grey. His features were lean and the prominent bone structure was hardly masked at all by the pointed beard. The gross disfigurement on the left side was softened by shadows but the pale scar tissue was evident even to the casual eye.

The boy sat at a bench, looking down a binocular microscope; the beam of the lamp was directed through the mirror on to a tiny watch-glass placed on the stage. The boy was massively built; he had a large head, dark hair, cut short, and a round face, amiable in its immaturity.

'The little beggar won't keep still.'

The man looked up from his book. 'Try adding a drop of glycerine.'

Incredibly, the great hand with its thick fingers performed the delicate operation of sucking up a little glycerine from a bottle into a pipette and adding one drop to the water in the watch-glass.

There was a smile on the smooth features. 'Ah, that's better; he's not so lively now. He looks like some sort of larva . . .'

'Is the body divided into segments?'

'Oh, yes.'

'Can you see a head?'

'Yes, he has a head—'

'And the rest of the body in two parts?'

'Yes—'

'Any legs?'

The boy peered down the microscope. 'Yes, he's got six legs on the middle – on the thorax.' He brought out the word with evident pleasure.

'So it's an . . .'

'An insect – I ought to have bin able to work that out, didn't I?'

'You need practice, that's all. Now let's see if you can decide whether it's a larva, a nymph, or an adult . . .'

The exchange continued to a resolution of the problem and the man returned to his reading. It was high tide and the houseboat was afloat so that there were creaks and chuckles to disturb the stillness. Once a duck squawked in fright and somewhere, distantly, a dog barked.

The boy said, 'Nice, isn't it?'

'What's nice?'

'Well, being on our own again. She's not going to come in and spoil it.'

'Shut up, Jumbo!'

The man's voice was peremptory, angry, and the boy's

features seemed to crumple. 'I'm sorry, Brian . . . Really I didn't mean to . . . I just thought . . .'

'Yes, I know. Don't get upset. But you mustn't talk like that.' He added after a pause, 'Play me something, Jumbo.'

'Shall I?'

'Please.'

The boy fetched an accordion from under a bench seat and, after a preliminary trial, started to play. It was a strange melody which seemed always on the point of repetition, of finding a theme, then losing it in a fresh adventure. The man discarded his book and sat back in his chair, eyes closed; the boy's face became serious and intent. After a few minutes he stopped playing and put the accordion aside.

'Time for supper.'

The man said: 'You're right, Jumbo . . . It is nice.'

Chapter Seven

Easter Monday evening

The triumvirate assembled in Wycliffe's little office. Kersey lit a cigarette and, ostentatiously, Lucy Lane threw open the window to the dusk outside. Wycliffe looked from one to the other but made no comment.

'It's time to look at what we've got.'

Each of them had a file containing copies of the reports and statements so far. Idly, they turned the pages, searching for inspiration which failed to come. Wycliffe, at his most dry and succinct, gave an account of his interview with Arnold Paul.

'You've got a copy of his statement and you'll see it puts him in the crosswires as far as means and opportunity are concerned. As to motive, it could be that Jessica really did stumble on something that would have put him and/or his brother on the spot. CRO have nothing on either of them. So, if the brother is bent, he's been lucky, or he's worked under another name.'

Kersey said, 'Perhaps they're not brothers.'

Wycliffe agreed. 'Which would implicate Arnold. I had a word with Geoff Cox of the Met Fraud Squad. He'd never heard of Philip but he knew Arnold and his bank – nothing against either, but he promised to ask around and get what he can in the way of background. Meantime, I arranged for Fox to go over the man's room and he's sent off a set of prints to CRO just in case.'

He turned to Kersey. 'What about the other statements? I haven't read them.'

Kersey grimaced. 'As bland as milk. When you read them you begin to think that there never was a woman lying there in the church with her head bashed in.'

'I believe you've got a line on the Vinter breakdown.'

Kersey said: 'Yes, he's got no form but the word breakdown is a euphemism for getting the sack. He was suspended in eighty-five for sexually assaulting a girl student. I got this from a mate of mine in Bristol CID. He knew about it because there was a police investigation but no prosecution. It was more than a bit iffy and Vinter was allowed to resign. The girl was no Persil-white virgin and the feeling was that Vinter misread her signals or that she was working off a grudge.'

Lucy Lane, turning the pages of her file, said, 'He would be an expert at misreading signals where women are concerned.'

Kersey shrugged. 'You would know about that. At any rate, it cost the poor bastard his job.'

Wycliffe cut in: 'None of which disqualifies Vinter as a suspect, so we need to keep an eye on him. All right. We already know about Geach, so it's over to you, Lucy – your interview with the vicar's sister – Celia, isn't it?'

Wycliffe looked bored. He saw this as a routine exchange of information to save everybody having to wade through the reports. At these sessions he discouraged discussion. More than once he had been known to say, 'There are times when listening to other people's ideas only confuses my own.' An attitude which was more defensive than bigoted.

Lucy Lane summarized her visit to the vicarage. 'Celia is a very intelligent woman, but there's something odd about her.' She hesitated, then plunged. 'I think she sent the first three notes herself.'

'Did you put it to her?'

Lucy, to Wycliffe's surprise, flushed; an unusual phenomenon. 'No, sir. She is a very formidable woman. If it comes to a confrontation I would want to be better prepared. I wouldn't want to start something I couldn't finish.'

Kersey looked at her in mock amazement. 'This woman I must see!'

Wycliffe let it pass. 'So, at least, you don't think she was responsible for the fourth note?'

'No. That took her by surprise. And, as you know, I'm not happy about that fourth note. I would like to have all four submitted for expert opinion.'

'Why not? We must also get something on the Jordans' background. Let's know who we are dealing with. Anything else?'

For a few minutes conversation drifted away from the case. Wycliffe and Kersey speculated, dismally, about the probable findings of the Criminal Justice Commission while Lucy continued to study her file.

Finally Wycliffe sat back in his chair, stretched, yawned, and looked at the clock. 'Well, nobody will listen to us; that's for sure. It's time for our meal . . . Lucy! Aren't you eating this evening?'

Lucy was still absorbed in her file. 'I was looking at his signature on my xerox of his statement.'

'Who are you talking about?'

'Geach.' Lucy pushed the open file across the desk and both men examined it. Wycliffe said, 'A bit florid.'

Kersey shrugged. 'Takes up a lot of paper, but so what? Chaps like Abe Geach boost their ego with a flashy signature.'

Lucy said: 'He signs himself Abe G Geach, but the last four letters are no more than a scrawl.'

Wycliffe was impatient. 'Come on, Lucy, if you've got

anything, let's have it. My signature ends in a scrawl too.'

'No comment, sir. But just read aloud the letters that are legible.'

Wycliffe muttered as though to himself, 'ABEGG . . . Well, I'm damned!'

'It must be chance,' said Kersey.

'It's certainly odd,' Wycliffe replied. 'But could there possibly be a connection?'

Lucy Lane said, 'I can't believe that it's chance.'

Wycliffe was studying the signature. 'Neither can I. Which means that whoever wedged the organ keys did it to draw attention to Geach.'

Kersey said, 'This is better thought about after a good meal.'

In contrast with the night before, several of the tables in the restaurant were empty and others were occupied by couples and threesomes there for a quiet meal. Wycliffe's table, in a corner by one of the windows, was a little removed from the others, a testimony to the discretion of the landlord.

The man himself came to take their order. 'Only one main dish tonight – *coq au vin*. It's the real thing – none of your boiled chicken warmed up in a prepared sauce but, if you don't fancy it, I can do you ham-off-the-bone with a decent salad.'

Coq au vin was agreed.

'I can offer you a red burgundy which goes very well.'

Kersey said, 'I'm beginning to like this place.'

They had reached the dessert stage before the case was mentioned and it was Kersey who said, 'It strikes me as bloody silly whichever way you look at it. I mean, if Geach did the killing he'd hardly put his signature to it – musical or otherwise, and, surely, the same argument would stop anybody else with an ounce of common sense from trying to incriminate him in that way.'

Lucy Lane, meticulously dissecting a pear, said, 'I suppose the fact that the organ was used draws attention to Paul as the organist—'

Wycliffe cut in, 'Full marks, Lucy, for spotting the signature business but it adds one more bizarre feature to this case which bristles with them already. Instead of looking for runners in the means, motive and opportunity stakes, we might try to work out the kind of person who could lay on such an exhibition.' Wycliffe picked up his coffee cup and put it down again. 'Think of it: after the woman was killed by a blow to the head, her body was dragged to the statue of Christ so that her hair could be draped over the sandalled feet . . . Either then, or before, she was undressed to the precise extent which would suggest obscenity without implying a sexual assault in the ordinary sense.'

Kersey was about to say something but Wycliffe stopped him. 'No, Doug, let me finish. After all that, he or she goes to the organ and wedges the appropriate keys, apparently to suggest Geach's involvement through his shared initials with the Schumann Variations, as well as a musical connection. Add to this that the bits of folded paper were carefully cut from a religious magazine, subscribed to by the vicar, and the whole seems to suggest a deliberate plan to involve, if not incriminate, several people.'

Wycliffe paused just long enough to sip his coffee, which had gone cold. 'Having laid on his charade, the killer then starts up the blower on the organ and simply walks away.'

He frowned in a final effort to give his ideas coherence. 'It's been my impression from the first that this tableau, or whatever one calls it, was intended to make a point beyond the death of Jessica Dobell. Now, of course, aside from all this, we have these anonymous notes which may or may not be the work of the killer but must be fitted into the pattern.'

He drank off the remainder of his coffee, made a wry face, and patted his lips with his table napkin. 'Let's think all this over and see if we can get some sort of notion of the kind of man or woman we are looking for – without trying to fit any particular individual into the frame.'

He looked at his watch. 'But not tonight. Tonight I'm having my walk.'

He set out to explore the village beyond the square and found himself in a pattern of three or four short streets made up, for the most part, of terraced houses with their front doors opening on to the pavement. There were shops, a Methodist chapel big enough to accommodate the whole population, and a pub. This was a fresh aspect of the village and it was where most of the villagers lived.

There was still light in the sky but curtains were drawn across many windows and fragments of TV programmes filtered through. From the pub came the murmur of voices and an occasional burst of laughter but over most of the village there was silence and the streets were deserted. It was half past eight.

These evening walks over the ground where he happened to be working were necessary to him, especially in small towns and rural communities. He had to get the 'feel' of the place, to have some idea of what it was like to live there. To start with he was an intruder, perhaps a threat. Sometimes he felt heir to the witch doctor, prowling at night among the huts of the villagers, peeking, prying and eavesdropping.

The notion appealed to him. Perhaps in the morning he should line up his suspects, place a dry pebble in the mouth of each, and woe betide the one whose pebble

119

stayed dry. (Add that one to his training school lectures on Modern Investigatory Procedures.)

A steepish hill was lined with more little houses, but these were stepped against the slope. An enamelled blue and white sign on the corner house read 'Bell Hill'. He remembered that the woman who wrote to him, the fortune-teller, or whatever she was, lived at the top of Bell Hill, at the junction with Church Lane ... Grace Trevena, that was it!

As he climbed the hill he found that he had decided to call on her. From witch doctors to fortune-tellers by easy stages. King Saul visited the Witch of Endor by night and modern police chiefs had been known to enlist diviners to find their missing bodies. Whimsical thoughts of the head of CID on his evening stroll. Did other apparently responsible and sage officials have such rag-bag minds? Sometimes it troubled him that the persona he presented to the world was such a fake.

Tilly's Cottage belonged neither to the rather dreary little terraced houses of Bell Hill, nor to the grander villas of Church Lane. Placed on a corner between the two it was a solid little house in its own garden, surrounded by pine trees. There was a light in one of the downstairs rooms.

Wycliffe opened the gate and walked down the crazy-paving path to the front door. His ring was answered by a female voice. 'Who is it, please?'

'Superintendent Wycliffe.'

He had envisaged a stringy female, close to forty, casting about for a tolerable route across the sterile plane of virginity. Instead he was confronted by a plump young woman with a mass of dark curls and a friendly grin.

'I'm Grace Trevena. So you've come. I've been wondering whether you would and thought you probably wouldn't.'

He was shown into a homely, comfortable living room

turned almost into a jungle by potted plants. An elderly woman sat knitting by an electric fire and, on the dining table, there was a portable typewriter, a few books with places marked, a box of paper and some carbons.

'This is my grandmother, who brought me up.'

The old lady acknowledged him with becoming formality.

Grace said: 'Will you have a drink? Sherry or gin – that's our limit, I'm afraid.'

He refused a drink but accepted a chair, and the girl resumed her seat at the table but turned to face him.

'I'm in the middle of my weekly article. I expect you've been told that I'm interested in the occult and that sort of thing. I've not got what it takes to do research but I learn from people who have and try to apply their methods. We have a society, and I run a little stall in Truro market where I sell the literature, cards, charts, and so on.'

She smiled as she spoke, so that one had the impression that it was all good fun. 'I'm telling you all this because it was how I came to meet Jessica in the first place.'

Wycliffe listened politely, the old lady's needles continued to click, and Grace never stopped talking.

'You don't look comfortable to me. Stretch out your legs and rest your head back. Make yourself at home. As I was saying, Jessica came to me for a Tarot reading and we ended up by doing a series.'

The plump girl's face was suddenly serious. 'It was worrying. I've never known such a series, so consistent, and so – well, threatening.'

'What was threatened?'

'Oh, her death – and death by violence. Of course I didn't let on to her. I mean, one can't. You do see that, don't you? I interpreted it as a crisis in her life but I was never in much doubt as to the nature of the crisis – if my reading was anything like right.'

'When did she first come to see you?'

'When was it, Gran? Seven – eight months ago?'

'It was last September, when we had the first decent weather of the year.'

She went on: 'I don't expect you to believe all this stuff about the Tarot and so on. I mean, you're not a convert, but I mention it because it led to us becoming quite friendly. Jessica confided in me. People do. When you take up this sort of work you get to be something like a priest – I mean, people rely on you to keep their secrets because it's your sort of profession . . .'

'Jessica told you things about her life?'

'Yes, she did, and I feel, now that she's gone, I'm free to talk if it would help to find out who killed her.'

'What did she tell you?'

'Oh, about the farm, about the Vinters, and about her affairs with men. She had quite a sense of humour when she got going. Of course, she was Aries – fairly typical – energetic, belligerent, and highly sexed . . . But not all that sure of herself underneath. I mean, she worried, and she had a sense of guilt which many Aries subjects don't . . . What are you, by the way? I'd put you down as a Leo.'

Wycliffe felt trapped, mesmerized. 'I was born on August the fifteenth.'

'There you are then! Fortunately you don't have the aggressiveness which sometimes goes with the Leo make-up. But as you get older, watch out for back trouble. Could be heart, but I don't think so.'

'You were telling me about Jessica.'

'Yes, I was. I can't keep to the point, can I? I'm a true Piscean – never know where I'm going until I'm coming back. Well, one evening last week she came here – Good Friday, it was, and I could see that she was worried and depressed. Even Arians have their fits of depression.'

Wycliffe, on the verge of losing patience, asked, 'What was she worried about?'

'Well, she started by asking if I'd seen in the local paper that Mrs Ruse, over to Tresillian, was dead. She reminded me that this was the mother . . .'

'Of the boy killed in a hit-and-run several years ago.'

She looked at him in surprise. 'So you know about that! Well, they never found out who did it and Jessica said that she knew who was responsible and that she had been involved. She'd been trying to put it out of her mind ever since, but with the mother dying, and people saying the poor woman had never got over her grief – well, it brought it all back as bad as ever.'

'She said that she was actually involved in the accident?'

'That was how I understood her.'

'Did she say who was with her?'

Grace looked embarrassed. 'No. I asked her if it was Johnny Glynn – I shouldn't have done, I know, I was just being inquisitive. But with all the rumours . . . Anyway, she said it wasn't Johnny; that he'd told the truth. She asked me if I thought this was the crisis the Tarot predicted and I was weak; I said it might be.'

'And?'

The fat girl looked down at her hands. 'She seemed very upset and said she supposed she'd have to go to the police. Then there was a bit about not having played fair with her sister and not wanting to make it worse. I didn't quite understand that.' She looked at Wycliffe, soft eyed. 'I wasn't much help to her, was I? She left more worried than she came. Then, the very next night . . .'

Wycliffe said nothing and she went on, 'I didn't know whether to tell you all this. I mean, I don't really know anything and I could easily get somebody into trouble. I decided to leave it to fate; I usually find that's the best way.' She looked at him, earnestly searching for approval. 'I wrote to you and gave you the option. If you didn't come to see me, well that would be that. If you did, it wouldn't have been my decision.'

Wycliffe leaned forward in his chair. 'Miss Trevena . . .'

'Call me Grace, please. Everybody does.'

'All right, Grace – you do realize that Jessica was murdered and that her murderer has not been caught. He or she could kill again. What I am saying is that anything you can tell me of her life could be important. You spoke of the men with whom she had affairs. Who were they?'

The girl's voice was low. 'She mentioned Mr Geach – I suppose that's why she felt guilty about her sister; then there was the man on the houseboat, and Mr Vinter.'

'No-one else?'

'No, I don't think so.'

Wycliffe became stern. 'Look at me, Grace!'

The brown eyes were solemn but not scared. The old lady's needles ceased to click.

'Think now, Grace! Was there anything else that Jessica told you about anyone – anyone at all, that reflected on them in a mean or discreditable way; anything they would not want to be known? If you tell me things that turn out to have no relevance then they will never be mentioned again, I can promise you that.'

The girl's brow wrinkled. 'I can't think of anything really . . .'

'But?'

'Well, it was quite a while ago now, just before Christmas. Jess was laughing about it.'

'About what?'

'Well, it seems so mean to tell you, but if I must . . . Jessica went to the church one morning, to get things ready for a christening in the afternoon, and when she opened the vestry door, the vicar was there with the Vinter boy. He was hugging the boy – fondling his hair. That was all . . . I mean, there was nothing dirty going on . . . But Jessica reckoned the vicar was a bit that way.'

'All the same, you were quite right to tell me.'

Unexpectedly, the old lady joined in. 'What Grace does with her cards and all that stuff is her business; it's nothing to do with me; I don't interfere. But I didn't like that Dobell woman in my house. There was something about her. I'm sorry she's been murdered but she's the sort of woman, in my opinion, who asked for it.'

A faint smile reappeared on the face of the fat girl. 'Now you know what Gran thinks.'

She saw him out, and he walked down Church Lane and back to the pub, thoughtful. The Hopton was quiet, the restaurant was closed and only a few regulars lingered about the bar.

'A nightcap, Mr Wycliffe?'

'No. No, thank you.' He was in no mood for Johnny. From the telephone in the passage upstairs he said 'Good night' to Helen.

In bed, with the light out, he lay staring through the open window at a rectangle of starlit sky. He listened to the few late drinkers being seen off the premises, the muttered partings, the footsteps; then Johnny locking up. There must be a private part of the house, for he did not hear Johnny climbing the stairs. In fact the silence was so complete that he found himself listening to it as though to something positive.

A lot had happened in this first full day. It seemed a long time since Lucy's kedgeree. But were they any further forward? He had been right about Jessica; there was a history of trauma which could explain her frenzied life style. The Ruse boy: she had admitted to some part in his death. But through action or by association? Was it guilt or guilty knowledge? Either way, could it have any significance as a motive for her murder? Vendettas reaching out across the years are material for fiction, but they are rare in fact.

In the matter of suspects and evidence: no material progress; just a lucky dip. Were there any suspects with a credible motive? The Vinters? Certainly there was bitterness, possibly hatred. But murder? What did they gain? Geach – to divert attention from himself had brought in Lavin, the houseboat man. At most it was a banal little tale of sex which must be kept from the wife – for her own good, of course. Still, he must talk to Lavin.

Wycliffe sighed, and turned on his side. He thought of Arnold Paul and his precious brother. He felt in his bones that despite appearances they were a sideshow. And the vicar? It was possible that the vicar was homosexually inclined, and not impossible that Jessica had used the fact against him. But murder? And in his own church?

Wycliffe decided that he had had enough. He thumped his pillow, made a convulsive turn, and to his own surprise, felt suddenly relaxed.

Chapter Eight

Tuesday

At seven o'clock on Tuesday morning, almost forty-eight hours after Jessica Dobell was found dead on the chancel steps, Michael Jordan and his sister, Celia, were at breakfast. Even at breakfast Michael was already wearing his clerical collar and vest. Celia's grey eyes regarded her brother across the table with diagnostic rather than sympathetic concern.

'You are looking ill, Michael.'

The vicar paused, a spoonful of All-bran halfway to his lips. 'The last two days have been a strain. I suppose it shows.' His manner was defensive.

'I warned you about that woman, Michael. She was not a fit person to have in the church.'

The vicar parried with a professional response. 'The church is for sinners, Celia.'

'For sinners who repent. That woman was blatant in her sin and you allowed her to profit from the church.'

'She profited very little, poor soul; she worked hard for what she got.'

Celia continued to stare at her brother as though by concentration she might read his mind, and he flushed under her silent scrutiny. She said, at last, 'I don't think you've told me everything, Michael.'

'What more could there be to tell?'

Celia sipped her coffee without taking her eyes off him.

'I've been thinking: you went across to the church on Saturday evening – at around eight it must have been.'

'I went to fetch my new service book.'

'So you said. Was the Dobell woman there then?'

Michael's flush deepened. 'Yes.'

'You didn't mention it at the time.'

'Would you expect me to? You know quite well that Jessica was often there of an evening, especially if there was a service the following day.'

'Perhaps that is why you found these evening visits so necessary.'

'Celia! What are you suggesting?' She had sparked off his anger.

But Celia was unimpressed. 'No, I was forgetting; women do not interest you.'

On the point of an angry retort, Michael remained silent. There was a lull. Celia finished her coffee, patted her lips with her napkin, then spoke conversationally, 'You've finished your cereal, will you have some toast?'

'No, thank you.'

Once more the grey eyes were on him. 'Did you tell the police that you saw her at eight o'clock?'

'No.'

'Why not?'

His boyish face was scarlet once more. 'Well, they didn't ask me and it seemed, well . . . irrelevant.'

Celia shook her head. 'No, Michael! You wouldn't hold back information of that sort without good reason. It was obvious that the police would wish to establish when she was last seen alive.'

Michael looked down at his empty dish and fiddled with the spoon. 'Are you suggesting that I . . . That you think I might have . . .' His voice trailed off.

'Killed the woman? No, I am quite sure that you would be incapable of killing anyone in any circumstances.'

'Well then, I don't see what you are getting at.' Sullen.

Celia poured herself another cup of coffee and added a dash of milk. She was cogitating and, once or twice, she looked across at her brother – thoughtful, speculative.

Michael was staring out of the window through which he could see the tower of his church rising above the trees.

Abruptly, as though the thought had just occurred to her, Celia demanded, 'Was there anyone else in the church at the time?'

'What? – No!'

After a long pause Celia said, 'I'm sorry, Michael, but you are prevaricating, if not actually lying. Either you saw or you have been told something which you are holding back from the police. That is foolish if not dangerous.'

There was a long silence and Michael was on the point of leaving the table when Celia spoke again, 'I had a policewoman here yesterday, while you were in Truro.'

'To see me?'

'No.'

Michael looked the question he was careful not to ask.

'She wanted to consult me about anonymous communications sent to the Dobell woman.'

Michael, already on his feet, sat down again. 'Anonymous communications? What did they say?'

'There were four of them, all quotations from the Bible and concerned with sexual depravity.'

Suddenly Michael had gone very pale. He said with great seriousness, 'The police must have heard something, Celia, otherwise why would they come to you?'

Her expression was smug. 'My work with the Women's Guild is supposed to put me in touch with the women of the village.'

'What did you tell the policewoman?'

'I told her that the fourth communication was not from the same hand as the other three.'

'How could you possibly know that?'

'It was obvious.'

Very carefully, Michael arranged his plate, cup, saucer and spoon. Without looking up he said, 'Recently, Celia, I have begun to feel that I am doing God's work here in Moresk. I thought you shared that feeling.'

'Well?'

'I hope we shan't be forced to move again.'

Celia stood up and began to clear the table. In a tight voice she said: 'Don't forget that it's Tuesday and I have my Fellowship meeting in Truro this morning. I shall catch the ten-twenty bus. Molly Symons has invited me back to her place afterwards so that I may not be home before you go to the Careys' this evening.'

Katherine Geach and Elsa were sitting at the kitchen table, drinking coffee. The old pendulum clock on the wall showed ten minutes past eight.

Katherine seemed to be studying the rings on her fingers. After a moment or two she said, 'I've been a fool, Elsa. Looking back, it's obvious that Abe had been seeing Jessica.'

Caution masked any expression there might have been on Elsa's freckled features. '*Seeing* her?'

Katherine snapped, 'You know exactly what I mean!'

Elsa shifted in her chair, pushed her cup and saucer away, and said, 'I've never heard anything of that sort and most gossip reaches me one way or another.'

But Katherine was not to be put off. 'Don't be difficult, Elsa! The only question in my mind is, when did it start?'

Elsa opened her mouth to reply when Julie came in, fully dressed. On holiday, it was unusual for her to be up before ten.

Katherine vented her annoyance. 'What's the matter with you? Can't you sleep?'

The girl ignored the question. 'Is there any coffee left?'

'In the pot, but you'll have to make your own toast if you want it.'

'I don't want any.'

Her mother's irritation subsided. 'Don't take any notice of me; I'm on edge.'

'I know. I'm going out, but I'll be back around lunchtime.' Julie drank a mug of coffee and a moment later she was gone.

Katherine called after her, 'You should take an anorak or something, it's going to rain.' But there was no response.

Elsa said, 'She looks all in. I didn't think this would have had such an effect on her. I heard her moving about in the night and once I thought she was crying.'

Katherine sighed. 'It's not what happened to Jess that's upsetting her, it's that bloody boy. I wish I knew what was going on there.' She added after a pause: 'I'm not much of a mother.'

Julie walked towards the foreshore and took the path along the river bank. The going was muddy but she picked her way. At the kissing-gate she gave a nervous glance up into the churchyard and hurried past. Her hands were tightly clenched so that her nails bit into the flesh. 'If only I can get him to talk!'

Since overhearing the conversation between her father and the policeman she had felt more than ever troubled and depressed. There were one or two girls at school who talked, glibly, perhaps for effect, of their fathers 'screwing around'. She was not, she told herself, old-fashioned about sex, but she had never thought of her father in that way. She had been naive; for that, apparently, was precisely what he did. And Aunt Jess had been one of his women. Did her mother know – or suspect?

But Aunt Jess had had other men – Giles' father, and the houseboat man, perhaps others. And now she was dead – murdered.

She could not take it in. She thought she had understood how things were at the farm. There was tension and bitterness, Giles had never made any secret of that, and it was obvious to anyone who spent any time at all there. It came about because her aunt seemed to take pleasure in humiliating the Vinters. And yet, despite that, it seemed that she and Giles' father were having sex.

No wonder the police . . . It was like something out of a tabloid newspaper. People would say – must be saying – 'Of course she asked for it!' And they would be speculating about which of her men . . .

But there was something else that troubled her even more deeply. It arose from a casual remark of her father's: 'Henry, down at the post office, says the bits of paper used to wedge the organ keys were cut from a religious magazine which he orders specially for the vicar.'

And it had come to Julie, irritatingly vague but compelling, a memory of having seen such a magazine, curiously mutilated. It was at the farm, but she could not recall exactly where, or in what circumstances.

As she drew level with the houseboat Jumbo came down the gangway with bags slung about his shoulders and carrying a battery of nets. He greeted her with his slow speech, seeming to listen carefully to his own words: 'Hello, Julie! I'm going out to collect spec-i-mens.'

Julie raised her hand but said nothing. She turned up to the farmhouse across the rough grass to the front door, and knocked.

It was opened by Giles. He pushed up his spectacles and regarded her with solemn attention but said nothing.

'I want to talk to you, Giles.'

The boy looked back into the house, hesitated, then closed the door. Still he did not speak.

Julie was at a loss, not at all sure what she wanted to say. In the end it came in the form of a bald question: 'Do you have any idea who killed Aunt Jessica, Giles?'

His blue eyes, enlarged by his spectacles, were cold, indifferent, and when he spoke his voice was toneless. 'What makes you ask me that?'

They were standing, looking towards the river where it was about half-tide. A band of mud separated the shingle from the water and gulls flat-footed around, searching for worms.

'I'm worried, Giles.'

The boy said nothing, he seemed to be staring across the river at the trees which overhung its banks.

Julie went on, 'Have you talked to Michael about it?'

'Why should I talk to Michael?' He sounded bored.

She felt as though she were trying to reach him through a barrier of cotton wool, and she floundered. 'Well, you seem to get on – I mean, it's obvious he likes you.'

Giles flushed and his manner became even more remote. 'I don't know what you mean. What would I have to say to him? Your aunt's death is nothing to do with us.' He added, after a pause, 'Anyway, I haven't seen Michael since before it happened.'

They were silent while Julie gathered her scattered wits to try again. 'Giles . . . Was Aunt Jess out all night sometimes?'

'Yes.'

'Do you know where she spent those nights?'

'It was no business of ours, and I've told the police all I know.'

'The police! Did they question you?'

'I went to them.'

133

'What did you tell them.'

'I told them something I thought they ought to know.'

Julie was getting nowhere but she was desperate to keep the contact going. 'They say the organ keys were wedged with pieces of paper cut from a religious magazine.'

He looked at her now but his expression did not change: 'So?'

Her courage failed her. She was utterly miserable. 'I don't know. I just wonder what will happen next.'

'That's simple. We shall have to go.' He was wilfully misunderstanding her. 'Your father has sent a man who used to be a farmer; he came yesterday and he's here again today. I expect he will take over.'

Julie was near to tears. 'I'm sorry, Giles. I hope it won't work out like that. I don't think mother . . .' Her voice trailed off because she could not say what she wanted to say with any conviction.

Giles regarded her with a steady gaze and, without raising his voice, in the same monotone as before, he said, 'I don't want to talk about any of this, Julie, and I don't want to talk to you. I would rather you didn't come here any more.' He turned and went into the house, closing the door behind him.

Julie stood, looking at the closed door. In just a couple of days it seemed that her whole world had fallen apart.

Shortly after nine Wycliffe, with his briefcase, presented himself at the front door of Trigg, and was received by the housekeeper, fair and freckled; a youngish woman, plump, and running comfortably to seed.

'Superintendent Wycliffe. I would like a word with Mrs Geach.'

He was shown into the room with the Russian samovar on the sideboard where Kersey had interviewed the contractor. After several minutes, Katherine Geach came in, looking every inch the lady of the house in tailored pale-grey trousers and a matching silk top.

'We can't talk in here, it's like a morgue.'

He followed her along a corridor to a very large room at the side of the house with a bow window which looked out across a lawn to the river.

There were plenty of blue and mauve chintzes, a neutral carpet, sage-green walls with hunting prints, and a white frieze, but Wycliffe's immediate attention was claimed by a grand piano, very much at home in a corner of the room.

'Do sit down, Mr Wycliffe. Would you like something? Coffee? A drink?'

'Thank you, but no.'

She was very pale, doing her best to appear relaxed, but tension showed in the set of her jaw and in her restless hands.

'I'm sorry to return to a subject that must be painful to you but I am anxious to know more of your sister's life.'

She eased the set of her trousers. 'I want to help, but I think you're probably better informed on that subject than I am.' A hint of bitterness.

Wycliffe refused that gambit. 'I'm wondering if you can tell me anything about her association with Jonathan Glynn, and whether she confided in you concerning the accident in which a young boy called Ruse was killed?'

It was not what she had expected and she did not answer at once.

Wycliffe went on, 'I don't wish to probe unnecessarily into your sister's life, but in searching for a motive for what happened I have to look at all the possibilities.'

A quick, troubled look. 'And you think there could be a connection?'

'As I said, I'm merely looking at possibilities.' From his briefcase he brought out Jessica's album. 'If you can bring yourself to look at the last few pages . . .'

She took the album and turned the pages, lingering here and there. When she reached the news cuttings, Wycliffe said, 'Three of those cuttings are concerned with the Ruse family – two with the original hit-and-run, the third with the recent death of the boy's mother.'

She spent some time on the cuttings, then turned back to the photographs. When she finally closed the book and handed it back, her eyes were glistening with tears. She said, 'You obviously know more than you have told me.'

'I know that immediately before her death your sister was considering going to the police with information about the boy's death.'

'I see.' She was shocked. She accepted that the sixteen-year-old tragedy might have traumatically affected Jessica's life, but it had not occurred to her that it could have been the reason for her death.

After an interval, she asked, 'Are you suggesting that—'

Wycliffe cut in with decision. 'I am not suggesting anything; I am seeking information. You must understand that this is only one of many lines of investigation and implies no suspicion of any individual.'

She considered this piece of police doubletalk and tried again. 'After my marriage Jessica and Johnny Glynn became very close. We assumed that they would marry . . . Johnny had a reputation as a bit of a wild man.' Her eyes lost focus as she seemed to relive some incident from the past. 'He drove a farm-truck about the lanes at breakneck speed and everybody expected trouble. Jessica was often with him.'

'Did your sister drive at that time?'

'Jessica never learned to drive. I've often wondered why. At any rate, there was strong feeling against Johnny after the accident but there was no evidence to suggest that he was anywhere near. All I can say is that Jessica was not the same girl afterwards, though I had no idea what it was that might have changed her.'

'She said, in any case, that she was not with Glynn that night.'

'I know.'

'Could it be that she was with someone else?'

Katherine made a despairing gesture. 'How can I possibly know? She talked to me about it, briefly and for the first time, only a day or two before she died . . . I have to admit, she left me with the impression that she was involved.'

'But she said nothing of the person she was with?'

'No.'

Wycliffe returned the album to his briefcase. 'I am sorry to have caused you further distress. I hope that you will keep our conversation to yourself.'

On his feet, he looked across at the piano. 'Are you the pianist?'

A quick smile. 'No, that's Abe's little indulgence. He used to play a lot when he was younger. He's really quite musical.'

She saw him to the door; once more the lady of the house. She even remarked that the primroses were especially beautiful this spring.

Back in his makeshift office, Wycliffe was looking out of the window at a pair of jackdaws perched on a boundary wall. They had their backs to him and, like an old married couple with nothing new to say to each other, they watched the world go by. A herring-gull, yobbo of the strand, alighted a yard from them and the pair edged their way crabwise to a discreet distance but were not otherwise disturbed.

In the back of his mind he was thinking about the Ruse boy and who might have been involved with Jessica Dobell in that hit-and-run. Did it matter to this present case? Was it feasible that having escaped a possible manslaughter charge, all those years ago, the man would resort to murder to avoid exposure now? Of course, although the law might be lenient after such a lapse of time, public opinion would not.

But murder? And murder in such a sensational vein?

Anyway, he would be talking to Tom Reed.

A tap at the door, and Kersey came in. 'Anything from the Lady of the Manor, sir?'

Wycliffe told him, not forgetting the piano.

Kersey was thoughtful. 'Interesting! It could have been friend Geach who took Jess for a ride that night. From the photographs the two couples seem to have been more of a foursome in those days.'

Wycliffe agreed. 'It's possible. It would explain what Jessica said to the Trevena girl; something about not having played fair with her sister and not wanting to cause further hurt – along those lines, anyway.'

Another tap at the door; this time the duty officer. 'The vicar would like a word, sir.'

'Ask him to wait a moment, please.'

Kersey said, 'Ah, the vicar! He's been keeping his head down; perhaps we should have made more use of him. If some of these parsons had their intelligence network computerized it would make Special Branch look like a bunch of amateurs.'

Wycliffe was thinking of Grace Trevena's rather pathetic story about the vicar and the Vinter boy. Put that way it sounded like a Victorian morality tale and perhaps that is what it was. He picked up his telephone. 'Ask Mr Jordan to come in, please.'

He was shocked by the change in the man. His baby face was pale and seemed to have lost its chubbiness. There was a darkness about the eyes and, above all, there was no sign of that smooth manner which seems to come with the collar and provides even the most timid clergyman with a measure of authority.

'Mr Jordan, this is Detective Inspector Kersey. Please sit down.'

The vicar looked at Kersey with obvious misgiving. 'I hope I'm not intruding, but I had to come . . .'

When he was seated he went on, 'It has been on my conscience though I cannot see how anyone can have suffered through my neglect. However, I mustn't try to condone it.' He had been looking down at his hands, now he met Wycliffe's eyes and said, abruptly, 'I was in the church on Saturday evening; I went there to collect my new service book.'

'At what time?'

'It must have been about eight o'clock. After eight, probably.'

Kersey snapped, 'You saw Jessica Dobell?'

'Yes, she was polishing the lectern.' He spoke in a low voice as though making confession.

'Presumably you spoke to her?'

'Something trivial – just a few words. I collected my book and left.'

'Did she seem as usual?' From Wycliffe.

'I think so. She made some remark about the weather – it rained all Saturday evening.'

'Was she alone?'

'I saw no-one with her.'

Kersey spelt out the question emphasizing each word. 'Did you see anyone either going to or coming from the church?'

Jordan hesitated, then, 'I saw no-one.'

Wycliffe said, 'You realize that you were probably the last person to see Jessica Dobell alive – other than her killer?'

He nodded. 'The thought has kept me awake at night.'

'But failed to persuade you to do your obvious duty.' From Kersey.

Wycliffe followed up: 'I cannot understand, Mr Jordan, why you were so reluctant to come forward. You are quite sure that you are concealing nothing else?'

The poor man had never before been subjected to interrogation. His pallor had given way to a deep flush and he was on the verge of breakdown. Wycliffe did not pursue the question.

'I understand that the dead woman visited the church at odd times whenever she thought there might be something in need of attention?'

'Indeed she did. Jessica was most conscientious.'

'I'm thinking of a morning in late December when there was a christening in the afternoon.'

The fresh shock was obvious. There was an interval while Jordan contemplated his plump hands and, when he spoke, his words were barely audible.

'So you know about that?'

'I want your version.'

'It was innocent, but very foolish on my part.'

Wycliffe waited, the fingers of one hand beating a silent tattoo on the desk top. The mild tension he created was more than enough to loosen the vicar's tongue. It was like taking sweets from a child.

'You see, Mr Wycliffe, the boy Giles is not happy at home . . . The situation is very difficult – a family unit living and working with a woman whose background and aspirations are – were – so different. I'm saying nothing against Jessica; she behaved as we all do, according to our lights. But Giles is a complex and sensitive boy, very easily hurt.'

Jordan looked up and was, perhaps, reassured by Wycliffe's bland, attentive manner. 'In short, Giles sometimes came to me to confide his difficulties. On the occasion you refer to he was particularly upset and I was moved by his distress.' The vicar shifted uncomfortably in his chair. 'Foolishly, I put my arm around his shoulders, he rested his head against me and I smoothed his hair. It was at this point that Jessica came in.'

'Are you homosexually inclined, Mr Jordan?'

Jordan looked at Kersey as though he had received a slap in the face. He did not speak for some time but when he did he had decided on a straight answer. 'I will tell you the truth. Since early adolescence my sexual inclinations have been towards my own sex but, with God's help, I have never, in any relationship, allowed my impulses to carry me beyond a simple caress.'

'Did Jessica ever refer to the incident she had witnessed?'

'Not to me, but I heard from Giles that she sometimes taunted him.' Jordan sighed. 'He was, understandably, deeply distressed and bitter.'

Wycliffe was puzzled by the man. It was probable that he had spoken the truth; certainly not the whole truth, but what was he stretching his conscience to conceal?

Probe a little deeper. 'I understand that you subscribe to the *Church Quarterly*.'

'I've done so since shortly after my ordination.'

'It seems that you are the only subscriber in this district.'

'Probably.'

'Are you aware that the folded paper used to wedge the organ keys was cut from a copy of that periodical?'

'I was told so by your officer.'

'How do you dispose of your copies when you have finished with them?'

'I don't dispose of them; I keep them for reference.'

'Will you check to see that you still have the issue for last September?'

141

The vicar made a little gesture of resignation. 'I have checked; that issue is missing.'

'Can you explain that?'

'I occasionally lend the odd copy to anyone who might be interested in a particular article.' He added, 'It doesn't bother me if they are not returned.'

Kersey interjected, 'You must have some idea who borrowed this particular copy.'

Jordan hesitated then, with obvious reluctance, he said, 'It was the issue which contained an article on the role of the Church in German reunification. Stephanie Vinter happened to see it and said she thought Laurence would like to read it. He is interested in the part played by the Church in the overthrow of Communism in Eastern Europe.'

Wycliffe was gazing at the vicar with disquieting intensity; then abruptly, with a gesture of resignation, he relaxed. What was the point of keeping him on the rack?

But his manner was still brusque. 'I want you to make a further statement about your visit to the church on Saturday evening, and the loan of your magazine to Vinter. At the same time I must remind you that holding back information, however privileged, could delay our investigation and might be dangerous. Somebody who has killed once has broken through a psychological barrier and may well find it easier to kill a second time.'

Wycliffe got to his feet. 'Mr Kersey will show you to the interview room where you will be given the opportunity to make a fresh statement.'

Jordan looked at him, pale and solemn, but said nothing.

Left alone, Wycliffe was still worried by the man. Law enforcement has always had special problems with tender consciences but it is no longer approved procedure to put to the torture their troublesome possessors.

Chapter Nine

Tuesday morning (continued)

When Kersey had taken the vicar to make his statement, Wycliffe left for the houseboat. He went alone, counting more than he cared to admit on the interview with the former biochemist. It was not actually raining but a pearly mist softened outlines with the effect of a lens that is slightly out of focus. The surface of the water was greeny brown, still and shining; it was hard to believe that the tides reached so far. He passed the kissing-gate to the church and, arriving at the reed bed, encountered a troop of bird-watchers, with their binoculars who charmed him with their twittered 'Good morning's.

As he approached the houseboat he could hear music – an orchestra; a radio or record player? Another musician? The orchestra gave way to a single female voice followed by an unaccompanied duet, and at the bottom of the gangway he stood still to listen. The sound seemed to fill the whole valley with trills and cadences which echoed back from the slopes and it was some time before he realized that the bearded Lavin was leaning on the rail looking down at him.

'You like it?'

An indeterminate grunt.

'"The Flower Duet" from *Lakme*, Heady stuff – an aural narcotic not to be taken by policemen.'

'Mr Lavin? Superintendent Wycliffe.'

'You'd better come up.'

On deck a short companionway led down to a saloon which was filled by the music. Lavin switched off the player.

The light, coming from a row of windows near the ceiling, had a greenish hue. Below the windows were aquaria, lined end to end, and below them again, bookshelves and cupboards. There was a bench with an impressive binocular microscope, and another with a sink and rows of bottles.

Lavin stood so that his left side was shielded. He pushed forward a chair for Wycliffe and sat down himself. Certain movements seemed to involve a painful strain. 'What do you want?'

'I am inquiring about Jessica Dobell.'

'She's dead. Your interest has come too late to do much about it.'

Wycliffe was aware of the tension in the man; his whole frame seemed taut, and his manner was aggressive. 'What I can do is to find out who killed her and why. You were on intimate terms with her so you are an important witness.'

'Well?'

'She spent nights here?'

'Occasionally.'

'When did your relationship begin?'

'Our relationship as you call it began five or six months ago.'

'Was it affection, love, or just sex?'

A twisted smile. 'I could ask what the hell that has to do with you.'

'If you answer my questions, Mr Lavin, it will save us both time.'

'All right. I suppose you need to know these things. It was sex – just plain sex.' He seemed to hesitate, then,

'Jessica had no conception of a relationship based on anything other than what was useful or profitable to her. Sex was the area in which I happened to be useful and available. No commitment.'

He looked down at his left hand which was deformed and white with scar tissue. 'I'm not to every woman's taste, but she was titillated . . .' He added at once, 'But I don't want you to think that the arrangement was one-sided. For a man as I am, sex at almost any price must be a plus.'

His head was turned away from Wycliffe so that it was hard to judge his expression.

He added after an interval, 'Poor old Vinter! His sphere of usefulness was on the farm, he didn't quite come up to scratch in bed. Stephanie was no good on the farm and not much use as a housekeeper. And the boy, Giles – the poor lad wasn't much use for anything in Jessica's terms.'

Lavin grimaced as though in sudden pain, and shifted himself in his chair. 'I suspect that there must have been others who passed – or, more likely, failed her tests.'

Wycliffe said, 'So you didn't even like her?'

A short laugh. 'No, I didn't even like her. But I didn't kill her though I'm not totally surprised that someone did.'

'Why do you say that?'

Lavin took time to think. 'There are crude expressions which would answer you precisely but, translated, I suppose one would say that she set out to stimulate a man to the limit of his sexual capacity then disparaged his achievement. Of course that would hardly square with the circumstances of her murder.'

'When did you last see her?'

'Ah!' For once he turned full face, his expression mocking. 'I saw her on Saturday evening when she was on her way to the church. I happened to be on deck as she passed.'

145

'Did she speak?'

'Casually. Of course, you have only my word for it that I didn't follow her.'

Wycliffe was trying to assimilate what he had been told; it shed fresh light on the dead woman and it also suggested that Lavin had been closer to the Vinters than he had supposed.

'Do the Vinters come here?'

'Laurence drops in for a chat quite often. He's an interesting chap, and knowledgeable; he's keen on natural history and the kind of work we are trying to do here.'

'Did I hear that he's interested in bats?'

'Yes, I believe he's doing a survey of the area for the county records.'

'What about Stephanie and the boy?'

A faint smile. 'Giles looks in occasionally to consult my bird books and he sometimes stays long enough to say "Thank you" when he's found what he wants.' Lavin shrugged. 'He's a strange lad. Recently he's taken to going about with Jumbo on collecting trips. They make an odd pair but they seem to get on, though I suspect that's because of Jumbo's high level of tolerance.'

'And Stephanie?'

A wry look. 'I've never been to bed with Stephanie if that's what you're suggesting.'

'But she comes here?'

'Once in a while, to listen to a new CD if I've got one. Now what free time she has is spent at Trecara with old Carey and his books. The place is falling down about his ears but I gather he's got a good library and Stephanie is helping him to catalogue it.'

'The Vinters seem a very intelligent family; isn't it surprising that they find themselves reduced to the situation on the farm?'

Lavin nodded with emphasis. 'Stephanie's got a first

class brain but she's totally unpractical. When it comes to the nitty-gritty of life she hasn't a clue, and Laurence isn't much better. There's no earthly reason why they should be shacked up here and treated like servants. With a bit of common sense added to their brains they could both land good jobs, whatever Laurence did or didn't do to his wretched student.'

'One more thing, Mr Lavin – the young man who lives here – I don't know his name or his status . . .' Wycliffe was aware of the compulsions which drive policemen to speak with such pomposity but at a loss what to do about it.

A broad grin. 'His name is Mark Wheeler though he prefers Jumbo, and his status is that of a friend. If it wasn't for his reputation – I don't care a damn about mine – I wouldn't bother to tell you that I'm not homosexual. What Jumbo's predilections are I can't say, though I fancy he's a late developer.'

'You came here together?'

'Yes. I was a single man with a decent salary, living just outside Nottingham. I had a house, a boat on the Trent, and a cottage near Newark. Jumbo came to me at eighteen as a sort of odd-job man . . . At the time I thought I might marry and I was preparing the ground.'

A brief pause, then, 'Jumbo doesn't know who his parents were and he's spent most of his life in homes of various sorts. He's too gentle for this world . . . Anyway, I've no close relatives, so we have something in common. We suit each other and when I had my accident it seemed natural what we should stay together. He likes it here and the kind of life we lead; he's becoming quite a good naturalist, all he needs is a bit of theory and the essential jargon.'

'Where is he now?'

'Out with young Giles, actually, getting samples – from the marshy ground around the tower.'

147

'One more question, Mr Lavin – do you know Arnold Paul, the church organist?'

'I would probably recognize him if I met him but I have never spoken to him.'

Wycliffe was running out of questions; in any case he was only fishing. Before the investigation could take a firm direction he needed to know the victim better, to discover the sources of that hatred which was manifest in the staging of her death.

He thanked Lavin and left. As he reached the bottom of the gangway the music began again. He was impressed by Lavin, he even liked the man. Lavin was ready to admit that he suffered the frustrations of his disability, but he was not perverted by them. It seemed that his self-analysis was sufficiently detached to be objective.

On the other hand Wycliffe was sure that he had not been told more than Lavin wished him to know. A killer? You do not decide on the strength of fifteen minutes conversation whether or not a man is capable of murder. But would Lavin have staged such a tableau? Would, or could Geach have done so? Would Paul? Or, assuming that he had a motive, would or could the egregious Johnny Glynn? Significantly, perhaps, he stopped short of adding Vinter to his catalogue of interrogatives.

It was at this point that a fresh thought occurred to him. As Franks had said, the killer could have been a woman; even a woman of no particular strength. And setting aside, he hoped, any male chauvinist tendencies, he thought he now saw, in the strangely logical yet freakish setting of the crime, more of female than of male psychology. Katherine Geach? Stephanie Vinter? There was no obvious reason why Katherine Geach would want to murder her sister, but the Vinter woman could be a different matter. The Vinters, man and wife, were credible suspects.

*　　*　　*

Lucy Lane drove to Truro and contrived to wedge her Escort into a tiny kerbside space somewhere near the offices of Nicholls and Greet in one of the Georgian houses in Lemon Street. Several of the houses in the street hid modern office blocks behind their deceptive façades but Nicholls and Greet practised no such deception; they fitted themselves into the domestic fabric of one of the houses with inconvenience and incongruity, but with consciences clear.

Harry Nicholls' office on the first floor retained its elaborate plaster cornice, its ceiling rose, its deep skirting boards, its multi-paned sash window and elegant panelled door. But, like its occupant, it showed every sign of running gently to seed. Harry Nicholls was fifty, a former scrum-half, now with thinning sandy hair, a high colour, a paunch, and an air of wistful bewilderment.

Lucy felt impelled to be brisk and bright. 'I think you know why I've come.'

The lawyer, concluding that any approach other than a strictly business one would be wasted on this attractive but severe young woman, said, 'The Dobell twins.'

'I understand there was an agreement between the sisters after their parents' death.'

Nicholls fingered a blue file but did not open it. 'Simple enough: ownership of the farm was shared equally between them under their father's will but it was agreed that Jessica should run the place, that Katherine would forgo any claim on the profits and would not be responsible for losses or debts incurred. Katherine's agreement was necessary to any change of use or the disposal of the property.'

'I believe that both sisters made wills at that time.'

'I'm not sure that I should discuss matters involving a living client but, in the circumstances – murder and all

149

that . . . Yes, they made wills each naming the other as sole beneficiary.'

'As far as their interests in the farm were concerned.'

'No, they both used the "all of which I die possessed" formula.'

'One wonders what Katherine's husband thought of that.'

Nicholls shifted around the files on his desk but said nothing.

'Those wills are still valid?'

'As far as I know.'

Lucy stood up. 'Well, thank you for being helpful, Mr Nicholls. I'm sure that what you have told me will be treated with discretion. I can't imagine that the wills are likely to figure in the case but . . .'

'No stone unturned. I know.' Nicholls got up to see her out. 'Do you play golf, Miss Lane?'

'No, why?'

'Or stay at four-star country hotels?'

'Not on my salary.'

'No, so you would hardly be interested in a development which offered such facilities . . .' A bland smile. 'Just a thought.'

He had opened the door for her to pass through. 'Perhaps you will excuse me now, I have another appointment.'

When Lucy returned to her car and a hovering traffic warden, she was thinking that she might have underestimated Harry Nicholls.

Wycliffe continued to walk feeling vaguely guilty because he was enjoying himself. He watched the ducks and the swans, he wondered what species of creature made that rippling arrow-like track on the water, swimming all but submerged, and whether the birds in disturbed flight over

150

the opposite bank were jackdaws or rooks. He thought how pleasant it would be to retire into such a valley, sheltered, perpetually moist, and usually silent. He often imagined withdrawing into such peace and seclusion but rarely thought of what he might do there.

Helen would say, 'You'd be bored within a week; in any case the place is an infallible prescription for rheumatism.'

'Stop the world, I want to get off!' It was a feeling he had often enough, but at other times he was more or less resigned to staying aboard the roller-coaster, screaming with the rest.

But this was a good place. Perhaps a place to die in. Death, he imagined, might come easily, unnoticed, stealing like a mist up the river.

He could see Trecara ahead, a jumble of decaying walls, windows, gables, roofs and chimneys. A low, battlemented wall separated the grounds from the river bank and, as he rounded a bend in the path, he came in sight of an absurd Victorian Gothic gatehouse, now lacking a gate. A car was drawn up there and two men stood by it, talking. One was the whiskered Carey, the other, Abe Geach. Wycliffe was mildly surprised.

They were within a hundred yards of him; they shook hands, Carey turned back to the house and Geach to his car. Geach caught sight of Wycliffe, decided not to see him, then changed his mind and came across the weedy gravel to meet him.

'Good morning, Mr Wycliffe! Finding your way around? Will you let me give you a lift back to the village?'

'No, thanks. I think I'll walk.'

Geach seemed reluctant to leave it at that. 'I've been having a chat with Carey about his house. It's in a terrible state; parts of it could collapse at any time. Pity! It's a fine old place but upkeep is the problem. Trigg is bad enough but this is three times the size and it's been neglected.'

He was talking too much.

'Are you undertaking restoration?'

'Well, it's been talked about, but Carey couldn't run to it. To put that place in good shape would set him back forty grand. It's a difficult building – a rabbit warren.'

'And the rabbits?'

Geach chuckled. 'There's old Carey – though he's not as old as you might think. I'm forty-one and he could give me ten years – no more; then there's his niece, and the Pascoes. The Pascoes, man and wife, must be in their sixties. They started there as servants in Carey's father's time; what they are now, God knows. I doubt if they ever get paid.'

They had come to a halt beside the contractor's car.

'Do the Careys have any friends?'

Geach pouted. 'The vicar is a regular visitor, I believe; and recently Stephanie Vinter. That set a few tongues wagging. She's supposed to be helping him sort out his library so perhaps he's hoping to raise a bit of capital.'

He had his hand on the car door. 'Sure you won't change your mind?'

'Thanks all the same.'

Geach, still uneasy, drove off up the road which was little more than a track. Wycliffe followed him with his eyes, and wondered. Had Geach, newly married, already started to look back over the fence? If it was he who had been with Jessica on the night the Ruse boy was killed, and now, sixteen years later, Jessica had threatened or even hinted at exposure . . . Geach had a great deal to lose.

But the bizarre staging of the crime?

Wycliffe walked up the track, through the pillared order of the larchwood. In a few minutes the ground levelled off and he was clear of the trees. To his right, the folly rose, apparently out of a marsh in which thickets of reeds and rushes were interspersed with scrub willows.

He was tempted to take a closer look, but resisted.

Then, looming ahead, and coming towards him, he saw a bulky figure laden like a Christmas tree. When the two were within a few yards of each other Wycliffe said, 'You must be Jumbo.'

The broad face beamed. 'And you're the policeman. I've seen you pass the boat.'

Wycliffe looked at the nets and at the battery of collecting bottles draped around the lad's neck. 'Mr Lavin told me you were out collecting.'

'Yes, in the marsh. You see, this is a freshwater marsh and Brian thought we ought to compare it with the marshes by the river which are a bit salt – because of the tide. Some of the animals and plants you get up here wouldn't like that, and some you get down there wouldn't like it up here.' His forehead creased in the effort of exposition. 'It's funny; some creatures and some plants are very fussy about how much salt there is but others don't mind much.'

Wycliffe said, 'I thought Giles Vinter was with you.'

Jumbo nodded. 'He was, but he didn't want to go home yet. I expect he's gone to the tower.'

'To the tower?'

'His dad is interested in bats and the tower is one of their roosting places. I think Giles is interested too.'

'Have you always been friendly with Giles?'

'No, only lately. He used to go around with Julie.'

Jumbo had very dark brown eyes and when he was speaking his expression was intent and serious. 'Brian – that's Mr Lavin, thinks that we might be able to write something about the valley and get it printed.'

Had anybody, so far, talked to Jumbo about the crime? He couldn't remember anything in the reports. 'Where were you, Jumbo, the evening Jessica Dobell was killed?'

'I was on the boat.'

'You didn't go out all that evening?'

'No.'

'So you couldn't have seen anybody – say, on the river bank?'

'Oh, I saw Jessica on her way to the church. Brian saw her too; he spoke to her – just said "Hullo" like.' His face clouded. 'That was the last time we saw her.'

'Mr Lavin told me that Jessica used to come to the houseboat sometimes.'

The boy's features went blank. He said: 'Yes.'

'Did you like that?'

A frown. 'I expect she was all right . . . But it wasn't the same when she was there. I don't think I liked her very much.' He added, after a pause. 'She spoilt things.'

Wycliffe went back to his earlier line. 'You saw no-one else on the river bank that evening?'

'Well, I saw Mr Vinter, but that was afterwards.'

'After you saw Jessica – how long afterwards?'

'I don't know really. I was still on deck, just leaning on the rail; it was dark.' He lowered his voice. 'A bit before, Mr and Mrs Vinter was quarrelling. I could hear them. You can hear everything on the river when it's dark. Mr Vinter shouted a bit but Mrs Vinter didn't raise her voice, then I heard the door slam and he went past the boat, but he didn't see me. I think he was upset.'

'Did Mr Lavin see him?'

Jumbo shook his head. 'I don't think so; he was in the cabin, working.'

Wycliffe said, 'I'm keeping you; I expect you want to get home with your specimens.'

Stray ends from other people's lives. A man quarrels with his wife, he walks out and slams the door; it happens all the time. But through a coincidence of time and place this quarrel would occupy Wycliffe and his detectives. If Vinter was ever arrested and charged it would figure in countless documents and records and would appear in the press. In solemn tones, worthy of the Recording Angel, counsel for the prosecution would say, 'Mr Vinter, on that Saturday evening when Jessica Dobell was murdered, you quarrelled with your wife . . .'

Chapter Ten

Tuesday morning (continued)

Wycliffe returned to the Incident Room, thoughtful and morose. Kersey was there.

'Nice walk, sir?' Kersey was nursing a mug of coffee. 'Like some? Potter has set up a snack bar in what used to be the kids' cloakroom.'

A constable went to fetch the coffee and Wycliffe sat astride one of the chairs, resting his arms on the back. 'On Saturday evening, after Jessica left for the church, the Vinters had a quarrel and Vinter took an airing along the river bank in the direction of the church.'

'Where did you get that?'

'The boy who lives on the boat with Lavin; he overheard the quarrel and saw Vinter leave.'

'Reliable?'

'I think so; he's not so stupid as people make out; in fact I don't think he's stupid at all. Uncomplicated, I'd say. Of course, what he's told us doesn't amount to much evidentially, it merely means that Vinter joins the club – Paul and the vicar were both coy about admitting not only that they were out and about on Saturday evening but actually in the church. Geach is supposed to have been working in his mobile office, but who's to say he didn't take a little walk? There's nobody in this case with anything like a respectable alibi except, perhaps, Johnny Glynn who seems to have been at the bar as usual.'

Kersey agreed. 'But, for what it's worth, Fox thinks the wellington boot that made his precious toeprint belonged to Vinter. It's not a hundred per cent, but Fox has the boot and he's getting an expert opinion. Chances are he'll get no more than a probable but even a possible could be a useful lever.'

He put down his coffee cup and lit a cigarette. 'And there are other pointers to the Vinter household. Whoever wrote the fourth anonymous note must have had access to the others in order to imitate their style and content, and choose the same stationery. The notes were sent to the farm, and Stephanie admits having seen one of them. Add to this that the vicar loaned his *Church Quarterly* to Vinter – the one from which the wedges for the organ keys were cut. Things are beginning to gel.'

Wycliffe was less euphoric. 'It would be a pleasant change. Anyway, we'd better have Vinter in for further questioning, on the record. If nothing else, he lied in his statement. I'm seeing Tom Reed this afternoon; if you have Vinter in about four, I'll join you when I can. Anything else?'

'Not much. We've filled in a bit of Lavin's background. He was employed in the research division of British Drugs. He qualified as a medical doctor before taking a post-graduate degree in pharmacology. The firm wanted him to stay on after his accident but he opted to go with an out-of-court settlement of damages. Nothing known against him; he was regarded as something of a boffin and a loner. All sorts of more or less good-humoured jokes about him and his boyfriend.'

While they were talking Lucy Lane arrived.

Wycliffe said 'Get yourself some coffee, Lucy. Potter has set up shop in the cloakroom.'

Lucy went out and came back with her coffee. 'I've talked to Nicholls, the lawyer. What we were told about the wills made by the two sisters is not quite right. According to Nicholls, if either of the two sisters died the other came into everything – not only the deceased's share in the farm.'

Kersey was unimpressed. 'So what? I don't see how it affects things. Of course Kathy gets Jessica's few belongings, whatever they are, but I don't imagine they would constitute a motive for snuffing her sister. Anything else?'

Lucy sipped her coffee. 'I don't know. As I was leaving, Nicholls asked me if I played golf or stayed at four-star hotels.'

Kersey laughed. 'He was winding you up.'

'I'm not so sure. It's occurred to me since that he could have been dropping a hint.'

'Of what?'

'There's been talk from time to time of business groups who want to cash in on Truro's prosperity with an up-market country park – hotel, golf course, swimming pool – that sort of thing. I believe that one or two schemes have already come to grief at the outline planning stage and I wondered if Nicholls was hinting at something of the sort affecting the future of the farm.'

Wycliffe was interested. 'I think you could have something. I happened to see Geach this morning, coming away from Trecara, being seen off by Carey. He seemed over-anxious to tell me that they had been talking about repairs to the house. It wouldn't surprise me if he had some deal in mind which could involve the farm and Carey's property.'

Kersey summed up: 'So the plot thickens as far as Geach is concerned. If he was involved in the RTA which killed the Ruse boy and our Jess was having qualms of conscience, plus the fact that she was being difficult about the farm . . . Well, you could say he was killing two birds with one stone.'

Wycliffe said, 'You have a talent, Doug, for making even your own brand of logic sound like fantasy. But Geach must be taken seriously. It's difficult to see him pursuing a double bluff with the Schumann thing but we know now that, musically, he was probably quite capable of setting it up.'

The three were beginning to loosen up; the atmosphere was coming right. Next door, telephones were bleeping; officers were tapping away at keyboards, nourishing the computer, scratching away in notebooks, or drinking coffee. Files were growing in number and bulk. They had settled in.

Wycliffe said, 'Before we get too bogged down, let's do what I suggested last night; let's try to work out some sort of specification for the criminal.' He turned to Lucy Lane. 'You have first go, Lucy.'

Lucy, taken by surprise, gathered her wits. 'Well, I don't think he's the sort to act on impulse. This crime was thought out in advance, planned, even to the cutting out and folding of the bits of paper to wedge the organ keys. Those bits of paper – so carefully cut, they bother me; the attention to detail for its own sake is obsessive.'

She paused, thoughtful, studying her finger nails. 'But the whole tableau seems to have been worked out beforehand and set up with almost loving care . . . Even the exact extent to which he would undress his victim was calculated. It's as though he got his kicks from brooding on every detail of what he would do. It seems to me that this adds up to a lot of hatred.'

Wycliffe was pleased. 'Good start! Hatred rather than lust?'

'I think so, yes.'

Kersey said, 'You talk about planning, but he didn't bring his own hammer.'

'No, but that makes another point – he knew the church

159

well enough to know where he could find one, and he avoided using a weapon which might be traced to him. I think he's accustomed to being in the church so that nobody would think twice about seeing him there. He also knows the organ and must have at least an elementary knowledge of music.'

Wycliffe said, 'Right! Your turn, Doug.'

Kersey grimaced. 'This is worse than being in the witness box.' He fished in his pocket for cigarettes and lit one. 'I see him as a twisted bastard, sexually repressed. If he had it in for the woman he could have killed her straight off, no need to set up this charade in order to tell the world that she was a whore.'

He blew out smoke and Lucy fanned herself defensively. 'I'd be inclined to think that at one time he must have been bitten by the religious bug. The whole thing has a rather nasty flavour of self-righteousness: judgement and condemnation . . . Then there's the Mary Magdalene stuff. He knew his Bible; and how many do these days?'

'You don't think the motive for the crime was sexual?'

Kersey screwed up his lined features in uneasy doubt. 'I was afraid you'd ask me that. I mean, there's obviously a strong sexual element but somehow I can't see it as a bloke killing his girlfriend just because she was having it off with somebody else. And yet . . .'

'Go on.'

'I was going to say that I still smell jealousy though somehow not of the woman . . .'

Wycliffe was approving. 'I go along with you there. Is that it?'

Kersey grinned. 'I wouldn't want to upstage you, sir.'

Outside the mists had cleared and the sun was shining. Through the open window they heard the church clock dole out a single stroke.

Wycliffe said, 'One o'clock, we shall be late at the Hopton, but I'd better say my piece.

'You've left me with the difficult bit – the nature of the hatred which seems to underlie this crime. Unless the whole set-up is a deliberate con, this hatred isn't only directed against the victim. She is the focus, but it reaches out to others – to Geach, as shown by the wedged organ keys, to the organist, to the vicar whose church is defiled, and even to the Church itself.'

Wycliffe paused, sitting back in his chair. 'In essence, I agree with both of you, and in particular with Doug's emphasis on jealousy allied to hatred. I can't see this crime simply as murder; it looks to me more like a comprehensive act of revenge and defilement.'

He shuffled some papers on his desk; he was uneasy, and it served him right. He had trapped himself into making some sort of analysis of the vague notions that were in his mind. Ideas, once put into words, demand the gloss of logic and thereafter are set in concrete. But having started, he soldiered on.

'It seems to me that we are dealing with a strangely disturbed personality and, though both of you speak of "he", in my opinion there is more of feminine than masculine psychology behind this crime. It could be that we are looking for a woman. I don't suppose Lucy will agree with that.'

But Lucy did, with reservations. 'You may be right about the psychology, sir, but if you are I don't think it necessarily means that we are dealing with a woman.'

'Perhaps a man in drag,' from Kersey. 'But does all this help to pin down the killer? I mean, is he, she or it on our list?'

Wycliffe said, 'Our next question, obviously. If I had to answer it at this moment, I would say, "No".'

They crossed to the pub for lunch. Carey and his niece

161

were well ahead with their meal, and today they shared their table with the vicar. From time to time Jordan glanced across at the police table, distinctly uneasy.

Kersey said, 'We're putting him off his lunch.'

By the time the police party had finished the others had already left and Wycliffe approached the landlord for enlightenment. As usual, Johnny was taciturn on the subject of personalities.

'His sister goes to Truro on Tuesdays and he lunches here.'

Stephanie Vinter spread a grubby blue tablecloth over one end of the kitchen table and laid three places with knives, forks and spoons. On the bottled-gas cooker a saucepan simmered, puffing out jets of steam. Stephanie's movements were listless, she was pale, her eyes were red and she had that curiously pinched look about the nostrils which goes with sleepless nights and distress of mind.

The back-door opened and Vinter came in; he'd left his boots outside and was in his stockinged feet. Moving like a sleepwalker, he went to the sink and began to wash.

'How are you getting on out there?' Stephanie spoke as though she were inquiring about some distant undertaking of which she had only hearsay knowledge.

Vinter paused in the act of soaping his arms. 'All right.'

'The man that Geach sent – what's he like?'

'He's called Sandry. He seems a decent sort – doesn't talk much.'

'Did he give you any idea of what they intend to do?'

'He doesn't know any more than we do. He's still employed by Geach and, as far as he knows, he's just helping out on a temporary basis.'

'It can't last.'

'No. Where's Giles?'

'He went out but he'll be back for lunch.' Stephanie put

plates to warm under the grill. 'Oh, there's a letter for you. It's on the dresser.'

Vinter finished washing, dried himself and went over to the dresser. With deliberation he slit open the envelope and unfolded the letter. 'It's from Jessica's lawyers.'

'Read it to me.'

'It says: "In connection with the estate of Miss Jessica Dobell, deceased, I shall be grateful if you will make an early appointment at this office to discuss with me matters arising which are of concern to you."'

'What does it mean?'

'Our marching orders, I suppose. What else?'

As he spoke, Giles came in. The boy stood inside the door, looking first at one parent, then at the other. 'Is something wrong?'

His mother said, 'No, I'm just going to serve out.'

They sat down to their stew in which the carrots were still hard. Stephanie said, 'We shall have to make up our minds; how much notice will they give us?'

Vinter, his fork halfway to his lips, put it down again. 'Let's leave it until I've seen the lawyer.'

Stephanie was about to protest but glanced across at her son and was silent.

Giles watched his parents but said nothing.

When the first course was almost over Vinter spoke to the boy. 'If, when we leave here, it meant you going to another school, how would you feel about it?'

Giles considered the question, then, 'When shall we go?'

'I don't know. We have no tenancy agreement so, as I was saying to your mother, it depends on the lawyers. But if it means another school we must make sure they use the same examining board.'

Stephanie got up from her chair. 'There's baked apple.'

She served the apple and they ate in silence. Suddenly

Giles dropped his spoon with a clatter. There was a fourth chair at the table, unoccupied, and he was looking towards it with his expressionless gaze. He said, in a conversational manner: 'Don't you miss her?'

Wycliffe drove into Truro along the devious lane which is its principal link with points east. Just above the town it blossoms into a dual-carriageway and the descent offers a glimpse of the three spires of Pearson's Gothic revival cathedral. The police station, at the bottom of the slope, by a busy roundabout, escapes being a sixties horror, for which somebody should get a small medal.

Wycliffe parked his car and was received by the desk man. 'Mr Reed is in his office, sir. You know the way?'

Wycliffe did.

They were served with coffee in china cups – with saucers, and Reed said, 'I only get this kind of service during royal visits.'

His little office was separated from the CID room by a glass partition. He fiddled with a little wad of typescript. 'I made a few extracts from the Derek Ruse file and there are one or two photographs . . .

'The date was January 3rd 1976 and the boy was fifteen at the time. At about six-thirty in the evening he was cycling home from the village of Trispen, to Tresillian, after spending the afternoon with a school friend.'

Reed must have spent time he could ill spare getting together his dossier and Wycliffe felt a pang of guilt. But exploring blind alleys is a growth industry.

Reed said, 'Derek Ruse was a popular boy and the case aroused strong feelings – especially when the medical evidence suggested that he might not have been dead when his body was pushed over the hedge into an adjoining field.'

The sun, hidden all the morning, had broken through

and was shining directly into the little office. With a massive forefinger Reed separated his collar from his neck. 'This damned office gets like an oven in the afternoons.'

He selected two photographs and passed them over. The first could have been taken in almost any of the minor lanes in the district; the second showed a field ditch by the side of a low hedge. In the ditch, the boy's crumpled body lay under his bicycle which must have been pushed over on top of him. His glazed eyes seemed to be staring up through the wheel spokes.

Reed said, 'That lane wriggles across country between Trispen and Tresillian, up hill and down dale, and it's barely wide enough for a hearse.' He added, after a pause, 'You see how we found him – that was next morning, and it had deluged with rain all night, washing away any traces there might have been.'

Reed sat back in his chair. 'CID took over, but I was kept on the case. The experts reckoned the bike had been struck higher up than would have been the case with a car, so we concentrated on commercial and farm vehicles. We covered the area for miles around, and got nowhere. Of course we realized there might be no trace of the collision left on a sturdily built vehicle with a good fender.'

He paused and looked at Wycliffe. Reed's baby-blue eyes were possessed of a singular innocence. 'No need to bore you with the details, the point is, names began to be bandied about – one name in particular, Jonathan Selborne Glynn. Johnny may seem tame enough now but he had a name as a tearaway then. His father farmed near Trispen and Johnny used to drive around the lanes, hell-bent, in a clapped out pick-up, usually with his girl-friend—'

'Jessica Dobell.'

Reed nodded. 'You're ahead of me, sir. Anyway, we'd had complaints, so it was natural we should think of him.

He admitted that he'd driven through the lane that evening – alone, he said, but he claimed it was more than an hour after the boy would have reached there on his bike. We might not have taken too much notice of his unsupported word but there were two reliable witnesses who saw him in the lane after half-seven that evening.'

Reed brought out a spotlessly white handkerchief to mop his forehead. 'Even the locals seemed satisfied, but I had my doubts. After the accident he could have driven back home and waited – there are plenty of farm gateways in which he could have turned the truck. All he had to do then was to drive along the lane an hour later and make sure he was seen. I put that to the DI, but of course he wanted evidence which I couldn't find.'

Reed spread his great hands. 'There were other suspects, but none that stood up.'

Wycliffe said, 'Well, all I can tell you is that shortly before her death Jessica Dobell confided in her sister, and in a friend, that she knew who was responsible for the hit-and-run and that she had been involved. She spoke of going to the police to tell what she knew.'

Reed stopped in the act of collecting his papers together. 'Did she mention Glynn?'

'In answer to a question, she said that it definitely wasn't Glynn and she added something else. She said that she wanted to go to the police but that she hadn't played fair with her sister and didn't want to make it worse for her.'

Reed looked at Wycliffe, incredulous. 'That adds up to Abe Geach. God, that would be a turn-up for the book! His name came up. Although he'd recently married her sister, it was rumoured that he'd been seen with Jessica in pubs far enough from home to feel safe. One story had it that he and Johnny had come to blows over the girl. Certainly Abe's Land-Rover was putting on a lot of night mileage at the time but we couldn't get anywhere in that direction.'

Reed massaged his chin until it shone. 'Well, sir! Where do we go from here? Is there a chance of reopening the file? I don't like loose ends even when they're ancient history.'

Wycliffe got up from his chair and walked to the window. For a minute or two he stood looking down at the frenetic gyration of traffic at the roundabout. Panic in the ants' nest.

'At the moment I'm more concerned with Geach as a possible murder suspect.'

Reed nodded. 'I see that – if she threatened him.'

'I'm willing for you to tackle Johnny Glynn in general terms about the hit-and-run. Let him know that he's no longer under suspicion, hint that the case could be reopened, and see what comes of it. No mention of any possible link with the present case. And remember, the new evidence, such as it is, is hearsay. I don't need to tell you that it wouldn't stand up in court.'

Reed said, 'Fair enough. That's all I could expect.'

Chapter Eleven

Tuesday afternoon

When Wycliffe returned to the Incident Room, Vinter was just arriving in a police car. He looked pale and drawn like a man on the edge of collapse.

The little interview cubicle was crowded, with Kersey and Wycliffe on one side of the table and Vinter on the other. On the table between them was a tape recorder and, on the wall, a notice setting out the rights of those undergoing police interrogation. An electric clock clicked the seconds away.

Wycliffe felt sorry for the man and was mildly reassuring. 'This interview is to clear up matters which have come to light since you made your statement, Mr Vinter. You should attach no more and no less importance to it than that.'

Kersey switched on the tape. 'This interview begins at 16.04 hours. Present: Detective Chief Superintendent Wycliffe and Detective Inspector Kersey. If you wish, the interview may be postponed and take place in the presence of your solicitor.'

'I feel in no need of a solicitor.'

Through the window of the little room noises reached them from outside; the occasional sound of cars manoeuvring to pass each other in the narrow street, people exchanging greetings, and gulls in squawking flight.

Wycliffe left the initial questioning to Kersey.

'You didn't tell us in your earlier statement precisely how you came to leave your teaching post.'

There was a pause while Vinter looked from Kersey to Wycliffe and back again, then: 'But now you've found out for yourselves, as I knew you would.'

'You were dismissed following an involvement with a girl student.'

'Technically, I was not dismissed, I was allowed to resign and so preserve my pension rights.'

It was strange. This man was wearing the clothes he wore on the farm – bib-and-brace overalls and a khaki shirt – yet he spoke in a cultivated manner with the precision of an academic. He had been warned of the interview in ample time to change but he had chosen to come in his role as a farm worker.

'Would you say that you are, by nature, a man inclined to violence?'

'I would not. In that instance I was the victim of a rather unpleasant young woman. Of course I am bound to say that, am I not?'

Wycliffe intervened. 'It is your relations with Jessica Dobell which concern us now.'

Vinter was looking down at his bony hands, clasped together on the table top. 'I was employed by her.'

Kersey said, 'But you had sex with her.'

The clasped hands tightened. 'I am not proud of that.'

'Another case of a designing woman?'

Vinter shifted on his chair. 'No, Jessica was highly sexed and I am not a monk.'

'Was your wife aware of the relationship?'

'No.'

Kersey sounded relaxed, understanding. 'Difficult, wasn't it? All together in the same house?'

Vinter seemed to be struggling to explain a situation which he had never before put into words. 'These encounters were casual, spur of the moment affairs . . . They did not take place in the house, but while we were working together – in the fields, the barn – any-where.'

Kersey said, 'Think carefully how you answer this, Mr Vinter. How did you feel about the woman? Were you fond of her? In love? Were you jealous of her having other men?'

Vinter looked at Kersey in astonishment. 'Why should I be jealous? I wished then, and I wish now, that I'd never seen her. We used each other sexually, that's the simple truth. Most of the time I hated her.' He added, in a low voice, 'But I didn't kill her.'

Neither of the policemen spoke and, after an interval, Vinter went on, 'I put my family in the position in which we found ourselves. I was to blame. We were servants, and Jessica wasn't slow to make us understand that. It wasn't a question of being overworked – I've very little idea of what could reasonably have been expected of us; it was her attitude. She was contemptuous of us for the very reason that we had put ourselves in a position of dependence. She could not understand people who lacked the strength of purpose which she had and her instinct was to humiliate them.'

'You are acquainted with Lavin, the houseboat man?'

Vinter's surprise at the abrupt change of subject was obvious and he answered as though with relief, 'Yes. He's the sort of man I can get on with, but I don't see as much of him as I would like. He is the sort of man I can understand.'

'I believe you have a common interest in natural history.'

'I'm trying to do a little work on the bat population of this area.'

'This means going out early and late?'

'Yes, I visit their known roosting places and try to find others.'

'Is Mr Carey another of your acquaintances?'

Was there a momentary twinge of concern? 'I know him.'

'I believe your wife is a fairly regular visitor at Trecara.'

'She is helping Carey with cataloguing his books.' He added, as an afterthought, but giving it some importance, 'Since he's been on holiday Giles has been going with her.'

It was Wycliffe's turn: 'In your earlier statement, Mr Vinter, you said that you did not leave the farm on Saturday evening.'

Vinter sat forward on his chair and looked directly at Wycliffe. 'That was a lie.'

'So we have discovered. Perhaps we can now have the truth?'

'My wife and I had a row.' A small gesture. 'It doesn't happen often but tension has been growing. I mean, Stephanie wanted us to move in with the Careys – Carey knows how unhappy we have been and he offered us a home for an indefinite period, with no strings . . . This was some time ago . . . I suppose it was very kind of him but what would it make me?' A longish pause, and then: 'The long and short of it is that I can't take his charity. Stephanie says I could help out around the place – earn my keep, but that would be just a façade . . . Anyway, we quarrelled and I stalked out.'

'Where?'

He looked blank. 'I'm sorry, what are you asking?'

'Where did you go? A simple question.'

'Oh, I walked along the river bank to the village, through the village and back by the road. I cooled off.'

'You didn't go into the church?'

Vinter shook his head and spoke in a low voice, 'No, I

171

didn't go into the church and I didn't see Jessica, but what is the good of me saying so?'

'At what time did you leave the house?'

'I'm not sure, but it would be about nine.'

'Did you see anyone, on the river bank, in the village, or on the road home?'

'There were one or two people about in the square but I didn't speak to anybody.'

'Anybody you recognized.'

'Tommy Noall was chatting to somebody on his garage forecourt but I doubt if he saw me . . .'

'There was silence in the little room; only the electric clock, clicking the seconds away.

'Are you interested in music, Mr Vinter?'

Vinter's blue eyes met Wycliffe's. 'Why don't you ask me if I know enough to have set up the thing on the organ?'

'Do you?'

'Yes, but I didn't do it and I can't make any suggestion as to why anybody would want to.'

'When you left home on Saturday evening what boots or shoes were you wearing?'

Vinter hesitated for a long time and Wycliffe did nothing to hurry him. After one or two false starts, he said, 'I was wearing my wellingtons.'

'You have more than one pair?'

'No.'

'You know that one of those boots is being checked against evidence found in the church?'

'Yes.'

'You have no comment to make on that?'

'No, except that I wasn't there.'

'One more question. I understand that you borrowed a copy of the *Church Quarterly* from the vicar, in which there was an article that interested you. What happened to it?'

'I thought I had returned it.'

'Can you remember the circumstances?'

A long period of hesitation which puzzled Wycliffe, then, 'No, I'm afraid not.'

'It was with pieces of paper cut from that issue that the organ keys were wedged – can you explain that?'

'No, I cannot explain it.'

Wycliffe recited, 'This interview ends at 16.34. It has been recorded and will be transcribed. You will then be asked to read the transcription and to sign it if you agree that it is a correct record.' He switched off the tape.

'And then?'

'You will be free to go but I strongly advise you to think carefully about your walk on Saturday evening and about what happened to that issue of the *Church Quarterly*. Two of my officers will return home with you to make a thorough search of the house for the magazine. I can obtain a warrant, but if you have no objection that will not be necessary.'

'I have no objection.'

Wycliffe returned to his office. He felt confused and depressed. A few minutes later he was rejoined by Kersey.

'So you're letting him go.'

'Yes.'

Kersey blew out his cheeks. 'So what? This is only the third day after all. What can you expect?'

Wycliffe fiddled with the papers on his desk. 'I know all that, Doug, but this woman wasn't found in some lay-by off the motorway; she was murdered in the heart of a small community of which she had been part for her whole life. Her associates are known, her life style is known, and the manner of the crime itself might be expected to point to the killer.'

Kersey said, 'I gather you weren't impressed by Vinter as a candidate.'

Wycliffe did not answer at once, then, 'Whatever I think there isn't enough evidence, material or circumstantial, to hold him, let alone charge him. Above all, there is no obvious motive. As far as I can see, Jessica Dobell's death did nothing to solve the Vinters' problems, it merely precipitated a crisis.'

Kersey persisted. 'So you don't think he's our man?'

'He still could be. For an innocent man, some of his answers were anything but spontaneous or convincing but, if he killed Jessica Dobell, there's a great deal more in all this than has so far surfaced . . . What was it Lucy said? Something to the effect that not much of what goes on inside Vinter shows – seven-tenths submerged. She could be right.'

Wycliffe sat back in his chair. 'When Franks said that we would be up to our necks in trick cyclists before we finished I didn't think it would start with me. But this case isn't going to be settled by studying bits of paper wedged between organ keys and toe marks on the bloody floor.'

It was unusual for Wycliffe to swear, and Kersey took note. 'So what's the agenda?'

'I want you to take Fox and Collis and search the farmhouse. Officially, you're looking for what's left of the vicar's magazine but that gives you an open brief. I've no idea what you might or might not find; that's why I want you there. Obviously if you find anything incriminating you'll act accordingly. Don't go until Vinter has signed his statement, then you can take him with you.'

Left alone, Wycliffe looked at the telephone, hoping that it would ring, and at the door, hoping that it would open. The investigation was losing its way; he had reached the stage of a punter picking winners with a pin. He needed a spot of luck. He trimmed his nails, emptied the little dish which Kersey had used as an ashtray, and tidied his files; placatory gestures to unknown gods.

And they seemed to work. At any rate there was a knock, the door opened and Dixon came in with a pink flimsy. 'Fax from CRO, sir. No record of prints from the Paul premises.'

Down the snake. But no sooner had Dixon returned to his post than the phone rang: 'DI Cox, sir. Met Fraud Squad.'

'Put him through . . . Geoff? This is Charles.' They had been at training school together but Cox had joined the Met and got stuck on the promotion ladder. It was from him that Wycliffe had sought information about the Pauls.

'When you phoned yesterday you mentioned that Arnold Paul, in an off moment, had called his alleged brother "Timmy". It rang a bell but I couldn't think why it should. Anyway it came back to me overnight. Arnold Paul was a witness for the defence in a case against a certain Timothy Raison a few years back. Raison was acquitted on charges of false accounting and misappropri-ation in a company of which he was managing director. That's history; more to the point, we've got a warrant out against him for jumping bail on fresh charges – perhaps a bit more serious this time. It sounds too much of a coincidence for there to be no connection so I'd like to send a chap down to talk to your friend.'

'Be my guest. But you don't see this Raison as a killer?'

Cox laughed. 'More of a twit. We meet a lot of his sort in our line, not very bright; they wade into trouble without noticing it and their success depends on others being bigger fools than they are. Of course, Raison is very small fry but intelligence isn't a conspicuous feature of the financial world – mostly it's cunning and greed.'

'He must have some sort of hold over Paul.'

'I'll keep you posted.'

175

The gods had failed him; he wasn't interested in crooked dealings which might or might not involve Arnold Paul.

It was almost six before Wycliffe heard from the searchers.

It was Kersey. 'I'm speaking on the car phone. The house seems to be clean. We did a thorough search. Vinter showed not the slightest interest and refused to monitor what we were at. He went back to his work about the farm. Stephanie didn't turn a hair; she followed us around but made no complaint or comment. It was uncanny.'

'Was the boy, Giles, there?'

'Working at his books on the kitchen table. I gave him the chance to be in on the search of his room but he hardly looked up – just said, "No, thank you."'

'Tuesday is pasty night. Cornish pasties, me han'somes! How's that then? The real thing: plain pastry, chuck steak, sliced potato, turnip and onion; nothing minced, nothing diced.' Johnny, doing his Captain Birds Eye act, seemed his usual self. 'Of course, there's the cold table if you prefer it.'

'How big are your pasties?' from Lucy Lane.

'Two just fit on a ten-inch dinner plate – perfect. But nobody eats more than one, and young women worried about their figures are allowed to leave a bit.'

So pasties it was.

Wycliffe's mind was on Vinter. He was uneasy and all his cop instincts told him that he should have held the man for questioning. He told himself that he would have had to let him go again, but his professional conscience was not appeased. On the other hand . . .

The pasties arrived – golden brown, beautifully 'turned in', with a slot in the top to let the steam out.

Johnny was there. 'My wife makes 'em; that's mainly

176

why I married her. You can use a knife and fork if you must, but the proper way is to pick 'em up and bite from the end – hold 'em in your table napkin but watch out for the gravy, it's hot.'

Kersey and Lucy Lane took Johnny's advice but Wycliffe, victim of his mother's aspiring gentility, used his knife and fork.

Lucy surrendered when only one-quarter of her pasty remained; the two men had cleared the crumbs. 'That was good!' – Kersey. 'Excellent!' – Wycliffe.

Johnny said, 'No dessert, no coffee, but a cup of tea with milk and sugar; then a walk. That's my recipe to aid digestion after a pasty, but if you don't like it, then there's sodium bi-carb on the house.'

Carey, with a gleeful flourish, laid down six of the seven tiles in his rack – 'H-R-A-T-R-Y. With your P, Jordan, that makes phratry.'

The vicar's smooth brow creased into a frown. 'Phratry?'

'Are you challenging?'

A self-conscious laugh. 'No – I know better than to do anything so rash. It's just that phratry is new to me.'

'It shouldn't be. The word has an excellent pedigree, going back to the Greeks; it means a religious or political division of the people – originally, I believe, based on kinship. Your turn, Alicia.'

Alicia studied her tiles and finally selected three: 'I am adding I-S-E to journal, to make journalise – which will annoy uncle.'

Carey grinned. 'There should be an Officer of State – like the old Public Hangman who burned books – charged with the duty of formally banishing such words from the language.'

They were in one of the few rooms that remained

habitable. It was small, with items of furniture too large for it brought from other parts of the house. Although the room was lit by electricity, the chill of an April evening was kept at bay by a paraffin stove, placed close to the table at which they were seated.

Tuesday evening Scrabble was a regular feature of life at Trecara, with the vicar as guest. For him, it was the social event of his week. The game ran its course with Alicia the winner.

'She has no compunction whatever in profiting from the dregs of the OED,' Carey said. 'Shall we have another game and try to teach her the elements of discrimination?'

Jordan smiled a dutiful smile but it was clear that his thoughts were elsewhere. There was no disguising the fact that he was preoccupied and distressed. He looked towards the window where the curtains remained undrawn against the darkness outside and rain trickled down the window panes. 'I really must get back or Celia will be worried.'

'Why don't you telephone? It's raining hard now but that probably won't last long. Tell her you'll be a bit late.'

The vicar hesitated. 'No, Celia likes to keep to a routine.'

Alicia said, 'I'll get the whisky.'

This too was part of the Tuesday ritual; just the one drink before Jordan left. Alicia went to get it.

Carey said, 'I can see that you are worried, and no wonder; it is a most distressing affair. And so inexplicable!'

Jordan fingered the tiles which he had collected together and boxed. 'I'm at my wit's end. I don't know what to do.'

Carey stroked his beard. 'If it would help to talk . . . ?'

Jordan shook his head. 'It is kind of you, Hector, but it's only with God's help that I shall see this thing through.'

Alicia returned with the drinks tray.

'Ah, Alicia, there you are!'

The two men drank their whisky; Alicia, her orange juice; then Jordan got up to go. He made an effort to sound normal. 'Another Tuesday gone by!'

Carey saw him off at the door. The rain had eased. Jordan said, 'Good night! And thank you, both.'

'Let me lend you a torch.'

'No – really, I don't need one.'

It was dark but in the country it is rarely so dark that one cannot see one's way. The weedy gravelled drive curved gently to the grandiose gatehouse. He felt a little relieved; the companionship, the whisky, and the mere admission of his distress had coloured his mood. Tonight he would pray, and tomorrow would be in God's hands.

The arch was ten or twelve feet wide – wide enough to add a certain dank clamminess to the air beneath it and to intensify the darkness. But he could see the dull gleam on the pool which always formed under the arch when it rained and he kept close to one side to avoid it. Then, suddenly, there was a movement close to him, perhaps he let out a startled cry. He experienced a crushing, pulverizing pain in his head, and then – nothing.

That night Stephanie went early to bed; she was prepared against another bad night with tablets Dr Sparrow had given her. She read a few pages of *Mansfield Park*, her current bedside book. It was long since she had read it and she was surprised to discover that the intervening years had made it possible for her to envy poor Fanny Price. After a few pages she put down the book, swallowed a Mogadon washed down with water, switched off her light and snuggled under the bedclothes. Within a short time she was asleep.

Some time later she was awakened by a sudden breeze

which blew a curtain of rain against her little window. Sleepily, she realized that Laurence had not yet returned from his bat-watching. Nothing unusual in that. Then she noticed the reflection of light coming from Giles' room and called to him, 'Don't stay up reading too late, Giles!'

'No, Mother.'

'Good night, dear.'

'Good night.'

Almost at once his light went out and Stephanie fell asleep once more. Her dreams were confused and several times they brought her to the edge of wakefulness, but she slept on. When she eventually woke it was from a mildly erotic dream, and her hand was between her thighs. She sighed, turned over, and realized that Laurence was still not beside her. It was light, with the pale-grey light of early dawn and it was still raining.

Chapter Twelve

Wednesday morning

Wycliffe awoke, feeling sure that he had been disturbed by some sound and, for a moment or two, unable to recall where he was. Then memory returned and so did the sound – a gentle tapping on his door. He sat up in bed and as he did so the door opened. It was Johnny, the landlord, in shirt and trousers.

'I'm sorry to wake you but Celia Jordan has been on the telephone. She wanted to speak to you personally but I insisted on taking a message . . .'

Celia Jordan? Wycliffe's brain was still clogged with sleep. The vicar's sister, of course. 'Well?'

'She says her brother is missing – that he didn't come home last night.' The landlord spoke with detachment, as though disclaiming all responsibility. 'She's a bit odd sometimes but I thought I'd better pass it on.'

Wycliffe, still coming round, looked at his travelling clock; it was a quarter past six. 'Perhaps you will knock on Mr Kersey's door, and on Miss Lane's, while I get dressed.'

Johnny withdrew. Wycliffe got out of bed and pulled back the curtains. At times in the night he had been aware of heavy rain, now it had given place to drizzle. His room overlooked the square and the creek where the usual pair of swans, padding about on the muddy shore, were the only sign of life.

In his dressing gown he used the pay-phone in the corridor to arrange for a patrol car to call at the vicarage. He was uneasy, apprehensive. He recalled his last words to the vicar: 'Somebody who has killed once has broken through a barrier and may well find it easier to kill a second time.' Pompous, but true. A pity he hadn't listened to himself with greater attention. He had hoped to induce Jordan to tell what he was holding back, but he had failed, and could now be facing the consequence.

Fifteen minutes later, with Kersey and Lucy Lane, he was sipping scalding coffee in Johnny's kitchen. Johnny was still inclined to backtrack. 'This could be a mare's nest. As I said, Celia's queer. I've heard talk that in his last parish – somewhere in Wiltshire – they had to put her away for a time.'

Lucy was sent to the Incident Room while Kersey and Wycliffe drove the short distance to the vicarage. A patrol car was parked outside and they were admitted by a uniformed copper. He reported in a low voice, 'My mate is with her in the sitting room, sir. She says she went to call her brother this morning and found that his bed hadn't been slept in. It seems he had a regular Tuesday evening date at Trecara – with the Careys – and he went last evening as usual. I phoned Carey just now and he says Jordan left there at about half-ten.'

'On foot?'

'Yes.'

'Do you know if he usually went by the road or by the river path?'

'His sister says he went by the road. The footpath doesn't save much between the vicarage and Trecara, and if it's wet or dark, it's difficult.'

Wycliffe said, 'I want you to stay here until relieved. If anything crops up get in touch with DS Lane at the Incident Room.'

Back in the car he and Kersey continued up Church Lane; they passed by the entrance to Jessica's farm, and a moment or two later they were at the top of the long track which led down to the manor house. At one time it must have been a well-maintained drive but now the surface was rutted and pot-holed – facts that were even more apparent in the car than they had been when Wycliffe walked it the day before. The mist was so thick that Kersey was deprived of his first close-up view of the tower, and as they jolted down through the larchwood even the tops of the trees were hidden.

They arrived in the open space before the gatehouse to find Carey waiting for them. His silky hair and beard glistened with drops of moisture.

'He's here.' Carey was deeply distressed and found difficulty in being coherent. 'We found him. Alicia went back to the house to telephone but you must have already left . . .' He passed a hand over his face and beard and seemed surprised to find it wet. 'It doesn't seem possible; I saw him off at the door – watched him go down the drive . . . I can't understand how I didn't hear something . . .'

Wycliffe formally introduced himself and Kersey, then the two detectives moved under the arch where Carey had pointed. The vicar was there, lying in a crumpled heap on the ground. The body lay on its right side, half in and half out of a shallow pool formed by the overnight rain. The cause of death was apparent, a massive injury to the left side of the skull above the ear.

For some reason there was not much blood, but what there was had drained into the blond, fine hair, and trickled in rivulets over the cheeks. Away from the actual wound the undamaged skin was pale and seemed to have shrunk over the bones so that the brow-ridges, nose, and chin were more prominent. The vicar's appearance had aged in death.

Kersey said, 'No theatricals this time; no props.'

Wycliffe nodded. 'Simple panic, by the look of it.'

'He must have known more than was good for him.'

Wycliffe was solemn. 'He certainly knew what we should have known – or at least guessed. But here we are, still in the dark. We've missed something vital, Doug, and this poor devil has had to pay for it.'

Kersey said, 'As far as I'm concerned, there's now only one horse in the race. Jordan must have seen Vinter in or near the church on Saturday evening and—'

Wycliffe, irritable, cut him short. 'Get on the car phone; contact Lucy at the Incident Room, and tell her to notify the sister. Then, the coroner and so on. Franks is still at the address in St Mawes – he's going to moan about this – twice in four days, but that's his problem. I shall be at the house with Carey but let me know when the circus begins to arrive.'

Carey had been standing well away from the two men, indifferent to the drizzling rain; now Wycliffe joined him. 'Perhaps we can go up to the house.' He added, 'This must have been a great shock.'

Carey said, 'I shall be glad to get back; I'm worried about Alicia; she says very little but things affect her deeply.'

Seen at close quarters it was more than ever obvious that successive generations of Careys had altered and added to the original house, each in their own idiosyncratic style. The process had culminated in the Victorian gatehouse, after which, perhaps mercifully, money must have run out. Now Wycliffe was to see the inside.

It was depressing. Carey led him through a bare hall and down a long passage, all stone floored and uncarpeted, into a sitting room at the back of the house.

Carey was agitated. 'Perhaps you will excuse me for a moment; I must find Alicia.'

Wycliffe waited in the little over-furnished room where the light was so poor that it was hard to distinguish any detail in the pictures on the walls. The furniture consisted of large pieces from different periods, presumably collected from rooms that had fallen victim to the progressive decay. He noted the cast-iron grate with its surround of Delft tiles, and the stacked, sawn logs beside it, but there was an oil stove in the middle of the room.

Carey was gone for some time. When he returned he was accompanied by his niece and he had changed his jacket and trousers.

The girl was very pale but composed. She said, 'I've seen you at the Hopton, Mr Wycliffe. I'm sorry to have kept you waiting, it was my fault, I made uncle change into dry clothes.' She turned to her uncle. 'Now you will want to talk – I shall be in the kitchen with Winnie if you want me.' Her manner was that of an affectionate mother with her child.

When she had gone, Wycliffe said, 'Just a few questions, Mr Carey. Jordan was a regular visitor here on Tuesday evenings?'

'Yes. I think he enjoyed those evenings. I know we looked forward to him coming.' He glanced at the table on which there was a Scrabble set. 'We usually played Scrabble.'

'So anyone who knew his habits could expect him to be leaving here at . . . at what time?'

'At about half past ten; that was his time, and that is when he left last night. I saw him to the door and watched him as he walked down the drive . . . It was dark, but a clear night.' Carey brushed his eyes with his hand; they glistened with tears. 'He was a good man, but not a happy one, tortured rather than comforted by his religion.'

'Presumably you neither saw nor heard anything unusual?'

'Nothing.'

'What was your impression of his state of mind?'

Carey frowned. 'Well, as you might expect, the poor man was terribly shocked and distressed by what had happened in his church – by the crime itself, and by its bizarre embellishments.'

Wycliffe waited, and when no more came he said, 'I think you were going to add something.'

Carey looked down at his hands. 'Yes, well, I suppose discretion would be out of place in the circumstances. Jordan had other troubles. Yesterday evening, after we had had our meal and while Alicia was in the kitchen helping Mrs Pascoe with the clearing up, he told me, in confidence, that he suspected his sister of having written the anonymous notes which were found in the dead woman's possession. It seems that she did something very similar in his previous parish with unpleasant though not tragic consequences.' After a momentary pause, Carey added, 'Not that he imagined for a moment that she had any part in the crime itself. There was no question of that.'

'I understand.'

Carey was uncharacteristically restless and troubled. Instead of staring at him Wycliffe chose to look at a portrait of a Carey ancestor which hung over the fireplace. It portrayed a strikingly beautiful young woman with a remarkable resemblance to Alicia.

Carey had followed his gaze. 'Elvira Carey. When she died in childbirth at the age of twenty-four, her husband built the tower to her memory.'

He had had time to recover his self-control though his manner was still uncertain and tentative. 'I have very little to go on, but I feel sure that Jordan's worries went even deeper. Looking back, I can't help wondering if he had some idea of the identity of the killer . . . There was something which he wanted to confide but could not bring himself to do. I feel now that if only I had seemed a little more receptive, if I had been a little more persuasive . . . Of course I had no idea that he was in any way threatened.'

Wycliffe was sympathetic. 'I understand how you feel. I had precisely the same impression – that he was holding something back, but I was reluctant to put pressure on him. Now, of course, I regret that I did not.'

'It distresses you?'

'Of course it does!'

Carey seemed surprised. It seemed a new idea that a policeman might have a conscience in such matters.

The rain had stopped and the skies were clearing. Watery sunshine brought fresh colour and life to the river and its banks, but under the arch of the Victorian gatehouse the preoccupation was with death. There a group of initiates began that sequence of rituals prescribed for the discovery of the dead victim of another's hand.

Dr Sparrow, manifestly grown in self-importance, was there to pronounce life extinct. DS Fox, attended by his acolytes, was there to record every minute aspect of the scene of the crime. Dr Franks, the pathologist, under direction from the coroner, had arrived to take charge of the body and supervise its removal to the mortuary, there to perform his peculiar rites. Screens had been erected to preserve all this from prying eyes, but there were none. Kersey, nominally in charge, was mainly concerned with how soon they would let him get back to the job.

Wycliffe arrived while Franks was still making his preliminary examination. The pathologist got up from his knees, brushing his trousers free of invisible dust – he invariably used a kneeling pad. 'Twice in four days of the only break I've had in months! Do I, in some mysterious way, attract these diversions, Charles? Or do you arrange them for me?'

'Neither. I'm quite sure the poor chap got himself topped just to spoil your holiday. Now, what have you got for me?'

Franks became judicial. 'I could say that the medical evidence is consistent with him having died between ten and eleven last night—'

'Good! And I suppose you could also say that death probably resulted from a blow delivered to the left side of the skull—'

Franks finished for him, 'causing a depressed fracture at the junction of the parietal, sphenoid, and temporal bones.'

'In other words, you've nothing to say that might be useful.'

There was a doorway which gave access to what had once been the gatekeeper's room; now it was stacked with boxes, broken furniture, and old beer crates. From the standpoint of the killer it had been simple. Knowing that the pool would force his victim to walk on that side, all he had to do was to stand back in the doorway and wait.

Franks was stooping over the body, taking another look at the wound. 'Perhaps I could add that from the angle of the depression it seems likely that the assailant was significantly taller than his victim. If I was asked nicely, I'd say he must have been not far short of six feet.'

Kersey looked at Wycliffe. 'Interesting, don't you think, sir?'

Wycliffe pointed into the little room with its store of rubbish. 'Perhaps he stood on a box to give him more clout. He had plenty to choose from.'

Franks laughed. 'You see what he's like when you try to help.'

Fox, hovering now, asked if it was all right to go through the dead man's pockets.

Franks said, 'Enjoy yourself.'

Fox had provided himself with a selection of the regulation tagged plastic bags. He explored the pockets which were sodden down one side. The trouser pockets yielded three pounds eighty-four in coin and a grubby handkerchief. The jacket side pockets were empty except for a raffle ticket and a supermarket receipt, but the two inside breast pockets were more productive: a wallet, a cheque book, a ball-point pen, and an engagement book. The wallet held fifteen pounds in notes, a cheque card, driving licence, and library card.

Wycliffe flipped through the pages of the engagement book then turned to Kersey. 'I want Vinter brought in for further questioning. And to keep the record straight we must organize the troops for another round of inquiries: where was everybody, why, and who saw what.

'Now, Fox: everything here is to be minutely examined. If we are to get any material evidence it must come from here. I'm serious about the possibility of one of those crates being used by the killer to stand on.'

Kersey said, 'Where will you be, sir?'

'Back at the Incident Room, keeping my head down.'

Lucy Lane had returned to the Incident Room after informing Celia of her brother's death and was bringing her notes up to date.

'How did she take it?'

Lucy swept back a stray lock of hair – the only sign that she had been turned out of bed and set to work in fifteen minutes flat. 'I find it hard to believe that she really "took it" at all, sir. That's the most charitable view. At first she said nothing. Then I suggested that it might help to talk and she said, "What about? You tell me that my brother is dead, that he was murdered; oughtn't you to be out with your colleagues looking for his killer? Instead of here, playing at being a social worker."

'As I was leaving, she said, "I must tell the bishop."'

Wycliffe said, 'Perhaps she really believes he's gone to a better place. I must admit it would be a comforting thought.'

He was still in his office, brooding, when his telephone rang. It was Kersey, speaking from the farm. 'I'm using the car phone. It seems that Vinter was out bat-watching last night.' Kersey contrived to make it sound like a perversion. 'And, according to Stephanie he hasn't been home since.'

'Wasn't she concerned?'

'Not so's you'd notice; he's often been away all night it seems. But the point is I've just discovered that the farm-truck is missing. It looks as though he's been back and gone again, this time in the truck.'

'He didn't take it last night?'

'Not according to the boy; he says the truck was still parked in the lane when his father left. I've asked Stephanie to check, and find out whether he took anything else while he was about it. The long and short of it is, sir – he's done a runner.'

Wycliffe did not miss the note of criticism. 'All right; phone in what you've got on him and the truck and I'll have it circulated.'

It was necessary to report to the chief. Oldroyd resisted the temptation to say 'I told you so.' Instead, it was: 'You had to make a decision Charles and, as it happened, you made the wrong one, but it's easy to be wise after the event. Any idea where Vinter might have gone?'

'It's by no means certain that he's gone anywhere.'

Oldroyd took a deep breath. The two men had worked together for many years and outside the office they were good friends. In the office there were frequent differences. 'You're holding back on this one, Charles. I take it you now know who you're after?'

Wycliffe was silent, and the chief prompted, 'Charles?'

'No, sir; I'm by no means sure.'

Oldroyd snapped, 'Then I hope you'll act as though you were.'

Wycliffe had scarcely replaced his phone when it rang again. It was Kersey. 'There's some money missing, sir; just a few pounds they kept for emergencies. Nothing else, according to her ladyship.'

'Cheque book? Credit card?'

'I asked her and she looked at me as though I was talking about the family silver.'

'How are they taking it – she and the boy?'

'Nobody could accuse them of dramatizing the situation.'

'What was he wearing?'

'Overalls. It seems he didn't stop to change.'

'A man in overalls, driving a farm-truck, with only a few pounds in his pocket, isn't likely to be making for sunny Spain. I'll pass you over to Lucy and you can give her the details for circulation. After that I want you back here to arrange a search of the vicar's belongings, in particular of his study and his personal papers . . . His sister? If she interferes she'll be obstructing the inquiry. Handle her tactfully, but no nonsense.'

When he put down the phone Wycliffe got up from his chair and stood, staring out of the window of his little office. Ahead, there was only the boundary wall, but overhead the sky was an intense blue and two seagulls, whiter than white, cruised and planed with effortless ease.

It was always his practice in a murder inquiry to concentrate on the victim, and Jessica's life, like anyone else's, was intimately woven into the pattern of the lives about her. To discover and trace all the threads was impossible; one must select, and he had selected those which seemed significant. They pointed to a limited range of possible suspects. The problem was to match the character of any one of these with the extraordinary circumstances of the crime. He had encouraged the drawing up of some sort of specification for the criminal but the plain fact was that none of the suspects had seemed to fit.

Now, overnight, the vicar had become a second victim and Laurence Vinter a fugitive.

Laurence Vinter . . . A man filled with hatred which could find no single target but nourished itself in the meticulous preparation of a tableau in which a brutal murder was no more than a centrepiece . . . A man who, threatened with exposure, had shown no hesitation in murdering a second time . . .

A tap at the door, which opened just as Wycliffe muttered to himself, 'Nonsense! It's not possible!'

Lucy Lane said, 'I've brought you some coffee, sir.'

And yet Vinter was on the run.

He turned away from the window and, for a moment, it was as though he hardly knew where he was.

'Are you all right, sir?'

He sat at his desk and seemed, suddenly, to relax. 'Yes, I'm fine, Lucy. I've just decided that I can't believe the impossible.'

'You're obviously not as good at it as the Red Queen. Perhaps you should practise more. Anyway, coffee.'

He was being mothered, indulged, and he rather liked it. Drinking his coffee, he said, 'I'm going to the farm amongst other places, Lucy, and I want you with me. Send a crime car with a DC to the farm to await our arrival. Mr Kersey is leaving a uniformed man there. Tell the DC to park in the farmyard for communications purposes.'

A few minutes later they were crossing the square together. News of the vicar's death must have got around but there were few people about. Two women outside the post office watched them go by, solemn faced and silent. There must be a sense of shock; probably a feeling of resentment against the police. Why did they let it happen? Despite all the publicity, fictional and documentary, violent crime, when it strikes home, still arouses an expectation of miracles. By the same token Wycliffe felt a responsibility for his failure to deliver.

The garage man had his head under the bonnet of a car and did not see them.

The tide was in, the creek and river were brimming. Swans and ducks cruised close inshore. Wycliffe and Lucy Lane walked along the river bank, past the kissing-gate to the churchyard, and on towards the houseboat.

Chapter Thirteen

Wednesday morning (continued)

Wycliffe said, 'Lucy, how many bats do you think there are likely to be within, say, a mile radius from here?'

'I've no idea: dozens, I suppose. Scores for all I know. Why?'

'I was just wondering.'

This was the beginning of a strange interlude in the continuing relationship between Wycliffe and his two closest associates. The next few hours would remain in the memories of Lucy Lane and Kersey as the period during which they had lost contact with him, when he neither heeded their opinions nor offered them encouragement or direction.

They were drawing level with the houseboat. No music this morning. The canoe floated astern. Jumbo, his arms resting on the rail, was looking down at them, his expression gloomy.

'Mr Lavin about?'

'He's in the cabin.'

'We'll drop in for a word.'

'You don't think we should be getting on to the farm, sir?'

'No hurry. I want to talk to Lavin about bats.'

Lucy followed Wycliffe up the gangway and Lavin came on deck to meet them.

'You'd better come below.'

In the cabin Lucy looked about her with interest. It was obvious that the routine of the boat had been disturbed. On a small trestle table at the foot of the companionway there was a coffee pot, a couple of used mugs, and eggy plates with crumbs of toast. A door stood open to a tiny cabin aft where there were two bunks with sleeping bags and a blanket or two.

Lavin, eyeing Lucy, was careful to present his uninjured profile. He closed the door on the bunks and found them seats.

Wycliffe said, 'You've heard about Jordan?'

'Yes.'

'May I ask how?'

'Rain or shine I go for a walk along the river bank in the early morning. This morning, as I was approaching Trecara, I met Vinter on his way home. He looked ghastly. I asked him what was up and he pointed back to Trecara, muttering something about the vicar, and hurried past.'

'What time was this?'

'Time? We don't take much count of time but I suppose it must have been between half-six and seven. He was in no state for a chat and he didn't want my company. I walked on and found the police at the gatehouse; they'd just arrived. Carey was there, looking like Marley's ghost, and he told me what had happened. But it was obvious enough; the poor devil was lying half in and half out of a pool of water with his head bashed in.'

'Have you seen Vinter since?'

'I haven't seen anybody. I had half a mind to look in at the farm but Stephanie isn't the sort to welcome visitors in moments of crisis.'

Wycliffe said, 'I came here to ask you about bats.'

'About bats?' Lavin's astonishment was obvious. 'What about them?'

195

'How many do you think there might be within the area that interests Vinter?'

Lavin shrugged. 'You should ask him. He concerns himself only with the immediate neighbourhood and, on the basis of figures he quoted to me, he's looking at a population of considerably less than a hundred. They seem to be spread over four species, mainly pipistrelles. About a third of them roost in the roof of the old tower, while the rest are scattered over a number of sites: house roofs, barns, an old adit . . . You name it. But what's all this about?'

'I've been wondering what Vinter did during those hours and whole nights when his bats failed to keep him occupied – especially out of season.'

Wycliffe received a quick look from Lucy Lane with whom the coin had dropped.

Lavin too. 'Don't you think you should ask him?'

'I would if I could. Vinter is missing.'

'*Missing*?'

'After seeing you it seems he collected a few pounds cash they happened to have in the house and cleared off – in the farm-truck.'

Lavin was incredulous. 'But that's absurd! You're not suggesting that he had anything to do with what happened to the vicar? The man was upset – distressed.'

'I'm not suggesting anything, Mr Lavin, I'm telling you what happened.'

Lavin was fingering his beard. 'There's something damned odd going on!'

'I agree. I also think that your friendship with Vinter was closer than you or he have led me to believe. Did he often spend the whole or part of the night here?'

There was an interval while Lavin decided how to react. He didn't argue or protest but he chose his words with care. 'I think you should understand how things were at the farm while Jessica was alive. The Vinter family were in an intolerable position, and poor old Laurence could hardly deny that it was he who had got them into it. There was bound to be tension between him and his wife and there was no outlet. It was difficult for them to have a discussion, let alone a row, that wasn't monitored by Jessica. And, above all, however they felt about each other, they had to share a room and a bed . . .'

'So?'

A faint smile. 'You are quite right. Until comparatively recently, Laurence would often spend the whole or part of the night on the floor in this cabin. We kept a mattress, a pillow, and a few blankets always ready for him.'

'He never clashed with Jessica's visits?' It was the first time Lucy had spoken.

Lavin looked at her as though he had just been reminded of her presence. 'Obviously he knew when she was away.'

'But recently he has not come so often?'

'He has not come at all at night. I suspect that he made another arrangement. We never discuss the subject. Of course, he looks in of an evening and at weekends and he knows that he is always welcome when it suits him to come.'

Wycliffe stood up, his manner was brisk. 'Thank you, Mr Lavin, you've told me what I wanted to know.'

Lavin saw them off. At the gangway, he said, 'Vinter is a man with a conscience. As a policeman you must know what a liability that can be.'

The sun was shining, the tide was at flood, there were green reflections in the water and everywhere there was stillness.

As they turned up towards the farmhouse Lucy Lane said: 'Bat-watching as an alibi for spending nights out of his wife's bed . . .'

'What about it?'

'Just the cosy accommodations which are possible between men where women are concerned.'

'And not the other way round?'

'That's our weakness.'

A uniformed constable stood by the front door which was a little open.

'DC Curnow is parked in the yard, sir. I believe there's been a message for you.'

Wycliffe tapped on the door and a woman's voice called, 'Come in!'

Stephanie was in the living room. She stood up as he came in, a book in her hand, a finger marking her place. The book was *Madame Bovary*. 'Have you anything to tell me?'

'I'm afraid not, Mrs Vinter.'

She was pale but otherwise she looked as Wycliffe had first seen her: the straight blonde hair with its meticulous central parting, the blue pinafore frock, and the blouse with a pattern of tiny rosebuds. Her hard blue eyes studied her visitors.

'What will happen when you find him?'

Wycliffe was abrupt. 'That depends on the circumstances. Where is your son?'

'He's up in his room. Do we have to stay here?'

'You are a free agent as long as we know where to find you.'

'Hector Carey has invited us to stay at Trecara until this . . .'

'Until this has blown over?' Wycliffe's tone was like a slap in the face.

She had the grace to look embarrassed. 'It is easy for you to be censorious, Superintendent.' She turned to Lucy Lane. 'You see, don't you? The plucky little woman should stand by her husband in all things.'

Wycliffe looked at her, his grey eyes appraising but also puzzled. 'You believe your husband to be guilty of murder – of double murder, Mrs Vinter?'

She flushed. 'You have no right to ask me that question, Superintendent.'

Still watching her, his eyes grave, Wycliffe said: 'No right at all.'

In the yard, Lucy said, 'You were rough on her, sir.'

'You think so?'

DC Curnow, all six foot three of him, was standing beside his car. 'Mr Kersey wants you to ring him, sir.'

Hens were stalking about the yard, pecking at anything which showed between the cobbles. A man in overalls, presumably Geach's nominee, was brooming out the goat house.

Wycliffe got into the car and phoned Kersey who sounded mildly put out. 'I've had the press here, sir, wanting a statement.'

'What did you tell them?'

'I referred them to the Press Officer at HQ.'

'Good! Is that all?'

'No. Not long after we put out the fax on Vinter there was a call from the Transport police at Truro Station. The truck is in the station car park, standing out like a sore thumb among all the private cars.'

'Did they follow it up?'

'Yes. A man in overalls took a single standard class ticket for Plymouth shortly before the seven twenty-one was due to leave.'

'Any evidence that he boarded the train?'

'They're trying to contact the conductor who checked the tickets. I've been on to Charlie Harris at the Plymouth nick and he's going through the motions.'

'Anything from the vicarage?'

'They've hardly got going, sir. I sent Dixon with a

WPC. I thought she might cope better with Celia.' Kersey added after a pause, 'You seem very laid back about the Vinter angle, sir. I mean, we've got a presumed double murderer on the run—'

'That I let slip through my fingers.' Wycliffe hesitated. 'I understand how you feel, Doug, and I don't want you to be too much involved with the Vinter saga. Then, if the sky falls, you'll be like Macavity.'

'What about him?'

'He wasn't there.'

Wycliffe got out of the car and stood, for a moment or two, looking about him, then he turned to DC Curnow. 'I want you to report back to Mr Kersey. Ask him to see that the constable here is relieved as necessary.'

Then to Lucy Lane. 'We are going to the tower.'

'Curnow could drop us off in the Trecara drive, sir.'

'No.'

They walked along the river bank. The screens were still in place around the gatehouse but there was no sign of activity. They continued up the slope, through the larchwood, and arrived on the marshy plateau without a word spoken. The tower loomed out of the scrub, looking more impressive because of the surrounding plain. They followed a raised, stony path which formed a causeway across the marsh to the door at the base of the tower. The lintel above the door was of slate and deeply incised with an inscription: 'Elvira 1833 – 1857. *Amor aeternus*.'

Lucy said, 'I wonder if he would have put up a monument if she'd died at forty-four instead of twenty-four.'

'You're a cynic, Lucy.'

'I'm a realist where men are concerned.'

The stout door, studded with hand-forged nails, was held fast by a crook in a staple. Wycliffe opened the door and they were faced with a spiral stair which wound upwards around a massive central pillar or giant newel post. As they climbed and made circuits of the pillar they came across small lancet windows through which they had fleeting glimpses over the countryside. Lucy counted sixty-eight steps before they came to another door, blocking their way.

Wycliffe muttered, 'Only a latch-lock.' And to Lucy's surprise he produced a length of stiff wire from his pocket, bent it into shape, and had the door open almost at once. 'My one parlour trick.'

The door opened into a circular room about nine feet in diameter. It was windowless except for a single slit in the circular wall into which someone had wedged a piece of transparent plastic, neatly cut to shape. Beneath the window there was a granite slab supported on pillars, like an altar. There was just enough light to see by.

Lucy said, 'It's a little chapel!'

The floor, swept clean, was tiled in slate and the wall had been decorated with murals but the paint had flaked off leaving only hints of what had once been there. Taking up most of the floor space was a camp bed, a wicker chair, a table with a lamp on it, a small bookcase with three or four shelves, and an oil stove of the old type with a fretted top.

Wycliffe said, as though to himself, 'This is where he does most of his bat-watching.'

Lucy sensed the relief in his voice. 'You expected this?'

'Something like it.'

There were army blankets folded neatly on the mattress, there was even a pillow of sorts. The shelves held several books as well as a tin kettle, a saucepan, a teapot, and a china mug.

Lucy watched while Wycliffe walked very slowly around, looking at everything, taking it in. He seemed to approve of what he saw, and finally he said, 'Do you ever feel you could settle for something like this, Lucy?'

She looked at him in astonishment. 'As a way of life? Starting from here I should end up with a cardboard box, under a bridge.'

Wycliffe nodded. 'You're probably right; it's a slippery slope.'

At last, with seeming reluctance, he said, 'We had no breakfast and if we don't go now, we shall get no lunch.'

'You are not going to search the place – or have it searched?'

'Later.'

They arrived at the Incident Room just as Kersey was leaving for the pub. He was subdued, almost sullen.

'The chief has been trying to contact you, sir. He seemed to be in a bit of a twist.'

'He'll be at lunch now.'

At the Hopton, Johnny Glynn was behind the bar as usual but Wycliffe thought the man gave him a strange look. No doubt Tom Reed had been talking to him.

The table usually occupied by the Careys was empty.

They ate in silence for a while but it wasn't in Kersey's nature either to sustain a grievance or to keep quiet for long. He said, 'Are you going to be around this afternoon, sir?'

'Yes.'

'No reports of any sightings from Plymouth. He must be lying low. In overalls and with hardly any money it can't be easy.'

Wycliffe said nothing and Kersey tried again. 'Fox found muddy footprints on one of the crates in the gatehouse. It looks as though somebody stood on it to get greater clout – as you said. He's taken it away to examine it for possible prints.'

'Good.'

The meal continued in silence and while they were still drinking their coffee Wycliffe got up to leave. 'I shall be in my office.'

Kersey turned to Lucy, half-accusing. 'Are you in on this, whatever it is?'

She told him what she knew.

'What did he mean about me being like Macavity – isn't that the name of his cat?'

Lucy grinned. 'Macavity was T. S. Eliot's Mystery Cat who, whatever feline crime had been committed, always had an alibi. He wasn't there.'

'What a thing it must be, to have an education.'

'You must have heard of the musical – *Cats*.'

'Perhaps. Anyway, it sounded a bit nasty to me.'

'I don't think he intended it that way; he's up to something and he's worried. He doesn't want anybody else involved.'

Kersey grinned. 'In case the sky falls.'

'I suppose so.'

In the afternoon there was a long session on the telephone with the chief. Acrimonious at the start, it ended in a resigned acceptance of a situation that couldn't be changed. 'Well, I hope you're right, Charles. If you're wrong, the media will roast us.' Oldroyd sighed. 'And in a year or two I was hoping to go out, peaceably, with my OBE. Clarice was looking forward to that.'

Oldroyd's prospective OBE was a perennial joke in the two families; so all was not lost.

As Wycliffe dropped the telephone the duty officer came in. 'Johnny Glynn from the Hopton wants a word, sir. He won't talk to anybody else.'

Johnny looked nervous, but determined. 'I could have said my say back at the pub but I don't want my wife involved.'

He sat down, looking about him with curiosity. 'I used to be in here pretty often as a boy, usually to get my backside tanned.'

'You wanted to tell me something, Mr Glynn?'

'Yes. Inspector Reed came to see me this morning. I'm sure you know what about. Anyway, I refused to talk to him.'

Wycliffe said nothing, and Johnny went on, 'I suffered quite a bit of aggro over this business the first time round. I told Reed and his boss at the time that I wasn't involved and that was the truth.'

'I think that is accepted.'

Johnny was flushed; little beads of sweat stood out on his forehead and his gestures were exaggerated. He was well primed. 'I was going to marry Jessica Dobell. It was understood. But she couldn't settle for one man and it was the other man she was with that night . . .' He shook his head. 'That finished me!'

Abruptly, he said, 'Do you mind if I smoke?' He brought out a pack of cigarettes, lit one, and leaned forward, confidentially: 'There's another thing I think you should know. It was Jessica who was driving that night.'

'I understood that she couldn't drive.'

Johnny spread his hands in a helpless gesture. 'The silly bugger was trying to teach her . . . In that lane, with a foot clearance when you're lucky!' He broke off. 'Well, you've got to remember, Mr Wycliffe, we were all a lot younger then – and a bit mad.'

Wycliffe said: 'The other man?'

Johnny sat back in his chair. 'No names, Mr Wycliffe. What I know came out in one hell of a row I had with Jessica at the time. I kept quiet then, when it would have helped me to speak out, and I shan't talk now. I've got my living to get in this village.'

He reached forward to tap ash into Kersey's little bowl.

'I came here because if you knew the facts you might ask yourself what was to be gained by stirring it all up. It was a bad business but there must be a limit. Anyway, this is a private chat – no witnesses, no statement.' He sat back, rather pleased with himself, and waited.

Wycliffe said, 'I've listened to what you have told me.'

Johnny waited a little longer, expecting more, but when no more came he stood up. 'Well, I must be getting back . . .'

At five o'clock Wycliffe went to the post office stores and bought a few things; at six he announced that he would not be in for the evening meal, and telephoned Helen; at six-thirty he set off with a borrowed rucksack slung over his shoulder.

He was in a strange mood, almost one of desperation. He *knew*, but in the absence of material evidence he could not act. And that fool, Vinter . . . One had to sympathize, perhaps admire, but it was wrong, and sure to prove tragically wrong in its consequences. Now he was virtually putting *his* job on the line in behaviour almost as quixotic.

He followed the path along the river bank which for him had acquired a symbolic significance. It was the link binding together the elements in his chain: Trecara with its folly, the farmhouse, the houseboat, the church, Trigg, and the old school which was his base.

In the valley it was already evening, the light had a golden hue and the birds were silent. The tide was running out and there were banks of mud being worked over by the gulls. A tidal creek or inlet is not a single landscape, but a cycle of landscapes following the changing patterns of time and tide.

Somewhere in the woods across the river there was a shot which put up a flight of flustered and flapping pigeons. Looking up into the churchyard, through the kissing-gate, he could see a woman on her knees, tending one of the graves.

There was no-one to be seen on the houseboat but smoke came from the cowled chimney. The farmhouse looked deserted but there would be a uniformed man on duty there somewhere. It was the thing to do, in case Vinter returned to his home. Wycliffe was not in a mood to appreciate the irony of it.

Smoke drifted idly upwards from one of the Trecara chimneys and the screens were still in place at the gatehouse.

He followed the track up through the larchwood and on to the marshy plateau. The tower stood out against a dark, towering cloud mass in the southern sky.

The nearer he got to his goal the more absurd his project seemed. He crossed the causeway, let himself into the tower and climbed the spiral staircase to the locked door. A moment later he was inside, and he felt better. It was considerably darker than it had been in the morning and he could just make out the objects which he knew to be there. He took a torch from his rucksack and swept the room with its beam.

Nothing had changed.

He had planned what he would do. First he would light the lamp and the oil stove. He had assumed that there would be enough paraffin, and there was. Life on his father's farm had taught him something about paraffin and bottled gas. Vinter's lamp was a monster, with twin wicks and a pink glass bowl on a fretted brass stand. It spread a pale but sufficient radiance over the little room. The oil stove did not flare, flicker, or 'yellow' and was soon casting the shadow of its fretted top on the ceiling. The place was becoming cosy.

He emptied his rucksack on to the table: a couple of cans of beer, a piece of cheese, some bread rolls, a bar of chocolate, a bottle of water, and a portable telephone.

Half past seven. He peered through the slit window; the clouds now covered as much of the sky as he could see. Soon it would rain and soon it would be quite dark. In the lamplight the paintings on the wall seemed to acquire increased definition; he could make out trees, a faun, a woman in a flowing gown. He noticed too that the boarded ceiling had been painted at one time but he could make nothing of the design.

There was a hatch which must give access to the dome and, presumably, to the bats. He wondered how Vinter got up there, then realized that the ceiling was low and that by standing on the table, a tall, active man could make it.

He was beginning to feel at home. Sometimes he felt not only that he understood, but that he had some kinship with those who deliberately narrowed their horizons, drew in their tentacles, and retreated from life.

He looked at Vinter's books: biographies, journals and diaries in French, German, and English, and recognized another bond; the attempt to live at second-hand.

He began his search of the room. It was no great task. He found what he was looking for, under the camp bed, in a shallow cardboard box without a lid. The box held Jessica's missing half-wellingtons in a plastic bag, a Bible, the mutilated remains of a *Church Quarterly* magazine, a few sheets of notepaper and some envelopes. He did not handle his finds but left them in the box in full view, on the floor.

He was just in time. There were footsteps on the stairs, slow, weary footsteps. Wycliffe turned down the lamp. It seemed an interminable time before there came a fumbling with the latch-lock and the door opened.

Wycliffe turned up the lamp. 'I was beginning to think you wouldn't come.'

Vinter stood just inside the door, holding on to it as though for support. 'Christ! I might have known.'

He came forward into the room, staggering with fatigue, and slumped into the wicker chair. He looked at the cardboard box with its contents.

'So you found them?'

'Of course; you knew they were there.'

'I put them there, didn't I?'

Wycliffe looked down at him and said, in a tone of mild rebuke, 'Don't play the bloody fool, Vinter, and don't treat me like one.'

Chapter Fourteen

Thursday morning

It was five in the morning, still dark and chilly, when a police car dropped Wycliffe off at the Hopton. He let himself in with the key Johnny had given him. In his room, he undressed, had a quick wash, and got into bed. He told himself that in the next few hours he must be in a position to show that his conclusions were inescapable. '*Inescapable,*' he muttered the word, drowsily – repeatedly, and its syllables seemed to acquire an hypnotic rhythm: in-es-cap-a-ble, so that he fell asleep.

The next thing he knew it was daylight and his little clock showed seven-thirty. He joined Kersey and Lucy Lane in the dining room for the tail end of the eight o'clock radio news.

'It has just been reported that during the night a man attended voluntarily at Truro Police Station in connection with the murders of Jessica Dobell and the Reverend Michael Jordan in the village of Moresk just outside the town. The man has not been named and a spokesman said that he had not been charged with any offence but was helping with inquiries.

'Yesterday, the police issued a description of Laurence Vinter, a farm worker, employed by the murdered woman, and wanted for questioning in connection with the crimes.'

There were several people at breakfast, more than on

any day so far, and Kersey warned, 'Press, on the next table; ears flapping.'

Kersey and Lucy were subdued, conscious of the need to get back into step, but unable to speak of what was uppermost in their minds, so the three dissected their kippers in silence. Even Johnny had his own reasons for keeping away, and it was a relief when Wycliffe said, 'Well, if we are ready . . .'

Outside it was a typical late-April morning with a moist softness in the air and the promise of a warm day.

Kersey went to buy cigarettes and newspapers at the post office and came back grumbling, 'They looked at me like I was Dracula.'

In his office Wycliffe's manner was still detached. 'Anything from the vicar's papers?'

Lucy said, 'I spent most of yesterday afternoon with Curnow and WPC Dash going through them. Apart from his professional records and correspondence, we found only sermon notes and little essays on knotty theological points. Student stuff. I've rarely seen anybody with fewer personal papers; certainly nothing in the nature of a diary.'

Wycliffe seemed resigned. 'It was too much to expect that he made a record of whatever he knew. Why should he?'

Kersey brought the conversation around to Vinter. 'So the official line is that he gave himself up.'

'He *did* give himself up.'

Lucy Lane asked, 'But what persuaded him to come back?'

'He wasn't going anywhere; there was nowhere for him to go. The Plymouth thing was a feint to get us off his back for a while. In fact he went no further than Truro, and spent yesterday skulking around, keeping out of sight as much as possible. He returned to the tower on foot, after dark, with a half-bottle of whisky and a supply of aspirin tablets. I suppose he hoped for the chance to do what he felt he must do, calmly and with a bit of dignity.' Wycliffe sounded oddly defensive.

Kersey looked at him in surprise. 'Suicide! You expected that?'

'Of course I didn't *expect* it!' Wycliffe sounded irritable. 'But after seeing his hideaway in the tower I felt sure that he would come back to it – that was all. I suppose it's what I might have done myself.' He made an apologetic gesture. 'At any rate, I was sure he wasn't stupid enough to go on the run.'

'But why suicide?' From Lucy Lane.

Wycliffe's eyelids were pricking and there was a heaviness at the base of his skull. He could have done with a couple of those aspirins.

'As Vinter saw it, our investigation, if it was allowed to go on, could lead to only one conclusion, and he felt that he couldn't live with the consequences of that.'

Wycliffe had been fiddling with the objects on his desk, arranging and rearranging them. (In stressful times he still missed his pipe.) He looked up. 'I don't know if Vinter loves his wife, he's certainly proud of her, yet it was he who brought on her the humiliations of life on the farm, and he can't forget that.'

Kersey was looking at Wycliffe, his lined features creased even more deeply by doubt. 'I don't know about Lucy, but I'm still at sea.'

'It's simple enough. Vinter intended to offer himself as a nice, tidy, uncomplaining scapegoat and, if he had succeeded, the evidence being what it is, we should have been forced to pack up and go home. You can't prosecute a dead man but you can saddle him with a load of guilt, and Vinter wanted to settle for that. It was my problem to persuade him otherwise. Even now he's biding his time in a police cell waiting to make some damn-fool confession.'

Lucy Lane said, 'But the circumstantial and some material evidence *is* against him.'

'Yes, and there's more in the tower. Fox is up there now, giving the place a thorough going over. In this case evidence likely to incriminate Vinter has been scattered about like confetti.'

He shifted uncomfortably in his chair. 'Although we worked out a specification for our criminal we made no use of it except to agree that it didn't fit any of our suspects. We laid stress on the planning, on the obsessive attention to detail, but we ignored the absence of any identifiable overall purpose. I said something about revenge and defilement but didn't follow it up. The crime was anarchic, not planned to achieve anything, only to disrupt.'

Lucy Lane agreed. 'A disturbed mind reacting to real or imagined frustration.'

Kersey fished in his pocket for cigarettes. 'Soon somebody is going to say "paranoia"; then I shall go.' He lit a cigarette. 'Back to Vinter, I've been reading the transcript, and I must admit there are times when you wonder if he wasn't deliberately landing himself in it, leaving himself open to suspicion. It took him a while to decide what he had on his feet when he walked by the river that night and he finally settled for wellingtons.'

Lucy Lane said, 'So he's shielding either his wife or his son.'

Wycliffe said nothing, and Lucy Lane looked at him with curiosity. 'What exactly happened last night, sir?'

He seemed put out by the question but after a brief hesitation he said, 'We ate some bread and cheese and drank a can of beer.' He gave Lucy a sidelong glance. 'We also talked, but not on the record, and there will be no report. It was two o'clock when I phoned Division, asking them to divert a patrol car.'

He sat back in his chair as though to signal that discussion was over, and turned to Kersey. 'I hope you realize, Doug, that I put myself out on a limb and it was no place for company.'

Kersey looked embarrassed. 'Being out on a limb has never bothered me unduly, sir, but I take your point. I understand.'

'Good. Now, I want you to look after things here and deal with Fox. Lucy and I will be at the farm. Keep me informed of any developments.

'Ready, Lucy?'

They were just leaving when the telephone rang and Wycliffe answered it.

Fox, pleased with himself. 'I've got two possibles, sir: an index finger and thumb of the right hand on one of the boots, and just a suggestion of a thumb on the magazine that needs enhancement. I'm pretty sure, but I'll do a full comparison check back at the nick.'

For once, Wycliffe's heart warmed toward his scenes-of-crime officer. It was not much, but it was something to put in the file.

The media people had lingered over breakfast but now they were gathered around the old school entrance. He pushed through them with a curt, 'No statement!'

Lucy made for his car, still parked in the square, and this time he made no objection. There were unusual numbers of people in the square, gathered in little groups as though they sensed that another act in the drama was about to be played.

As he got into the car he said, 'Of course, this case will never come to court.'

When they were driving out of the square, Lucy said, 'So you've made up your mind.'

'I should have seen it earlier. Instead I talked nonsense about female psychology. It was only on Tuesday evening

213

that I came to terms with the idea. Of course Jordan knew, and I should have guessed as much from his attitude. But by Wednesday morning Jordan was dead, and it was too late.

'I even warned him, without being clear in my own mind what I was warning him about . . . This case has been a shambles from the start, Lucy.'

They drove up Church Lane, past the church, and clear of the houses. Lucy pulled up at the farm entrance and Wycliffe got out to open the rickety gate. The goats were browsing as usual and, in the sunshine, Elvira's tower looked more like a misplaced lighthouse than ever.

Gingerly, Lucy drove down the rutted track to the farmyard entrance and stopped at the second gate. Wycliffe did not get out immediately and Lucy sensed his reluctance.

'How will you handle this one, sir?'

'As gently as possible. Vinter is in custody and we are asking his wife and son to make further statements. That must be our line for the moment. Of course any formal interrogation will be on the record with a lawyer and, perhaps, a psychologist or one of that ilk, sitting in. But I would like a chat beforehand.'

They were still in the car, watching the hens pecking over the cobbles. Vinter's stand-in was tinkering with an ancient tractor. He looked across at them, but showed no particular interest.

Wycliffe pushed open the car door. 'Let's get it over!'

The house door was shut; Wycliffe knocked, but there was no response.

The man with the tractor called to them, 'I haven't seen anybody this morning but you could try around the front.'

They walked around the house to the front door which was slightly open. Wycliffe knocked again with no result so he pushed the door wide and called out. The narrow

214

passage hall was almost blocked by two large suitcases, and by books, tied in bundles and stacked against the wall.

Giles was standing at the far end of the passage looking vague. 'My mother isn't here.' He was not wearing his glasses and his face looked oddly naked and vulnerable.

'It seems you're moving out.'

The boy looked at the cases and the books. 'Yes. Mother is down at Trecara, getting our rooms ready.'

Lucy followed Wycliffe through into the sitting room and the three of them stood facing each other in semi-darkness. The curtains had not been drawn back.

Wycliffe said, 'Perhaps we could have some light.'

Lucy Lane drew back the curtains and the three of them sat down.

Wycliffe said, 'You're not wearing your glasses.'

'No, they fell off, and I stepped on them.'

'Haven't you got a spare pair?'

'Yes, upstairs.'

'Then why not go up and get them?'

The boy sat, hands on his thighs, massaging them in a curious stroking movement that rocked his body to and fro. He was very pale. He said nothing for a time, then, 'No, I'll get them later.'

The rocking movement continued and the blue, unfocused eyes seemed to shut him off from real contact.

Wycliffe said, 'You know that your father is in custody?'

A flicker of the eyelids. 'He is not my father.'

'Not your father?'

'My father died before I was born. He was a famous mathematician. That man is my stepfather.'

'Have you always known this?'

'I have always thought that he could not be my father. He is a stupid man.'

215

'Very well. Your stepfather wants to confess to the murders of Jessica Dobell and Michael Jordan.'

The rocking movement ceased, but there was no other response. He sat, motionless, his eyes unfocused.

'Do you think your stepfather is guilty of those crimes, Giles?'

The boy clasped his hands tightly together and there was a long silence before he said, 'He deserves to suffer; more than any of them.'

Lucy Lane asked, 'More than Jessica Dobell?'

The blue eyes were turned on her and a hint of a smile trembled on his lips. 'She's dead.'

Wycliffe wondered at the mental deterioration which appeared to have taken place in such a short time. 'Why did you dislike Jessica so much?'

The rocking movement was resumed and he spoke in a harsh voice: 'She was an animal! She tried once to get me to . . .'

Lucy Lane asked, 'What did she try to get you to do?'

'I don't know.'

Lucy tried again, 'Do you disapprove of all people who enjoy sex, Giles?'

The question disturbed him. Two or three times he looked from Lucy to Wycliffe and back again. Finally he shook his head and did not reply.

Wycliffe said, 'I thought you were fond of Julie Geach.'

For the first time Giles raised his voice. 'I don't want to talk about her!' He made oddly defensive movements with his arms as though warding off a blow. 'Her father called me a . . . No, I won't talk about it. I won't!'

Lucy Lane looked across at Wycliffe, a look which asked clearly enough, 'How far do we go with this?'

Lucy was right to sound a warning note, but for him there were other considerations than the Rules of Evidence.

Almost holding his breath, Wycliffe asked, 'Why did you attack Michael Jordan?'

The boy trembled as though in an effort of self-control but he managed to speak calmly, 'I didn't want to hurt him.'

'So why did you?'

The rocking movement recommenced and for some time he did not speak. Then, very quietly and reasonably, he said, 'I set them a puzzle which I knew that nobody could solve . . . I wanted to see what they would do. I wanted to make them suffer and pay for everything . . .'

'And the vicar?'

'He saw me with that woman's boots in the churchyard. I didn't know, but he told me, and he said that I must tell them, that I must go to you.' His hand, resting on his thighs, were squeezing the flesh so tightly that he must have suffered pain. 'He threatened me. He shouldn't have done that . . .'

In the silence that followed, the telephone startled all three of them. Lucy went to answer it. There was a brief exchange, and she replaced the receiver.

'That was Mr Carey; he says that he was expecting your mother earlier this morning but that she hasn't arrived.'

For a while the boy gave no sign that he had heard, then, in a flat voice and looking straight ahead, he said, 'She's upstairs.'

Wycliffe signed to Lucy to stay and started up the stairs.

The door of the Vinters' room was wide open. The curtains were drawn across the little window, but there was enough light to see the form of a woman on the bed. At close quarters he could hear shallow, irregular breathing. He swept back the curtains, letting in the light.

Stephanie Vinter, wearing a dressing gown over her nightdress, was lying across the bed. A good deal of blood had seeped into the honeycomb quilt from a wound in her

217

head, concealed by her hair. As he stood over her she opened her eyes but there was no sign of recognition. She moaned briefly and her eyes closed again.

Wycliffe went to the top of the stairs. 'Ambulance, Lucy! She has a head wound with some loss of blood but she's semi-conscious . . .'

Back in the room he saw on the floor an old-style desk lamp which he remembered as being on the bedside table. Its base was stained with blood. The boy's spectacles lay beside it where they had fallen and been trodden upon.

He turned to find Giles standing in the doorway. 'She isn't dead, is she? . . . I couldn't sleep and when it was getting light I came in to talk to her . . . We sat on the bed, and I told her . . .' He had difficulty with his speech, choking on the words. 'She tried to tell me that I should . . . She said we would go together . . . I couldn't believe it! . . . I was angry and I picked up the lamp and my glasses fell off . . .'

Thursday evening

It was ten-fifteen and the three were sitting at their table in the restaurant after a late snack meal. The kitchen had closed long ago and they were alone in the room. Through the glass doors they could see the usual group of regulars clustered on stools around the bar.

On their table was a bottle of burgundy; Kersey picked it up and held it to the light. 'There's another drink in there. Shall we split it?'

Lucy put a hand over her glass and Wycliffe shook his head.

'All right; mustn't let it go to waste.'

Wycliffe said, 'Vinter was at the hospital with his wife

this afternoon. It seems she's conscious. I wonder what will happen there.'

Lucy said, 'I wonder more what will happen to the boy.'

'It won't be up to us, thank God! And I doubt if the lawyers will have much say. He's spending the next two or three days under observation in the psychiatric ward at the hospital and it's from there that the magistrates will take their cue.'

Kersey finished off the wine. 'Was Vinter the boy's father, or wasn't he?'

Wycliffe yawned behind his hand. 'Does it matter? The trick cyclists will enjoy finding out. But, whether he was or not, the boy's hatred was directed mainly against him.'

Lucy Lane said, 'I'm going to work on Johnny for some more coffee.'

Kersey watched her go. 'She's coming on, that girl.' Which from Kersey was praise indeed.

Wycliffe was twisting his wine glass by the stem, watching the reflections in the bowl. 'It's been an eventful week: two murders, a psychotic teenager in custody and his mother in hospital; the Met investigating the dubious dealings of the church organist and Abe Geach just one step nearer his four-star dream.'

'You sound bitter.'

'Do I?' Wycliffe sat back in his chair. 'Causes seem so disproportionate to their consequences. Just imagine that Vinter hadn't played the fool with his girl student, or that the Ruse boy had set out on his cycle ten minutes earlier, or that Giles Vinter had drawn a different number in the gene raffle, or that almost anything had been just that little bit different . . . It's no wonder Jessica went to a fortune teller.'

Lucy came back. 'Johnny is bringing the coffee. He says there's to be a service of rededication in the church tomorrow morning and that Jessica's funeral will be on Monday afternoon.'

Katherine Geach was sitting up in bed. The clock radio on her bedside table showed a quarter to eleven. The curtains were not drawn and a top window was open to the darkness and the stillness outside. She had a magazine open on her lap but she was not reading, she was looking at herself in the dressing table mirror. Five nights ago her twin sister, Jessica, had been brutally murdered, but here nothing had changed. Had she? She looked in the mirror and felt guilty.

She could hear Abe splashing about in the bathroom. A minute or two later he came in, wearing his dressing gown. He slipped it off and got into bed beside her. After a minute or two his hand reached between her thighs. So far, since Jessica's death, she had refused him.

'Oh, all right.'

He put his arms round her and held her tightly for a while. 'That's my girl! Now let's get that bloody nightdress off.'

In the village of Moresk things were returning to normal.

THE END

Wycliffe and the House of Fear

W.J.BURLEY

To Muriel, without whose collaboration
and constructive criticism there would
have been no books

Prologue

Extract from the *Cornish Gazette* dated 15 June

Well-known Cornishwoman in Yachting Tragedy

Mrs Julia Kemp of Kellycoryk was lost over-board while sailing with her husband and a friend about two miles south of St Anthony Head on Tuesday afternoon. Mr Kemp was at the tiller of his eighteen-foot yacht *Winifred*, and Miss Clare Jordan, a friend of the family, was in the well of the boat with him. Mrs Kemp had chosen a position on the foredeck, her back propped against the mast. The weather was fine, and with a following breeze conditions were ideal.

When they were almost due south of St Anthony Head they were passed at some distance by a container ship heading up channel. The turbulence of the wash from this vessel caused the *Winifred* to pitch and roll and although Mr Kemp shouted to his wife she failed to be warned in time and fell into the sea where she was lost to sight almost at once.

Mr Kemp launched the life raft, lowered the foresail, and started his outboard motor. A

7

distress rocket brought other craft to the scene and the search continued, to be joined later by a search-and-rescue helicopter; all to no avail.

Mrs Kemp, the mother of two teenage children, was an accomplished painter and for several years was prominent in the cultural life of the county with a special concern for the visual arts.

Chapter One

Roger Kemp was working in his library; a pleasant room, square and high, with bookshelves reaching to a generous frieze. There was a richly moulded cornice and the ceiling sported an improbable selection of plaster fruit and flowers, but every plaster surface was encrusted with the grime of years.

Roger worked at a big table littered with books, papers and charts, in the middle of which a black cat curled asleep, sleek and slim as a serpent.

Five minutes past eight on a sunny morning; Roger had been at work since six. An electric radiator close to his chair fended off the early morning chill. For at all times, even in summer, the old house was never free of a chilly dampness, and year by year Roger watched while eroding moulds made inroads on wood and plaster, paper and fabrics.

He consoled himself with the idea, and sometimes believed, that in the long run, whatever happened to Kellycoryk, to him, or to the family they would all survive in his *History of the Kemps of Kellycoryk*, a record of almost five centuries of industry and endurance.

Sometimes he wished that he could shut himself away in this room, a scholarly recluse. The Kemps were Catholics and, as a young man, Roger had been tempted by the cloistered life. The obligation of

9

chastity would have troubled him little, yet through some element of the perverse the course of his life seemed to have been moulded, even warped, by women.

A tap at the door and his sister, Agnes, called, shrill and peremptory, 'Breakfast in ten minutes!'

The black cat raised its head, fiercely alert, watching Roger with yellow-green eyes. Roger reached out a reassuring hand. 'It's all right, Coryk.'

He returned to his manuscript, fingering the pages, and read aloud from the passage he had just written. Then he addressed the cat. 'Will anybody ever read that, Coryk? Will any publisher ever give it a chance?'

The cat showed no particular interest but when Roger got up from his chair, in a single clean leap Coryk was on the floor at his feet. They moved to one of the twin windows and Roger stood looking out. A large pond, almost a lake, with rushes at the margins, separated the house from a wilderness of laurel and rhododendron. Beyond the wilderness he could see the grey roofs of the cottages in the cove and the sea beyond, broad and empty and sparkling.

He caught sight of his reflection in the window, distorted by imperfections in the old glass. They seemed to exaggerate the drooping eyelids, the prominent nose and sagging jowls, the distinctive Kemp features which became more pronounced with age. Now, looking at his own reflection, he thought he saw his father's face.

'Breakfast, Coryk!' The cat paced him out of the room and down the dim passage to the kitchen. The family had their meals in the kitchen where an Aga maintained a cosy warmth even in the coldest weather. It was a large, bare room with adzed beams, cream-washed walls and a floor of slate slabs laid over with sisal matting. A naked bulb suspended from a central beam competed with the greenish-grey daylight which filtered through the parboiled glass.

On the big table, which was only partly covered by a cloth, there were packets of breakfast foods with a selection of crockery and cutlery from which people helped themselves. On the Aga, along with a saucepan of stock, was a rack of toast, a jug of milk, and a giant-sized blue-enamelled coffee pot with a chipped lid.

Crispin, Roger's son by his first wife, and Agnes were already at table. Crispin was nineteen, dark haired, pale faced, quiet and withdrawn. He was removing the top from his boiled egg with the same precision and concentration which he brought to everything he did. He looked up as his father entered, his eyes as limpid and guileless as a spaniel's. Roger never ceased to wonder what went on behind those eyes and at the genetic lottery which had given him two children so alike in looks and so different in temperament. Isobel, Crispin's sister, was a reincarnation of her dead mother.

Agnes said, 'Your egg is in the saucepan, it will be boiled hard by now.'

Agnes had a feminine version of the Kemp features, the drooping eyelids and dark colouring, but the heavy jowls were less in evidence.

Before retrieving his egg Roger went through to the old wash place and came back with a saucer of cat food which he put on the floor beside his chair. Only then did he fetch his egg from the stove.

'Isobel not down yet? She'll be late for work.' Isobel worked at a health food shop in Truro.

'She's on holiday this week and next.' Agnes said it as though the very fact was a personal affront.

Three or four years older than her brother, Agnes saw herself as a self-sacrificing spinster, trapped by her sense of duty into dependence.

Roger prepared his egg while Agnes sipped her coffee, continuing to hold the cup to her lips with both hands while watching him over the rim. For no apparent reason there was tension in the air.

Roger spoke to his son: 'Last evening I was up at the Northern Garden taking a look at your work, Crispy. You must have cleared nearly an acre; and Frank has made a good job of the roof of the old lodge . . .' His voice trailed off as he realized that even this modest show of enthusiasm was somehow out of place.

Crispin was attending classes in horticulture and, with the help of a part-time employee, he was clearing an area in the Northern Garden in the hope of starting a commercial nursery.

Agnes said, 'You'll need capital for glasshouses or plastic tunnels or whatever they are; then there's equipment, as well as fertilizers, plants, seeds . . . Where do you think the money's coming from?'

Roger ventured, 'I think we might manage it.'

Agnes ignored him. 'Of course there wouldn't be any problem if Bridget would show a spark of interest. After all, she is your stepmother and she wouldn't miss a few thousands, but I'm afraid you'll have to wait a long time if that's what you're counting on.'

There was a sound of movement from the back premises and Bridget herself came in, followed by a slightly overweight Labrador. She wore a half-length fawn suede coat with trousers, and a waterproof hat over her red hair. She was petite, delicate as porcelain, but she looked flushed with health and vitality. The dog, after a preliminary reconnoitre, settled in front of the Aga.

Coryk, tail erect, back arched, hissed so that Roger had to soothe him.

Bridget said, 'Timmy and I have had a lovely walk, it's a wonderful morning and the gorse is unbelievable . . . the colour, and the scent!'

12

Two years ago Roger had married Bridget, the daughter of a shrewd and prosperous businessman who had promptly died of a heart attack, leaving her in charge of an expanding and profitable business in the leisure industry.

'Goodness, it's warm in here!' Bridget slipped out of her coat. Underneath she wore a gaily patterned blouse like a sunburst in the gloom.

Agnes said, 'There are eggs and there's toast.'

Bridget looked about her and decided, 'No, I think I'll have some muesli; I need to lose weight.'

Agnes, her eyes on Bridget, buttered a piece of toast. She seemed to be waiting, and when Bridget was settled she said, 'We've just been talking about Crispin's scheme for the nursery. It's really a question of where he's going to get the capital.' She spoke as though the business had been a subject for family discussion.

Roger stopped in the act of chewing a mouthful of toast, and Crispin looked at Agnes in disbelief.

But Bridget was saved from comment. Isobel, wearing her dressing gown, drifted in. She rubbed her eyes like a sleepy child and asked in a plaintive voice, 'What time is it?'

Agnes said, 'There's a clock on the wall.'

It was true that in features and colouring Isobel resembled her brother, but she was a striking girl; a mass of almost black hair accentuated her pallor and her lips appeared dramatically red. As her late mother had once remarked, 'Like blood on snow.'

She pulled out a chair and sat down, stretching and yawning. 'It feels like the middle of the night.' She reached for a bowl and for the cornflakes packet but realizing that she would have to get up for the milk she abandoned the idea.

Instead she sat back in her chair and announced, 'Mother spoke to me last night.'

Roger felt that he was about to be drawn into some kind of vortex. He said, 'What on earth are you talking about?'

'It was rather marvellous, actually.' Isobel was becoming animated. 'A little group – just seven of us; we've been meeting for three or four weeks with a medium called Teresa from St Endel Churchtown. She tried to make contact with Mother twice before and last night it worked.' Isobel's manner was brisk and brittle.

Crispin was watching his sister uneasily but no-one spoke, and she went on, 'It was Mother's voice, just like having her in the room.'

Agnes said, 'You don't remember your mother's voice.'

'Of course I do! I was sixteen, for God's sake! I remember everything about her, how she looked, how she smiled, how she dressed . . . You remember, don't you, Crispin?'

Crispin said nothing and the ticking of the clock was left to fill the silence.

Then Isobel began again. 'Mother was very upset. She said, "I've longed to speak to you, Isobel, but I can't do it unless you help me. You must try to reach me as I struggle to reach you . . . There are things I want you to know, but it's very difficult to break through—" '

The girl spoke in a low, tense monotone when quoting her mother's words but broke off to speak normally immediately afterwards. 'That was all . . . It was like being cut off on the telephone . . . Of course I shall go on trying; I shan't give up now. Teresa, as a favour, has agreed to try again tomorrow night.'

It was Bridget who spoke finally. She sounded remote and judicial. 'Of course, what you do and what you believe, Isobel, is up to you, but before you are led to do something you might regret I should make sure that you are not being exploited by this woman.'

Isobel looked at her with a glazed expression. 'That's what I would expect you to say.'

The arrival of the daily maid put further discussion on hold. She came in through the back and stood in the doorway, a young girl from the cove, Jane Clemens; fresh, if inclined to be raw, with a manner which made it clear that she was nobody's doormat. She looked at Agnes. 'Where do you want me to start?'

Agnes said, 'Surely you know by now. It's Monday, so you change the beds.'

The girl shrugged. 'It's all the same to me.'

As she crossed the room there was a momentary exchange of glances between her and Crispin, not lost on Agnes.

Wycliffe looked out of the window of the living room at a tranquil, sunlit sea, at the slow ripples that produced a lace of foam on the shingle, and decided that they had come to the right place. A little way up the shallow valley, Kellycoryk House was visible between the trees, the low pitched roof with overhanging eaves seemed to rise out of a shrubby wilderness.

Wycliffe was convalescent; overwork, a bad bout of influenza followed by bronchitis and a touch of pleurisy had kept him out of circulation for several weeks. Now, before returning to the treadmill, on medical advice and on orders from his chief, he was having a holiday 'away from it all'.

'Away from it all' materialized into this cottage, one of a dozen or so, stone-built and slate-roofed, scattered in an irregular crescent about the margin of a tiny, rocky cove facing south into Veryan Bay. The Wycliffes had visions of walks along the Cornish cliffs, through the lanes and over the moors.

A stream divided the little community into two, but it was reunited by a bridge (Max Wt 2T). Beyond the bridge the stream spread out and all but lost itself in the shingle on the shore.

There was no sound, and no sign of life anywhere.

The choice had been Helen's, made because she had discovered that the name, Kellycoryk, is Cornish for elf wood or rather, wood elf; also because the cove was managed by Coast and Country, a leisure company with a good reputation in the business. Helen's best decisions were often based on a nice blend of whimsy and calculation.

Half-past ten; they had made a leisurely trip. Helen was inspecting the accommodation and finding it to her liking. There was electricity, with provision for a wood fire in the living room. There were two bedrooms, an adequate bathroom and kitchen; a TV and a telephone.

Mrs Moyle, the woman who supervised the lets, lived with her family in one of the other cottages. Thin and wiry, her grey hair cut short, she had a youngish face betrayed by fine wrinkles on her upper lip. She was polite but distant.

Helen said, 'Do all the cottages belong to the leisure company?'

'They don't any of them belong; they're only leased from the estate.'

'So the cove is still part of the Kellycoryk estate?'

'Like it always was.'

Wycliffe tried his hand. 'Does anybody live in the big house?'

'Live there? Of course they do. The Kemp family live there like they always did.' She had no intention of being drawn into gossip.

Helen, with her taste for Victorian novelists, had mentally labelled her Mrs Tightlip.

Helen said, 'Well, there's nothing we need do here.

16

What about a walk to the village, buy a few things and perhaps get some lunch?'

Mrs Moyle volunteered, 'If you want lunch, Jack Sara's wife at the New Inn is a good cook.'

They walked along the road they had driven earlier; it was overhung by a low cliff and there was a notice, 'Crumbling cliffs. Beware of falling stones.'

'What are we supposed to do? Dodge?'

The road rose steeply to surmount a promontory which separated the cove from the larger inlet and village of Porthendel; a broad stubby headland, pushed raggedly into the sea.

Wycliffe said, 'It's called Jacob's Head, according to the map.'

Down the further slope they came to the village where a crooked jetty defended the tiny harbour.

Old fish lofts had found other uses: one was a café, another a picture gallery, while two more had become desirable waterfront residences. The Wycliffes strolled happily, not saying much; words that were spoken usually came in answer to the other's thoughts. Wycliffe reflected, We are an old married couple, becoming smug; because we like it that way.

They turned up a narrow, steep slope into the village square. It was not really a square but a triangle at the junction of three roads, itself on a slope. A few visitors, in pairs or in family groups, drifted around the square, down to the waterfront and back again, while a café, with tables outside, served morning coffee to those who wished to take the weight off their feet.

There were several shops; a newsagent's on one corner was also the post office; no company shops. The New Inn had a board outside: 'Lunches 12.00 – 2.00.'

'We'll come back to all that.'

They were attracted by 'Clare Jordan's Old

17

Curiosity Shop'. At first sight it was an ordinary little shop selling bric-à-brac, but the bygones were of more than average quality. Clare Jordan, whoever she was, had an eye for small pieces of china and glass, and the knack of displaying them.

Helen said, 'See those dogs?'

She was looking at a pair of china 'comforter' dogs, white glazed, with spots or splashes of copper lustre. Recently Helen had developed a taste for that kind of thing, presumably in line with her Victorian reading. 'They would look good on the kitchen shelf. I wonder what she wants for them. Shall we ask?'

They could see two women in the shop; one of them, presumably Clare Jordan herself, was seated on a chair by a door leading to an adjoining room. She was in her middle forties, well preserved, with a bony physique innocent of curves. The other, standing by her, was a thin, pale girl with a mop of dark hair. She wore a jade-green tunic which barely reached her thighs and black leggings. The effect was dramatic.

As Wycliffe opened the door the older woman was saying, her voice raised, 'You have become totally unbalanced about your mother, Isobel. Obsessed! If you—' She broke off on the instant and turned to her customers. The girl however continued to stare at her and Wycliffe was made uncomfortable by those coldly appraising eyes.

Helen opened negotiations for her dogs. The woman quite recovered her poise and her business sense, while the girl turned her back on all three of them, waiting for the strangers to go.

It was obvious that the confrontation or whatever it was would be resumed when they left, and it was not long before they did, Helen, with her dogs snug in a cardboard box.

Helen said, 'We interrupted something.'

They decided on a drink before lunch and went to

the New Inn where they joined a group around the bar. The landlord said, 'Lunch? If you want lunch somebody will be along in a few minutes.'

At one end of the bar there was a group of tables railed off. No slot machines, no pool table, no canned music; Helen purred, and they took their drinks to one of the tables behind the rail.

Others began to arrive and several tables were occupied. A plump woman in a white coat put up a chalkboard. 'Meal of the Day: Chicken with mushrooms and courgettes; sauté potatoes. Apple pie with Cornish clotted cream.'

Colours nailed to the mast. No compromise, no options.

'Shall we have a half-bottle of something?'

'Look!' Helen nodded towards a couple just seating themselves at a table for two in a far corner of the bar. 'The woman from the dog shop and the girl. They seem to have settled their quarrel, if it was one.'

Wycliffe studied the pair with interest. 'From the look of them I wouldn't bet on it.'

When the plump woman came to take their order Helen asked, 'Who's the girl with the woman from the antique shop?'

The landlady looked across at the pair and smiled. 'Striking girl, isn't she? Isobel Kemp, from Kellycoryk, Roger Kemp's daughter by his first wife. And just like her mother; a real beauty she was. Clare Jordan is related to them somehow.'

Wycliffe was beginning to enjoy himself. He loved to find out about people. Even as a child, when taken somewhere new, it had intrigued him to discover people of whose existence he had known nothing. He would watch them with a sense of wonder and afterwards he would think of them going on with their lives when he wasn't there. Helen said that it was this inquisitive streak that had made him a policeman.

After their meal they did their shopping and Wycliffe bought a local history book on Kellycoryk and the Kemps.

The afternoon was overcast and misty so that Roger, in his library, was working by artificial light. He brooded over a letterbook which held correspondence between his great-grandfather and the Tehidy estate. The crabbed script frequently defeated him and in any case his mind was elsewhere. Isobel's absurd tale of her medium troubled him and he tried to tell himself that it was nothing more than another of the girl's odd whims.

At forty-six Roger felt that time had stolen a march on him. It seemed that the transition from vaguely hopeful and aspiring youth to despairing and stressful middle age had been visited upon him unjustly. At times he felt like some defenceless sea creature who puts out an exploratory tentacle only to have it bitten off.

The telephone rang and he picked it up.

'Is that you, Roger . . . ? It's Clare. Is it safe to talk?'

'I suppose so.' His manner lacked enthusiasm.

'Isobel came to the shop this morning. At first she pretended she wanted to buy a present for Agnes's birthday but it was obvious that she was out to make trouble. She's been going to seances and she says she's had a message from Julia.'

Roger felt the tension rising and his fingers gripped the telephone. 'I know.'

'Has she said anything about us?'

'About *us*?'

His emphasis on the word seemed to offend her. 'Don't play with me, Roger! Yes, about us! She as good as asked how much you gave me to set me up in the business.'

'But that's nonsense!'

'All right, but in almost the same breath she started to talk of discovering what really happened when her mother died. I mean, it was blatant. To get her out of the shop I took her to lunch at the pub but it made no difference. She said that she expected to know more when her mother spoke to her again.'

Roger was barely articulate. 'But she can't—'

Clare cut him short. 'I'm worried, Roger, and we've got to talk – not over the telephone. I'll expect you this evening.'

Roger was cut off. He replaced his phone and stared at it as though he had been bitten. Then he held his breath; it was a trick he had learned in childhood. When there was something that he did not want to think about he would hold his breath until the pressure in his head was almost unbearable, then when he started to breathe again he could usually think of something else. It had become a survival technique.

The Wycliffes were back in their cottage in the cove. Helen was arranging the kitchen to her liking while he sat in a wicker chair by the window of the living room, leafing through his book on the Kemps and Kellycoryk. It turned out to be one of those little gems of local history, published on a shoe-string.

He learned that the family had arrived at Kellycoryk at about the time when Henry VIII of England and Francis I of France were displaying like peacocks on the Field of the Cloth of Gold. As Catholics, the Kemps of Kellycoryk, unlike some of their namesakes, had the good sense to keep their heads down during the religious upheavals. But there must have been some bad moments with the influential, time-serving Trevanions almost next door at Caerhays.

The Wycliffes' cottage was sideways on to the cove

so that from his window Wycliffe could look down to the sea or up the valley to Kellycoryk House. The mist was like a thin veil; it did not exclude the view but added a certain fuzziness like a slightly out-of-focus lens.

He was thinking about the contemporary Kemps and becoming increasingly interested in that gloomy-looking house almost hidden in a seeming wilderness.

'I think I'll take a look around the cove. You don't feel like coming?'

'It's not worth it; I've got things to do and I'm quite happy here.'

Their cottage was nearest the shore and he had to pass three or four others before reaching the bridge. A group of children, presumably on their way home from school, were playing by the stream – three girls and a boy. The scene reminded him of those idealized versions of rural life by Victorian painters. Two of the little girls wore skirts.

On the other side of the stream he should have followed the road by the crumbling cliffs, but he looked up the valley towards the gates of Kellycoryk and decided to take a closer look. In fact, there were no gates, only a pair of massive granite gateposts and a well-weathered notice: 'Kellycoryk Estate. Strictly Private.' There was a gatehouse, but the roof had fallen in and the window frames were empty. A weedy drive, just wide enough for a car, disappeared between the encroaching laurels.

There was no sound anywhere except the gentle rippling of the stream and the breaking of lilliputian waves over the shingle in the cove. Even the children were silent. So far Wycliffe had only seen the roof of the house and wanted a closer view. After a couple of twists the drive opened out and he was surprised to find a virtual lake between him and the house. The surface was largely covered by a green scum and

22

rushes were taking over the shallows, but what he had come to see was the house; and there it was in clear view.

It was not large as country houses go, a single block of two storeys with dormers above, and here too there was evidence of neglect and decay. In places the stucco-facing had flaked away exposing underlying brickwork, and rampant ivy reached to the windows of the first floor. From where he stood he could see, on the east side of the building, an area of low scrub from which, here and there, broken walls emerged, presumably the site of an earlier house.

While he stood there a car, a blue Mondeo Estate, appeared from around the side of the house, skirted the lake and came towards him. Instinctively he dodged into the laurels, and then felt foolish. The car passed, and he saw a woman at the wheel. For an instant their eyes met and he had a glimpse of red hair and the impression of a beautiful, doll-like face.

Gradually the sound of the car died away but he could still hear it a couple of minutes later as it climbed the slope to the village.

He walked back to the bridge; the mist was thickening into fog; the children had gone indoors, and he could no longer see the sea.

Crispin got into bed, pulled the bedclothes over him and switched off his bedside lamp. His curtains were undrawn, the mists had cleared with the turn of the tide and through his window he could see the stars. As his eyes accommodated he could pick out the familiar objects in his room.

This time each night before he fell asleep was important to Crispin. Once he had closed his bedroom door he began to feel secure – not against any physical danger but against the more subtle threat of emotional intrusion. In all the encounters of his day Crispin took

23

refuge behind a mask of placidity, usually interpreted by others as coldness or indifference. But that mask was his defence against intimacy of any sort; the cut and thrust of ordinary relationships scared him and he could not bear to contemplate the consequences of becoming involved.

Crispin had constructed for himself a tiny world where contacts were few and life was predictable. The boundaries of Kellycoryk defined its physical limits and he went outside them only of sheer necessity.

But sex had become a problem, strangely disturbing, even menacing, to his world. It was solved to some extent, almost accidentally, by the girl who came to help with the cleaning, and encounters with her, two or three times a week, entered into the routine of his days. But there could be no doubt that they profoundly disturbed that uncertain equilibrium he had so painfully contrived.

Drifting off to sleep he was aware of a slight sound and he saw his bedroom door opening.

'Are you asleep, Crispy?' It was Isobel. She was in her nightdress and she came to stand beside his bed. 'I want to talk to you.'

Crispin dreaded this approach; usually it meant that his sister was about to involve him in something of which he wanted to know nothing. 'Can't it wait until tomorrow?'

'No.' She pulled back his bedclothes and got in beside him.

He could feel her naked thigh against his and he moved away.

'Don't go away, I'm cold. In any case, you'll fall out the other side.'

'We shouldn't be here like this.'

'Why not? When we were children we used to sleep in the same bed.'

'That was different. We're not children now.'

She made an irritable movement. 'Are you going to let me talk or not?'

He said nothing and she went on, 'What I said about Mother I almost think was true, Crispy. She really seemed to speak to me and I believe there are things she wants to tell me.'

'What things?' The words were forced from him.

'I don't know yet. I hope there will be other sessions and that she will speak again.' She added after a moment, 'But I can guess what it's about.'

He was disturbingly aware of her body and his emotions were wildly confused. He was desperate to put an end to the situation. 'How can you if she didn't tell you?'

'Never mind, I think I know . . .' She broke off. 'Do you remember all that happened around the time Mother died?'

'Of course I remember it!'

'Did you believe what they told the police?'

He said, bleakly, 'I suppose I believed it – yes.'

'Who was on the boat besides Mother and Father?'

'Clare was on the boat.'

Crispin was troubled by the way in which she had once more succeeded in putting him at a disadvantage. Now he was being subjected to some sort of test. It had always been the same. She would cross-question him, catch him out, and so re-establish or confirm a certain ascendancy which she had had over him since infancy.

Isobel demanded, 'Where was I the day Mother died?'

A momentary hesitation. 'You were away on a school trip somewhere. You were supposed to be away all that week.'

'Yes, and Aunt Agnes was staying with her friend in Torquay, so there was you, and Mother and

Father and, of course, Clare was still living with us then.'

'Yes.'

Isobel took a deep breath. 'It was a Tuesday when it happened so you were at school. Were they quarrelling the night before?'

'I don't know.'

'What was she like next morning – before you went to school?'

Crispin spoke very slowly as though each word came with difficulty. 'I didn't see her. You know how it was; Clare used to get the breakfast when Agnes was away.'

'Yes. Now about what they told the police; they said that Clare was in the well of the boat with Father who was at the tiller, but that Mother was on the foredeck – why?'

'I think they said she wanted to sunbathe.'

'Yes, she wanted to sunbathe!' Isobel was derisive. 'Mother would never sunbathe; she was too worried about her skin; she had to be, because she was pale like me.'

Crispin said nothing.

'It would have been so simple.' Isobel sounded thoughtful.

'What would?' The question seemed to be forced from him.

'I don't know. How did Clare manage to buy her shop not long after Mother died?'

'Clare had her shop before Mother died.'

'But she was renting it as a lock-up and she lived with us. When mother died she bought it, then later went to live in the rooms over the shop. She couldn't have done it on her own; where did she get the money from?'

He almost shouted, 'I don't know and I don't want to know, Isobel!'

26

Isobel ignored him. 'Anyway, Clare was settled in her own shop and after two or three years Father married Bridget.'

They were quiet for a few moments; Crispin was tense, waiting, when Isobel burst out, 'It's this bloody house; that's what it comes back to.'

'The house?'

'Yes, the house, this place . . . It cripples us all. I get to hate the very sight and smell of it . . . I wish it would fall down, burn down – anything so that we could get out and live like other people. But Father is a Kemp and so we have to skimp and scheme and pretend . . .' She broke off. 'And you're just as bad, with your bloody nursery; as though, even if it worked, it could make any real difference.'

Crispin was silent; he lay rigid and still. There was a brief interval of quiet then Isobel bounced up in the bed and put her arms around him. 'Now I've got that off my chest you can warm me up before I go back to my own bed.'

He struggled to free himself and she laughed, a rare occurrence with Isobel. 'What's the matter? Are you afraid you might be tempted to rape me or something? It would be different if I were Jane Clemens, wouldn't it?'

'Isobel! Stop it!' The words were hissed at her, and he was gripping her arms so tightly that she was frightened, and became quiet at once. 'All right, I'm listening.'

He said nothing for a moment and when he did speak his voice was controlled. 'I want you to drop all this, it can do no good. You've no idea what you are doing – no idea!' He seemed to have difficulty in finding words and there was another pause before he added, 'You will end up by . . .' Again he broke off, then finished lamely, 'You will make things worse.'

27

She was uneasy and, feeling slightly foolish, she took refuge in a childish retort. 'That's what you think!' And she slipped out of bed and was gone.

Left alone, Crispin lay rigid, every muscle taut, fingers and toes clenched, head throbbing.

Chapter Two

Tuesday 4 May

The morning was clear and bright and fresh. The Wycliffes were enjoying a holiday breakfast, semi-lethal, with an egg and a sausage.

From where he sat, Wycliffe was looking out of the window at the sunlit sea. 'Well, what's our programme for the day?'

Helen said, 'I thought we might walk the coast path to Portloe, Kiberick, and the Nare. I think we could probably get lunch in Veryan.'

'It sounds like a lot of miles.'

Helen was dismissive. 'Nonsense, Charles!'

Like most of Helen's plans, it worked; lovely cliff scenery, an abundance of spring wild flowers, and the delight of Portloe where they had coffee in a restaurant almost overhanging the cove and watched a fishing boat being winched up the beach. Then on to Kiberick, and Veryan for lunch. After that they had a less spectacular but pleasant trudge back through the lanes to St Endel Churchtown, little more than a mile inland from Porthendel.

In a dry-stone wall opposite the church a pair of ornamental gateposts marked what must once have been the imposing northern entrance to Kellycoryk. Now the only barrier was a rickety farm gate. Near the gate a substantial little building, with shuttered windows, must at one time have been a lodge.

Helen, arms on the gate, looking over, said, 'Somebody's been working in there – clearing the ground. I wonder if they're going in for reclamation.'

Over a considerable area the ground had been cleared and a start had been made digging out roots. The clearance had uncovered a track leading from the gateway into the wilderness beyond.

'What's left of the original drive.'

Helen said, 'There must still be a way through. Let's take a look.'

It was a waste of time to argue and in any case Wycliffe's curiosity would overcome his ingrained conformity. At least they managed to open the gate and avoid the indignity of climbing over.

Once out of the clearing they were treading a narrow path through a mixed jungle of rhododendron and camellia with frequent woodland trees, some well established, others in the thrusting sapling stage. Two centuries ago a garden had been carved out of the wood; now, slowly but surely, the wood was reclaiming its own.

At intervals they glimpsed broken walls and remnants of buildings which must once have been features in an ornamental park. The path they were following was largely notional, broken at intervals by sudden inexplicable changes of level, and from time to time there were muddy patches. Here and there the burgeoning growth had been cut back to maintain some sort of passage.

Wycliffe said, 'Don't you think we've had enough?'

'Let's see if we can reach the stream.'

Away to their left they could hear running water and the path seemed to be making broadly in that direction. Then, abruptly, the stream was in front of them, swirling between constraining banks. There was a bridge, whose generous width defined the scale of the original drive, its ornamental balustrade now almost lost under matted ivy. On the other side, in a large clearing, there was a substantial house with outbuildings.

Faced with the alternative of turning back they crossed the bridge, which meant passing close to the house. A neatly painted notice set on a post read: '*Chylathva*. Beware of Jackals.'

A sizeable patch of ground to one side of the house was enclosed by chicken wire, and within it a dozen or so hens pecked and scratched and clucked in apparent contentment. Helen, once a keeper of chickens, said, 'White Leghorns.'

Near the front door of the house, at first unnoticed by the Wycliffes, a dark-haired young woman with a stick was bent double, poking away at what appeared to be a choked drain. She glanced up without special interest. 'Looking for somebody?'

Wycliffe said, 'We're trespassers. We are renting one of the cottages in the cove and we wondered if there was a way through.'

The woman – she was in her thirties – stood up and swept back trailing hair from her face with a bare arm. 'There's a way through if you follow the stream. It's true Roger doesn't like people about the place but he won't eat you.'

Helen said, 'What about the jackals?'

The woman grinned happily. 'That's Francis – Roger's brother, I live here with him and, like all the Kemps, he's never grown up.' She turned back to her drain. 'Anyway, there's a good track from here direct to the Porthendel road if you don't fancy the stream walk, but don't let Roger put you off.'

Wycliffe said, 'Nice woman.'

In fact now the going was much easier; they simply followed the course of the stream and a few minutes later they were in sight of the big house.

Ahead their way seemed blocked by a long run of

low outbuildings with decaying roofs, but as they drew nearer they saw that a broad archway gave access to a yard with the house beyond. At this point, abruptly and noisily, the stream plunged through a large grating into an underground culvert and disappeared.

'It must go under the house and come out in the lake.'

'Surely we don't have to go through the house yard?'

'It looks as though we do.'

The yard was reasonably well paved, but the outbuildings, presumably the former stables and coach house, were in a ruinous state and there was rubbish everywhere, from a massive sofa with escaping stuffing, to an ancient powered mower, red with rust. A newish open shed with a corrugated asbestos roof at the east end of the yard provided cover for the blue Mondeo, a museum-piece Volvo, and a white Mini.

Helen said, 'Wouldn't you think they'd do something about tidying this up?'

There was no-one about and they made their way around the east end of the house with the overgrown ruins of a former building on their left. Wycliffe, out of his recently acquired knowledge, said, 'The original Tudor house.'

It was as they came round to the front, in sight of the lake, that they saw a man: stocky build, tweed suit and flat cap – the very model of a country gentleman. He had his back to them, apparently watching ducks on the lake as they dipped, bottoms up, for food. At his feet, instead of the traditional retriever, a black cat performed its acrobatic and elegant toilet.

The man turned, saw them, and came over; he had the heavy features which seem to characterize some of the oldest families and altogether he could have been an intimidating individual but Wycliffe sensed at once that he was more nervous than they.

Wycliffe spoke first. 'Charles Wycliffe. I'm afraid that we're intruders, without much excuse other than interest. We are staying at one of the cottages in the cove and our curiosity about Kellycoryk got the better of us.'

There was an inarticulate response, not unfriendly, then, 'I'm Roger Kemp.' A wry smile. 'I take it you've come by the Long Drive. I know it's hard to believe, but in the twenties there was a carriage drive from the northern entrance all the way to the house.'

Wycliffe, an incurable catophile, stooped to stroke the cat but Kemp stopped him. 'I wouldn't if I were you; Coryk can be quite nasty with strangers.'

Wycliffe said, 'He seems very much attached to you.'

Kemp was pleased. 'Black cats and Kemps and Kellycoryk go together. The story is that a seventeenth-century ancestor was awakened by the first Coryk when his bed-hangings caught fire.' A shy smile. 'And to prove it we have a painting of that heroic Coryk with a badly singed tail.'

Wycliffe tried to develop the conversation. 'I've been reading a most interesting little book on the Kemps and Kellycoryk. Your house and family have a long and enthralling history behind them.'

For some reason the compliment was not well received. Kemp frowned. 'I'm afraid Miss Scott's book can scarcely be called history.'

It was Helen's turn to change the subject. 'Does the stream actually go under the house?'

'Not under the present house, no.' Kemp's manner had become decidedly less friendly. He looked at Wycliffe. 'It hadn't occurred to me, your name is unusual – you must be—'

'The policeman. I'm afraid so.'

Not for the first time in such circumstances Wycliffe wished that he had been born a Smith, a Jones or a

Brown, but he would not have expected his identity to have had any significance for Kemp. In fact there was a decided drop in temperature and an awkward pause before the man said, 'I suppose you are down here on holiday?'

'Yes, a spring break.'

'Well, I can only wish you good day and a pleasant holiday.'

As they were making their way around the lake Wycliffe said, 'What came over him?'

Helen was in no doubt. 'An antipathy for policemen; it's not uncommon.'

But Wycliffe was following his own line. 'A strange man. Not the sort I would expect to have married two very attractive women.'

Helen, still smarting from Kemp's snub, said, 'You know next to nothing about his first wife; you may have glimpsed the second, though you can't even be sure of that.'

'You only have to look at the daughter. She didn't get her looks from her father.' He went on, 'Three Kemps: Isobel, we saw in the dog shop and the pub; Roger, we've just met, and I feel sure that the woman I saw driving the Mondeo was his second wife. Now we know there's a brother called Francis, who lives with a very pleasant young woman who clears drains.'

Helen couldn't help laughing. 'Is this some sort of game?'

'Call it a jigsaw puzzle. But there are pieces missing, and so far we haven't fitted in the lady of the china dogs.'

'Does she?'

'Oh, I think so. The landlady in the pub said she was a relative, and we interrupted a rather heated discussion between her and Isobel, something about Isobel's mother – that would be the first Mrs Kemp . . .' Wycliffe broke off, then added, 'It's just occurred

34

to me that we don't know what happened to her – did she die? Or was there a divorce?'

'You'd better ask Kemp when you see him again.'

But Helen's sarcasm was lost on her husband. 'No, I need to be a bit more subtle than that.'

Helen looked at him with affection. 'After all these years you never cease to surprise me, Charles. What has got into you about these people?'

They left Kellycoryk and arrived at the cove. Evening comes early to these south-facing coves; although the sun still shone there was a muted quality to the light which reminded Wycliffe of his boyhood, of summer Sunday evenings in chapel.

Helen said, 'Look at my shoes . . . and your trousers! A shower, a sherry, and a meal. How about that?'

Roger watched the Wycliffes as they made their way around the lake and down the drive. He had made a fool of himself. He had got out of the habit of talking with strangers. And then to discover that this one was a policeman . . . He realized that Isobel's activities were worrying him more than he would admit, but to imagine that this man . . . That, at least, was nonsense.

He turned away from the lake and walked back to the house, paced by the cat. He made for his library and once there Coryk leapt on to the table and curled up amid the litter of papers. Roger sat in his padded chair, leaned back and stared at the ceiling, his favourite position for relaxation.

Above his head the ceiling was defaced by a pattern of cracks; a pattern he knew so well that he could have drawn it from memory. Yet he saw them differently at different times; sometimes as a branching tree, sometimes as a river delta, occasionally as similar to the lines of destiny which are supposed to occur in one's hands. Once, not long ago, he had dreamed that he was sitting in his chair looking up at those cracks when they started to widen, and at such a rate that before he could move to protect himself, with a great rending and crashing, the whole ceiling had collapsed, burying him under a mountain of rubble. Miraculously he was unhurt, but helplessly imprisoned.

He still shivered at the memory of that dream.

The gathering was in a private house. The room was lit only by the light which diffused through the curtains drawn across the bow window. Four women and two men sat around an oval dining table. Teresa, the medium, was at one end, Isobel at the other.

Teresa wore a gown of yellow silk which, even in the dim light, produced subtle and changing reflections. Her long, pale hands rested on the table but her face was not visible. She sat, slumped in her chair, with her head drooping, chin on chest; only her dark hair with its central parting was clearly seen.

She spoke without lifting her head so that her voice sounded muffled. 'Tonight I shall not use either of my spirit guides. I shall try to communicate directly with the spirit of our departed sister. At our last meeting her distress and her anxiety to communicate were such that I feel able to rely on her co-operation to this unusual extent.'

There was an interval, then the medium's voice resumed. 'If you will now concentrate on her given name – Julia. Repeat the name Julia to yourselves, over and over again, and at the same time *will* her to be with us and to speak.'

A brief silence, then came the sound of stertorous breathing, a garbled flow of words or near words, then silence again. This sequence was repeated, but the second time it was interrupted by the striking of the church clock which was so close that they could hear the mechanical whirring and clacking which punctuated the eight strokes.

36

One of the men, whose bald head shone in the dim light, muttered, 'You should have thought of that, Margot,' and was shushed by the others. Teresa seemed unaffected. More garbled speech, then a different voice, clear and authoritative, demanded, 'Is Isobel here?'

Margot, a plump figure with mauve lights in her hair, prompted. 'Answer your mother, Isobel!'

'I'm here, Mother.' Isobel sounded self-conscious and uncertain. After an interval, during which the medium breathed deeply and slowly, the voice came again, but this time the tone was less peremptory. 'You must ask *them* questions, Isobel . . . Keep asking them. There are things I cannot tell you . . . You must find them out for yourself . . . I haven't much time . . .' She sounded breathless.

'I want to know exactly how you died, Mother.' There was a tremor in the girl's voice.

This time the silence was so long that it seemed there would be no response but it came at last though the voice was weak. 'You know *how* I died, Isobel.'

And that was all.

Teresa moved in her chair, sitting bolt upright, and she said in a tired voice, 'Did I make contact?'

There were murmurings of assent and approval.

Margot said, 'It was very successful, Teresa. Isobel should be grateful to you.' She got up from her chair and went to the window where she drew back the curtains. At the bottom of the garden the church tower with its clock rose above a tall yew hedge. The sun was setting and the tower was caught in an orange glow.

Margot, bustling, said, 'Let's move into the other room. I'm sure we all need a drink.'

Bridget Kemp was seated at her work table by the window. The curtains were undrawn and the window panes shone blankly against the darkness outside. The little digital clock registered five minutes past eleven. The desk lamp cast only a semi-circle of light out into the room so that most of it was in shadow. Bridget's tiny fingers seemed to dance over the keyboard of her word processor as a memorandum took shape on the screen.

'Inter-office memo to Ian Curtis from BK. 4.5.93.

'Reference: April returns. For the second month in succession, there are items for which the information provided is totally inadequate . . .'

Bridget took pleasure in most things that she did, not least in reminding her staff of their obligations and their dependence.

There was a gentle tap at the door and she turned to see Roger in his dressing gown coming into the room, manifestly unsure of his reception. Surely he didn't imagine . . . No! The thought was stillborn. She looked, to make sure that he was not followed by his cat.

'I hope I'm not disturbing you but I wanted a word . . . I could hear you tapping away, so I knew you were still at work.'

Bridget stood up and drew forward a chair as though for a visitor.

Roger wedged himself into a tub chair that was too small for him. His drooping lids and sagging jowls gave him the look of a grieving mastiff.

'I'm worried, Bridget.'

'Oh?' As though the fact came as a surprise. 'What about?'

'You know what about. About us, about the future, the estate – everything.'

Her attitude was that of a doctor with a difficult patient. 'Well, the remedy is in your own hands.'

He tried to shift in his chair but the chair moved with him and he looked ridiculous.

She went on, 'There's no way in which you will persuade me to spend money on this place chasing your dream, Roger. I've said that often enough, but you don't seem to understand that I mean it. You can't live on sentiment, even five centuries of it. But, apart from anything else, you don't even make use of the assets you have – for one thing, income from the farms could be doubled with proper management; and your brother lives off you, he pays no rent for a property which, renovated, and offered in the right market, could bring in a good income. Instead, you pay his council tax while he dabbles with his paints, producing stuff which no-one could possibly buy, pretending that he's a neglected genius.'

'Francis got nothing under Father's will.'

Bridget made a dismissive gesture. 'Your father's will! Your father was a realist, Roger. He knew that the Kemp legend couldn't be sustained for much longer and it's obvious that he fully expected you to sell up. He made provision that if and when you decided or were forced to do so, Francis and the others would receive a proportion of the capital sum raised. I've told you, though I doubt if you believed me, that two years before the old man died he was putting out feelers about selling the place. It was common talk in the business. All the company is asking of you is a long lease which would be wholly in your favour.'

This, with variations, was more or less familiar ground, a sort of preamble to serious discussion; then Bridget broke into new territory: 'Now there is Isobel; if you allow her to go on the way she is going you may find yourself in another kind of trouble and that would do none of us any good.'

'I don't know what you mean.'

'I think you understand only too well.' The doll-like features and the blue eyes looked innocent of any possible threat, but the voice was hard.

Roger's gaze shifted around the room as though in search of inspiration while she watched him with total detachment.

The silence was absolute until broken by the distant barking of a dog.

She waited, unmoving, until Roger said, 'I suppose we could continue to live here?'

Bridget sighed. 'You know exactly what the company is offering, Roger.'

Although Coast and Country was virtually hers, Bridget always spoke of 'the company' as if it were some entity with a life and will of its own over which she had no control.

Roger eased himself out of his chair and stood up, then: 'Yes, well . . . It seems to be the only way out . . . I agree.'

'You mean that you will accept the company's offer?'

'Yes.'

'Good!'

Wednesday 5 May

Wycliffe was awakened by quarrelling gulls. The curtains of the little window were undrawn and he was looking out at a blue sky with fluffy white clouds. He eased himself out of bed with difficulty but avoided disturbing Helen. Then, in shirt, trousers and slippers, he left the house by the front door.

It was a morning, as somebody once said, 'Fresh from the hand of God.' In the low light most things had a dual existence, in substance and in shadow; the sea alone had definition and wholeness, glittering under the sun. The cottages were silent and blind and Wycliffe was surprised to see a man on the shore, staring out to sea, solitary and enigmatic, like a figure from a Friedrich painting.

Wycliffe crunched over the shingle towards him. 'A beautiful morning.'

The man turned. He was in his middle to late thirties, loose limbed and dark, with unquiet eyes and the taut features of a man at odds with himself. 'Yes, it is a beautiful morning, but if you live in this place most mornings are.'

'You live here – here in the cove?'

The man pointed to one of the cottages. 'That's mine; at least I rent it. I've lived there for more than ten years.' He went on, 'I know who you are. As you can imagine there are not many secrets among the cove community.' He held out a very clean, bony hand. 'My name is Harvey – John Harvey. Come and have a coffee with me.'

Wycliffe looked at his watch; it was half-past six; Helen would not be about for another hour.

John Harvey's cottage was on the east side of the cove, opposite the one where the Wycliffes were staying, and even nearer the sea. In fact it was built out on a rocky promontory and in a south-westerly gale spray, at least, must have been carried over the roof.

Parked at the side of the cottage and, to some extent, sheltered from the sea was a rattle-trap Deux-Chevaux. Harvey said, 'I call him Boanerges because he makes such a hell of a row.'

In the living room most of the wall space was occupied by books though at the bottom of the stairs an area of white wall had been reserved for a framed oil-painting of the cove as seen from the sea. Wycliffe was impressed; the painter had caught that sense of remoteness, both magical and sinister, which he had experienced when he first set eyes on the place.

Harvey said, 'I sometimes think that my books will

eventually squeeze me into the roof space; one of the penalties of being a bachelor – most women are great pruners. Anyway, I'll make the coffee while you make yourself at home.'

It was strange, the man's manner was casual, even playful, but Wycliffe suspected an underlying purpose. He was interested and, as always, the books drew him. He glanced over the shelves, searching for some sort of focus, but found none. The fiction content was small and restricted to a few English, French and Russian classics, but the non-fiction ranged through the sciences, philosophy, history and the arts with a fine lack of discrimination. Wycliffe, survivor of that endangered species addicted to self-improvement, wondered if he had stumbled upon a kindred spirit.

Harvey came in from the kitchen with two mugs of coffee. 'So what do you make of my books?'

Wycliffe grinned. 'I gather you've set out to discover the secret of life, the universe, and all that.'

A quick, appreciative laugh. 'I'm working on it, but I don't get far. I guessed a little milk but no sugar. Am I right?'

Already they seemed to be on a footing which is usually only achieved after much longer acquaintance.

Wycliffe sipped his coffee.

Harvey said, 'Why don't we sit down?'

They sat, and Harvey went on, 'Don't you find this life of ours frustrating and more than a bit galling? I mean, it's thrust upon us without a by-your-leave and snatched away again with neither a please nor a thank you. We start with a howl and if we are lucky we go out with no more than a whimper.' He looked at Wycliffe with a quizzical expression that was almost comical. 'Don't you think the gods owe us something more than that?'

Wycliffe was uneasy at having his night thoughts so casually exposed to the light of day. He merely nodded and changed the subject. 'Do you mind if I ask what you do?'

'In the sense that you are a policeman . . . ? I'm a doctor, a GP. I share a practice with a woman partner and we have our surgery in Porthendel.' He smiled. 'I see that I'm going too quickly, presuming on a brief acquaintance, but it's a novelty to have someone to talk to and, as a policeman, you must see the apparent futility of it all, at least as clearly as I do. As the old fairy-tales, myths, faiths and theories, religious and scientific, wear thin, masses of people feel that they are up a creek without a paddle. Is it surprising that they ask themselves, "What the hell?" '

Wycliffe took refuge in gentle irony. 'So you're really looking for a more convincing fairy-tale.'

'Something like that. Aren't you?'

On the face of it, here was a lonely man making the most of a chance to talk to someone other than his partner and his patients, but Wycliffe thought he could detect a more subtle purpose.

'How did you come to settle here?'

'I came here while my elder sister, Julia, was married to Roger Kemp. She was his first wife.' He added after a pause, 'By the way, is it true that you are interested in Kellycoryk and the Kemps?'

'I know hardly anything about them. I've read a little book about the house and its history. They seem an intriguing family.'

Harvey smiled. 'They're certainly that.'

Wycliffe's interest in the man was growing and he wanted to prolong the acquaintance but he had a limited tolerance of psychological striptease, especially before breakfast. On the spur of the moment he said, 'I don't suppose you would care to join my wife and me for a meal this evening?'

'I would like that very much. Your wife won't mind? I promise not to bore her with my chatter.'

43

'She will be glad to meet you.' He prayed without much confidence that this might be so. Anxious to put it to the test, he looked at his watch. 'I must be getting back. My wife will think I'm lost.'

Wycliffe was seen off at the door; a few yards of sparse and stony turf separated the house from dark rocks splashed with orange lichen, a shingle beach, and then the sea.

'Thanks for the coffee . . . See you about seven, then.'

Wycliffe crossed the bridge and arrived back at the cottage to find Helen downstairs in her dressing gown.

'Nice walk?'

'I've just had coffee with a chap called John Harvey, he's a doctor, and Julia's brother.'

'Who's Julia? Should I know her?'

'Julia was Roger's first wife; her brother lives in a cottage across the cove.'

'Did you find out what happened to her?'

'No, it only cropped up and I didn't have a chance to ask.'

Helen, in the act of putting coffee into the percolator, turned to look at him. 'Does he live alone?'

'Apparently . . . I've put my foot in it. I've asked him over for a meal this evening.'

Helen said nothing.

'Are you annoyed?'

'Not really. I suppose we owe the poor man something if we are going to pump him about his relatives.'

'We?'

'Well, I can't pretend I'm not curious.'

Isobel, lying in bed, stared at the ceiling and tried to impose a pattern on the cracks. As a little girl, with Crispin, allowed to amuse themselves in the library, she had watched her father doing the same thing, and she had understood. Sometimes she wondered if, after all, she had more in common with her father than she was inclined to admit. Perhaps it would have been possible . . . But it was too late now.

A few minutes ago the old Volvo had chuntered out of the yard; Agnes, on her weekly visit to a supermarket in Truro.

Now Radio 2, subdued to incomprehensibility, just held the silence at bay.

Her father would be in his library and Crispin, if he wasn't at the Northern Garden, would be somewhere in the house, as unobtrusive and remote as a mouse in the woodwork.

She had grown up surrounded by unused or empty rooms in a house which she hated, a house that was no longer a home, buried in a wilderness. At school she had envied the other girls who seemed to lead defined lives in real houses.

She spoke to her ceiling. 'I wish . . .' But she could not even formulate her wish.

There was a tap at the door and, to her surprise, Crispin came in. He looked secretive. 'Agnes has gone to Truro . . .'

'What about it?'

He went to the window and stood, looking out. 'I was thinking about what we talked about the other night and there's something I want to show you.' He added after a moment, 'I think you should see it.'

'See what?'

'It's in the ruins. I don't want us to be over there when Agnes gets back.'

'All right, if I must.' She was wary of upsetting Crispin again.

She got out of bed and in almost the same movement pulled off her nightdress. Crispin made for the door. 'I'll wait for you.'

Isobel caught sight of herself in the glass; she

45

was frowning. What makes me do it to him?

A few minutes later they were in the yard. Through a gap in the boundary wall they entered an area of tussocky grass and scrub where uneven dwarf walls emerged to a height of a foot or two in some forgotten plan. Otherwise there was little to show for the Tudor building which had once been the home of the Kemps. From somewhere away to their left they could hear the stream as it plunged underground. The whole area had been a favourite place to play when they were children.

Crispin led the way through the ruins to a flight of steep granite steps, sixteen of them, leading below ground to a stout, padlocked door which carried a faded warning in red paint, 'Danger! Keep Out'. The steps were maintained to give access to the underground stream.

Isobel said, 'You haven't got a key.'

'I don't need one.' Crispin went to work with a piece of stout wire and in a short time the door was open. Padlock and hinges were well oiled. As they passed through the door the sound of the stream which had increased as they descended the steps now came at them in a subdued rush.

They were in a tunnel, arched over, nine or ten feet wide and of indeterminate length. The water slid smoothly in its stone channel only to be swallowed up in the darkness a few yards ahead. There was a narrow, paved walkway beside the stream, coated with slime, and the air was dank. The lack of headroom forced them to stoop as they walked.

Crispin said, 'Come on, it's in Mayne's Closet. I've got a torch.'

None of this was new to Isobel though childhood visits had been rare and strictly controlled. She followed Crispin along the walkway for twenty yards or so until they reached a narrow opening in the tunnel wall just large enough for an average man to squeeze through.

Scarcely any light from the entrance reached this far and Crispin played his torch through the gap. It opened into a cavity which seemed to have been cut from the rock itself.

'Come on.'

They were standing in a little room about six feet square. Against one wall there was a raised slate slab like a shelf, known in the family as Mayne's Bed, after the sixteenth-century seminary priest who was supposed to have taken refuge there. Now it had more the appearance of an altar, with two brass candlesticks placed one on each side of a plaster cast of the Virgin. Each candlestick held a half-burnt candle. Crispin directed the beam of his torch to an inscription cut into the slate:

Julia Constance Kemp née Harvey
died 13 June 1988, aged 37 years.
Pray for her Soul.

Isobel could scarcely control her astonishment. 'Did you do this?'

Crispin snapped, 'No, of course not! He did.'

'He must come here regularly. How did you find out?'

Crispin turned away without answering but Isobel took the torch from him and continued to examine the surface of the slate. 'It must have taken him ages to cut these letters.' And then, abruptly, 'He's got the date wrong! It was the fourteenth.'

Crispin, as he watched his sister, was becoming increasingly agitated. He took her roughly by the arm and said, 'Let's go!'

Outside Isobel asked, 'Does Agnes know?'

'I've no idea.'

The Wycliffes spent a good day exploring the eastern limb of the bifurcated Roseland peninsula, below Gerrans. They visited the lighthouse at St Anthony, lunched at Place, walked to Percuil, and explored the lush, sheltered creeks on one side, and the exposed cliffs and beaches on the other. They arrived home shortly after five, very tired.

'We've got a couple of hours, so let's start with a shower.'

Helen had never set herself up as a cook; she had a number of simple menus which she could lay on to order; usually they were basic and tasty, but without frills. This one was likely to be more basic than most.

'It's more or less what we would have had anyway. A cold soup, stir-fry chicken with boiled rice and herbs; fresh fruit salad to follow. I hope he likes garlic.'

Wycliffe said, 'I think he wants to talk.'

Harvey arrived shortly after seven, wearing a suit, and Wycliffe thought he noticed a subtle change in him, a certain reserve. Perhaps it went with the suit or it could have been due to a shyness with women. At any rate, with Helen's calculated informality they drank sherry in the kitchen and moved, together with the soup, into the living room. By that time conversation was free and easy.

Inevitably it turned to crime and criminality, to individual responsibility and, of course, to the old chestnut, heredity versus environment. Wycliffe said that was a chicken-and-egg situation while Helen cunningly went on to suggest that families with a well-documented historical lineage must provide a rich source of material for research into inheritance patterns. Wycliffe followed suit with, 'The Kemps, for example.'

By this time they had reached the dessert and were comfortably afloat on Wycliffe's Chablis.

Harvey said, 'Of course my connection with the family is not all that close; my sister married Roger Kemp. At the time I was a schoolboy but later, as a newly fledged GP, when an opening cropped up here it seemed tailor made. At that time the whole cove was in Roger's direct gift and this cottage was available, so here I am.'

'Your sister died?' Helen put the question gently.

'She was drowned in a boating accident five years ago leaving the two children. Isobel was sixteen and Crispin fourteen.'

The Wycliffes murmured genuine expressions of sympathy and Helen said, 'Terrible for the children.'

'Yes, it affected Isobel in particular. It seems to have influenced her development in an unhealthy way. Only recently she told me that she was attending seances in the hope of getting in touch with her mother.

'Anyway, getting back to the subject, what you say about the lineage is quite true. In fact, Roger is supposed to be writing a history of the family. Being Catholics they've kept their line more obviously distinct, and so they're even better grist for the researcher's mill.'

'They dutifully married into Catholic families?'

'Oh, invariably. As Charles will tell you, I'm an apostate.' Harvey grinned. 'Grand old word that! But Julia was a devout adherent and the present Mrs Roger at least goes through the motions.'

After a fair amount of wine Harvey was now on to brandy with his coffee and it was beginning to show in a metaphorical unbuttoning.

'My sister was a very unfortunate girl. She was intelligent – perhaps too intelligent – and talented. She could have done almost anything; she could certainly have made a name for herself as a painter.' He broke off. 'You may have noticed one of her paintings at my place, Charles. But Julia was also one of life's misfits, hypersensitive, only interested in what was beyond her reach, and deeply frustrated.'

Harvey sighed. 'A very unhappy young woman, and difficult to live with.'

He brooded over his coffee, fiddling with the handle of his cup. 'The atmosphere at Kellycoryk didn't help. It was a strange household; Roger tried, but he was incapable of understanding her . . .' He pushed his cup and saucer away. 'Of course, Clare was there then.'

'Clare?' Wycliffe playing dumb.

'Clare Jordan, who now has the antique shop. She is Roger's cousin and she lost her parents when she was a child. She was brought up at Kellycoryk along with her three cousins . . . Anyway, Roger did his best according to his lights but he was incapable of coping with Julia. Nobody was to blame. It was inevitable.'

Wycliffe risked, 'What was inevitable?'

Harvey looked at him, his brown eyes suddenly wary, then he seemed to make up his mind. 'I know we all pretend that it was an accident, but I am quite sure that Julia committed suicide. I don't believe for one moment that she fell overboard.'

'But the inquest verdict was accidental death?'

'There was no inquest; the body was never recovered.'

Wycliffe was hesitant, wanting to know but not wanting to appear inquisitive. 'But Roger was able to marry again.'

'Yes, he applied to the High Court and was granted leave to presume death.' Harvey smiled. 'Roger would never have thought of such a thing; his future father-in-law organized all that.' A flavour of bitterness?

Harvey drained his coffee cup and Helen refilled it.

Wycliffe drew the curtains over the darkened window and for a while they sat in silence. Already the Wycliffes had ceased to hear the constant swish of little waves rippling along the shore.

Wycliffe said, 'It's sad, even for an outsider, to see an historic estate like Kellycoryk sinking into decline; it must be very hard for Kemp.'

Harvey nodded. 'All the harder when there's money in the family. Bridget, his second wife, is a rich woman. But she works hard for it, and if she's unwilling to put her money into the place, being realistic, who can blame her?'

'She is actually in business?'

'Oh, yes. Bridget *is* Coast and Country; she has a staff, of course, but she's the drive behind it.'

'The company that leases the cove?'

'Exactly. Odd, isn't it?'

At shortly after midnight Wycliffe said, 'What about a nightcap?'

'No, thanks; it's been a lovely evening for an old bachelor but I have to work in the morning.' They saw him off, and watched him as he made his way across the cove. There is no such thing as total darkness on the shore.

Later, in bed, Helen said, 'A very interesting man; but that was very odd about his sister.'

Wycliffe yawned. 'There's something going on here but we shan't be around to discover what.'

Chapter Three

On Thursday evenings Bridget had a regular date with the Wilsons in St Mawes to play Scrabble. As usual it was after midnight when she left for the drive home and, as usual, Ann and Gerry came to their gate to see her off.

Gerry said, 'Your night again, Bridgie. But *ziphiiform* – I ask you! Three i's and a z! You wait, young woman; next Thursday the Wilsons will have their revenge if it means swallowing the *Shorter Oxford*, both volumes.'

Bridget laughed; she was on a high. Winning was what life was about. She let in the clutch and the car took to the slope with a screech of tyres. She switched on the radio, an orchestra, muted and treacly, but company.

The road home was narrow, twisted, undulating, and often forked, but she knew every inch. The night was quiet and clear and on the higher ground a half-moon and stars made the car lights superfluous. The little houses she passed were in darkness. Bridget enjoyed the run home at night; she took a pride in her driving skills as in all the other things that she did well.

She was coming to Hendra Croft, a copse and a patch of green verge, less than three miles from home, when her headlights picked out a familiar figure, standing on the verge, holding on to a tree branch, and signalling her to stop. She pulled in, two wheels on the verge.

'Thanks, I was counting on you, I've twisted my ankle and knee and I can't walk very well . . . If I can get into the back I can hold my leg out straight . . .'

Bridget got out of the car. 'Hold on to me . . . Now!'

Bridget prided herself on calm efficiency in all circumstances and it worked. She got back into the driving seat. 'Are you all right? Try not to move about more than you have to.'

Bridget fastened her seat belt.

Isobel awoke from a sleep which had been troubled by dreams, and was finally disturbed by the sound of a car in the yard below: Bridget, of course! Isobel looked at her bedside clock: the green numerals glowed in the near darkness: 01.17. She was later than usual. Why couldn't she leave her car in the drive instead of waking everybody up? Not Bridget! Isobel turned over and tried to settle once more.

She could not say whether she slept or not but the next thing she knew she was listening to what seemed to be surreptitious movements in the yard. Her window was open and she could hear plainly. There was someone down there; no doubt about that. To her surprise, her little clock showed 02.31, so she must have slept. The sounds continued, there were footsteps, and finally she got out of bed and went to the window.

Isobel's room was at the east end of the house and from her window she had a full view of the entrance to the yard and of the open shed where the cars were kept. There was a moon and though the sky was cloudy there was sufficient light to see that Bridget's car was not in the shed but parked immediately beneath her window with the driver's door wide open. As she watched, she saw her father walk around the car to the driver's side. His manner was stealthy, he looked about him as though in fear, then got into the driving seat and closed the door with scarcely a sound. The engine started, and the car reversed out of the yard and out of her sight. She heard it come to a halt on the gravel in front of the house then move off down the drive and away.

Isobel found herself shivering though the night was mild. She could not imagine what was happening and she was overcome by a sense of unease.

At a quarter to four by her little clock she was again disturbed, this time by sounds from the room below. It was as though someone had tripped over a chair and was making clumsy efforts at recovery. The room which adjoined the library was little more than a corridor, its main furniture a giant settee on which her father would sometimes spend the night rather than trouble to undress and go to bed.

He had been doing it more often lately so that she had wondered whether it was a sign of something.

Had she fallen asleep? She thought not, but she couldn't be sure. She got out of bed and went to the window; Bridget's car had not been returned to the yard. She waited until her father had had time to settle in the little room below, then, very quietly, she let herself out into the corridor and crossed to Bridget's room. With infinite care she opened the door. There was enough light to see that the room was empty and that the bed had not been slept in.

Isobel returned to her own room and lay on the bed staring at the ceiling now dimly visible in the early morning light.

Friday morning 7 May

It was twenty minutes past eight by the wall clock in the kitchen and the Kemps were at breakfast. Outside the skies were overcast and a thin rain fell half-heartedly out of low cloud.

There was no conversation. Roger was forcing down the ritual egg and toast. From time to time he looked up from his plate as though he would speak but no words came. On the floor by his chair Coryk had already finished a dish of food and was lapping away at a saucer of milk. Roger was aware of Isobel looking at him; she had scarcely touched her bowl of muesli; her gaze was unnerving and when she met his eyes it was he who turned away.

Agnes watched them both. Crispin ate his egg, dipping small portions of toast in the runny yolk. His soft brown eyes gave nothing away.

Roger felt the pressure building, the intolerable pressure of silence. Somebody must speak; somebody must make the obvious remark or – or what . . . ? He could not keep it up any longer. In a weak voice, which sounded unreal, he said, 'Bridget is late getting back this morning.'

The expression on Isobel's face left him in no doubt.

Agnes was pouring herself a second cup of coffee. 'I don't think her ladyship has been out this morning. When I came down Timmy was whining to go out and he's in the yard now.'

Roger cast about for the right response and took refuge in irritation. He snapped, 'Why didn't you say? It's obvious if the dog's here, Bridget hasn't been out; she could be unwell.' Even to him it sounded hollow.

Agnes looked at him. 'What's the matter with you? Tell me if I'm wrong, but I assumed that she could stay in bed if she wanted to.'

55

Roger flushed and mumbled, 'I'd better go up and see what's happening.'

In Isobel's ears none of the things being said sounded real; more like a play-reading by poor actors.

Roger let Coryk out for his morning prowl then went up by what had once been the servants' stairs; they were covered with linoleum which had worn through in places. His movements were slow and deliberate; it was essential that he should think about everything he did and said. He could not guess how much Agnes knew already but she had always been able to see through his every subterfuge.

And Isobel . . .

The bedrooms were on either side of a central corridor and only half of them were in use. Bridget occupied the master bedroom, centrally placed in the front of the house. Only a year after their marriage he had moved across the corridor to a room at the back and since then he had tried to wipe from his memory all that had led to that.

He went through the motions, knocking on Bridget's door, then waiting before he opened it; a charade, but the only way he knew of making sure that he had a credible tale to tell. And that way he might come to believe it himself. He muttered repeatedly, as if in prayer, 'I must keep my nerve.'

Everything in the room looked as he had last seen it two nights earlier, the night when he had finally capitulated.

'You mean that you will accept the company's offer?'

'Yes.'

'Good!'

The words, the scene, and the atmosphere were stamped on his memory.

But now the room was empty; the bed had not been slept in.

56

Roger paused for a while to think what he was about, then left, closing the door behind him. He crossed the corridor to his own room which could hardly have been in greater contrast. He must be careful to do exactly what he would say that he had done so that he would make no mistakes. He went to the window and looked down into the yard. There was the accumulation of rubbish which he had come to accept as part of the place and no longer saw, like the outbuildings with their crumbling roofs and walls. If you allowed yourself to see all that, then . . .

By standing with his forehead pressed against the glass and looking to the right, he could see the vehicles in their lean-to shed, the old Volvo, Isobel's white Mini . . . But no Mondeo Estate.

Satisfied that he knew his part, Roger left the room, but in the corridor he realized that there was no way in which he could return to the kitchen and say, 'Her car isn't there,' or 'Her bed hasn't been slept in' – not with Agnes and Isobel watching him.

He went down the main stairs to the front hall and turned into his library, leaving the door ajar so that Crispin would find him. There he sat in his padded chair and leaned back, as if to study his cracks in the ceiling.

He needed a little more time.

With faith, justified in the event, that the weather would clear, the Wycliffes set out early to walk the coast path to Gorran Haven. By the time they reached the Dodman the sun was struggling through a pearly mist, the sea seemed lumine-scent, and Wycliffe claimed that he could already see Rame Head, twenty-five miles away. Helen said it was mist.

They squatted by the daymark, enjoying the view. Helen said, 'I can't help wondering about Kellycoryk.

I've been thinking about what you said last night – that there's something odd going on there.'

Wycliffe, chewing a grass stem and offering free board to some ghastly parasite, seemed to have lost interest. 'It's not our problem anyway.'

They walked to Gorran Haven, had a snack lunch in the village, looked in at the church in Gorran Churchtown, then walked home through a tangle of lanes and field paths. It was still short of three o'clock when they reached Jacob's Head at the top of the slope above their cove. Two police cars were parked on the track leading to the point and a uniformed man lounged, somnolent, against one of them.

Helen said, 'Go on; find out what's happening, and I'll expect you when I see you.'

The policeman recognized Wycliffe and was returned to life. 'I'm on radio watch, sir.' He pointed to the roofless ruin of a little building some distance away. 'DI Reed is just the other side of that, sir.'

Around the corner of the building Wycliffe found a dark-blue Mondeo Estate and a Cliff Rescue Land Rover, parked close. And Tom Reed was there, in conversation with a young man wearing a climbing harness.

'You're quick off the mark, sir.'

Reed was a man of some bulk; his hair, now no more than a fringe to his bald patch, was red; he had a high colour, and arresting blue eyes. It surprised people to discover that he was also a man of perception and delicacy of feeling.

Wycliffe said, 'We're staying at a cottage in the cove.' (A fact of which Reed, in common with the rest of the division, was well aware.) 'I happened to be passing. Anyway, what goes?'

Reed ran a finger around between his collar and his neck. 'As you're staying in the cove you must know something of the Kemps, sir. Well, at nine this morning, Roger Kemp reported that his wife was missing from home. She hadn't returned after spending yesterday evening with friends in St Mawes.' Reed made an expressive grimace. 'If my wife didn't come home one evening I reckon I'd know about it before breakfast next morning. But there! We move in different circles.

'Anyway, nothing to get too excited about if what one hears of the family is true. According to gossip, the lady herself isn't exactly Caesar's wife.'

Reed raised his massive shoulders in an expression of distaste. 'Missing persons are a pain in the neck! It's not even a crime to go missing. I've sometimes thought of having a go myself. Anyway, my chaps went through the motions. They established that Mrs Kemp spent the evening with a family called Wilson in St Mawes, playing Scrabble – a regular date apparently, every Thursday. She left in her car around midnight and according to the Wilsons she was in good health and humour. That, as far as anybody will admit, is the last time she was seen.'

'And the car?'

Wycliffe was looking at the missing woman's car. It was clumsily parked, sprawled over a little mound close to the ruin. The driver's door was open wide and the keys were in the ignition. It seemed to speak of strong emotion: panic? despair? fright? . . . 'This is definitely her car?'

'Yes, sir. And that's odd too. Some anonymous member of the public phoned the nick early this afternoon to ask whether we had any interest in a blue Estate parked on Jacob's Head. That's how we come to be here.'

'It could have been here since last night?'

Reed was dismissive. 'As far as the majority of Joe Public is concerned it could have been here since last week, or last year, that is if nobody nicked it in the meantime.'

Wycliffe said, 'What do you make of it?'

'I don't, sir. The implication is that the lady drove here with the intention of doing away with herself. It's the place for that kind of thing. As you see, the facilities are laid on, so to speak.'

A short distance from where they were standing, on the western side of the promontory, the ground fell away steeply for a dozen yards or so, a grassy slope stippled with sea pinks, ending abruptly in a sheer drop.

Two men in harnesses were crawling over the slope splayed out like crabs with a depleted set of appendages.

'They're searching for anything which might confirm that she went down that way,' Reed said. 'It's known locally as Simmond's Drop, after a chap who topped himself here donkey's years ago, but others have done it since.'

From where he stood Wycliffe could see the drop in profile; where the grass ended a forty-foot wall of rock plunged vertically into clear water.

Reed said, 'No froth, just a surge, which means the water's deep. It's all tailor-made. You don't even have to jump, all you have to do is to jog pleasantly down a nice grassy slope – admittedly, you couldn't change your mind – and let gravity do the rest. No nasty rocks to cut you up at the bottom either.'

Reed was becoming carried away by his expositions but Wycliffe was an understanding man. 'You think that's what happened to her?'

'No.' Reed sounded confident. 'It seems obvious, but somehow I'm not sold on the idea. That car . . . In my experience suicides are rarely in a state of frenetic excitement. Their behaviour can seem pretty well normal until the last minute. In fact, I think I'd be more ready to put this down as a possible suicide if she'd closed the windows and locked the doors when she left her car.'

Wycliffe agreed. 'Of course there are other possibilities; she may be wandering around in a state of shock.'

'You mean she might have been raped or something?'

'It might account for the way the car was left. Anyway, whatever has happened to her you must get on to Search-and-Rescue for a helicopter and let your chaps loose on the cliffs and adjacent fields between the Cove and Porthendel.'

He added, 'You haven't examined the car at all inside?'

'Haven't had the chance, sir. We only arrived shortly before you. One thing I did notice, the driver's seat is custom built and the controls have been modified; an expensive job. I understand she was very small.'

They worked round the car peering through the open door and through the windows. Nothing unusual. The load space between the back seats and the tail-gate appeared to be empty except for a tartan-patterned rug lying in a crumpled heap on the floor.

Wycliffe said, 'I'd like to see if there's anything under that, but watch yourself. If this is a not very clever attempt at a set-up we don't want to queer our own pitch.'

'I'll bear it in mind, sir.' Reed, very dry.

He contrived to open the tail-gate with a minimum of finger contact and lifted the rug clear uncovering a purse-handbag: lizard skin, small and elegant.

Reed said, 'Funny place to keep a handbag. Anyway, she was no champion of animal rights.' He turned to Wycliffe. 'Do we or don't we?'

'We'll chance what SOCO might say for once but

I think you should send for them and for a vehicle recovery wagon. Also, as I said, notify the coastguard and Search-and-Rescue.'

From the look on Reed's face it dawned on Wycliffe that he was taking over the case; he drew back. 'Of course, it's your case, Tom.'

All the same he had something approaching a certainty that the woman had not merely walked out, or committed suicide. The abandoned car, keys in the ignition, driver's door wide, had a contrived look; it was stagy. And the handbag, left where it was found, seemed to give his misgivings substance.

But the contents of the handbag were not immediately helpful though they might become so: a Clinique compact and lipstick, a comb, a few tissues, a foil pack of six Panadols with four tablets left, driving licence, insurance certificate, and a little case holding three credit cards, a blood-donor card, and several tenners, folded small.

Reed was studying the donor card. 'AB Rhesus negative. That puts her among a small minority for a start.'

A few minutes earlier the cliff road, the promontory, and the broad expanse of the bay with its cliffs, beaches, coves and headlands had been, for Wycliffe, holiday country; now they were rapidly becoming no more than the background to an inquiry.

Wycliffe took an Ordnance map from his pocket and spread it on the bonnet of the car. 'She must have left St Mawes by the A3078 but then it's a question of finding out which route she was in the habit of following after that. It's possible that she was seen. The chances may be slim at that time of night but it's worth looking into, especially if she stopped or was stopped on the road.

'I should watch your step on this one, Tom. If it turns out to be something more than a suicide it's sure to attract a lot of attention. For a start, get a formal statement from the Wilson people. Ask them about her state of mind; not only last evening, but during recent weeks. Have a talk with the husband and take it from there. It's just possible that this might turn into a murder inquiry.'

The cove, when he reached it, looked as peaceful as ever but, unusually, a little group of women gossiped beside the stream. They acknowledged him, but he was conscious of a change in their attitude. Did he imagine it or was he no longer just a visitor, but an intruder, perhaps a threat?

He found Helen seated outside the cottage, reading Trollope. '*The Eustace Diamonds*. I found it in the living-room cupboard along with some other books.' She looked up at him. 'So you're back. To stay, or just passing through?'

'Kemp's wife is missing.'

'I know. Mrs Tightlip told me. Even she couldn't resist passing it on. Is that what it was all about up on the headland?'

'They've found her car up there.'

'Are you going to be involved?'

'Not at the moment, anyway.'

The Kemps had their evening meal in a small room which had at one time been a boudoir for the lady of the house and was now their dining room. In it a few items had been gathered together from the rest of the house, remnants of past times. There was a sideboard, disproportionately large, a half-dozen Victorian balloon-backed dining chairs, and a Regency gate-table. On the walls there were family portraits in heavy gilt frames, so coated with the grime of years that the identity of the sitter as well as the quality of the painting were speculative.

Agnes served lamb stew from a large tureen. Roger

sat, staring at the tablecloth, and seemed surprised when Agnes passed him his plate of stew. She said, 'There's bread if you want it.'

Roger picked up his fork and in a low voice he said, 'I suppose you all know they've found Bridget's car up on the headland with her keys in the ignition.'

Isobel looked from her father to her brother. Crispin was staring at his plate and his expression seemed frozen into immobility. He looked ill.

Agnes said, 'Aren't you eating, Crispy?'

The boy started, 'What . . . ? Sorry!'

Agnes looked from one to the other, trying to fathom the minds of each, and for once she decided to say nothing.

They were late having their meal and the room was in near darkness. Roger got up and went over to the light switch. 'Let's have some light, for God's sake.'

Isobel had not touched her food. Abruptly she pushed back her chair, stood up, and left the room.

Roger watched her go. Once or twice Agnes seemed on the point of speaking but each time she thought better of it. Finally, Roger dropped his fork with a clatter and got up from his chair. 'I think I'll . . .' His voice trailed off as he shuffled out of the room with Coryk at his heels. Agnes waited for him to close the door behind him then she began to collect together the dishes, scraping the plates into a bowl. She looked at Crispin. 'Do you know what's going on?'

The boy shook his head. A moment later he said, 'I think—'

Agnes finished for him. 'Like your father, you think you'll find somewhere else to be miserable. I don't blame you, boy.'

Although it was almost dark Crispin followed his usual route to the Northern Garden until he reached the balustraded bridge; there he stopped in front of his uncle's house. The night was mild and the door stood open to the lighted room where Molly, Francis's girlfriend, sat at the table, eating something with a fork, and reading.

Crispin had always been attracted to Molly; despite the gap in their ages he felt more at ease with her than with anyone he knew. She talked to him in plain language, no holds, no subjects barred, but she never pressed him to say more than he wanted to and that was usually very little. He was never quizzed.

She looked up and saw him. 'Oh, it's you! What are you hanging about out there for?'

He went in. Molly was alone and Crispin was relieved.

'Frankie's gone to see a man about a picture – at least, that's his story. I expect there will be a few drinks in it somewhere. Cup of coffee?'

Molly pushed back her plate, took a cigarette from a packet on the table and lit it.

Crispin pulled out a chair and sat down. For more than a year he had been a regular visitor at Chylathva, usually when his uncle was not there. He would sit by the fireplace while Molly went on with whatever she was doing, listening to her line of staccato chatter and putting in a word or two if he felt like it. After a certain time, a quarter of an hour or so, he would get up and go, though sometimes he would stay to clean out the hen house or do a little weeding in Molly's kitchen garden at the back.

One morning he arrived as usual and as there was nobody in the living room he called out. Molly answered him from the kitchen. 'I'm in here.'

He found her standing in a galvanized bath, naked, washing herself.

'We aren't very strong on plumbing, but we manage . . . What's the matter? Haven't you seen a naked woman before . . . ? Anyway, now you're here you can scrub my back.'

Things had never progressed from there. Normal relations were resumed when Molly put on her clothes.

She looked at him now. 'What's the matter? Bridget not turned up yet? I shouldn't worry; Bridget can take care of herself.'

'They've found her car up on Jacob's. Keys in the ignition.'

It took Molly a moment or two to grasp the implication of the news then, 'They're not thinking she . . . God! There's a turn-up for the book. Who found the car?'

'The police.'

'They surely don't think she committed suicide? No way! That woman liked herself too much for that—' Molly broke off. 'Anyway, here's my lord and master.'

An old banger chuntered to a stop outside and a moment later Francis came in. Francis was a younger version of his brother, but either he had escaped the more extreme version of the Kemp features or they had yet to reach full maturity. He carried a framed picture under his arm which he propped against the wall. 'Morris wants to see what else I've got. He's interested . . . Hi, Crispy! Any news of Bridget?'

Molly said, 'They've found her car abandoned on Jacob's Head.'

Francis looked unbelieving. 'And Bridget?'

Crispin broke in. 'They don't know where she is.' He went on speaking in little bursts. 'There's something I've got to tell you . . . It's what I came for . . . I must tell somebody.'

Francis reached for a cigarette, lit it, and sat down. 'All right, lad; let's hear what you've got.'

Crispin started to speak in a low voice and haltingly, but he seemed to gather confidence as he went along. 'She went to play Scrabble with the Wilsons last night as usual. They say she didn't come back to the house.'

'Well?'

A momentary hesitation, as though he hadn't quite decided to talk, then, 'She did come back. Something outside woke me, I got out of bed to look and Bridget's car was parked in the alleyway right under my window.'

'Anything else?'

Again there was a delay before the answer came. 'Yes, I saw Father get in and drive away.'

Francis, deeply disturbed, glanced across at Molly and wished that she wasn't there. 'You're not hearing this.' He turned back to Crispin. 'Did you see anybody else?'

'Nobody.'

'Could there have been anyone in the car with him?'

'There could have been but I didn't see anybody . . . What do I do?'

'Have you been questioned by the police?'

'No.'

'Have you spoken to your father about it?'

Crispin made an emphatic little gesture of negation. 'No . . . No, I couldn't do that.'

'Have you told this to anybody else?'

'No.'

Francis was thoughtful. 'It's up to you, Crispy, but if it was me I'd say nothing and know nothing.'

The three of them sat in total silence, and no sound came through the open door. Outside it was quite dark; inside, the light from a low-voltage bulb over the table attracted moths but failed to reach the corners of the room.

Francis shifted vigorously in his chair. 'I've no idea what happened to Bridget but I wouldn't worry too much about what you say you saw. Your father has always had a knack for turning misfortune into something like calamity. He's never learned to leave ill alone.'

He was watching the boy with an intensity of expression which Molly had never seen before. 'Do you understand what I'm talking about?'

Crispin was subdued. 'I think so – yes.'

'Good! Then all you've got to remember is that your father is not a violent man. He couldn't be if he tried . . . Right?'

Crispin nodded.

Francis got up from his chair, 'Have you got a torch?'

'No, but—'

'I'll run you home in the car but I shan't come in.'

Isobel lay on her bed, staring up at the ceiling in the near darkness, her thoughts in turmoil. She realized that for months she had been playing with a bizarre possibility, a fantasy; now that fantasy seemed to have become real in a different and even more terrible form.

She had been deeply wounded by her mother's death. Without warning, the one person capable of reaching into the depths of her emotions had gone. And it had happened while she herself was away from home on a school trip; she felt betrayed.

'It's your mother, Isobel . . .' It was her English teacher who broke the news. 'You must be brave, dear . . . It happened in a boating accident . . . Of course, you must go home at once . . . Somebody will travel with you . . .'

Neither then nor at any time since had she shed a tear, but there was an emptiness at the centre of her being and a vague, unfocused feeling of resentment. There had been nothing to punctuate her bereavement, no opportunity to say her goodbyes, no funeral at which she could begin to formalize her grief. For five years she had lived with a feeling of helpless negation until, by chance, she made contact with the medium and somehow the idea had occurred to her that her ineffectual, bumbling father might have deliberately contrived her mother's death.

Had she ever accepted that as a real possibility? What would she have answered if she had faced herself with the question 'Do you really believe that your father murdered your mother?' The truth was that she had refused to do any such thing because she knew what the answer must be, and that answer would have deprived her of a scapegoat.

But now . . . What she had seen made anything believable. And Mayne's Closet – how did that fit in?

Saturday morning 8 May

A fine morning; a pearly mist over the sea which would melt away when the sun strengthened. Wycliffe walked on the shore half hoping for another encounter with Harvey but aware of his own ambivalent position if the doctor showed himself. However, the door of the cottage remained closed and the windows blind.

At breakfast he was subdued.

Helen said, 'You want to hang about this morning until you hear from Tom Reed.'

'I must admit—'

'Don't worry.'

He moved restlessly about the little house, living room to kitchen and back again; he stood, staring out of the window at a placid, unresponsive sea. He could hear the helicopter droning along the coast in search of Bridget Kemp's body, and once, with a sudden roar, it passed low overhead. He sat in his wicker chair and read a few paragraphs of Jean Scott's book on Kellycoryk.

All the time he wished that he was back in his office with the right to pick up a telephone and demand to know the state of play in any of the cases on hand. He

69

told himself that it was unreasonable, childish and absurd; but that was poor consolation.

Release came at two-thirty with a call from DI Reed.

'Not much to report on the search, sir; the fly-boys have been out all morning but there's nothing so far.'

'And the car?'

'Forensic are working on it but there are a few pointers: only one person's prints on the steering wheel and those are identical with prints all over the place. Some on the wheel are smeared as though the last person to drive it wore gloves. Of course, that could still have been the woman herself.'

'Anything from the rug or the load space?' Reed always saved the tit-bit (if there was one) until last.

'Yes, they found several hairs – red hairs, stained with traces of blood, adhering to the rug. They're checking the blood against the grouping on her donor card. They also found spots of blood on the floor under the rug and on the headrest of the driver's seat. They also recovered several black and white woollen fibres from the rug which could have come from the little jacket she is supposed to have been wearing.

'It adds up, don't you think, sir?'

Wycliffe had no doubt of it. Injured or dead, Bridget Kemp was carted in the back of her own car to Jacob's Head. He said, 'Obviously we need to know more about that journey which began when she left St Mawes at around midnight and ended on the headland, we don't know when.'

Reed said, 'Anyway we seem to be looking at a suspicious death, almost certainly murder – with no body.' One of Reed's profound sighs came over the line, a sigh which seemed to give expression to a weariness with the world and the ways of men. 'It's time to bring your people in, sir.

'Just one more point. I've got a statement from the Wilsons saying that Bridget has been quite her usual self recently. No crisis; no special worries as far as they could tell. It seems they've known for some time that the marriage is little more than a convention but no particular upset recently.'

After talking to Tom Reed, Wycliffe took time off to put his thoughts in order. It was almost thirty-six hours since Bridget Kemp was last seen and the evidence now pointed strongly to foul play. As Reed said, there were reasonable grounds for getting the show on the road.

He telephoned his deputy, John Scales. 'I've run into trouble, John . . . You've probably seen something of it in the reports.'

The upshot was that a van should be stationed in Porthendel until an Incident Room was established there and that DI Kersey and a DC would travel down at once. Back-up to be provided locally.

Doug Kersey had worked with Wycliffe for more than twenty years, first as a sergeant, later as a DI.

'And Lucy Lane, how's she fixed?'

'Lucy's been preparing papers for the CPS on the Union Street stabbing, but if she's through with that she could join the team. I'll check with her.'

'Well, when she's available . . .'

Wycliffe was beginning to relax, to feel in control of the situation. It was strange, his whole attitude had changed; gone was the air of diffidence which belonged to his off-duty persona and in its place was a certain appearance of authority which went with the job, like a parson's collar.

Helen noticed it and said, 'Holiday's over.'

It was early evening when the message came through that an Incident Van was parked in an open space behind the square and that DI Kersey, DS Lane, and a DC were there, ready for a briefing if that was convenient. Arrangements had been made for their accommodation in the village.

The disappearance of Bridget Kemp had at least taken on the trappings of a real case and it was time for him to behave accordingly; even so, he left his car outside the cottage and set out to walk to the village. He wanted to get his thoughts into some sort of focus. As usual they were vague, and peripheral. He was trying to imagine what it must be like to *be* Roger Kemp, a lineal descendant of four hundred years of Kemps, and heir to the family estate, that decaying house in a wilderness which was Kellycoryk.

He thought how strange it must feel to be living in the same house, using the same rooms, even perhaps the same furniture as your ancestors had done for nearly two hundred years, and then to have next door the ruins of another house in which their ancestors had lived for more than two centuries before that.

If that had been his background, what would his response have been to the threat of dispossession? Resignation? Or a desperate resolve to fend off that moment when the break would come, a determination not be the last Kemp in Kellycoryk? He was inclined to think that he would fight; not perhaps from courage but from fear, the fear of change.

To which category did Roger belong? And if he was a fighter, how would he fight?

Of course, money would always be the final arbiter and two wives with money of their own had disappeared in suspicious circumstances. Was it possible that this heavy, seemingly mild-mannered man had gone to the limit to preserve what was his?

It was one of those south-coast evenings when the whole of nature seemed to pause, all movement suspended; the sea was glassy, the sky windless, gulls perched on rooftops, starlings spaced themselves like well-drilled soldiers on overhead wires, and ceased their chattering. In the harbour it was the same; moored boats matched their reflections and a solitary old man sat on a bollard and stared at nothing.

Wycliffe made his way up the slope to the village; the square was deserted but although it was far from dark there were lights in the dimness of the pub and in a restaurant where he could see people at the tables.

He found the Incident Van tucked away behind the Old Curiosity Shop in a part of the village he had not yet seen. There was the school with its playground, and a small car-park adjoining. To one side of the car-park was a single storey, newish-looking building with a red-tiled roof. A sign outside read: 'Porthendel Surgery. Dr John Harvey and Dr Enid Scoles.'

The van was in position with a police Land Rover beside it. Doug Kersey's battle-scarred Escort stood next to Lucy Lane's pristine old Viva. A few sightseers had gathered, but when nothing happened they would soon go away and the van with its occupants would become part of the scene.

Quite suddenly he experienced misgivings about picking up the threads again, resuming established intimacies, taking his place once more in the hierarchy – a certain shyness after several weeks away. It was absurd, but it was real.

In the entrance cubicle a technician tinkered with the communications unit. He passed through to the main cubicle. The three were seated round the little table: Kersey, Lucy Lane, and a newcomer to the squad whom Wycliffe scarcely knew, DC Lanyon – Clive Lanyon.

Beaming, self-conscious smiles. 'Good to see you back, sir . . . You look better.' . . . 'Good to be back . . .' The ice was broken, and he sat down. It wasn't going to be too difficult. He took the plunge, sketching in the background and reviewing the facts.

'Bridget Kemp went missing on Thursday night, returning from a visit to friends in St Mawes. The disappearance was reported by her husband on Friday morning and on Friday afternoon her car was found abandoned on Jacob's Head, near here. On the face of it she, like others before her, had thrown herself over the cliff known as Simmond's Drop . . .

'There are reasons against that. The main one is that SOCO have found hairs and bloodstained fibres in the back of her car which strongly suggest that injured, or dead, she was confined there . . .'

The exposition continued for about fifteen minutes and included a succinct account of the people involved and of their relationships. DC Lanyon made the occasional note, Kersey seemed to be asleep, and Lucy Lane merely listened.

When Wycliffe had finished, Kersey, chafing at the constraints which the cubicle imposed on his length, stretched his arms above his head and yawned. He summed up in true Kerseyish style: 'So we've got a suspected murder with no idea where or how it happened, and no body. We're not sure if she went into the water or whether she didn't, and, if she did, whether her body will ever be recovered.'

Wycliffe was used to this. 'All quite true, Doug, and just a few of the questions I want answered.'

Lucy Lane, always one to think before she spoke, asked, 'What's the husband like?'

Wycliffe realized with a slight shock that he couldn't begin to answer the question. He said, 'You'll have to meet him.'

DC Lanyon, like any sensible new boy, said nothing until he was asked to, then he was enigmatic. 'First time round, sir, again there was no body, but there was no suspicion of violence either, not in police circles, anyway. Though others made up for it.'

Wycliffe's knowledge of Lanyon was scanty,

derived from official assessments and a couple of interviews: thirty-three, married with a daughter, good record, resourceful and quick thinking. Lanyon spoke slowly, with a slight drawl and in appearance he bore a striking resemblance to the Prince of Wales. Wycliffe wondered if he was cultivating the voice and manner to match.

'What do you mean, by "First time round"?'

'With the first Mrs Kemp, sir. When she had her boating accident I was in uniform – community policing in St Mawes.'

'Are you saying that there was a lot of talk?'

'Just that; there was no evidence to back it up, but everybody knew that the Kemps were on their beam ends and that Mrs Kemp's money would have kept the ship afloat a bit longer. From what you've just said it seemed possible that history might have repeated itself.'

'You were concerned in the original investigation?'

'Such as it was, sir, the ordinary police inquiry into the circumstances surrounding such a death.'

'Were you satisfied with the inquiry?'

'As far as it went, and there was no evidence that would have justified taking it further. There was no inquest because the body was never found.'

Wycliffe considered, and reached a decision. There had been two Mrs Kemps; it was becoming increasingly clear that the second had died by violence, while the first was lost in an accident which at the time had aroused gossip, if not actual suspicion.

He turned back to Lanyon. 'So your job is clear; you pick up where you left off six years ago. There must be something in the files, obviously you start from there but go over the ground until you're in a position to reconstruct all that happened on that day. If you need help, ask for it. Report to Mr Kersey.'

They could hear staccato bursts from the

communications unit in the next compartment. It was beginning to feel like home and Wycliffe was getting into his stride.

'Tomorrow is Sunday; you've got a chance to settle in and get to know the terrain, and we shall get down to business on Monday. A WPC from sub-division has been assigned to the case and she will work mainly with you, Lucy. In the first instance I want you to concentrate on the two young people, Isobel and Crispin.'

He turned to Kersey. 'Tom Reed's people are going over the route Bridget took on Thursday night in case she was seen, but I want you in on that and I think we'd better get Fox down.' Fox was the scene of crime officer attached to the squad.

'It seems established that she started that trip alive and driving her car, but ended it injured or dead in the back. Where and when did the change take place? Did she return to the house? Kemp has told Reed that she did not, but we need more than his unsupported assertion.'

Kersey muttered, 'You can say that again, sir.'

'All right, but this is the point, whatever Kemp says, in getting to the headland the car must have passed through the village and at that time of night the place isn't exactly alive with traffic, so there's scope.'

Kersey nodded. 'Point taken. Anything else?'

'Yes, you're going to need extra hands. Let me know the score and I'll arrange it.'

Chapter Four

Sunday/Monday 9/10 May

Sunday was a fallow day. Helen went to church at St Endel and Wycliffe mooned about the cottage and cove. Officially the team was off duty; there is a limit to permissible overtime on a case where murder has not been conclusively established. In the evening they walked on the cliffs and went early to bed.

On Monday morning, an early breakfast.

Helen said, 'So you're definitely back in business.'

'It looks like it. I'm sorry.'

She grinned. 'Liar! Anyway, I expect I shall be able to amuse myself. But don't let it get you down; you're still officially convalescent.'

The atmosphere in the little living room was gloomy; the wind had backed around to the south-west and freshened, ripples on the shore had become waves and the sound of their breaking reached into the cottage as a murmurous background.

The telephone rang and DI Reed's voice boomed, 'It's possible that your body has been found, sir.' (Wycliffe noted that he had acquired ownership.) 'Not far down the coast from where you are. The report comes from a retired coastguard so he should know what he's talking about. Out for his dog-walking morning stroll he spotted the body, trapped between rocks at the foot of a cliff, an inlet known as Grant's Cellar. Of course there's no certainty that it's the

Kemp woman but our people have to respond as they would to any report of the kind.

'Apparently land access is difficult so there's a small team, with a doctor, going round by boat from Porthendel. Sergeant Conway is in charge and they should be leaving harbour within the hour. I thought you should know, sir.'

Good old Tom. Always the diplomat. Translated, it meant, 'This one is ours until it turns out to be Bridget Kemp but it's up to you if you want to put your oar in.'

Wycliffe tried the little hotel where Kersey and company were staying but they had already left and he spoke to Kersey at the Incident Van.

'Sub-division have it organized but we'd better be prepared to take over.'

'You're joining the party, sir?'

'If I can make it in time.'

Helen said, 'So you're off already. According to the forecast it's going to be windy so watch out for yourself and wear your waterproofs.'

Wycliffe drove over the cliff road to the village and parked on the quay along with several other vehicles including a patrol car. A small group of spectators created an air of expectancy. The tide was ebbing, almost half-gone, and the surface of the water in the little harbour rose and fell in regular undulations so that Wycliffe wondered what it would be like outside.

'DS Conway, sir.' Wycliffe knew him of old; six foot three, curly fair hair, and a large pink, amiable face. 'We've got a good boat, the *Dorothy*, and a good boatman, a chap called Matty Choak. He and his mate have had experience of this sort of thing—'

Conway was interrupted by the arrival of the doctor, a middle-aged man, an outdoor type, smoothed and weathered like driftwood. He came towards Wycliffe, hand held out. 'Sanders, police surgeon. We met once on a Home Office course. They pick on me for jobs like this because I do a bit of sailing. Evidently it qualifies me for retrieving dead bodies from inaccessible shores at inconvenient hours.' He broke off. 'Is it the Kemp woman?'

'That's what we want to find out.'

The doctor nodded. 'Odd business. Odd family.'

As they pulled away from the quay the church clock at St Endel chimed the half-hour, half-past nine, and the strokes carried fitfully on the breeze. Already spectators were gathering in little groups.

Matty Choak was at the tiller; lean and cadaverous, a man of very few words. He was assisted by a little fat chap, who seemed to wear a permanent grin as though in compensation for his chief's taciturnity.

'Grant's Cellar; is that it?' Matty demanded of the sergeant.

'Just below Kellycoryk Cove.'

This was received with a nod.

In addition the boat party comprised a constable, and two men from the mortuary service who had amongst their gear a light stretcher which folded into a surprisingly small bundle.

The south-west wind created quite a swell and the old launch, broad-breasted and truculent, took it on her port bow, punching into the waves and shedding sheets of water inboard. Wycliffe had a love affair with the sea not shared by his balancing organs and he wondered whether he was going to disgrace himself.

It was not far; within a short time they were off Kellycoryk. The little cove, its grey-brown cottages with lichen-covered roofs looked like a picture postcard. Ahead the low coastline of mainly friable cliffs stretched away into the mist. The three-hundred foot platform of the Nare, no more than a couple of miles away, was a vague blur between sea and sky.

Soon they were nosing into Grant's Cellar and shelter. The Cellar, a shallow cove like an amphitheatre, was backed by shelving cliffs, girdled by gorse in flower. To the west the cove was bounded by a small promontory, a crumbling cliff, with a tumble of ominous looking tide-washed rocks at its foot.

At a signal from Matty the fat man eased back the motor and the *Dorothy* cruised more slowly towards the maze of half-submerged rocks. Two walkers, a man and a girl, watched from the cliff top. As the boat edged closer three or four herring gulls rose screaming and wheeling in the air.

Matty said, 'The bastards have just found her, in a few minutes they'd have been here by the score.'

Wycliffe could see a pale form, apparently stranded in a shallow gully between two rocks now clear of the retreating tide. Even at a distance the red hair was unmistakable.

Another signal, the engine was knocked out and, rising and falling with the surge, they were gliding between the blackened rocks. When it seemed that they must go aground, the fat man put the motor briefly into reverse before knocking it out again so that they came almost to rest within a few yards of the rocky shore. During the approach nobody had spoken a word.

The mortuary men stood up, steadying themselves against the movements of the boat. Matty said, 'I want one of you with me, and bring that stretcher. Take your shoes off; you're going to get more than your feet wet.'

He removed his sea boots and, barefoot, clambered over the side. The surging water reached almost to his waist. 'Hand me the stretcher and grab hold of my arm . . .' The younger of the mortuary men managed it without much difficulty. 'Watch your step, the bottom's uneven and slippery.'

80

The two men waded ashore then picked their way over or between the slippery rocks to the body and the boat party watched while, with infinite care, the dead woman was lifted on to the stretcher and covered with a plastic sheet. The return journey took longer, and at one point the fat man let in his engine and drew the launch back a yard or two from the shore.

At last the two men reached the boat and the stretcher was eased over the gunnel and laid on the bottom boards of the launch.

Matty said, 'Poor little woman, there was nothing to her.' Then, 'Let's get out of here, boy!' And with the engine in reverse they drew away into clear water. Wycliffe felt redundant.

Dr Sanders looked at Wycliffe, who nodded. An early medical opinion could be important as post-mortem changes are speeded up when a body is transferred from water to air. The plastic sheet was drawn back.

Wycliffe, though familiar with death in many forms, was always moved, perhaps by the awareness of mortality that is in all of us. Bridget Kemp's body (there could be no doubt that it was hers) was still clothed, and the fact had probably contributed to its early recovery. The clothing corresponded with the description given to the police: a black and white hound's-tooth jacket (which was buttoned at the front) and a white skirt which, surprisingly, was still on the body. But there normality ended; there were no shoes, and the tights had been reduced to threadwork while the soles of the feet and palms of the hands were white and thickened. The face, neck and legs had suffered from abrasion as well as from attacks by fish, crustacea and molluscs.

With a following wind the going was easier and Sanders crouched to examine the body, making notes as he worked, and by the time he got to his feet they were off Kellycoryk on the return trip.

'She hasn't been in the water more than two or three days; it's just possible that she died of drowning but I think not. There is significant injury to the base of the skull, in my opinion, aggravated rather than caused by bites. There is too much swelling to decide the nature of the original injury but it could have been the cause of death.'

'A blow?'

'A blow which broke the skin – possibly; but you'll have to wait for the post-mortem. In other words, I can't tell you much, but you probably didn't expect me to.'

Matty snapped, 'Isn't somebody going to cover the poor woman up?'

His only other remark came as they were passing through the heads into the harbour: 'Good thing we got her when we did. Wind's backing an' there's rain and a blow on the way.'

It seemed that half the village must be on the quay to see them come ashore. Wycliffe recognized the innkeeper among them. The body, now decently covered, was carried up the steps and placed in the mortuary van.

Kersey was there. 'So it was her.'

Wycliffe said, 'See that Conway deals with the coroner, arranges for the ID, and gets the body across to Franks for the autopsy.'

'What did Sanders think?'

'That she didn't drown. Where's Lucy Lane?'

'At the van with the WPC from sub-division, waiting to know if this changes her programme.'

'No. Let her break the news officially to the family, then she can carry on with her interviews there. By the way, Fox should arrive soon and I want you to use him in tracing that car journey. I'm going back to the cottage to get out of this wet gear and I'll see you later at the van. What are you grinning at?'

'I was thinking that your break has done you good, sir.'

Two reporters tried to waylay Wycliffe but he referred them to Kersey and drove off along the waterfront.

Sub-division's contribution to the team joined Lucy Lane in the Incident Van; a WPC called Milly Rees. Lucy had worked with her before but that was five years ago when Milly was new to the job. Now she was an old hand.

Lucy said, 'Our brief is to break the news at Kellycoryk then interview Crispin and Isobel, the son and daughter by his first wife.'

In the car Lucy said, 'How's it going then?'

'So so. Nobody's straining themselves to give me a shove up the ladder, but you're in the same boat by the look of it, Sarge.'

'You intend to make a career of it?'

'Five years must mean something. Perhaps I'm waiting for some guy with money to fall for me. You mightn't think so but qualified candidates are thin on the ground. Anyway, I manage with what comes along.'

Lucy listened with mixed feelings. Once she had had no doubts but now, with relatives beginning to treat her like a maiden aunt, and with a growing addiction to hot-water bottles, she sometimes wondered.

She said, 'You haven't changed, Milly.'

And Milly said, 'Snap!'

As they turned into the drive at Kellycoryk a sudden gust of wind brought raindrops splashing on the windscreen and contorted the laurels on either side. By the time they reached the house it was raining hard.

Agnes Kemp opened the door to them. She looked haggard.

'Miss Kemp? I am DS Lane; this is WPC Rees.'

Agnes seemed almost indifferent. 'I heard they've found her.'

'Yes, Mrs Kemp's body has just been recovered from a cove a little way down the coast. Would you prefer to tell your brother before we talk to him?'

'No, he knows already. He's in with his books, as usual . . . This way.'

Milly muttered something as they followed Agnes down a short passage off the hall. Agnes pushed open a door and said, simply, 'The police.'

In the large, dimly lit room, Roger sat at a table littered with papers and books, and in the midst of it a black cat, roused from sleep, turned on them a suspicious green-eyed gaze.

Roger removed his spectacles and looked up at them, blinking. His eyes were vague, as distrustful as the cat's, though less threatening. His cheeks were pale and flabby.

Lucy showed her warrant card. 'This is WPC Rees and I am DS Lane. I gather you've already heard the news.'

Kemp said nothing and Lucy went on, 'Your wife's body was found stranded in the little cove known as Grant's Cellar, just west of here.'

Kemp was apparently unmoved. He seemed to be communing within himself and he muttered, 'Grant's Cellar.' He looked up, as though realizing that some explanation was called for. 'Elias Grant was a notorious smuggler of the seventeen-nineties and that cove is where he used to bring his stuff ashore. In the end he got himself shot in a fracas with the Revenue men.'

Lucy, at a loss, said, 'May we sit down?'

'What? Yes, pull up some chairs. So it's like I thought.'

'What did you think?'

'That my wife killed herself. I said so to the policeman who came here when they found her car.'

Heavy velvet drapes and the book-lined walls absorbed much of the light which came from the windows on this grey day. Leather-bound volumes which were probably never opened crowded the shelves. Undoubtedly some of them were valuable but they were as much a part of Kellycoryk as its bricks and mortar. Books and ledgers, plans and maps, letterbooks and boxes of documents were piled on the floor.

Lucy had an odd feeling that the whole place, and Kemp with it, was caught in a limbo between past and present, without a future. She made an effort to rid herself of a growing sense of malaise.

'Do you know of any reason why your wife might have taken her own life?'

He thought about that. 'No, but why else would she drive to the headland and leave her car like that? In any case her body has been found.' The brown eyes sought the policewoman's as if in an appeal to reason.

Lucy was about to speak but Kemp forestalled her, his manner suddenly querulous. 'I'm not going to identify her; John Harvey can do that; he's a doctor.'

Lucy tried to conceal her distaste. 'I've no doubt that will be acceptable to the coroner. Now, Mr Kemp, I have to tell you that there are features connected with your wife's death which require investigation.' Lucy at her starchiest.

The heavily lidded eyes opened wide. 'Investigation? But surely it's obvious; she killed herself.'

'The post-mortem will tell us more, but there are indications that it may not be so straightforward. You will be kept fully informed but in the meantime we need to talk to those who knew her best; her family, friends, and business associates.'

Kemp was becoming uneasy. 'She had no family apart from me, my sister and my two children.'

'But surely, your brother Francis is a near neighbour?'

'Francis? What has he got to do with it? Bridget had no connection with him . . . None!'

He was gathering together the collection of papers in front of him into what could only have been a meaningless heap, and he disturbed the cat.

Lucy, with instructions not to put on pressure at this stage, was soothing. 'Just one question, then perhaps we could have a word with your sister. I think you told Inspector Reed that you only realized that your wife was missing at breakfast on Friday morning?'

He nodded. 'That's right.' For some reason the question seemed to give him confidence. 'Like many couples these days we do not share a bedroom.' It was as though a child, stumbling through a recitation, had suddenly come upon more familiar lines.

'So you don't think she returned here that night?'

'No, of course not.'

'Well, thank you . . .'

Kemp was already on his feet. He opened the library door and, as he did so, Lucy glimpsed a dark-haired girl – Isobel, presumably – hurrying off down the passage. Her father must have seen her but he gave no sign. He turned to the two policewomen. 'I'll fetch Agnes,' and he followed his daughter towards the back of the house.

They waited in the hall. The black and white tiled floor was patterned with cracks and in need of scrubbing, the oak panelling was coated with the grime of years, but the cantilevered spiral staircase with its wrought-iron balustrade still conveyed something of the elegance which had once belonged to Kellycoryk.

Milly muttered, 'The Munsters at home.'

Kemp was gone long enough to make Lucy think that Agnes had required either briefing or persuading. When she came she was alone and inclined to be aggressive. 'You wanted me?'

'We wanted a word with you and with your nephew and niece.'

'Isobel has just gone out.'

'And Crispin?'

'He's moping in his room, poor lad. Not like him at all; he's usually out there working long before now but he's taken all this to heart.' Her expression had softened in speaking of the boy.

'May we have a word with you first?'

She hesitated. 'All right. You'd better come to my room.'

Agnes's room, a bed-sitter on the ground floor, was sizeable but crowded with furniture like a store. There were good pieces, obviously gathered together from other rooms, and among them a grand piano. ('That was Julia's.') There were shelves of books and a television to show how Agnes spent her free time.

She glanced over her room and seemed to think that some comment was needed. 'I bring things in here to rescue them. At least it's dry, and I keep the room more or less warm.'

She found them seats, and sat down herself. 'So she's dead. I suppose you'll think I'm callous and perhaps I am. I wished her no harm but I'm not going to pretend that I'm heartbroken. You think she killed herself?'

'From what you know of her would you think that likely?'

Agnes hesitated. 'I don't know. We lived in the same house but we had very little to do with each other outside basic housekeeping.'

'Would you say that she was an unhappy woman?'

'I wouldn't say one way or the other. My guess is

87

that she lived that part of her life which mattered to her most away from here altogether.'

'In her business?'

'I suppose so, that and other things. Anyway, she didn't spend time with the family except at meals. When she was home she was mostly in her room.'

Not surprisingly, Agnes was being cautious.

Lucy looked across at the bed; a single, slatted oak, from the twenties. 'Obviously you sleep in this room. Do you mind telling me when you went to bed on Thursday night?'

'Between ten and eleven, as usual. I get up early.'

'Did you hear anything during the night – a car, footsteps, anything?'

'No. One thing I can do is sleep.'

'So Mrs Kemp could have returned here from St Mawes at, say, half-past twelve or later without disturbing you?'

'She could've done, but it doesn't look as though she did, does it?'

Lucy was beginning to respect Agnes. 'Just one other point. My colleagues and I have to talk to all members of the family, including your brother, Francis. Can you put us in the picture there? I mean, I know he lives on the estate but I've no idea where, and I know he's living with somebody, but that's about all.'

Agnes's smile was enigmatic. 'Francis! Yes, well . . . Anyway, you can get to their place through the estate on foot but with a car you have to go to Porthendel then, halfway up the hill to St Endel Churchtown there's a track into the woods that leads to Chylathva where they live – I'll spell it for you.' And she did.

'An odd name. Does it mean anything?'

'In Cornish it means "House of Murder" because there's a story attached to the place about a chap who used to encourage visitors only to chop them up and

88

bury them under the floor. It was Francis who dug up the old yarn and revived the name. God knows why, but that's Francis.'

'Thanks.' Lucy allowed herself a mild joke. 'I'll tell our people to watch out for themselves. Perhaps we could have a word with Crispin now?'

'If you must. As I said, the boy's upset. Anyway, his room is upstairs, turn right, and the last door on your right, just past the back stairs.'

At least Agnes wasn't making difficulties.

They climbed the spiral staircase and walked along a broad corridor. Everywhere there was evidence of neglect, of dust and damp and decay. A narrow, steep staircase on their right led down, presumably to the kitchen area; beyond it there was another door.

Lucy knocked and a voice said, 'What is it?'

They entered the room which was small and cheerless. A single bed, a cupboard, a table and chair, and homemade shelves stacked with books and magazines. What was left of the available wall space was covered by photographs pinned to a cork base.

As they went in the boy got up from the bed. 'I'm sorry; I thought it was my sister.'

'I'm DS Lane and this is WPC Rees.'

Crispin stood up and looked vaguely at the single chair. 'I'm sorry.'

Milly, always equal to such occasions, said, 'Don't worry, boy, I'll sit on the bed beside you.'

Lucy told him of the recovery of his stepmother's body and of the impending post-mortem. He listened with no change of expression in his soft brown eyes, but he said, 'We always called her Bridget.'

'Oh, yes. I understand. Now, there are a few questions we have to ask you . . .'

Crispin waited, apparently unruffled.

Lucy got up from her privileged chair and went to the window which overlooked the alleyway between the east end of the house and the back yard. 'I understand that Bridget often returned late at night. I suppose she kept her car in the yard?'

'In a sort of lean-to shed like the others, yes.'

'Did the sound of the car sometimes wake you?'

'Sometimes – yes.'

'And on the night she disappeared?'

Crispin did not answer. He was seated on the edge of his bed, leaning forward, his hands clasped between his knees. He was very pale. Milly, at his side, watched him with compassion. 'Get it off your chest, boy.'

He turned to look at her, his expression oddly sagacious, so that momentarily their roles seemed to be reversed. He said at last, 'I didn't hear it arrive but I heard it leave.'

'It woke you?'

'Something did, some noise down in the alleyway—'

'What time was it?'

'It was half-past two; I looked at my little clock.'

'Go on.'

'I got out of bed and looked out of the window. The car was parked with the driver's door wide open but, as I watched, Bridget reached out from the driving seat and pulled the door shut. The engine started and the car was backed away to the front of the house where I couldn't see it any longer but I heard it drive away.'

'You say Bridget reached out to shut the door. It couldn't have been anyone else?'

A small frown. 'Well, it was her car and I thought it was a woman's arm, that's all I can say.'

'Did you form any conclusion or make any guess about what was happening? I mean it must have struck you as unusual for Mrs Kemp to arrive home, then drive off again in the middle of the night?'

The boy considered the question. 'Well, I didn't think about it. Bridget had her own life and very often she didn't tell anybody where she was going or what she was doing.' He added with a faint smile, 'I suppose as a family we are all a bit like that.'

'And when the car was found on the headland, what did you think then?'

'I thought that she must have killed herself.'

'Do you still believe that is what happened?'

'Yes.'

'Did you have any reason to think that she might do such a thing?'

'No, but I didn't know very much about her. I mean she had another life quite separate from her life with us.'

'Did you mention this to your father or to anyone when it was known that your stepmother was missing?'

'I don't think I did. I mean, her car was missing too, so it seemed obvious that she had gone off in it.'

'But surely you must know her better than you say. You've lived in the same house with her for over two years.'

'We had nothing to do with each other.'

A conversation stopper.

Lucy was looking at the photographs pinned to the walls. 'Are these all of Kellycoryk as it used to be?'

'Yes.'

Some of them were so faded as to be almost unrecognizable but there were enough to show that Kellycoryk must at one time have ranked with the finest of the county's gardens. Every photograph was neatly labelled with the location and date, and where there were figures their names were listed.

Milly said, 'Doesn't it make you feel a bit sad to have these around you all the time?'

'No.'

There seemed little more that could be said. Time to report back.

Outside, Milly said, 'Poor boy; he looks like one of

the undead in search of a nice unoccupied coffin. And that room! It's more like a cell.'

Lucy said, 'I'm not so sure,' but she did not say what she was unsure about. She spoke to Kersey on the car radio.

Kersey was emphatic. 'Obviously what the boy said is vital. It shows the car was back in Kellycoryk before being driven to the headland. Get him to come in and make a statement, Lucy. Kid gloves.'

When Wycliffe returned to the van he found Kersey with a 1:25000 Ordnance Survey map spread on the table. 'What's this in aid of?'

'I had a call from Tom Reed. His chaps have reports of two sightings on Thursday night which could be interesting. Take a look.'

Kersey's blunt forefinger indicated a junction labelled Tippett's Shop. 'It's about eight miles from St Mawes and less than four from Kellycoryk. A resident says that a dark-blue estate passed through there between quarter and half-past twelve.'

'Could well have been her. I suppose it's something. You mentioned two sightings . . .'

'Yes, and the other is more interesting in a way.' Kersey's finger travelled further along the narrow road for something more than a mile and stopped at a junction with a little patch of green. 'A small copse. It's called Hendra Croft and it seems there's a bit of a lay-by where you can pull off the road. It's less than three miles from the cove.'

'So?'

'A motorist says he saw an estate car, probably blue, make unknown, parked without lights there at around one o'clock in the morning. Thought nothing much about it – a couple having fun. The car's lights came on just after he'd passed and he thinks the car pulled out behind him but he's not sure of that.'

'What have you done about it?'

'Fox arrived and he's now at Hendra Croft looking for any traces that might have been left in the lay-by. I suppose it's a forlorn hope after all this time but worth a try.'

Isobel drifted into the cottage living room where John Harvey was making a scratch meal from a mug of soup and a chunk of wholemeal bread. She dropped two or three novels on the table. 'I've brought your books back. Is that your lunch?'

'What does it look like?'

She moved over to the bookshelves and stood with her back to him. 'I suppose you've heard?'

'Yes. They want me to identify the body; I think your father must have refused, not that I blame him. Perhaps they didn't ask him. Anyway, did you want something? I've got to go to Truro for the ID, then I've got surgery at three.'

Harvey watched her as she removed a book from the shelves, leafed through the pages, and returned it. He saw a strip of bare back as she reached upwards. She was young and lithe, and supple – appealing, and she knew it. Always playing with fire. Bringing things to the brink then dodging. And always trying to prove herself; where no tension existed Isobel felt driven to create it.

She said, without turning round, 'They're up at the house now, two females, talking to Crispin, I think; that or searching her room. They wanted to talk to me but I escaped.'

'You'll have to face it sooner or later.'

'Do they know how she died?'

'They didn't say, but that's what the post-mortem is for.'

'Do they think Father killed her?'

Harvey was roused. 'For God's sake, Issy!'

'Somebody did.'

'Leave it to the police. Just answer the questions you're asked.'

'Is that what you're going to do? It might be difficult for you.'

He pushed away the remains of his meal and stood up. 'What are you after now?'

She looked him up and down. 'You must be quite a weight on top of a girl, Johnny. I felt sorry for poor Bridget sometimes, but perhaps you let her go on top? It must have been like grappling with a little red monkey.'

At the door she turned. 'Don't worry; I shan't tell.'

Kersey came in from the communications cubicle with Lucy Lane's message. 'I told her to bring the boy in to make a formal statement. If he's telling the truth we've got the car, at two-thirty in the morning, driving away from Kellycoryk, probably with a woman at the wheel.'

Wycliffe said, 'So if the two reported sightings on the road were of Bridget's car, the provisional timetable is, it leaves St Mawes at around midnight; it's seen at Tippett's Shop, eight or nine miles from St Mawes, between a quarter- and half-past twelve, and again at Hendra Croft at about one. Then at two-thirty it's being driven out of Kellycoryk.'

'By a woman?'

Wycliffe nodded. 'I'm inclined to ask, which woman? Anyway, if all these reports apply, there's a lot of time to be accounted for.'

By one o'clock, after his sea trip, Wycliffe was feeling hungry and decided on the pub. He could probably have had lunch at the cottage but he had worked himself into the feel of things and he did not fancy being wrapped in cosy domesticity just yet. Matty

Choak had been right about the weather; as Wycliffe and Kersey left the van the wind was blowing curtains of rain over the village.

There was the usual lunchtime cluster around the bar and several of the tables were occupied but they found a table for two in a corner by the serving hatch.

Already the landlady was treating him like a regular. 'So you've brought a friend. It's fish today – hake. A very good fish if it's cooked properly and you'd better make the most of it before the French and the Spaniards get away with the lot.'

Kersey said, 'A nice drop of bitter to go with it and I shan't complain.'

When they were settled and Wycliffe was brooding over hake snatched from the very jaws of thieving continentals, Kersey said, 'Why would this woman, driving home alone late at night, pull off the road and cut her lights? Because she felt ill? To pick somebody up?'

Wycliffe said, 'There's a different question. We know that somewhere along the line she was attacked, and, alive or dead, her body was bundled into the back of her car. Where did it happen? Possibly at Hendra Croft, perhaps at Kellycoryk. But the boy's evidence suggests that she was still alive when the car was driven away from the house.' Wycliffe took a mouthful of fish with a little spinach. 'This is good! Plenty of dill in the sauce.'

Kersey said, 'I don't believe that boy.'

Wycliffe cleared his mouth and took a sip of his lager. 'Neither do I.'

Chapter Five

When they returned to the Incident Van after lunch the SOCO van was parked nearby and DS Fox was waiting for him. Although he had worked with Fox for several years Wycliffe had never achieved the same rapport with him as with other members of the team. Fox was very tall and thin, he had an inherent stoop, and a protuberant nose so that he looked rather like a choosy bird in search of a worm of which he could approve. But within defined limits he was good at his job.

'I was lucky to get there before the heavy rain. The ground was fairly soft already and there was a certain amount of grass, but there were two identifiable tyre marks where the wheels on the nearside were off the road.'

Fox could not be hurried but his story confirmed the likelihood that Bridget Kemp's car had been parked in a lay-by at Hendra Croft.

'Two wheels were on the soft ground and left impressions of the tyres. I've checked the tracks against the tyres on her car and while there are no absolutely convincing distinguishing features, there's good agreement. Of course it's nearly four days since the car was seen there; if I'd been—'

'Anything else? Footprints? Signs of a struggle?' Wycliffe tried to hurry him.

'There was trampled grass and the imprint of a small high-heeled shoe, probably size three.'

'It's all on record?'

'Of course, sir. I have a cast of the print and all the photographs will be in my report.' Fox on his dignity. 'I've also taken a surface skim which can be examined in the lab just in case there are traces of blood.' Fox was thorough.

Was this, then, the scene of the crime? If so, what had happened later at Kellycoryk?

A small high-heeled shoe. Probably Bridget had worn high-heels to make her seem taller. It was easily checked against the description Reed had put on file. The grass had been trampled. A struggle?

Like Poirot, Wycliffe should have been 'given furiously to think' but furious thought was not in his line. He liked to accumulate images and impressions and to allow them to form patterns in his mind. He remembered passing that copse -- wind-battered hawthorn, or was it hazel? He could visualize the Mondeo parked just off the road in the darkness, then caught in the headlights of the approaching car . . .

If then, the copse was the scene of the crime, why had Bridget's car been driven to Kellycoryk instead of direct to the headland?

Good question.

Wycliffe thought the time had come to tackle Kellycoryk himself. He had been putting off that encounter for reasons which he did not fully understand. Lucy Lane had returned there with her WPC and he would join them.

The rain was clearing and the sun, about to break through, edged the sombre clouds with brilliance. The imposing gateposts and the laurels and rhododendrons that threatened to close over the drive reminded him of that first evening when, like a guilty schoolboy, he had drawn back into the shrubbery to watch Bridget

Kemp drive by in the blue Estate that was now acquiring notoriety in its own right.

He parked on the weedy gravel close to the front door and his ring was answered by the ubiquitous Agnes. He showed his warrant card.

'I know who you are. We've got two of yours here already.'

Wycliffe was struck by her resemblance to her brother. The heavy Kemp features, tolerable in the males, were an infliction when visited on the females, and it was not surprising if she looked on the world with a jaundiced eye.

'They're up with Isobel. Up the stairs, turn right, and it's the last door on your left.'

It suited him to join the others; he did not want to talk to Kemp at this stage. For the moment it was enough that he had arrived at Kellycoryk, the house which had so intrigued him from the moment he had first caught sight of it. He climbed the staircase from the empty, dimly lit hall, which smelt of mould, to a broad but dingy corridor where paint was peeling from the walls. Desires fulfilled can have a sour taste.

He knocked on the last door to his left. It was open a little and he pushed it wide.

'A word?'

Lucy joined him outside and closed the door behind her.

'We've just got started, sir. She's been avoiding us – always out when she's wanted. No special reason, I think; just bloody-mindedness.'

'I'll stand in for a bit.'

It was an odd little scene in the circumstances; Isobel was seated on her bed, Lucy had been sitting in the only chair, and the uniformed WPC squatted on the floor, feet tucked in, hands clasped about her knees. Leave out the uniform and it could have been almost any three young women gossiping.

'I said I'd stand in and I meant stand.'

Lucy grinned and returned to her chair.

A brief introduction, barely acknowledged, and then Lucy resumed. 'This room and that of your brother are the only bedrooms with windows that overlook the alleyway between the front of the house and the yard. We have evidence that your stepmother's car returned here on Thursday night, the night she disappeared. Your room is immediately above where it would have come in. Did you hear it?'

She hesitated. 'I almost always hear her come back. Thursday night it was a quarter-past one.'

'Did anything strike you as different from other nights?'

'You could say that. After waking me up she usually makes a mess of getting the car into her space; then you hold your breath until she slams the door. That night I heard her drive in, but the engine was cut at once and there was no door slamming.'

Wycliffe thought, Spiteful, and too talkative anyway. He said, 'This is very important, Miss Kemp—'

'Call me Isobel, that's my name.'

'All right, Isobel. Did you hear her walking away from the car?'

'No. I usually do; she wears high-heels to make her seem taller and they make a noise on the cobbles, but that night I didn't hear anything and I got out of bed to see what was happening.'

'What did you see?'

'Well, the car was just below my window; she hadn't quite made it into the yard. I could see over the roof of the car that the driver's door was wide open.' She paused before adding, 'I wondered if you got like that playing Scrabble.'

'You thought she was intoxicated?'

99

'What would you think?'

'You didn't see her?'

'No.'

'Did you see anybody?'

'No. I went back to bed and to sleep.'

'So you didn't hear the car being driven away again?'

'I don't think so; I might have done.'

'Your brother says that from his window he saw the car being driven away and he thought it was a woman's arm that reached out to close the door.'

'There you are then.'

Lucy Lane decided that it was her turn. 'How did you get on with your stepmother?'

'I didn't. I had as little to do with her as possible.'

'Any particular reason or just general incompatibility?'

'Both.'

Wycliffe was taking in details of the room. It was wildly untidy, with clothes littered over the bed and floor. There was a shelf of books above the bed, a mixed bag, ranging from obvious school texts, through Penguin classics to sci-fi and horror. But the most striking feature of the room was its one picture, a portrait in oils, the head-and-shoulders of a young woman. It was obviously a self-portrait. For a moment Wycliffe thought the sitter must be Isobel, then he realized that it was her mother. There was something compelling about the eyes even beyond that of any self-portrait; they were secretive, withholding more than they revealed.

Lucy Lane was saying, 'Will you tell us the particular reason why you did not get on with your stepmother?'

Isobel glanced at her mother's portrait before replying. 'She set out to take my mother's place.'

'But wasn't that to be expected when she married your father?'

She made an angry movement, was about to speak, then changed her mind.

'You were going to say?'

'Nothing.'

Wycliffe said, 'Is it true that you have recently been trying to get in touch with your mother through a medium?'

'Yes. Is there something wrong with that?'

'No. I merely wondered if anything in particular happened to bring this about?'

'I wanted to find out more about Mother's death . . .' She added, after a pause, 'I was away when it happened; on a school trip.'

Throughout the questioning Isobel had been sitting with her hands tightly clasped in her lap though from time to time she released one hand to sweep back her hair in a movement of either impatience or nervousness.

It was Lucy Lane who asked, 'What gave you the idea of a seance?'

The girl did not answer at once then she seemed to make up her mind. 'I got to know Teresa – a woman in the village who's a professional medium.'

Wycliffe was intrigued by the girl. She was playing a part which she had rehearsed and it was going to be difficult to discover what she was hiding, or why.

Lucy went on, 'And Teresa arranged these seances for you?'

'No, it doesn't work like that. There's a sort of group that meets regularly at Margot Sweet's house and she invited me to come.'

'When you went to these seances did you learn anything which was new to you?'

She hesitated, then stood up. 'I've had enough of this. You don't understand! You are supposed to be trying to find out what happened to Bridget. You are not really interested in my mother.'

Wycliffe intervened. 'But if I say that I am interested in what happened to your mother, would that make a difference? Remember that if there were suspicious circumstances surrounding your mother's death it would be my business to investigate them and your responsibility to help me.'

Her reaction was immediate; the mask slipped to reveal a frightened girl. 'I'm not saying that there was anything like that . . . I just wanted to know what had happened – that's all. This is something in the family. It is none of your business!'

There was no more to be said and they left her. Outside, in the corridor, Wycliffe asked, 'Which is Bridget's room?'

Lucy went to a door halfway along the corridor and pushed it open. The contrast was dramatic; a bright, airy room, part-bedroom, part-workroom, distinctively feminine yet business-like.

There was a white desk by the window, an ultra-modern computer, and filing cabinet to match. The bedroom furniture was also white: the bed, the alcove which incorporated a dressing table and mirror, the row of sliding doors which concealed a fitted wardrobe. The carpet was ivory, and thick.

'Surprising the difference money can make, don't you think?' Agnes's harsh voice; she was standing in the doorway watching them. 'I knew something must've happened to her; she wouldn't have stayed away from choice, she was too comfortable here.'

Wycliffe picked up a silver-framed photograph from the dressing table. It was the same beautiful, doll-like face he had glimpsed that first evening in the drive.

Agnes said, 'Taken a month or two back; she was always having her photograph taken, a one-woman admiration society.'

Wycliffe said, 'Did she have any men friends?'

'You mean, was there a man? I shouldn't think so. Her only chance would have been with a man who had a thing about dolls.'

Lucy was sliding the doors of the wardrobe backwards and forwards. One section was hung with dresses; another with coats, summer and winter weight; there was a rainwear section, another for skirts and short jackets, and yet another for trousers and casual wear.

Agnes said, 'She had enough to choose from. Of course, she had to have almost everything made specially, she was so small.'

Agnes was aggressive and unpleasant but Wycliffe was beginning to feel a sneaking regard for her; perhaps it was sympathy. But rarely had he come across such an instance of two women speaking of a dead relative with such spite.

He noticed four or five books on a shelf by the bed including a missal, bound in limp leather, edged and lettered in gold. 'She was a practising Roman Catholic?'

Agnes shrugged. 'She went to Mass.'

'Was she much involved with the rest of the family?'

Agnes smiled with her thin lips. 'I'd say she was more like a paying guest who knew exactly what she expected for her money. To think of her taking Julia's place!'

'You were fond of the first Mrs Kemp?'

Agnes hesitated. 'You couldn't be *fond* of Julia but she was a real woman, and she tried to make something of Roger.' A brief pause, then, 'Anyway, if you want me I shall be in the kitchen. There's still work to be done.'

When Agnes had gone Wycliffe turned to Lucy Lane. 'What's your broad impression?'

'Of the family?' Lucy considered. 'They're hardly

a family in any real sense; they live in their separate cells, physically and mentally isolated, as far as I can see. Have you talked to Roger?'

'No, I think I'll wait until I have the result of the autopsy. You and Rees had better get busy here. Lock the room when you leave and keep the key.'

It was something of a shock to come out of the gloomy hall at Kellycoryk into bright sunshine. As he drove between the gateposts he looked across the cove and saw Helen in the little garden of their cottage. It seemed a remote and different life.

He was in a strange mood. He had broken into Kellycoryk . . . It occurred to him what an absurd expression that was. But that was how he felt. His atttitude to the place was strangely ambivalent and he was still avoiding a confrontation with Roger Kemp. He felt like a boxer circling his opponent but reluctant to make contact. It dawned on him that his problem was uncertainty as to whether Roger really was his opponent or even the central figure in his investigation. In a murder case Wycliffe always started from the premise that the victim, like every other human being, had existed at the centre of a complex web of relationships and that it was in the unravelling of those relationships that an explanation of the killing must be sought. So far the process had only begun.

Which brought him to the brother. Why not take Francis next? A nebulous and enigmatic figure as far as Wycliffe was concerned. Time to bring him into focus. He had already seen the house – Chylathva, that was it! Lucy had told him it meant 'House of Murder'. The young woman he and Helen had seen there must be living with Francis.

The House of Murder . . . Buried deep in Elf Wood. Yes, well . . . He must watch out or he might be pixilated.

A message came through on his car radio asking him to ring Dr Franks. He had reached the waterfront at Porthendel so he pulled off the road on to the quay and phoned from his car.

'Charles? I thought you were recuperating.'

'I am. What have you got for me?'

'I gather there is no problem over identity so we won't go into that. As you must have seen for yourself she's been knocked about a bit—'

'Cause of death?'

'Well, she wasn't drowned. Most of her injuries were incurred post-mortem and are consistent with being buffeted by rocks and attacked by fish and other marine creatures.'

Wycliffe and the pathologist were friends of many years' standing but their encounters were always mildly abrasive. Franks, a socializer, with a fondness for women, brought out a puritanical streak in Wycliffe so that he became defensive.

Franks went on, 'I'd guess she'd been in the water four or five days—'

Wycliffe reiterated. 'Cause of death?'

'Oh, didn't I say? She was shot, Charles.'

'*Shot?*' The very last thing Wycliffe had expected to hear.

'So it seems. At any rate I found a bullet bedded in the cord between the axis and the third cervical. Seriously, she was shot through the back of her neck.'

Wycliffe gathered his wits. 'Would there have been much bleeding?'

'Not a great deal probably. No major vessels were involved. Forensic may be able to tell you something from her clothes – what's left of them. Incidentally, I'm not surprised your man missed it. The tissues around the wound of entry were swollen through immersion and he probably thought she'd had a clout there.'

'What about the bullet?'

'Small calibre, not much penetration; 6.35 or what we call a .25 Auto, something in that line anyway. Of course you can't take aim with a thing like that; it must have been fired with the muzzle touching, or almost touching the poor woman's neck. But your ballistics people will tell you more about that.'

Wycliffe was shaken though he was not quite sure why. Should the fact of the woman having been shot come as such a surprise? The truth was that he found it difficult to associate firearms with the people who, it seemed, might be involved.

'Is that it, then?'

'That should be enough to keep you busy, old chap; anyway it's all I've got. I'll let you have my report sometime tomorrow.'

Shot! And by what amounted to a toy gun. He could not get used to the idea. Yet he recalled that spattered blood had been found on the headrest of the driver's seat. Somehow, illogically, he felt that this must change his whole view of the case. Perhaps he had formulated in the back of his mind some hazy idea of the psychology of the killer and this did not fit.

He needed time to think, or rather to let his mind lie fallow so that images, recollected phrases, odd incidents would rise to the surface, making connections, patterns which dissolved and reformed. It was his nearest approach to what he regarded as logical thought.

As good a time as any to talk to brother Francis. He drove through the village and up the hill towards St Endel Churchtown. He found the track off on his left, turned in, and drove through the wood over ruts and ill-sited boulders for about two hundred yards.

And there was Chylathva seen from the other side: no gate, no fence, just a clearing in the wood; and in the middle, the four-square house, stark, with blind windows and a plank door which stood open. The whole scene straight from the Brothers Grimm.

There was a sign on a post, similar to the one he had seen on the other side of the clearing, but this one read, '*Chylathva*. Beware of Snakes in the Grass.' No mention of jackals.

Wycliffe was looking forward to meeting Francis Kemp. There was not a soul in sight; not a sound.

He left the car and walked up to the front door. It stood open into a large, low room, sparsely furnished. Opposite the door there was a granite fireplace with a grate full of grey ash, and beside it, in a rocking chair, the dark-haired girl sat motionless. One hand rested on the arm of the chair, while in the other she held a cigarette from which the smoke rose in a perfect spiral. It was more like a painting than reality; static, an instant caught in time.

He coughed, and the girl looked across at him, unconcerned. 'Haven't I seen you somewhere before?'

He held up his warrant card and introduced himself. 'I came in the hope of talking to Mr Francis Kemp.'

She got up in a vigorous movement that left the chair rocking. Older than he had first thought, up to mid-thirties; a good figure, but her features were losing their youthful moulding and becoming sharp. She wore a skimpy jumper, clinging to her body like an extra skin, and tight trousers. 'He's gone out. When I heard the car I thought he'd come back.'

'Who are you?'

She drew on her cigarette and exhaled slowly, closing her eyes against the smoke. 'I'm Molly Bishop; I live with him. What d'you want him for? Is there news of his sister-in-law?'

'Mrs Kemp's body was found this morning on the shore a little down the coast from here.'

'Drowned?'

'No.'

She stood, her cigarette poised. 'She could have been murdered?'

'We know that she was.'

'Oh, Christ! Do you want to sit down? He shouldn't be long.'

The room might have been a pleasant one: wainscoting, with unrendered granite above, and a timbered ceiling. It was neglected and smoke stained. The furniture was basic; where it was upholstered, stuffing was in evidence. The end wall was almost entirely taken up by a giant canvas, a painting of a bus queue at a request stop. The queue comprised both sexes, all ages, and a fair sample of races. Their expressions were vacant, resigned. The scene was ordinary enough, except that all the figures were naked, and looking at them recalled to Wycliffe's memory those mind-bending pictures of the Holocaust.

'Would you buy that?'

Wycliffe temporized. 'I wouldn't have anywhere to put it.'

'Neither would anybody else, but that's mostly the kind of thing the bastard paints. Of course, he's a Kemp; they're all dreamers. Frankie's thing is being a great painter. If only he'd settle for being good, he'd make a living, but like the rest of 'em he's pig-obstinate.'

'How long have you been with him?'

'Three years, but I'm a local girl.' She grinned. 'A P'rendel sprat – that's what they call us from the village. I've got a job, some mornings, some evenings, in the village pub and he teaches afternoons twice a week at the college in Falmouth. If it wasn't for that we'd be lucky to eat some weeks. I hounded him out this morning with a few of his smaller pieces to try his luck at a gallery in Truro. He shouldn't be long now but if they haven't shown any interest he'll come back pissed. He says I nag him, but if I didn't . . .'

When she stopped speaking the silence was total.

'Is it you who keeps the chickens?'

Her face lit up. 'Yes, and I've got a little allotment out the back.' She broke off. 'There he is now.'

It was a moment before Wycliffe heard a car engine and a little later an old banger spluttered gratefully to a halt, close to the window. A car door slammed and a man came into the room.

'Ah! The sheriff. I know why you're here.'

Francis Kemp was several years younger than his brother, taller and slimmer, his features were less heavy. But he was still, unmistakably, a Kemp.

'You've found Bridget's body; I heard it on the radio.'

'A radio in a pub.' From Molly.

Francis ignored her. 'You know how she died?'

Molly said, 'They say she was murdered.'

Wycliffe cut in, 'There is evidence that Mrs Kemp was intercepted while driving home from St Mawes on the night she disappeared. She was killed and her body placed in the back of her car. The car was then driven to Kellycoryk where it remained in the yard for more than an hour before being driven on to the headland where the body was disposed of.'

Francis, astride a kitchen chair with his arms resting on the back, listened, apparently incredulous. 'I can't believe this. How exactly did she die?'

'She was shot.'

'Shot?' Francis looked at Wycliffe in amazement.

'That surprises you?'

'Yes, it does. I don't know why but I can imagine Bridget being strangled or bludgeoned – but shot!'

Wycliffe said nothing but he was inclined to agree.

Francis was seemingly reluctant to drop the subject. 'May I ask what sort of gun?'

'A small-calibre pistol. Any reason for your question, Mr Kemp?'

'No, just interest.'

'I see. Did you see much of your sister-in-law, Mr Kemp?'

'As little as possible. She had a low opinion of me; in particular, because I don't pay Roger rent for this place; in general, because she disapproves of those who neither toil nor spin with obsessive enthusiasm. I tried quoting the Gospel at her but Bridget wasn't impressed by the lilies of the field as role models.'

It was hard to see this man as Roger's brother. 'How about the rest of the family? Do you see much of them?'

'Depends what you mean by the family. I drop in at the house a couple of times a week when Madam is from home. Clare pays us a visit when she feels like a bit of slumming.' A wry grin. 'But Clare's all right.' Francis yawned. 'Oh yes, and then there's John Harvey. When I feel in need of a bit of sanity I look John up – usually early in the morning.'

'Were you still living at home when Julia was drowned?'

The question, perhaps the background knowledge which it implied, seemed to surprise Francis. His answer was curt. 'No, I'd already left.'

'But you lived there for a time after your brother married her?'

'I was only nineteen and still at art college when they married.'

'And after you finished at college?'

'I lived at home until Father kicked me out.'

'How old were you then?'

'Twenty-three, twenty-four – something like that. Anyway, it was just after Mother died.'

'And when did you come to live here?'

'When Father died and Roger succeeded to the ball and chain. I must have been about thirty; I'd been bumming around London for years; Rog took pity on me and let me have this place.' A quizzical look; 'You seem very interested in me, Mr Wycliffe.'

'Background, Mr Kemp. Background . . . Have you any idea how Mrs Kemp's death is likely to affect the estate – or you for that matter?'

A faint smile. 'Good questions. I should hope it will mean a nice bit of lolly for poor old Roger, but I've no idea what the arrangements were between them. After the three years, or whatever it is, that he's been with her, he deserves something.'

'And you?'

'What's good for Roger is good for me.'

'I suppose you are familiar with the place called Hendra Croft?'

'I should be; I've lived here most of my life. It's a couple of miles out on the St Mawes road. Why?'

'It seems likely that on her way home Mrs Kemp was flagged down by someone well known to her and then assaulted.'

'Why do you say well known?'

'Because it is unlikely that a woman driving alone after midnight would stop to pick up a stranger.'

Francis nodded. 'That figures but the whole thing is incomprehensible. I mean, to shoot a woman and then drive her home in the back of her car . . . No man in his right mind would have done that. It doesn't make sense from any point of view.'

For a moment or two he was thoughtful then, abruptly, 'It could have been a woman. If a woman wants to work off a grudge she'll take any damn-fool risk.'

'Francis has a high opinion of women.' From Molly.

Wycliffe said, 'Do you have any particular woman in mind?'

Francis brushed this aside. 'No. Just a general observation on the sex.'

Wycliffe got back to business. 'I shall ask everyone connected with the family this question, Mr Kemp, so don't take it amiss. Where were you at around midnight last Thursday?'

'Tucked up in bed with Molly. I certainly wasn't at Hendra Croft laying in wait for my sister-in-law.'

It was all very smooth. Wycliffe had never met with such cheerful insouciance from a witness in a murder inquiry. Time would tell.

As Wycliffe was leaving Francis said, 'What do you think of my painting?'

Wycliffe tried to say something enigmatic. 'Does the bus ever come?'

Francis frowned. 'Of course the bloody bus never comes. What do you think is the point of the picture?'

It was after four when Wycliffe arrived back at the Incident Van. Kersey was there with Clive Lanyon.

'Lanyon's got a bit of news, sir.'

'You managed to dig out the file?'

Lanyon grinned. 'Archaeology they call it, sir. But there wasn't much in it. Most of what there was, was mine anyway. Nothing to make you think again about the incident.'

'Is that the news?'

'No, sir, not quite. Kemp had his moorings off the Percuil boatyard; they kept an eye on his craft and laid it up in the winter. I was there this afternoon and had a word with Mike Garland who runs it. He let fall something, quite casually, that didn't come out at the time. On the morning of the accident when Mrs Kemp was drowned, Kemp arrived at the yard around eleven. He had with him Clare Jordan, the woman who now runs the antique shop in

Porthendel. She's some sort of relative and, at that time, she lived at Kellycoryk and often went out sailing with them.'

'So?'

'The point is, Mrs Kemp wasn't with them. Kemp said she'd had to go to St Mawes and they were picking her up there.'

'Why didn't this come out at the time?'

'Well, sir, when you come to think of it, why should it? I must admit I never thought of questioning Garland and why should he have thought it of any importance? That sort of thing happens.'

'So what's your programme now?'

'I want to begin reconstructing that day by questioning the Kemps about Mrs Kemp's trip to St Mawes. I don't want to wade in if it's going to upset the inquiries already going on there.'

'Fair enough. Carry on, but put DS Lane in the picture and be guided by her.'

Alone with Kersey, Wycliffe said, 'Interesting. It could mean anything or nothing, but it's somewhere to start.'

Things had been happening in his absence. The village hall had been rented and was being equipped from central stores as a fully fledged Incident Room.

'You can see it from here – the slate roof, next to the school. Ready for us in the morning. And the chief wants you to ring him.'

His master's voice. Wycliffe telephoned.

Bertram Oldroyd had joined the force in the same year as Wycliffe; they came from similar backgrounds and they had much in common, including a firm but compassionate approach to policing.

'So you've managed to find yourself a job, Charles. Tell me about it.'

Wycliffe did his best.

'So this chap has lost two wives in five years. Oscar

Wilde had a word for that sort of thing. Neither died from natural causes and both had money in their own right. Seems to me the man must be a jinx, or stupid enough to think he can get away with the same thing twice. A lot of them are.'

'Anyway, you've made it your problem, Charles, and I'm not going to ask you if your break has done you any good. I'll just remind you that you've got Kersey down there; he's a good copper, so let him do most of the barking.'

Wycliffe had got what he wanted, a free hand.

He turned back to Kersey who might well have heard what the chief had said. At any rate Kersey was prompted to launch into one of his summings up, which seemed to clarify his own ideas but confuse Wycliffe's.

'Now that Franks has confirmed that the woman was murdered – not that there was ever any real doubt . . .' Kersey paused to light one of his own-rolled cigarettes, then resumed, '. . . We can assume that the scene of crime was Hendra Croft and that her body was transferred to the back of her car and driven to Kellycoryk before being dumped in the sea at Jacob's Head. But why take it to the house? Perhaps his first idea was that it should be found there, but he changed his mind later.'

Wycliffe, in an attempt to be mildly co-operative, said, 'For whatever reason, he must have handled the body twice, and though Franks says there need not have been much blood, there was obviously some, and the killer would have had a problem, working in near darkness, to avoid getting blood on his clothing. Perhaps we should follow that up. Possible suspects – what were they wearing on the night?'

Kersey said, 'Would you like to make a list, sir?'

Wycliffe grinned. 'No, I'll leave the easy bits to you, but remember women are not excluded. The dead woman was a featherweight and, if what the boy said is true, it was a woman's arm that reached out to close the car door.'

'In my opinion,' said Kersey, 'that was to protect his father.'

Chapter Six

Monday evening 10 May

After the evening meal Roger sat at his table in the library and tried to work up his most recent notes but he could make nothing of them; they might have been written in Sanskrit. He dropped his ballpoint and sat back, staring at the accumulation of papers. Coryk stirred uneasily. The house was quiet. More than that; as he listened, it seemed to Roger that it had become filled with a positive and hostile silence.

He got up from his chair and crossed to a little bank of switches near the door. He flicked two of them and a couple of rarely used ceiling lights came to life relieving the gloom with their dusty yellow radiance. It was sufficient for Roger's purpose. He stood looking up at a framed oil-painting which hung between two of the bookcases, a three-quarter-length portrait of an Elizabethan Kemp. Resplendent in his black velvet cap (with plume), white ruff, striped jerkin and short black cloak, the gentleman sat with his left arm extended to fondle a sleeping black cat curled up on a table at his side. The most conspicuous feature of the cat was a tail devoid of fur over the terminal inches.

For Roger the picture had become a sort of icon which he had contrived without difficulty to set alongside the holy pictures and statues, the paraphernalia of the church, which had captivated him as a child and remained the source of whatever emotional content his religion possessed.

Usually the picture had a sedative effect, but not tonight. He had convinced himself, against the odds, that he was in the house alone. Normally this would not have troubled him but tonight, for some reason, he could not endure it.

Coryk still curled up on the work table, watched him, sensing his restlessness.

Roger spoke quietly. 'I'm going out.' Surreptitiously, as though in fear of being detained, and followed by the cat, he crept down the passage and into the yard by the side door. It was only as he passed out of the yard, through the archway, that he felt he had made good his escape. At this point Coryk had reached the border of his territory and there he would wait until Roger returned.

It was mild and very still. In the gathering dusk, with no clear purpose except to get away from the house, he followed the stream until he reached Chylathva.

The front door was open and he could see into the lighted living room. Francis was seated at the table eating something with a spoon, and reading. That open door (they closed it only in the coldest weather) seemed to Roger to typify something fundamental in the difference between him and his brother; a difference which, secretly, made him envious.

He hesitated to make his presence known. Standing there, unseen, watching, he felt that he had some power which he would lose as soon as contact was made. He told himself that it was absurd and walked towards the door. Francis heard him and looked up. 'God, it's you! Come to collect the rent?'

There it was; the bantering reception which put him in his place. And yet it was he who made it possible for Francis to live there with his woman.

'Have a seat. How long is it since we've seen you up here . . . ? Must be months.'

Francis was eating some concoction from a large bowl, which seemed to be halfway between a soup and a stew. He cleaned the bowl with a chunk of bread which he stuffed into his mouth. Then, still chewing, he said, 'It's one of Molly's nights at the pub.'

Roger was by no means sure of what if anything he had come to say. He looked around the room and saw the giant canvas propped against the end wall; it would have been hard to miss. He looked at it vaguely, with no shred of comprehension, only puzzlement. But as far as he was concerned that applied to all Francis's work as well as to the man himself.

Francis was watching him. 'Don't you ever feel like that?'

'Like what?'

'Exposed – naked – vulnerable, waiting for something, God knows what.'

Perhaps Francis had not wanted a conversation stopper but he had found one. Roger felt threatened by the kind of intimacy to which he was temperamentally incapable of responding. So the brothers sat looking at each other across the table in silence. For both of them the encounter was difficult; there was no question of an immediate putting of cards on the table; it was more a matter of sounding out attitudes.

Francis made the first move, a conventional expression of sympathy. 'I was sorry to hear about Bridget, Rog . . . So it was murder.'

'She was shot.'

'I know. Wycliffe came to see me.'

Roger was shaken. 'Wycliffe was here? It was a sergeant and a constable who came to see me – both of them women. What did he want?'

'I suppose he was sussing us out.'

Roger was finding it difficult to sit still. 'They asked me if there were any guns in the house.'

'What did you tell them?'

'Obviously I told them there were not, that the only guns we ever had were sporting guns and that they were sold before father died.'

Francis was watching his brother with a sardonic expression. 'Tactical reticence, or a lapse of memory?'

'I don't know what you mean.'

Francis shifted irritably. 'For God's sake, Rog! You're not talking to the cops now. Wycliffe told me that Bridget was shot with a small-calibre pistol.'

For a moment or two Roger seemed paralysed then, incredulous, he said, 'He told you that?'

Francis was unrelenting. 'I was thinking of the one that used to be in that chest in what we used to call the junk room. As though the whole bloody house isn't full of junk. Have you looked to see if it's still there?'

Roger, reluctant, admitted, 'Yes, I did look and it isn't there, but it could have gone at any time in the last thirty years.'

'And I could have won the Turner Prize. Anyway, if the gun's gone, what about the cartridges? There was a little cardboard box with a yellow label.'

'I don't remember any cartridges.'

Francis was unbelieving. 'Your memory must be failing, Rog. You should eat more fish.'

Roger was on tenterhooks. 'But what you're saying would mean that it was somebody who knew about the gun and had access to the house.'

'Well? Who do you think killed her? Dick Turpin?'

Roger smoothed the plastic table-covering with the palm of his hand. 'I can't take much more of this.'

Francis stood up. 'I've got a drop of whisky I keep for special occasions.' He went into the kitchen and came back with a half-bottle, two glasses and a jug of water on a tin tray. 'Help yourself.'

When they were both sipping their drinks Francis said, 'I'm not trying to snatch the mat away, Rog, but if we don't face facts ourselves the police will soon be doing it for us.'

There was an uncomfortable silence and it was left to Francis to break it. 'It seems that Crispin heard Bridget's car return and saw it parked in the alleyway.'

Roger looked like a man under torture. He muttered, 'That's what he told the police.'

'Where were you sleeping that night?'

'I don't know what you mean.'

Francis's patience snapped. 'For God's sake, Roger, did you kill the woman?' He added almost at once, soothing, 'Don't bother to answer that, I know you couldn't kill a rabbit, but whether you like it or not you're sure to be a prime suspect.

'Now, lately, you've been kipping down on the sofa in the side-room; is that what you did on Thursday night?'

Roger nodded.

'Then all this business with Bridget's car went on outside your window. Are you saying you heard and saw nothing of it?'

Roger looked helpless. 'I think I was drunk . . .' A pause, and his voice and manner gathered conviction. 'Yes, I've taken to having a whisky or two last thing, to make me sleep, and that night I overdid it.'

Francis sat back in his chair. 'Ah, well, if that's the way you want it. There's just one more thing. Is Clare in on any of this?'

Roger was sharp. 'Clare? What do you mean? Is she *in* on it?'

Francis shook his head. 'Look, Rog, you're in hock to each other, I know that. Perhaps neither of you is in a position to rock the boat. But you know Clare, and she knows about the pistol. If she sees any advantage in dropping you in the shit she won't stop to ask herself whether she's playing according to the rules.

'All I'm saying is, keep her guessing.'

Roger had put down his glass and was staring at his brother in amazement. 'I don't know what you're talking about!'

Francis remained calm. 'Don't work up a froth, Rog, it's wasted. You've never taken me in.'

Roger got up to go, wishing profoundly that he hadn't come.

Francis saw him off. It was dark. 'I can't run you home, Molly's got the car, but I'll lend you a torch. Mind how you go.'

With the help of the torch Roger found his way back to the archway. As he entered the yard a plaintive miaow came out of the darkness and Coryk rubbed about his legs.

Wycliffe was home early for the evening meal. Helen was in the kitchen. 'I went to Truro this morning and stocked up, then I had lunch at Trelissick. The garden looked so fresh after the rain.'

A shower, then duck à l'orange, by courtesy of M & S. Not bad with a glass or two of nicely chilled Barsac.

'Are you going out? There's a promising play on the box.'

'I think I'll go out. I need a walk.'

At a little after eight he left the cottage and stood for a moment or two, hesitant, before setting out across the bridge and on to the cliff road which led to the village.

He was thinking of the two young Kemps, Isobel and Crispin. Both dark-haired and pale; by some remarkable genetic dispensation they had escaped the heavy features of the Kemps in favour of their mother's fine bone structure and delicate facial muscles. The boy in particular looked fragile – vulnerable.

What sort of time had they given him at school?

Adolescence for both of them must have been blighted in that house of gloom. Isobel had responded with aggression, and Crispin? Lucy had summed him up as 'an iceberg, seven-tenths submerged.' But icebergs are cold right through. Or are they? Wouldn't there be tremendous pressures in the middle that might raise the temperature? He had no idea; his physics had always been weak.

He could not have said whether he had set out with the intention of calling on Clare Jordan but he had arrived outside the shop. There was a light in one of the upstairs windows; he pressed the bell and stood back so that he could be seen. A moment later he caught sight of her looking down at him and shortly after that she was unlocking the shop door.

'I'm sorry to disturb you . . . Superintendent Wycliffe.'

'I know. The comforter dogs. You'd better come upstairs.' She was neither welcoming nor antagonistic.

He followed her through the stockroom behind the shop and upstairs to a room which ran the whole length of the house with a window at each end. The room was well used, the furniture, random in provenance, was worn and functional; makeshift bookshelves were crammed with paperbacks and there was a quality hi-fi and a TV. A coal fire burned in an open grate.

'These evenings turn chilly and I like to be comfortable.' She had been sitting, reading, and her book was open and face down on the arm of her chair, Iris Murdock's *A Severed Head*.

She waved him to a chair.

As she sat down and composed herself it occurred to him that she was a good-looking woman, who, while making no attempt to disguise her age, made the best of herself. Her dark hair, skilfully cut, showed streaks of grey, her features were regular and strong; a hard woman, perhaps the sort who might well prefer to see life through Murdoch's distorting mirror.

'I can guess why you are here; you want me to tell you what I can about Bridget. I heard at lunchtime that her body had been recovered. A tragedy. Unfortunately, I've had little contact with Bridget recently and I can't say that I knew her very well.'

'I think I should tell you before we go any further that her death was neither suicide nor accident, but murder.'

'Murder! But how? Who would want to—?'

'She was shot with a small-calibre pistol. As to who, that is what we have to discover, and it will help me if you can fill in some background; relationships within and outside the family, not only as they are, but as they have been in the past.'

'But why come to me?'

'Because you are a relative, and I understand that you were brought up at Kellycoryk with the Kemps. At the same time, you are probably not so deeply involved emotionally with the present tragedy as the immediate family.'

It was specious, but she was prepared to go along with it. 'I see; you evidently know my story in outline at least. To put the record straight, I am Roger's second cousin; I was orphaned at the age of six and brought up with Roger, Francis and Agnes by their parents.'

'So that you are almost like a sister to the three Kemps.'

She raised her shoulders slightly but said nothing. 'When did you leave?'

A quick look. 'I left when there was a prospect of Roger marrying again.' A brief pause before she added, 'You might say that I took the opportunity to *escape*.' A faint smile. 'I am not ungrateful for what they did for me but the Kemps are a strange family and life at Kellycoryk was a strange experience. You felt – I was going to say, imprisoned, but that's not the word – cut off, is better – isolated from normality by a whole system of ideas, assumptions, prejudices – call them what you like.' She finished. 'There you have it!'

'Thank you for being frank.' He wasn't sure that she had been, but one step at a time. 'In particular I wanted to ask you about the first Mrs Kemp and the boating accident in which she died.'

This did take her by surprise. 'Is that relevant?'

'I have no idea. It is impossible to say what will prove important and what will not. What I can say is, once it is known that Bridget Kemp was murdered, gossip and guarded press comment will force me to look into the circumstances of the death of her predecessor, whether I wish to or not. But, by the same token, the investigation will carry no imputation of guilt against anyone at all.'

It was smooth, but she was not wholly reassured. She would play for time. She glanced at her watch. 'I usually have a cup of tea at about this time; will you join me . . . ? Do you like Earl Grey?'

'Very much.'

She went into an adjoining room, presumably a kitchen, and Wycliffe could hear her busying herself with cups and saucers. A shrewd woman who would tell him only what she wanted him to know, and that would be edited with skill and finesse.

She was soon back with a prepared tray, hand-painted bone china, rich-tea biscuits, and a prepared response.

'Now, about the accident . . .' She nibbled a biscuit, neat and crumbless. 'It was a tragedy . . . As you must know, I was there; and I shall never forget the feeling of utter helplessness . . . We were out sailing with Roger; he was very keen on sailing at that time. Julia and I were close friends. She fell overboard while sunbathing on the foredeck. She had always refused to wear a lifejacket, and poor Roger was really not skilful enough to manoeuvre the boat and pick her up. It was as simple and tragic as that. Within seconds, sailing down wind, we were hopelessly far away . . .'

'It couldn't have been suicide?'

A pause, then, 'Who can say? It could have been, I suppose. Julia was a charming, highly talented woman, a musician, a painter; she wrote poetry, some of which was published . . . But there was a core of instability; she seemed to suffer from chronic frustration. In some strange way she was never able to take any satisfaction in what she achieved, her sights seemed always to be set on the unattainable.'

Wycliffe brought her back to earth. 'No marital problems?'

A shrewd glance. 'You have been listening to gossip, Mr Wycliffe. It is true that Julia and Roger were incompatible, but if you mean another woman, I very much doubt it.'

'Thank you. That is very clear . . . Yes, most helpful.' Wycliffe gave the impression that he was preparing to get up and go but he had no intention of letting the lady off the hook just yet.

'Just one other matter. Where did you board Mr Kemp's boat that morning?'

She looked startled, but recovered. 'At Percuil boatyard where he kept it.'

'You were still living at Kellycoryk at that time so presumably you drove there with him and Mrs Kemp?'

A momentary hesitation. 'Well, no. In fact, Julia

had business in St Mawes that morning and we picked her up there.'

'You mean that Mrs Kemp had left home earlier and driven to St Mawes. Presumably she had her own car?'

'Yes, a little white runabout, I think it was a Mini. Anyway, it was the one Isobel has now.'

She got up from her chair and retrieved a lump of coal which had fallen into the fender.

Wycliffe sat back and waited. 'I'm trying to get the picture. Who else was in the house at that time – presumably the children and Agnes?'

'Normally they would have been but, as it happened, Agnes was staying with a friend in Torquay – she used to go there for a fortnight every year – and Isobel was away on a school trip of some sort – Stratford, I think it was, for the Shakespeare thing.'

'What about Francis? Had he moved out?'

'Oh, yes. Francis was already established in the cottage.'

'So that leaves Crispin.'

'Yes.' For the first time she was getting flustered. 'I really can't see why you are going over all this when it all happened *before* the accident.'

Wycliffe felt that he had gone far enough. 'Yes, of course. So Mr Kemp crossed to St Mawes and picked up his wife. From the pier?'

There was irritation in her expression and her voice. 'In fact, Julia got someone to row her off to join us. The pier is almost always congested in the season.'

'I see. None of this seems to have come out in the inquiry into the accident.'

'But why should it? As I said, it all happened before.'

Wycliffe seemed reassured, but he made one more point. 'Mrs Kemp's car must have been stranded in St Mawes.'

'What . . . ? Oh, yes, I suppose it was. Roger must have made arrangements to have it brought back at some time. I don't remember.' She added, annoyance breaking through once more, 'Does it matter?'

'Probably not; but there is another aspect on which I would like your opinion – Isobel's attitude.'

'Isobel?' She was briefly disconcerted.

'Yes. Isobel came to my attention when my wife bought the china dogs. Isobel was here with you. It was obvious that we had interrupted a discussion, apparently acrimonious, concerning her mother.'

She gave herself time to think. 'How extraordinary! I had no idea that you could have gathered so much. Of course, Isobel was greatly affected by her mother's death. She was only sixteen – a difficult age for most girls.' A longish pause. 'I hardly know what to say. Quite suddenly – in the past few weeks really, and for no apparent reason, Isobel seems to have decided that there was something sinister about her mother's death.'

'Can you suggest anything that has happened recently which might have set her thinking along these lines?'

She did not answer at once, then, 'I know that she has got mixed up with some absurd spiritualist group. I believe it centres around a woman in St Endel Churchtown who claims to have mediumistic powers. The thing is organized by a woman called Margot Sweet, a well-to-do widow. They have meetings – seances I suppose they call them.' She broke off. 'I don't know the details but I have the impression that it is since Isobel became involved with them that she has got this nonsense into her head . . . A great pity; she is very intelligent and, fundamentally, a pleasant girl.'

Clare had already said as much as she wished to

and she was anxious for him to go, but Wycliffe had other ideas.

'When you left Kellycoryk about three years ago and came here, Isobel must have been eighteen and Crispin, sixteen. You had lived with them throughout their lives, from infancy to adolescence.'

'So?'

'You must have established an intimate relationship of some sort with both of them. I can see that with Isobel, because her mother's death affected her so deeply, her relationships might have suffered, but what about Crispin? Does he still keep in touch?'

Clare frowned. 'Crispin is a very different proposition from his sister. I've never been able to make up my mind about how deeply he felt his mother's death.' She shifted in her chair. 'Anyway, I see very little of him now.'

Wycliffe was already on his feet, and they were making the correct noises preparatory to his leaving, when she broke off abruptly as though a fresh thought had occurred to her. 'You mentioned that Bridget was shot with a small-calibre pistol; has it been found?'

'No. Obviously it is important that we should find it.'

She made a deprecating gesture. 'It's quite silly, but I happened to recall that there *was* a pistol at Kellycoryk. We used to play with it when we were children – until we got caught.'

'Can you tell me about it?'

She hesitated. 'It's a long time ago. We found it in a chest in one of the attics known as the junk room. It was small – more like a toy – but when Uncle Jos caught us with it he was angry. He said it was real and might even kill somebody.'

'Was there any ammunition?'

She shook her head. 'If there was, we never used it. As I said, to us it was only a toy.'

Wycliffe had got more than he could have expected from the visit and he allowed himself to be shepherded out into the darkness. He crossed the square feeling vaguely uneasy and in need of something more than Earl Grey. He went into the bar at the New Inn.

Later he walked home along the coast road; a half-moon emerged fitfully from the clouds; the crumbling cliffs looked pale in its light, and full of shadows.

Helen was still watching her television play.

Wycliffe went up to bed and took his history of Kellycoryk with him. When Helen came up he said, 'It says here that, during the religious troubles under the Tudors, the Kemps hid Cuthbert Mayne, one of the seminary priests, in the tunnel which takes the stream under the old house. Mayne was later hung, drawn and quartered in the Market Place in Launceston but the Kemps weren't implicated.'

'Lucky them.'

Helen had come to bed to go to sleep.

Tuesday morning 11 May

After a restless night Wycliffe was out on the shore before seven. There was a low mist over the sea with no defined horizon; the sea itself was calm but it seemed to breathe, rising and falling in a slow rhythm. Wycliffe had not spoken to John Harvey since their meal together; now his door was shut and his windows were blind. The Deux-Chevaux was in its usual place. Was Harvey avoiding him because of the latest developments at Kellycoryk?

Wycliffe was disappointed; at this stage he would have preferred a chance encounter to a formal visit. He was turning away when Harvey's door opened, and there was the man himself.

'Looking for me? Come on in. I'm late; I was called out last night on an emergency . . . Coffee's ready.'

Not surprisingly Harvey's manner was different, a certain brooding preoccupation. 'I suppose you are directing the inquiry into Bridget's death?'

'Yes, but there is nothing official about this visit. All the same, I was hoping that you might fill me in on some of the background.'

Harvey did not reply at once. He went into the kitchen and returned with two mugs of coffee.

When they were both seated he went on, 'I assume that this is now a murder inquiry?'

'Certainly.'

Harvey sipped his coffee. 'I doubt if I can be of much help. Since Julia died I've had very little to do with Kellycoryk. Isobel comes here; I think she sees me as a link with her mother, but as to the others . . .'

'Francis Kemp?'

Harvey was taken by surprise. 'Well, yes. I'm afraid it's difficult to think of Francis as a Kemp. Anyway, he's like me – and you, for that matter – he gets itchy feet in the early morning and he sometimes ends up here. He's a good wits' sharpener when he's in the mood.'

A brief interval to keep the right tempo, then Wycliffe said, 'You mentioned Isobel just now.'

Harvey showed slight irritation at being pressed. 'Yes, well, she's been making it fairly obvious recently, with little or no justification, that she's not satisfied with the accepted account of her mother's death.'

'You suggested to me the other night the possibility that your sister may have taken her own life. But off the record, I can't ignore the bare possibility of a connection between these two deaths, neither of them natural, occurring in the same family within a period of five years.'

Harvey sat back in his chair. 'Well, I can't accuse

you of pulling your punches. I suppose I should be grateful for your confidence but it opens up a bleak prospect.'

'Did your sister have friends or connections in St Mawes?'

'In St Mawes? Yes, she did. There was a woman called Holland – June Holland, who wrote poetry . . . Oh, yes, and there's a gallery where she sometimes sold pictures . . . There must be others but they don't come to mind at the moment. What's this about?'

'It seems that on the morning of the day she died she drove to St Mawes to keep an appointment and was picked up there by Roger and Clare Jordan who had sailed across from Percuil.'

Harvey frowned. 'Does that mean anything?'

'I've no idea. I'm trying to understand the circumstances.'

Harvey got up to put his empty mug on the table. 'Anyway, tell me what you want to know and I'll see what I can do.'

'You've given me a picture of your sister as a highly talented young woman and, if her portrait is anything to go by, she was a very attractive one. Why did she marry Kemp? It could hardly have been for his money. You see – I am not mincing words.'

Harvey's lips were pursed. 'It certainly wasn't for his money. Of course, Roger's father was alive then but everybody knew they were struggling to hold on to Kellycoryk. In any case, Julia was well off in her own right due to a legacy from an aunt with whom she had been a favourite.'

'So the question remains.'

'I think it must have been a whim – a romantic whim if you like; she was only a girl at the time. After all, Kemp had an essential qualification, he was a Catholic, and the idea of becoming the chatelaine of an historic country house probably had its appeal.'

Harvey hesitated before adding, 'And one can't rule out sex; Kemp seems to attract some women sexually, though I'll never understand why.'

'Did you approve?'

Harvey looked at him in surprise. 'Me? I wasn't consulted. I was still a schoolboy and very much the kid brother.'

Wycliffe was content. From his chair he could look through the open door at the cove where the mist was thinning and the sea looked silky; this was the way he liked to conduct an investigation, to listen, letting information flow over him and putting in only the occasional prompt. Unfortunately such situations rarely last long.

'When your sister died, what happened to her money?'

Harvey grimaced. 'In her will she left everything to Kemp.' He broke off and looked at Wycliffe with his first sign of irritation. 'But what is all this? Why are we talking about Julia who's been dead for five years, when it's Bridget who's been murdered?'

Wycliffe gave in with a good grace. 'I did explain, but all right, let's talk about Bridget; another attract- ive, well-off and youngish woman who, apparently, fell for Roger.'

'That was different. Old Jago, Bridget's father, was alive then and he and his daughter made a good pair.' Harvey shook his head with a tolerant smile.

'Can you enlarge on that?'

A brief hesitation. 'I suppose it can't do anybody any harm now. In my opinion they made up their minds they wanted Kellycoryk. There wasn't a dog's chance of persuading Roger to sell, so they went about it another way. After all, Roger was a widower, house- trained and a Catholic. You might say that it was a reasonable match, but by no stretch of the imagination could you call it a romantic one.'

Wycliffe was incredulous. 'You mean that she married Roger in order to get a foot in the door . . . ? But what was the attraction? Surely, as a business proposition Kellycoryk could be nothing but a liability?'

Harvey looked knowing. 'They saw it as an ideal spot, made for their purpose. Fifty acres of woodland-cum-garden; a hundred and fifty of farmland; a stream, a lake, and an historic house fronting on a sheltered cove.

'They would undertake to restore the house and gardens and regenerate the lake. That would win over the conservationists and, at an appropriate time their plans would emerge: an up-market leisure complex. No Mickey Mouse fun-trap for kids and the mentally retarded, but a haven of rest and recreation for those with enough money to lose sleep over and get neuroses about: a golf course, fly-fishing in the newly stocked stream and lake, discreet water sports based on the cove, perhaps a little rough shooting in the woodland . . . And finally, with a few modifications and additions, fully in keeping, of course, with its historic past, the house would become an hotel.'

Harvey grinned. 'Everybody happy – except Roger, poor old bastard.'

It occurred to Wycliffe that Harvey was more closely acquainted with what was happening at Kellycoryk than he acknowledged.

'If you are right, do you think Roger had any idea that he was being used?'

'To start with, no; but he wasn't long in finding out when it became clear that none of Bridget's money would be available to rescue the place except on her terms.'

They chatted for a while and Wycliffe was on the point of leaving when he was called back. Harvey looked sheepish. 'There's one other thing that you may hear elsewhere but I'd rather you heard it from me.'

Wycliffe waited.

'Bridget and I had what's usually called an affair . . . It didn't last long, there was no commitment on either side. Just plain sex. Anyway, it was over before this happened . . . Now you know.'

'Did you meet here?'

'God, no! We met after hours at the surgery. My partner is tolerant.'

'Who else knows?'

'Isobel; I've no idea how she found out.'

'Would she be likely to tell anyone else?'

'I don't think so. Isobel likes to conserve her capital.'

Wycliffe walked back over the bridge to his own cottage. The mists had cleared and the sea glittered in the sunshine. Three older children from the cove were straggling along the cliff road to the village and the bus that would take them to school in St Austell.

Helen was preparing breakfast and the radio was on for the news; the usual mix of terrorism, famine, street crime, and political chicanery spiced with sex scandals. It put his murdered woman into a horrifying perspective and he felt depressed.

'I suppose you will be tied up all day.'

'It looks like it.'

'I met a very pleasant woman from the village yesterday, a retired schoolteacher, and we thought of going across to Caerhays; the gardens are open and, according to the radio, it's going to be a fine morning with rain this afternoon.'

Roger had given up all pretence of work but he sat at his table which carried its usual load of books and papers. From time to time he stretched out a hand for his ballpoint in a reflex movement but withdrew it again. His head felt physically too small to contain the chaos of images and fears, of ideas and suspicions, along with the futile emotions of anger and remorse which accompanied them. From time to time he let out a sigh or a groan causing Coryk to open a wary eye.

Agnes came in without knocking. She crossed the room to his table and stood looking down at him; her face was drawn and very pale but her deep brown eyes, the Kemp eyes, seemed to burn in her head.

'Well?'

'I don't know what you mean. Why are you looking at me like that?' Roger's voice was tremulous, like that of a child threatened with punishment.

'I want to know.'

'Know what?'

'For God's sake, Roger, be a man for once! What happened that night? You were down there. Did you kill her?'

'Kill her? Of course I didn't kill her. My God, what do you think I—'

'Somebody did; somebody drove her car back here and left it in the alley with her body in it, and somebody drove it away again.' She broke off and looked at him with hard eyes. 'When will you ever face reality, Roger? In trying to save this bloody place you are destroying us all.' She finished as though in exasperation. 'I should have thought once was enough.'

He looked at her with fear in his eyes. 'I don't know what you're talking about.'

'I'm talking about Julia. I don't know what happened five years ago and I don't want to know, but I'm quite sure it wasn't the tale you and Clare served up between you. I'm only surprised that you got away

135

with it at the time but you can be sure that it will all be raked over now.'

Roger sat, staring at her, without a word.

'You've nothing to say to me? You mightn't think so but I'm trying to help you – and all of us.'

She waited but when there was still no response she turned away. 'I don't know which you need most, Roger, a lawyer, a doctor, or the priest.'

Chapter Seven

It was the day for taking possession of their new quarters. The village hall was within hailing distance of the van that had housed them until now. They had space, and Central Stores had disgorged the required furniture and equipment; much of it, through chips and cracks, coffee stains and cigarette burns, familiar from past encounters. At least it brought with it the right smell.

Wycliffe had a little office at the front which looked out on the car-park with almost the same view as from the van. Already the paperwork had been transferred from sub-division and he had a neat little pile of reports on his table along with a copy of the *Western Daily*, folded back to display a marked news item.

Body of Missing Woman Recovered

Yesterday morning the body of Mrs Bridget Kemp of Kellycoryk was recovered from a cove known as Grant's Cellar in Veryan Bay. Mrs Kemp failed to return home from a visit to friends in St Mawes on Thursday evening and her abandoned car was found on Jacob's Head near her home the following day. The circumstances of her disappearance and death are being investigated and an inquest will be held.

Mrs Kemp leaves a husband, a stepson and stepdaughter.

This is the second time in five years that tragedy has visited the family. In June 1988, Mrs Julia Kemp was drowned in a boating accident while sailing with her husband off Falmouth.

Wycliffe passed the paper to Kersey. 'Sting in the tail there. They don't even mention the presence of Clare Jordan. If they're doing that now what will it be when they know she was murdered?'

And soon they would know, for there was to be a press briefing at half-past ten.

He leafed through the reports. Franks, the least verbose of men, had contrived to spread his findings over several pages of typescript for the benefit of the coroner and the lawyers. The core was, of course, that Bridget Kemp had died as a result of being shot, at near-contact range, in the back of the neck, with a small-calibre pistol.

A report from Ballistics confirmed and enlarged on this: the bullet removed from the dead woman's neck was a 6.35mm, what the British call a .25 Auto and, in the opinion of the experts, it had been fired from a 'Baby Browning' type, pocket self-loading pistol.

Wycliffe was reflective. 'If I was in the back of a car the last thing I would think of doing would be to shoot the driver – unless, of course, the car was stationary.'

Kersey, caught in the toils of impending self-denial, was groping in the bottom of his tobacco pouch for a few shreds of shag to roll his last cigarette. Accepting failure, he said, 'I've been thinking on those lines and

I've worked out a possible scenario: Bridget, on her way home, is flagged down by someone she knows, waiting in the lay-by at Hendra Croft. Instead of going around the car to get in beside her, her passenger gets in the back and before she can pull away she gets it in the back of her neck, spattering blood on the headrest. The guy then gets out, removes her body from the driving seat, stows it in the load space, and drives off.'

Wycliffe finished for him. 'To Kellycoryk where he leaves the car for more than an hour before driving to Jacob's Head and finally disposing of the body.' A profound sigh. 'I find your bit more credible than mine, but I suppose they have to be fitted together. A couple of points: you don't account for Bridget getting out of the car and leaving her footprints in the mud; you've also assumed that her attacker was a man, but if young Crispin is to be relied upon, the car was driven away from Kellycoryk by a woman.'

'Yes, and you know my opinion about that.' Kersey had scraped together a few tobacco shreds and contrived to roll a thin spill which he now lit as though performing some sacred rite.

Wycliffe was still turning over the reports in the hope of discovering something that he did not already know.

The team met for a briefing. Wycliffe told Lanyon to follow up Julia Kemp's appointment at St Mawes on the morning of the day she died. 'I know it's five years ago but if she had regular contacts in St Mawes, people will remember her. Her white Mini might help. Talk to Clare Jordan and see what else you can dig up.'

Lucy Lane was downbeat regarding the second Mrs Kemp. 'The woman must have been almost pathologically circumspect. All her computer discs are protected; there isn't a scrap of writing anywhere. In fact, there's nothing much of anything except her clothes and her photographs to tell you about the woman. I think we should get DS Shaw down to work on the discs; for all I've found she could have been a couturier's dummy.' Lucy being acid. She went on, 'I've got together a few details of her company: Coast and Country have their offices in St Mary's Street, Truro, and the manager is called Curtis – Ian Curtis. Her solicitor, business and personal, is Ralph Beasley, of Beasley and Fiske, an old friend of her father's.'

Wycliffe said, 'I'm surprised they haven't been in touch.'

DS Fox handed in his report on the investigations at Hendra Croft. Like all Fox's reports it could have been framed and preserved for posterity, but it confirmed that the heelprints at the scene resembled those made by shoes in the dead woman's possession. The shoes she was actually wearing at the time were not recovered with the body.

Kersey's little firework had burned itself out and he had discarded the pitiful remnant to save his lips. He said, trying to look involved, 'So we now know the scene of the crime and the nature of the weapon used to commit it.'

Wycliffe told of the pistol which had been a plaything for the juvenile Kemps. 'Obviously we must search for the gun, starting from there. Let's hope the killer doesn't have another use for it. I'm seeing Kemp this morning with Lucy and I'll set that ball rolling.

'What we need now is to go over every bit of the route from Hendra Croft, through Porthendel and on to the cove. I want everybody who lives along that route and anybody who was driving or walking along it after, say, ten on Thursday night, to be found and questioned. Remember, it's not only sightings of the blue Mondeo Estate that we're after. If the killer was waiting for Bridget Kemp at Hendra Croft, he or she must have got there somehow – most probably on foot.

'Sub-division will provide assistance if necessary and Mr Kersey will be in charge. All reports and queries to him.'

The telephone rang. 'Ralph Beasley, the dead woman's solicitor, sir.'

Thought waves?

The voice was quiet and cultured. 'Mr Wycliffe . . . ? Ralph Beasley. I act for Coast and Country and for Bridget Kemp. I returned from abroad last evening in response to an urgent message from the office . . . There are things I would like to discuss with you . . . Perhaps we might meet? For several reasons it would be helpful if we could meet in the firm's offices in St Mary's Street . . . Thank you; that will suit me very well. This afternoon, then.'

By half-past ten there was a gathering of the press and TV. The Incident Room had come just in time, otherwise the cameras would have had him posturing in the car-park.

It was obvious that the news had leaked out. From the start it was clear that they wanted answers to questions rather than a statement.

'The post-mortem and a ballistics report show that Mrs Bridget Kemp was shot in the back of the neck with a small-calibre self-loading pistol.'

'Have you any idea where the crime took place?'

'There is evidence to suggest that she was shot from behind whilst sitting in the driving seat of her car when the car was parked beside the road at Hendra Croft.'

'So the killer was in the back and was, presumably, known to her.'

'That is speculation.'

'Has the weapon been recovered?'

'No. We are looking for a self-loading pistol of small calibre.'

'Is it the case that Mrs Kemp's car returned briefly to Kellycoryk before being driven to Jacob's Head where it was abandoned?'

'I am not prepared to comment on that question at this stage.'

Soon the questioning shifted, as he knew it would, to the first Mrs Kemp.

A wizened little man who worked for an agency started the ball rolling. 'So we know how, if not why, or who by, Mrs Bridget Kemp was killed, but are we any wiser about her predecessor, Mrs Julia Kemp?'

'I can only refer you to the news reports at the time.'

A woman reporter tried her hand. 'Are the police re-opening their investigation into the death of the first Mrs Kemp?'

'I am not aware that there was any police investigation. The coroner's officer made the usual inquiries and was satisfied that a tragic accident had occurred.'

And that was that. Not too bad, but there would be other days.

Coffee, and Wycliffe was on his way to Kellycoryk with Lucy Lane and WPC Rees, but this time it was to interview Roger Kemp. For reasons that were not clear to him he had put off this encounter until he could do so no longer. He had in his mind the memory of a sad figure, alone, except for his cat, hands in pockets, watching the ducks feed on the once ornamental pond now being choked out of existence by invading rushes.

They had to ring several times before the door was answered by a young woman who said she was the daily help. 'She's gone into Truro to do the shopping; he's in the library. I dunno where Isobel and Crispin are.'

They made for the library unescorted. Wycliffe tapped at the door then opened it. Roger was seated at his work table and at first sight Wycliffe thought he was asleep, then he saw that his eyes were wide open. He was lying back in his chair, staring up at the ceiling.

It was a moment or two before he became aware of them, then he sat bolt upright and faced them with vacant eyes. He was unshaven and looked like a man who had not slept for nights.

Wycliffe went through the routine introduction and it was received with dawning recognition and a tired gesture which could be interpreted as both an acknowledgement and an invitation to sit down.

Milly Rees found chairs for them. It seemed impossible to establish meaningful contact and Wycliffe found himself making a bald statement of fact. 'I think you already know that your wife did not take her own life, Mr Kemp, and that the pathologist's report makes it clear that she was shot.'

Roger reached out to stroke his cat as though the contact provided reassurance. He still said nothing.

Wycliffe ploughed on. 'As far as you know are there any firearms in this house, Mr Kemp?'

This prompted a definite, almost an emphatic response. 'No! In my father's time there were sporting guns, but they were sold off years ago. At no time since have we had guns of any sort in the house.'

Wycliffe persisted. 'I have in mind a small self-loading pistol which you and others sometimes played with when you were children.'

Roger's eyes widened and he shifted uncomfortably in his chair. 'That was a very long time ago.'

'But you remember it?'

'I suppose so, but—'

'Will you describe the gun as far as you are able?'

Roger spoke in a low voice, scarcely audible. 'It was

a little pistol. We thought it was a toy until father found us with it . . . It had a butt that was made of bone or ivory . . .' His voice trailed off.

Wycliffe said, 'I believe it was kept in a chest in one of the attics along with a lot of other things. Have you looked to see if it is still there?'

After each question there was a long interval before an answer came and during that time Roger's gaze shifted about the room and his hands were rarely still. 'Yes, I have to admit that I've looked and it isn't there. It must have gone a long time ago.'

'Where would it have gone?'

A slow shrug as though the question was unreasonable.

'We need to search for that pistol, Mr Kemp.'

Wycliffe felt that the time had come to change the subject. 'We have evidence that the crime was committed at Hendra Croft, that your wife was flagged down on her way back from St Mawes and attacked. The car was then driven here and remained in the yard for an hour and a half before being driven to Jacob's Head, where her body was disposed of.'

Kemp made no move to confirm or contest this version of events. Wycliffe gave him time but all that came was, 'I don't understand it.'

The light was fading by the minute and it looked as though the promised rain was arriving early. The walls of the room with their shelves of books receded into the gloom and what light there was seemed to fall upon Roger's large, pale face.

Wycliffe said, 'You can offer no explanation of why your wife's car was returned here, where it remained for some time, before being driven off to the headland?'

When it seemed that Kemp would not answer, he murmured, 'No.'

'Where do you sleep, Mr Kemp?'

144

'Sleep?' The question seemed to startle him. 'My bedroom is in the back of the house, overlooking the yard.'

'And you heard nothing of the arrival of your wife's car nor of its later departure?'

'Nothing.'

By that tacit understanding which seemed to exist between them, Lucy realized that it was her turn. She said, 'Your wife ran a very successful business, Mr Kemp, and it is common knowledge that you have difficulty in maintaining the estate. Were there quarrels over money?'

Again there was an interval before he answered. 'No. There were no quarrels. There were discussions.'

Wycliffe intervened. 'It is said that Mrs Kemp was prepared to make a very significant contribution to restoring the property, but only as part of a Coast and Country leisure project. Is that so?'

'Yes.'

'But you refused to agree to this?'

Kemp brought his large, soft hands together on the table top and spoke in a tired voice. 'No, I did not refuse. It was not what I would have wanted but I came to the conclusion that it was the only possible way in which Kellycoryk could survive. I came to a provisional arrnagement with my wife and it was intended that we should enter into a formal agreement.'

'When was this agreed between you?'

'On Tuesday evening.'

'Two days before she disappeared.'

'Yes.'

'Did anyone else – *does* anyone else know of the arrangement?'

Roger raised his shoulders in a dismissive shrug. 'I suppose Bridget might have discussed it with her associates and I mentioned it to my family.'

'How is your wife's death likely to affect the proposal?'

'I have no idea.'

'Do you know the contents of your wife's will – assuming that she made one?'

'No; it was something that we never discussed. You will have to talk to her solicitor.'

'I am doing so, this afternoon.'

Kemp spread his hands in a small gesture as though this disposed of the matter.

'Presumably you have made a will?'

'No.'

'Are you under any constraints in dealing with the property, such as entail or conditions laid down in your father's will?'

Roger frowned, and it was a moment or two before he answered. 'If I were to sell the property, my brother, my sister and my cousin, Clare, would each receive one-sixth of the proceeds of the sale.'

'So you would get half. Will that be the situation if your agreement with Coast and Country Leisure goes through?'

Roger shifted uneasily. 'No. The agreement would involve leasing, not selling the property so the provision would not apply.'

Another two or three minutes and Wycliffe was satisfied that he had got all that he was likely to for the moment.

Outside, Lucy wanted to know what he thought of the interview. 'The business of the will and the leasing of the property is interesting.'

'And the rest?'

Wycliffe was casual. 'All of them seem to have reason to lie, or think they have, so you pays your money and you takes your choice.'

'You didn't refer to his first wife.'

'No, I thought we would see how Lanyon gets

on first . . . You and Rees had better start trying to trace that pistol, though I doubt if you'll get very far. I only hope that whoever has it hasn't thought of a further use for it. Will you be at the pub for lunch?'

Tuesday afternoon 11 May

When Wycliffe set out for Truro the rain had stopped and a thin mist allowed hazy sunshine to filter through. The roads in this part of Cornwall were made originally for passage between farms and hamlets; they stagger across the countryside with abrupt and bewildering changes of direction, but the names of the places they link together are compensation in themselves: Great Polgrain, Goviley Major, Tippett's Shop, Paradise Cottage and Bessybeneath . . .

Wycliffe arrived at the river and made a slow but majestic crossing by the chain ferry. He was greeted in the city by the cathedral and town clocks chiming a quarter-past two out of sync. Reluctant to play musical chairs in search of a parking space, he asserted his privilege and found a space in the yard of the police station.

Truro is one of those country towns where the old ways have not yet been entirely squeezed out by greedy supermarkets and rapacious developers. There are still substantial businesses which have remained in the same family for generations, and there are doors off side streets which lead to mysterious offices above shops.

The offices of Coast and Country were above a jeweller's, reached by way of a glossy black door reminiscent of 10 Downing Street, and carpeted stairs. At the top, on a sort of landing, a blonde sat at a desk and asked, with no interest at all, 'Can I help you?' That question which has become almost a provocation.

Before he could reply, a youngish Uriah Heep packaged in bulging pinstripes came out of one of the doors, hand outstretched. 'Chief Superintendent Wycliffe . . . Ian Curtis . . . Good of you to come . . . This way if you please . . .'

From a chair, next to the inevitable upholstered swivel, another man stood up and Curtis said, 'I think you spoke to Mr Beasley on the telephone – Mr Ralph Beasley, Chief Superintendent Wycliffe.'

Beasley was an older man, lean and bony, with white hair and a little white moustache over teeth, yellowing and irregular, but his own.

'So Bridget is dead, Mr Wycliffe.'

'I'm afraid so, and, if you have not heard already I must tell you that she was murdered.'

'Murdered!'

Wycliffe recounted the circumstances and Beasley appeared deeply distressed.

'I should explain that I have known Bridget from the very day of her birth and I was closely involved with her father both as a business associate and a friend. You might say that Bridget inherited me in both capacities.' A dry chuckle, instantly suppressed. 'Technically, I am a co-director with Bridget, and the firm's solicitor, but I should add that my holding in the company is a nominal one.'

It was becoming clear that Curtis was only there for form's sake.

Wycliffe was appreciative. 'My job is to find out who murdered Mrs Kemp and why. To do that I have to look into the details of both her business and private life.'

Curtis spoke for the first time, playing with the cord of his telephone, 'You may rest assured, Superintendent, that there was nothing in her business life to give rise to anything of the sort.'

Beasley cut in. 'Of course I agree with my colleague, but that does not mean that there will be any obstacle to the fullest investigation.'

They were not yet getting down to business. Wycliffe looked out of the window; the view was taken up entirely by part of the south porch of the cathedral; it was almost as though one could reach across the narrow street and touch the biscuit-coloured stone or the leaded panes of the lancet windows.

Wycliffe said, 'The company appears to be very prosperous.'

'It is. Bridget inherited her father's acumen and caution along with his business. The company is sound and, despite the recession, increasingly profitable. We have a policy of planned and gradual expansion, capitalized out of our own resources, and that is proving entirely successful.'

Wycliffe smiled. 'That could be a quote from the chairman's report if you had such a thing. I have a more personal angle in mind. I believe Coast and Country had an interest in the acquisition of Kellycoryk with a view to its development as a leisure centre of some sort.'

For once Beasley was caught off guard, and from the look on Curtis's face it was clear that this was news to him. Beasley recovered his poise. 'I must admit that the idea has been looked at as a vague possibility.'

Wycliffe sat forward in his chair. 'More than that, surely. I understand that Mrs Kemp made a virtual take-over of the estate by the company a condition for providing any assistance towards its upkeep and restoration.'

Beasley, now on his mettle, was terse. 'Of course I cannot say what discussions may or may not have taken place between husband and wife.'

Wycliffe followed up his advantage. 'I quite

understand that. But my information is that Mr Kemp came to an arrangement with his wife along those lines shortly before her disappearance and that this was to be the subject of a formal agreement. Did she not mention it to you?'

Beasley shook his head. 'No, I was abroad. But you must see that such an agreement in no way suggests a possible motive for murder – rather the contrary, surely?'

'Unless there is someone determined to prevent such a development taking place.'

A gesture, signifying that this was wild speculation.

Wycliffe changed the subject. 'I understand that you act for Mrs Kemp in her private capacity also. Presumably she has made a will?'

Beasley hesitated, weighing the situation, then reached a decision. He turned to Curtis. 'I am sure you realize, Ian, that this is a matter which in no way concerns the company . . .'

Curtis did not wait to have it spelt out; he got up with apparent relief. At the door he turned. 'I have some things to do in town. I shall be about half an hour.'

When the door had closed Beasley said, 'You were asking about Bridget's will. Unfortunately there is no will. This may seem incredible to you but in the years since her father died I have tried over and over again to persuade her but to no avail. It was always, "There's plenty of time for that." ' The lawyer spread his bony hands in a helpless gesture.

'So who inherits?'

Beasley shrugged. 'The rules governing intestacy are complicated but broadly, in this case, it seems that the beneficiaries will be the husband and his children.'

'But they are his children by a former marriage – not hers.'

'That doesn't affect the position. Speaking as a lawyer, I can see a lot of trouble ahead.'

And speaking as a policeman, Wycliffe could say amen to that.

'And Bridget Kemp's estate includes the company?'

'It will include her holding in the company which amounts to ninety per cent of the share capital.'

Wycliffe had learned more than he bargained for and he was prepared to settle for that. Twice during their discussions they had been interrupted by the chiming of the cathedral clock which seemed to be just above their heads; now, as he stepped out once more into St Mary's Street, the chimes went through their full hourly gamut and the clock struck three.

An interesting three-quarters of an hour but he was not sure where it had got him. And, wherever that was, where did he go from there?

'Oh, it's you.' Molly Bishop came out of the kitchen, wiping her hands on a grubby towel. 'Long time no see. Where've you been this past few days . . . ? Well, don't stand there looking like an undertaker who's lost his corpse. You can come in; but if you're here to see your uncle it's his afternoon at the college.'

'I know.' Crispin was standing in the doorway but he came into the room.

She pushed forward a kitchen chair and sat herself in the rocker. 'Take the weight off your feet. So it's me you've come to see. I suppose things are in a bit of a state at home.'

'Yes.'

'Can you do with a drink? You look as though you need something. There's a can or two of lager in the fridge . . .'

'No . . . No, thank you.'

'I reckon you need something. Is it just to talk to Molly? You're all wound up inside. You've got to learn to let go.' Crispin sat on a kitchen chair, staring into the empty grate, both hands gripped tightly between his knees.

Now she asked him, 'Have the police been since they found out Bridget was shot?'

'They were there this morning, talking to Father.' He stopped, clearly on the point of saying something else.

'Come on! Out with it!'

'I lied to them about what I saw.'

'That won't be a new experience for them.'

'I told them it was a woman who drove Bridget's car away. I made it seem that I thought it was Bridget herself.'

'Well?'

'As I told you before, it wasn't a woman at all, it was Father.'

'You were trying to protect your father. Well, that's natural enough but I know how you feel. Anyway, I expect they'll manage without your help.'

She was looking him over with a critical eye. 'It might do you a bit of good if you found somebody to go to bed with, Crispy. What's the matter with the girls around here? Won't they play?'

Crispin flushed and mumbled, 'She won't have me any more.'

Molly pounced. 'Oh, so there is a she! Then why has she gone off you all of a sudden?'

Crispin lowered his voice so that it was barely audible. 'She says there's something wrong with me, with our family, that we're not right in the head. Her mother thinks so and she will probably stop her coming to work in the house.'

'Ah! So Jane Clemens is your girl. Well, the Clemenses are good ones to talk; Jane's grandmother died in the lunatic asylum, her uncle did time for interfering with little girls, and her aunt goes to Truro hospital for regular treatment, nobody knows quite what for.'

Crispin got up from his chair and moved towards the open door. 'Anyway, I'll do the hen house.'

She called after him; he turned, and was astonished to see her face suffused with tenderness. Her voice too was uncommonly gentle. 'If you go on like this, boy, you're going to make yourself ill. Come upstairs with Molly – and don't worry about Francis, he just thinks of me as an animated mattress anyway.'

Back in the Incident Room Wycliffe found DC Lanyon preparing his report.

'Anything fresh?'

Lanyon was careful. 'Not exactly fresh, sir. I followed up your tip about the first Mrs Kemp's contacts in St Mawes. The man in the gallery who sold her paintings remembers her well enough. He reckons she could have made a real name for herself but there wasn't the output – just the odd one when the mood took her. She would never get together enough work for an exhibition.'

'And the woman who wrote poetry – Holland, wasn't it?'

'June Holland, sir. Yes, she's still around. I didn't know what to make of her story.'

'Try me.'

'She says that the day Julia was drowned they were supposed to have spent together, but Julia didn't turn up.'

'She didn't see her at all that day?'

'No.'

'So what did she think when she heard about the accident?'

'That Julia had forgotten about their arrangement or decided she would rather go sailing. Apparently reliability wasn't her middle name.'

'Yet she had an appointment at St Mawes which she is supposed to have kept.' Curiouser and curiouser. 'Have you found any other contacts she had in St Mawes?'

'Two more, but one, an elderly painter, is dead; the other, a woman, is away at the moment.'

'So Julia definitely did not keep her appointment and you've found nobody who admits to seeing her in St Mawes that day.'

'That's what it amounts to, sir.'

'All right; keep at it. I shall be at Kellycoryk.'

Wycliffe drove down through the village towards the waterfront; a dry afternoon after the rain but a high ceiling of cloud. The cafés were serving cream teas to stave off any pangs of hunger there might be before the evening meal.

Wycliffe felt set apart, caught up in a strangely unreal drama of violence among the remnants of an old family struggling to survive. He was uneasy; the logic of the evidence pushed him towards conclusions which conflicted with his instinct. It had emerged that Kemp's first wife, Julia, was not with him on that day five years ago when he and Clare Jordan boarded the boat at Percuil. Now it was clear that she had not kept her appointment in St Mawes either. In fact, there was nothing to show that she had been there.

Had she been on the boat at all? And if not . . .

Bridget, Kemp's second wife, had undoubtedly died by violence. She had been shot, almost certainly, with a little pistol which had come from the junk room in Kellycoryk. Kemp had benefited from the death of his first wife and looked set to do so on a grander scale from the death of his second.

Wycliffe wanted to get closer to the two young Kemps. Like Kersey, he did not believe what the boy had said, and the girl had avoided saying very much at all that was to the point.

He drove along the cliff road and crossed the bridge. The cove was deserted and, under a grey sky, the scene was like a steel engraving; the rocky promontories stood out in silhouette against the silvery plain of the sea. He turned up the drive to the house and as he reached the open ground by the lake he spotted Crispin crossing the alley from the house to the ruins. On an impulse he made straight for the alley and pulled up halfway along it. The boy was still in sight, in fact he had stopped and was looking back.

Wycliffe got out of the car and started after him, only to be surprised by the hard going; the tussocky grass, the brambles, unexpected hollows, and meaningless lumps of masonry defied any attempt at setting a course.

Crispin waited, but did not come towards him. Strange lad; such self-control and lack of spontaneity . . .

Wycliffe, out of breath but anxious to sound relaxed and friendly, said, 'This is a bit of luck, I came to see you.'

Crispin acknowledged the greeting with that colourless courtesy which seemed to come naturally to him.

The boy wore jeans and a waterproof jacket of which the left-hand pocket sagged under some weight.

Wycliffe tried again, looking about them and recovering his breath. 'Interesting place. Have you ever tried to make a plan of the old house?'

'No. Father has one which somebody made a long time ago.'

It was going to be up-hill work. 'I've been reading Jean Scott's book about Kellycoryk and she has a lot to say about the Tudor house.'

'Yes.'

'She mentions a sort of priest's hole under the old building which, she says, still exists.'

There was no response. It was like trying to see through a mirror and Wycliffe was about to revert to being a policeman when the boy said, 'You are talking about Wayne's Closet. Yes, it is still there; it's in the tunnel that takes the stream through to the lake.' He added a moment later and more casually, 'Do you want to see it?'

'I would like to.'

Together they scrambled over the rough ground and reached a small clearing where a flight of worn stone steps led down between moss-grown walls to a heavy padlocked door.

Wycliffe could hear the muffled sound of the stream beneath their feet.

'Down here.'

At the bottom of the steps Crispin went to work with a picklock; the door swung open on oiled hinges and they were greeted by the sound of a smooth rush of water. Wycliffe could see a little way into the arching tunnel, the narrow walkway and the gleaming surface of the stream, before it all vanished into the darkness.

Crispin produced a large electric torch from his pocket. 'You'll have to be careful; it's slippery in places.'

'You come here often?'

'No.'

Wycliffe followed the boy along the paved path while the beam of the torch was lost in the distance. What with the narrowness of the path, the slippery stone slabs underfoot and the inward curve of the walls which made them stoop, he hoped they had not far to go. In fact they soon reached the gap in the wall which he might easily have passed without noticing.

'It's in there.'

156

Crispin slid through the gap and Wycliffe followed, to find himself in the little cavernous room. The torch beam picked out the rocky walls, the stone slabs of the floor, and the shelf-like recess in one of the walls at about waist level.

'They call it Mayne's Bed because he lived here and slept on that ledge when Sir Richard Grenville and his men were after him in fifteen seventy-seven.' Crispin held the beam steady on the stone slab. 'Of course he was caught later, and executed, but they didn't get him while he was with us.'

The hint of pride in the boy's voice was not lost on Wycliffe but at the moment he was more interested in the little statue of the Virgin and the candlesticks with their stubs of candle.

'Who put all this here?'

'Father.'

'In memory of Mayne?'

'No, of Mother.' He took a box of matches from his pocket, struck one, and lit the candles; they flickered weakly before achieving a steady flame. 'Father comes here to pray. He thinks nobody knows.'

Crispin turned the beam of his torch on to the inscription on the stone slab, not well seen by candle-light. The letters had been laboriously and inexpertly cut, but the inscription was easily legible.

Wycliffe read aloud, 'Julia Constance Kemp, née Harvey, died 13th June 1988, aged 37 years. Pray for her Soul.' He turned to the boy, 'I thought your mother died on the fourteenth.'

Crispin directed his torch beam on to the date. 'That's what he put down.' His manner had the detachment of a guide.

It dawned on Wycliffe that in the moment or two of hesitation after Mayne's Closet was first mentioned the boy had decided that he should see it. He wondered why. More important, what if anything did it mean in the context of the death of Kemp's first wife?

They walked back through the tunnel, Crispin relocked the door and they climbed the steps. Wycliffe sat on the dwarf wall at the top; there were primroses growing between the stones.

'As I said, I want to talk to you. I know this is painful but I have to look again at the circumstances of your mother's death. Whether we wish it or not people and the press are already making connections between her death and that of your stepmother. Of course I have to be prepared to deal with that situation as it arises.'

Crispin sat on the wall beside him, his manner resigned. 'All right. What do you want me to tell you?'

'I want you to think back to the morning of that day when your mother lost her life. I believe Isobel was away on a school trip and your aunt was staying with a friend in Torquay, so you were here with your parents and Clare Jordan. Is that correct?'

'Yes.'

'Presumably you went to school as usual?'

'Yes.'

'Did you see your mother that morning?'

'No. Clare got breakfast; she often did; Mother didn't get up very early.'

'Did you hear anything of their plans for the day?'

'I knew that Mother was going to St Mawes. I thought it was to see a friend who writes poetry. She mentioned it the night before.'

'Was there any talk of your father and Clare going sailing?'

'I don't remember. I expect I was thinking more about not missing the school bus.'

'And when you got back in the evening?'

'When I got back there was nobody home but that wasn't unusual if Agnes was away. When they came home Father told me what had happened and he got in touch with the school party to break the news to Isobel and arrange for her to come home. He must have telephoned Agnes too because she arrived back next day.'

'Was anything said about your mother having joined the boat at St Mawes?'

'No, I only heard about that afterwards.'

Wycliffe decided to sharpen the probe. 'I'm sorry, but I have to ask you this question: did your mother and father quarrel much?'

'No. I don't think Father ever quarrels.'

'But your mother would get angry with him sometimes?'

'Sometimes; yes.'

'Did you gather that there was any sort of trouble between them on the night before the boat trip?'

'No.'

Wycliffe was puzzled by Crispin's attitude, so apparently detached and uninvolved yet he felt sure that underneath there was intense emotion. Without meaning to he was staring at the boy in a way that many would have found intimidating but the brown eyes met his gaze with no hint of concern, let alone of fear.

He slid off the wall. 'Well, thank you for showing me Mayne's Closet.'

Crispin stood beside him. 'I thought you should see it.'

'Are you coming back to the house?'

'No, I'm going for a walk.'

Chapter Eight

Tuesday 11 May

Wycliffe retrieved his car from the alley and parked in front of the house. There was no other car, so Lucy and the WPC must have given up their search for the little pistol; a needle-in-a-haystack routine anyway. The killer had either pitched it into the lake or was holding on to it for possible future use.

He rang the bell.

The response time seemed to get longer with each visit, and he was beginning to wonder whether there was some fresh crisis when the door was opened by the girl who helped with the housework. Her aggression was obvious.

'I want to speak to Isobel, is she in?'

The girl shrugged. 'I don't know who's in or who's out; they don't tell me.'

'Miss Agnes?'

'She's out.'

'Mr Kemp is in his library?'

'I suppose so.'

'Then please tell him that I shall be upstairs for a little while.'

She was about to make some sharp retort but thought better of it. Instead she said, as though reciting a lesson, 'My family doesn't want me being mixed up in all this. Mother says I shouldn't be working here so I've told them I'm leaving.'

Wycliffe looked at her as though she had not spoken. 'If you will just give Mr Kemp my message.'

In modern police investigation, every move, every interview, every scrap of evidence is recorded in the pious hope that through processes of evaluation, comparison and correlation (largely carried out by computers) indicators will emerge to guide the investigator in the way he should go.

Wycliffe did not knock the system, it was immensely useful; apart from anything else, in most cases it guaranteed that bland pre-digested diet preferred by the CPS and the courts. But for cases like the present one, involving a small group of closely interrelated people, Wycliffe believed that it was essential to see life through their eyes, to stand in their shoes, to become familiar with their backgrounds and aware of the constraints and antagonisms which informed their relationships.

That was what he tried to do and he was making progress. Now he was about to snoop around the upper floor and attics of the old house and if he was alone, so much the better.

He began with the attics, which he had not yet seen. At the east end of the first floor corridor near where the back stairs came up and Isobel and her brother had their rooms, another staircase, steep and narrow, led upwards. This was uncarpeted and so was the long, narrow passage at the top. On either side of the passage plank doors opened into rooms where, in other days, the servants had slept.

He decided to take a look in each, though Lucy and her assistant in their hunt-the-thimble routine must have given them at least a cursory glance. There were seven doors; the first four attics, two on each side, were empty except for buckets and enamel bowls strategically placed under damp patches. The windows were so thick with grime that it was difficult to see out and some panes had been replaced by plywood.

Opening the door of the next room – one at the back of the house – he had a surprise. It was twice the size of the others, the two dormer windows were reasonably clean and fully glazed. There were paint-stained floorboards, a couple of easels and a painter's donkey: no prizes for guessing that the room had been a painter's studio. There was even a paint table with rows of tubes laid out ready for use, and a stoneware jar holding a collection of brushes.

'Were you looking for something?' Isobel must have followed him up the stairs and was standing in the doorway.

'Was this your mother's studio?'

She nodded. 'They've been in here this morning.'

'Who keeps it like this?'

'I do. When Mother died they let me bring all her clothes up here.' She gestured vaguely to a couple of cupboards which occupied one wall. 'Everything else of hers was up here anyway.'

He was disturbed by the change in the girl; she had lost her aggression; vitality had gone out of her and she looked at him with dull resignation.

'Do you mind if I look around?'

A gesture.

Between the windows there were shelves crammed with books: a miniature library on the history of art and a mixed bag of fiction and biography.

Wycliffe looked around the room. No desk, no filing drawers; in fact, very few drawers of any sort. 'Surely your mother must have left papers – letters, that sort of thing?'

'She didn't leave much. Mother wasn't one for keeping things.'

'And what she did leave?'

Isobel looked at him intently for a moment or two,

then turned away. There was a catch in her voice. 'I wish I could trust you.'

Wycliffe was moved; for an instant this was his own daughter a few years earlier with something on her mind, something to tell.

He said, 'I will tell you exactly how far you can trust me, Isobel, then you must make up your own mind. It is my job to find out who killed your stepmother and why. It is also my job to explain, if I can, circumstances surrounding your mother's death which seem to cast doubt on the idea that it was accidental. All I can say is that anything you tell me will remain confidential as long as it is not directly relevant to what I have to do.'

There was a sound of heavy footsteps on the stairs leading to the attics, then on the bare boards of the passage outside. It was strange. They stood, waiting, looking at each other, until the footsteps ceased and Roger Kemp stood in the open doorway. The situation had features of a confrontation, but it was nothing of the sort; Roger was behaving more like an intruder. He looked from one to the other, and at the room which had been his wife's, in mild astonishment and muttered, 'I had no idea . . .'

Wycliffe wondered how long it was since he had last seen the inside of this room.

Kemp repeated, 'No idea . . .' Then, recovering himself, he turned to Wycliffe. 'They told me you were up here, but I see that Isobel is looking after you so . . .' His voice trailed off. He stood his ground for a little longer, then turned away. They waited while his footsteps receded along the passage and down the stairs.

Isobel looked at Wycliffe and her expression seemed to say, 'You see?' Then, aloud. 'Is it possible that he . . . ?' She did not finish her question but the incident seemed to have given her confidence. She said,

'Mother had a lover.' And a moment later she added, 'She was pregnant by him when she died.'

'She told you this?'

'No! Just now you asked about her papers. Well, among them was a notebook in which she scribbled down odd things that happened, things that were on her mind, things that she intended to do . . . It wasn't a diary but something like that.'

Wycliffe nodded. 'And in it she mentioned her pregnancy?'

'Several times. And she was always referring to "Pasto" as she called him. I suppose it was her pet name for the man. I don't know who he was.'

She spoke baldly and Wycliffe realized the effort it was costing her.

'Was she distressed about her pregnancy?'

'No, she seemed pleased. At one point what she wrote seemed to mean that she was intending to leave Father and live with the other man, but then there were difficulties.'

'You still have this notebook?'

She flushed. 'No, I burned it.'

'So you've known about this ever since your mother died?'

'No, I found the little book less than a year ago when I had all the books out of the shelves because some of them seemed to be going mouldy. It was hidden at the back.'

'And that's what started you asking questions.'

'I wanted to know if Mother had taken her own life because there seemed no other way out, or if she had been deliberately . . .' Her voice let her down but a moment later she added with emphasis, 'I still want to know.'

Wycliffe was well aware of what all this had cost the girl and he did not want to prolong her distress but there was something else he needed to know. 'I suppose you know of the little shrine in Mayne's Closet?'

She nodded. 'So Crispy has told you about that. I'm glad.'

Wycliffe sat in his chair and brooded.

Kemp, a man with an obsession. Had that obsession cost the lives of his two wives . . . ? There was no real evidence concerning the first – and no body. But the second? If Kemp had killed his second wife what could have persuaded him to drive her body to Kellycoryk and leave it there for hours before finally disposing of it?

A good question to which there was no obvious answer.

Wycliffe was alone in his makeshift office and the little room was catching the early evening sun, making him feel drowsy.

But Roger was not the only one with a motive. Under the provisions of his father's will if Kellycoryk was *sold*, Roger would receive half the proceeds while Francis, Agnes, and Clare Jordan had one-sixth each. But if the property was leased as proposed, any possible carve-up would be indefinitely postponed.

Although Kellycoryk as a unit might be a liability, broken up into lots: the hundred and fifty acres of farmland, fifty of woodland, the lake, the house, Chylathva, the cottages and cove, would surely bring in enough to make a one-sixth share attractive . . .

Commonplace greed is the motive for most crimes, from theft to murder, but he could see little that was commonplace in the events at Kellycoryk . . . *And there is nothing commonplace about madness!* The words which he had come across somewhere recently seemed to erupt into his thoughts.

He was in a strange mood. In those few cases in

which he had become personally and deeply involved there had come a time when, without any particular regard for the evidence, indeed without much conscious thought of any sort, he had reached a conclusion which had served him as a guiding principle through the rest of the case.

There's nothing commonplace about madness.

Fragments of memory, phrases read or spoken, scenes witnessed, even the odd word or gesture, seemed suddenly to correlate in his mind, to form the outline of a pattern and to suggest a coherent view of what really mattered.

Molly, speaking of Francis: 'I live here with him and, like all the Kemps, he's never grown up.' And later. 'Of course he's a Kemp; they're all dreamers. Frankie's thing is being a great painter. If he'd only settle for being good . . .'

And Clare Jordan: 'You might say I took the opportunity to escape . . . life at Kellycoryk was a strange experience. You felt cut off, isolated from normality by a whole system of ideas, assumptions, prejudices . . .'

Isobel: 'I've had enough of this! You don't understand!'

And Crispin, who said very little . . . Perhaps too little . . .

Then a visual memory of Roger Kemp lying back in his chair, staring at the ceiling with Coryk curled up among the papers on his work table.

And two, more moving, visual experiences of that very afternoon: in Mayne's Closet, standing by Crispin as the boy shone his torch on the words inscribed by his father on a memorial stone to his mother.

And later, in what had been Julia Kemp's studio – that fleeting moment when Kemp had faced his daughter across the floor as though across some unbridgeable gulf, muttering to himself, 'I had no idea . . . No idea.'

Wycliffe became aware that he was stiff and uncomfortable in his chair. It was evening, the light was golden. Time to go home.

He arrived back at the cottage and pulled off the track to park. He cut the engine but did not immediately get out of the car. The sun must be low over the Nare, the sky was almost cloudless and the sea shone. Already there were lights in the cottage and he could see Helen moving around, perhaps laying the table for supper. In a moment or two she would look up and see him but for once he was reluctant to return to the domestic routine.

At least he was clearer in his mind about things that had previously confused him. The crime he had been called in to solve was the murder of Bridget Kemp, and he was becoming convinced that it had little to do with wills, with Coast and Country, with whether or not the Kemps would continue at Kellycoryk, with who might gain or who might lose if this or that course were adopted. Rather it was an explosion of hate . . . Perhaps not even that; but a release of inner tensions which had become insupportable.

But who was suffering these suppressed and insupportable tensions that could find release only in violence? Roger? His brother Francis? He had to admit that to him the Kemp brothers seemed essentially weak and ineffective, bumbling rather than vicious. But Isobel? Agnes? Crispin?

Helen had spotted him sitting in the car; she waved. Time to go indoors.

Pork spare ribs after marinating in a witches' brew of apple, onion, lemon, and garlic, grilled and served with mushrooms and sauté potatoes. Wycliffe gave the occasion his seal of approval with another bottle of the light and fruity Barsac.

They talked about the cove and the remnants of an almost feudal relationship which had survived into the present century and received its death blow in the aftermath of the First World War.

Helen said, 'But five of the cottages are still occupied by families who owe their tenancy to former service with the Kemps. Mrs Pascoe, who has the cottage by the bridge, told me that her husband's family had been at Kellycoryk almost as long as the Kemps. He himself was employed there as a boy, but now he works for a builder in the village.'

When Wycliffe set out on his walk the sun had gone down and the sea had taken on a translucent greenish hue. By the time he reached the cottage by the bridge he knew that he had already decided to call on the Pascoes.

There were lights on upstairs and down, and muted pop music, all enveloping, pulsated in the air. He walked up the path and knocked. His knock was answered by a woman with whom he already had a nodding acquaintance. She was fortyish, pleasant, and he remembered that she walked with a slight limp.

'I wondered if you and your husband could spare me a few minutes?'

'Mr Wycliffe . . . ! Come in, do! But you must take us as you find us.'

He followed her into the living room. 'This is Jim, my husband.' Jim had the newspaper spread on the table among the supper dishes, a brawny man with a dark moustache. The raucous pop music, dominant now, came from upstairs.

He said, 'Our two girls, twelve and fifteen; they say they can't do their homework without that row.' He raised his voice. 'Turn that thing off, Jean! We've got company.'

Peace descended like the heavenly dove and Jim said, 'There! Isn't it nice when they turn it off?'

It was Wycliffe who felt at a disadvantage. 'As your cottage is so close to the bridge I wondered if either of you heard a car arriving at or leaving Kellycoryk on the night Mrs Kemp disappeared?'

Pascoe looked at his wife. 'Ask her. I go to bed to sleep.'

Mrs Pascoe nodded. 'Yes, I often hear Mrs Kemp's car when she comes in late and I did that night. I can't say when it was exactly but she woke me. Then, some time later, when I'd got off to sleep again I heard a car driving away – up the hill out of the cove. O' course I couldn't say whether it was the same car.'

This was a bonus. It was not what he had come for; that was more difficult if he was to avoid stirring up gossip. He said, trying to sound casual, 'I've become interested in Kellycoryk and, knowing that your family were for so long part of the place, I thought I would like to talk to you.'

Jim folded his newspaper. 'You're welcome, Mister, but I can't tell you anything about the family as it is now. I've not worked there for more'n ten years, and then the first Mrs Kemp was still with us.'

Wycliffe said, 'It's not so much the people as the place that I was hoping to learn something about, in particular the old house and the tunnel. Perhaps I should say that I've read Jean Scott's book and that I've seen the tunnel and Mayne's Closet.'

Pascoe grinned. 'You must be somebody special; but there, I suppose you are.'

'I have to admit that I'm interested. Is it supposed to be some sort of secret?'

'I don't know about secret exactly, but the Kemps don't like it talked about. God knows why after all this time, but that's how they are.'

Pascoe looked at his wife, then at Wycliffe, and seemed to decide. 'Well, everybody round here knows the story and there's no reason why you shouldn't. It seems that the old house, the Tudor house, used to get flooded pretty regular, and a certain John Kemp, way back in the seventeen-fifties, decided to deepen the tunnel. To do it he drafted in men from the mines, and the bed of the stream was lowered by four feet, say about six feet below what is now the walkway level.'

Pascoe, warming to his story, tilted back his chair. 'Now this John Kemp was a bit of an antiquarian and, through his work on the tunnel, he got interested in Mayne's Closet. The story goes that in that sort of built-in stone chest they call Mayne's Bed, he found a collection of church silver rightly belonging to St Endel church. It must have bin hidden there long before to keep it out of the hands of the King's men an' somehow it got overlooked when the Pope came out on top again with Queen Mary.' Pascoe looked at Wycliffe. 'You don't need me to go on from there.'

Wycliffe finished for him. 'You're saying that more than two centuries ago John Kemp found the little hoard and disposed of it on the black market of the time.'

Pascoe chuckled. 'Anyway, that's the story that's come down through the families in the cove. All I can say is, if it's true, the Kemps had better luck then than they've had since . . .' He broke off. 'Ah, that looks better!'

Mrs Pascoe had come in from the kitchen with cans of bitter and glasses. 'We sometimes have a glass about now if we got company.'

It was after ten when Wycliffe left, and he was seen off at the gate by husband and wife. Nice people. He felt guilty about something without being quite sure what.

The sky had clouded over and it was very dark, only the sea shone dimly and he had to pick his way over the bridge and along the track back home.

Wycliffe had a restless night. A freakish notion which had been lurking on the fringes of his thoughts was beginning to acquire a sort of credibility and he was impatient for morning and the chance to try it out. Caution would have to be his watchword or he ran the risk of falling flat on his face in the proverbial mire.

He had to deal with Helen's plaintive question. 'Can't you sleep?' And later, with her resigned diagnosis. 'It must be those spare ribs.' He noted this second observation at a quarter-past two. Then he did sleep, and dreamed a dream which sometimes turned up with appropriate variations when he was under stress. He was a young constable again, a greenhorn in the witness box, being cross-examined by defending counsel, cold and supercilious: 'These events took place on the thirteenth of the month. You agree with that date, Constable?'

'Yes, sir.'

A pause while counsel surveys the courtroom to let the point go home, then, 'Are you possessed of second sight or some other means by which you are enabled to foresee the future?'

'No.'

'Then how does it come about that your notebook record of the occurrence is dated the twelfth?'

By shortly after six he was awake again. He eased himself out of bed and went downstairs, made coffee, and walked on the shore. No sign of Harvey though his Deux-Chevaux was parked by the cottage. It was misty, not actually raining, but wetting. He was restless. It would be another two hours at least before he could get to work without giving too much of a build-up to a possible fiasco. Resigned, he went back to the cottage, found Helen's Trollope in the window seat, opened it at random and started to read. At half-past seven when Helen came downstairs she found him in his chair fast asleep.

At nine he was closeted with Kersey and Lucy Lane. 'I don't want to ask permission; I think we must go for a warrant.'

At eleven o'clock, in two cars, they were on their way up the drive at Kellycoryk. Wycliffe was in the first car, with Lucy Lane, Kersey and Fox. A uniformed constable and a technician called Knowles, who knew about locks, travelled in the second car. Avoiding the front of the house, the two cars parked in the alley which led to the yard and marked the boundary between the 'new' house and the ruins of the old.

When they were all out, Wycliffe said, 'I'm leaving it to you, Lucy. Take the constable with you, tell Kemp that we propose to investigate Mayne's Closet, show him the warrant, and leave it at that.'

The four men, Fox with his camera gear, the technician with his case of tools, set out over the sodden grass, picking their way between the maze of walls. It was raining now, a thin rain drifting before a fitful breeze. When they reached the steps which led down to the padlocked door they could hear the water, a muffled, unremitting scurry of sound. Knowles made short work of the lock, the door opened, and daylight reached feebly into the darkness of the tunnel. Kersey switched on a powerful hand lamp.

Wycliffe said, 'Mind your heads and watch out for your feet, it may be slippery.'

The confined stream moved with a smooth rush, its sound echoing beneath the arching walls. Kersey's lamp made swirling patterns of light on the rippling surface.

Wycliffe led the way. 'It's not far.'

They reached the narrow entrance to Mayne's Closet. 'I want you in there first, Fox. Photographs of the place before we disturb it. Make sure that the inscription on the slate is readable.'

Kersey said, 'The things we do for a living.'

Fox inserted himself into the cavity. Kersey passed him the lamp, and Fox set about becoming acquainted with the amenities of Mayne's Closet while the others waited in darkness.

Intermittent clicks, burrs and flashes punctuated the next few minutes before Fox said, 'I think that's it.'

He was joined by Wycliffe and Knowles where, at least, they could stand upright.

Wycliffe went to the recess. 'I think there must be a cavity under the slates; lift them without damaging them if you can.'

After the fashion of good tradesmen the world over, with slow deliberation, Knowles removed the statue of the Virgin and the two candlesticks to a place of safety in one corner. Then, selecting a chisel from his bag, he inserted the blade beneath the slate at one end and began tapping it with his hammer, working along the whole length and back again several times until, gently, the mortar was shaken loose. This done, he lifted the slates undamaged and rested them on the floor.

Wycliffe's cavity (he felt a proprietorial interest) was narrower than might have been expected because the supporting wall consisted of foot-thick slabs of granite. There was a strong, almost choking smell of decay, dank and putrid. The cavity seemed to be stuffed with black, rotting straw.

Wycliffe picked up a short crowbar from Knowles's kit and, directing the light into the cavity, he began, gently, to push the straw to one end. At a depth of about a foot he uncovered the staring eye-sockets of a human face.

He turned away. 'All right; let's get outside.'

Fox went first through the gap, followed by Knowles and his tools, with Wycliffe bringing up the rear. Waiting on the walkway in darkness Kersey was unaware of what, if anything, had been found.

Wycliffe shepherded them back to the entrance and up the steps into the open air with, for more reasons than one, a sense of relief, but his manner was terse and sombre. 'I think we've found Julia Kemp but now it's a matter for Franks and the professionals.'

It was still raining, gossamer threads of rain; but there had been a spectator. Crispin was moving off, unhurried, and, apparently, untroubled by whether he was seen or not.

Wycliffe should have been pleased. Earlier he was concerned at the possibility that he was making a fool of himself but now his hunch had paid off and there was good reason to hope that he would soon know what had really happened to the first Mrs Kemp. But any satisfaction was mingled with a gut feeling that all this was bringing him no nearer to solving the murder of Bridget Kemp.

On the car phone he enlisted his experts.

Chapter Nine

Wednesday morning 12 May

Roger was at his table, the ritual papers and books spread out in front of him. In the midst of it all Coryk slept, disturbed now and then by feline dreams, or by indigestion. But it was days since Roger had added anything significant to the heap of manuscript in the open filing tray.

Outside it was overcast and raining; in the library an ancient desk lamp shed its yellow light over the littered table and shone on Coryk's glossy black fur. For several days now, Roger had kept a small glass by his hand and a two-litre bottle of cheap red wine on the floor by his chair. From time to time he would top up the glass, his movements surreptitious, although there was no-one to see.

He felt trapped, finally overtaken by the past. For five years he had lived with the knowledge that it was possible, at any time . . . Now that time had come and in circumstances which he could never have imagined even in his worst moments. There was a tap at the door; it opened, and Crispin came in. Roger could not remember the last occasion when Crispin had come into the library, or sought him out anywhere. The boy came to stand by the table, his pallor jaundiced by the lamplight. He wore jeans and a nondescript jacket, he was rarely seen in anything else, and he seemed totally indifferent to the weather. Now, jeans and jacket were darkened by rain, his hair was plastered to his head, and drops of moisture glistened on his forehead.

Roger tried to sound ordinary. 'You're wet, Crispy.'

Crispin said, 'They've been in Mayne's Closet for an hour. They've just come out.'

Roger shook his head like a man in a trance but said nothing.

Crispin went on, 'You know what they've found.'

Father and son stared at each other, wordless.

Any further exchange was prevented by another tap at the door, and Agnes came in, white faced and sombre. 'The police again.'

Wycliffe and the dour inspector who had brought the news that Bridget had been shot.

'Detective Superintendent Wycliffe and Detective Inspector Kersey.'

Wycliffe said, 'Mr Kemp, I have to tell you that remains which we believe to be human have been found in the recessed portion of Mayne's Closet.

'Obviously there will be an inquiry to establish the identity of those remains and how they came to be there. If you have any comment or explanation which you wish to offer, we are here to listen. On the other hand you may prefer to wait until we have more positive information.'

Roger did not know what he had expected from the police, he had refused to allow himself to speculate, but this was not it. Wycliffe was mild-mannered and matter-of-fact; even his hard-faced companion did not behave aggressively . . . And there were no uniforms. Roger fumbled with his papers while choosing his words; finally he said, 'Yes . . . That will be best.'

Crispin looked on, his face expressionless.

Wycliffe continued, dryly official. 'In order to assist our inquiries we shall need photographs of your first wife with any details of distinguishing physical characteristics which you are able to provide.'

Roger looked about him as though in search of help which he failed to find, then he said, 'Agnes . . . Yes, Agnes will give you what you want . . . And John Harvey . . . John is Julia's brother – and he's a doctor . . .'

They left Kellycoryk finally with half a dozen photographs and a few details of Julia's physique. Outside, Kersey said, 'I know all that I've said about that guy but I still don't know what to make of him. He could fit almost anywhere in my book between a well-intentioned if self-centred bungler and a psychotic killer. But whatever he is, he was expecting to be led away in handcuffs.'

When they were getting into the car Wycliffe, perhaps a little on the defensive, said, 'I don't want this to go off at half-cock, Doug. When we move we must be sure of our ground.'

They were lunching at the New Inn, Kersey, Lucy Lane and Wycliffe. There were not many customers for Mrs Sara's lamb stew, which was a pity. But it meant they could speak freely.

Kersey said, 'I don't understand what put you on to it.'

Wycliffe wasn't quite sure himself and he had no intention of trying to rationalize the hotch-potch of experiences and notions which had led him to the stone chest.

He said, 'You probably noticed that although Julia Kemp was supposed to have drowned on the fourteenth of June, the inscription on the slate slab, cut by Roger, puts her death at the thirteenth.'

'A mistake.'

'I thought so at first but then it occurred to me that she might really have died on the thirteenth and the story of her drowning could have been a cover-up . . . I mean, when a body is found an inquiry is inevitable, but in a case of drowning nobody is all that surprised if the body fails to turn up.'

Kersey paused with his fork halfway to his lips. 'A cover-up? Are you suggesting that Kemp not only murdered his first wife but that there wasn't even the trappings of an accident at sea?'

'I think it's possible, even likely, that Julia Kemp was already dead when Roger and Clare Jordan set out for their boat trip on the morning of the four-teenth. The boat trip was a charade. Julia had an appointment in St Mawes which she never kept. She did not board the boat with her husband and Clare Jordan at Percuil. Neither, in my opinion, did she join them at St Mawes.'

Lucy said, 'All this means that Clare Jordan was his accomplice.'

Wycliffe shrugged.

'But if what you are saying is true, surely Kemp would have taken the trouble to get his date right.'

Wycliffe said, 'I think that can be explained, but I'd rather it waited until we have proof that the body we found in Mayne's Closet really is that of Julia Kemp.' Abruptly, he turned to Lucy Lane. 'Do Roman Catholics bury their dead in a special cemetery or a specially allocated part of a cemetery?'

'I don't think either. As far as I know, it's simply a question of the ground being consecrated. Why the sudden interest, sir?'

'Would you say that Mayne's Closet was con-secrated ground?'

Lucy was intrigued. 'You would have to get a professional opinion on that. I can imagine some ecclesiastical committee sitting for weeks to decide it. My father's customers are mainly Methodists – if they are anything – but most of his flock opt for cremation anyway.' Lucy, with characteristic objectivity.

Kersey was finding it all difficult to take. 'Shouldn't

we at least be pulling in Kemp and the Jordan woman for questioning?'

'They won't run away.'

The afternoon brought watery sunshine. By four o'clock there was a flurry of activity in the ruins of Tudor Kellycoryk, probably more than at any time since the old house became a quarry for materials from which to build the new. With the approval of the coroner the body was to be removed for identification and post-mortem examination.

Cars, and a plain van, were lined up in the alleyway between the house and the ruins. Four men, all kitted out in protective clothing, picked their discriminating way down the steps, and through the tunnel to the reclusion of Mayne's Closet and the grisly remains which had been hidden under his stone bed. One of the men was Franks, the pathologist, two others were scientific officers from Forensic, and the fourth was Fox with his camera and lighting equipment. Wycliffe had put in an appearance to satisfy protocol but proceeded no further than the entrance to the tunnel. Twenty minutes went by before Franks, still in full kit, complete with mask, rejoined him.

'You do find me some nice jobs, Charles. Sometimes I think I would have done better as a sewage operative if that is the politically correct job description. I can't tell you much until we get her out. She's been there some time – years, probably, but it's not going to be easy to make an assessment.'

Franks brooded, thinking aloud. 'The body is clothed, and in what amounts to a sealed stone coffin. Insect activity would have been minimal . . . Unless that bloody straw made a difference . . . The temperature in the chamber probably doesn't vary much either side of eight to ten degrees . . . The humidity is hardly a factor if the coffin was sealed . . .'

Franks sighed. 'On balance I'd say the conditions favour preservation, but we shall have to see. Anyway, identification shouldn't be a problem and it should be possible to establish the cause of death without too much difficulty. You're expecting this to be the body of the first Mrs Roger Kemp?'

'I shall be surprised if it turns out to be anybody else.'

'And she went missing five years ago so that gives me somewhere to start.'

Two men in white came out of the tunnel and went up the steps.

Franks said, 'They've gone to fetch the shell so we shan't be long now.'

Wycliffe said, 'I've arranged for Dr Harvey to attend for identification purposes. Although he's a doctor, as the dead woman's brother it will be a pretty gruesome business for him, but he's agreed.'

News of the discovery had leaked out and half a dozen reporters, four men and two women, some with cameras, had tramped through the ruins to the top of the stone steps where a uniformed man held the pass.

The presence of Wycliffe was an unexpected bonus and they gathered round.

'What's the story? Another body?'

'There's no story yet. All I can tell you is that this morning a body was found in a chamber off the tunnel which carries the stream beneath the old house.'

'Mayne's Closet?' From one of the women.

'You've evidently done your homework. Yes. Actually the body was concealed in a sort of stone chest known as Mayne's Bed.'

'How long has it been there?'

'That is what the pathologist will try to find out.'

One of the men looked suspicious. 'What's all this about Mayne's Closet? Are we talking about ancient history or another crime? I mean, you wouldn't be here if they were just digging up some corpse from way back.'

'We shall know more after the post-mortem. Until then . . .'

That evening the Wycliffes departed from routine and had their meal at a little restaurant in Portloe which, with a disregard for furnishing and décor that was almost French, concentrated on the food and wine. With a certain feeling of smugness they walked there and back, so avoiding the need to nominate a sacrificial abstainer to drive the car.

On their homeward trek, above and ahead of them, was a cloudless turquoise sky, but behind them, over the Nare, the sunset was hidden by a bank of dense cloud. Wycliffe, who liked to sound like the Ancient Mariner, said, 'Rain tomorrow.'

Thursday morning 13 May

But the day dawned with limpid clarity; high, pale cloud obscured the sun, and the sea was a silvery plain; only the smallest ripples broke along the shore.

The breakfast-time radio news had the story: 'At Kellycoryk in Cornwall, home of the Kemp family, police yesterday afternoon discovered the body of a woman concealed in a subterranean stone chest in the ruins of the old house. The police are already investigating the murder of Mrs Bridget Kemp, wife of the present owner of the estate, whose body was recovered from the sea last Monday. She had been shot through the head.'

Wycliffe arrived at the Incident Room while parents, in cars and on foot were delivering their offspring to the school, and elderly visitors, on early-summer packages, collected their newspapers from the post office. But Kersey too turned up with a selection of the newspapers. 'They go as far as they can without actually saying that this is the body of Kemp's first wife.'

Kersey was in a contentious mood. 'I suppose, sir, that we now sit about waiting until Franks delivers himself of what we already know. In the old days we'd have had Kemp and the Jordan woman banged up by now.'

There were times when Wycliffe could be irritated by Kersey's moods and this was one. 'No, we do not sit about waiting, we try for a breakthrough in the Bridget Kemp case where we are sure of our facts. Bridget Kemp was shot a week ago and it's three days since her body was recovered, but we've not got very far. There's little doubt that she was shot at Hendra Croft and driven to Kellycoryk in the load space of her estate car. The car remained in the alleyway beside the house for well over an hour. Isobel says she saw it from her window with the driver's door wide open; her brother claims that he saw it being driven off by someone he took to be a woman. I've no doubt the car was there, though I don't necessarily believe the young Kemps' versions of what they saw. In any case, we've nothing to suggest who the killer was or how he or she got to Hendra Croft.'

Kersey was taken aback. 'But surely if Kemp was responsible for the death of his first wife—'

Wycliffe cut him short. 'There is no real evidence that Kemp killed anybody, but if you believe that he did then you should go all out at finding factual evidence which will justify holding him. I think you might be wasting your time. Kemp is a sitting duck and a bit of a fool, but there are other targets.'

Wycliffe looked at his old friend and his manner softened. 'We go back a long way, Doug, and times have changed. I suggest we keep the broad view for a bit longer, at least until we understand the link, if any, between her killing and the death of her predecessor.'

Kersey's grin was sheepish. 'You're the boss.'

Lucy Lane, witness to the exchange, was having a rare glimpse of the depth of the relationship which existed between these two so different men.

They were interrupted by the telephone. 'Dr Franks for you, sir.' Franks too, had started early.

'I tried to get you at the cottage, Charles, but Helen said you'd already left. I'm having the day off and I want to get in some sailing. I've worked half the night on your latest offering.

'Your body, Charles, was female, aged between thirty-five and forty, dark-haired, medium height – about one metre sixty-five. From what evidence remains, including the clothing, I would say that she was of medium build; about sixty kilos, stripped. As far as I can tell her skull and facial bone structure are consistent with the photographs. If necessary we can use dental records and there is quite a bit of soft tissue remaining.'

'Clothing?'

'I'm coming to that. She was wearing a cotton nightdress and a brushed nylon dressing gown. Nothing on her feet. She wore a plain gold wedding ring and she had a gold cross on a chain about her neck. I should add that Dr Harvey is in no doubt that it is the body of his sister. He was very distressed.'

'Cause of death?'

Franks decided that he was being pressurized. 'Don't try to rush me, Charles! However, your woman seems to have died of a severely depressed fracture of the skull in the nieghbourhood of the parietal/occipital suture.'

'A blow?'

'You may not have noticed, Charles, but a blow of some sort is the usual means by which skulls become

183

fractured. The possibilities are that she was struck by someone, that she fell, or that she was pushed.'

'Was the impact with a smooth surface?'

'No, in my opinion with a sharpish edge.'

'So, your informed guess?'

'I don't know how informed I can call it, but in my view the likelihood is that she fell.'

'Fair enough. Anything else?'

'The way in which the body was positioned in that chest thing probably means that it was placed there after rigor had passed off, probably twenty-four hours or more after death.'

Wycliffe was saying his thanks when Franks played his trump: 'Don't you want to know that she was pregnant?'

'Ah!'

'You don't seem all that surprised.'

Wycliffe was evasive. 'Well, it's not unheard of in a married woman of thirty-seven, is it? How long?'

'Sixteen weeks or thereabouts. Anyway, I'm off sailing; if you find any more save 'em for another day.'

So Isobel's story had not been fantasy.

Kersey was unimpressed. 'Apart from her pregnancy he's told us nothing much we didn't already know. At least we can get going, but what's it to be? What sort of charge can we bring?'

'For a start, the most you can expect is conspiracy to conceal a death and/or pervert the course of justice. And a nit-picking lawyer might blow holes through either or both. Let's hear what the pair of them have to say under formal questioning.

'I want you to invite – yes, *invite* in the first instance – Kemp to come with you to sub-division for questioning in connection with the death of his first wife. Bring Clive Lanyon in on this.

'Lucy Lane and WPC Rees will do the same with Clare Jordan. At this stage they will both be helping us with our inquiries. We'll keep it that way for the time being. I shall join Lucy at sub-division.'

Kersey said, 'Do I mention Julia's pregnancy?'

Wycliffe, placatory, said, 'You don't need my advice, Doug. Play it by ear.'

DC Lanyon pressed the recorder button and recited the preliminary incantation. 'This interview begins at 11.05. Present Detective Inspector Kersey and Detective Constable Lanyon. Let me remind you that you are not under arrest and that you do not have to say anything but what you do say . . .'

Roger Kemp, in a grubby shirt and a crumpled suit, sat in the little windowless interview room looking about him with vague unfocused eyes like a man newly awakened from sleep.

Kersey opened the questioning. 'With the finding of your first wife's body in Mayne's Closet do you now admit that the account you gave of her being lost overboard on a boating trip was a fabrication?'

It seemed that the question took a little time to sink in but the answer when it came was definite. 'Yes.'

'I must remind you again that you are entitled to have a legal adviser present at this interview.'

'I don't want a lawyer.'

'So your wife was already dead on the fourteenth of June when that trip took place?'

'Yes.'

'When did she die?'

'The night before.'

'Think carefully before you answer this question. Were you present when she died?'

'Yes.'

'Will you describe the circumstances?'

A profound sigh and a long pause. In the silence they could hear the traffic on the roundabout outside the station. 'We were in the bedroom, going to bed, and there was a quarrel.'

'What was the quarrel about?'

Roger spread his plump soft hands in a helpless gesture. 'I don't know . . . Couples do quarrel.'

'Was it anything to do with your wife being pregnant?'

Roger winced as though he had been struck. '*What?*'

'The pathologist says that your wife was fifteen or sixteen weeks pregnant when she died. Didn't you know?'

A long pause. 'Yes, I did know. She told me that night. I didn't think they could tell, not after all this time . . .' He added after a moment, 'You see, it was not my child.'

'She told you that too?'

Roger looked at Kersey's rubbery, expressive features and looked quickly away. He mumbled, 'She had no need to tell me; we had had no relations of that kind for nearly a year.'

'So that was what the quarrel was about?'

Asking questions of Roger was like interrogating a computer, one watched the changing patterns flicker across the screen until a resolution was achieved.

'No, it was because she wanted me to divorce her.'

'So that she could marry this other man?'

'Yes . . . I would have accepted the child as mine but that was not enough.'

In an identical little room, adjoining, Clare Jordan sat, apparently at ease. Her hair was perfectly controlled; she must have had a recent visit to the hairdresser's. No tinting; those grey streaks testified to wisdom and experience. She wore a plain cornflower-blue frock with a string of pearls, and she carried a white pigskin handbag. Middle-aged virginity tastefully preserved and packaged.

186

Wycliffe and Lucy Lane were about to tax her with questions not very different to those put by Kersey to Kemp. After the prescribed ritual and a few questions to lead in, Wycliffe asked, 'Was Julia Kemp with you on the boating trip?'

'No.'

'She was already dead?'

'Yes.'

'When did she die?'

'The night before.'

'Were you present when she died?'

'Yes.'

'Will you describe the circumstances?'

There was a brief pause while she set her ideas in order. She was a model witness, no word wasted. 'At that time Roger, his wife, his fourteen-year-old son and I were the only ones in the house. At something after eleven, when the boy and I were both in bed, I heard a quarrel going on in their bedroom which was next to mine.'

'The room used by Roger Kemp and his wife?'

'Their bedroom – yes.'

Wycliffe asked, 'Were quarrels between Roger Kemp and his wife frequent?'

'No, but they did occur from time to time, and when they did they tended to become violent – on Julia's side, that is. I have never known Roger raise a hand to anyone.'

After a moment of hesitation she added, 'I knew the risks if Julia became hysterical and when I thought that point was being reached I decided to interfere. I slipped on a dressing gown and went to their room.' She paused, as though reliving the moment in her memory, then: 'When I entered the room they were both standing between the bed and the old fireplace. Julia was clinging to Roger with one hand and hitting him with the other.

187

At the same time she was hissing abuse.'

Lucy said, 'Was Roger resisting?'

'No. But as I came into the room he took hold of both her arms and forced her away from him, he held her for a moment, then he released her. There was no violence in what he did, but as he let go of her arms she just crumpled up; she seemed to slip backwards and, as she fell, she struck her head against the corner of the marble mantelpiece.

'Of course I went to help Julia but at first Roger seemed paralysed with shock. He just stood looking down at her, where she lay with her head in the open grate. When he recovered a little I got him to help me lift her on to the bed. There was some blood from the wound in her head – not a lot, and there were no other signs of injury. All the same it was obvious that she was dead. I did my best to revive her but there was no hope.'

Wycliffe said, 'You were quite sure of that?'

'Quite sure. I trained and worked as a nurse before I went into the antiques business. Julia was dead, there's no doubt of that.'

Clare Jordan was pale and her hands were clenched. She had the gift of graphic narrative and while she was talking, for Wycliffe at least, the little interview room had become that bedroom at Kellycoryk.

There was an interval and he said, 'Would you like to take a break? A cup of tea or something?'

She shook her head. 'No, I'm going through with this.'

Lucy Lane asked, 'Did you see or hear anything of Crispin during all this?'

'Nothing. But that is not so surprising as it sounds. Crispin had the little room right at the east end which is still his, while the bedroom Roger shared with Julia was more than halfway along the corridor. In any case these quarrels between Roger and Julia, though they could be violent, were never very noisy.'

'All right. Will you tell us what happened next?'

Clare Jordan took a handkerchief from her bag and patted her lips. 'I assumed that we would call a doctor at once but Roger pleaded with me, begged me, to wait until morning.'

'Did he give any reason?'

'He said that he wanted to be alone with his wife, to pray at her bedside. Roger has always been a puzzle to me. In some respects he seems to have a faith that is simple and childlike. Yet sometimes I have the impression that his religion is no more than a kind of superstition.'

Lucy Lane said, 'Anyway, you left him alone, as he wished.'

'Yes. I went back to my own room.'

'And?'

'For a long time I lay in bed, listening, and heard nothing. Then, I hardly know how to explain or excuse it, I fell asleep . . . In circumstances that I would not have believed it possible to sleep, I slept . . . Whether it would have made any difference if I'd stayed awake, I don't know.'

Lucy Lane said, 'And when you did wake?'

'When I woke it was getting light. I got out of bed and went to the other room. There was no sign of Roger nor of the body. The bed was as I had last seen it, tumbled, and with a blood-stained pillow case, but apart from that there was nothing to show what had happened.' She broke off abruptly, and said with a helpless little gesture, 'I think, after all, I would like that cup of tea.'

Lucy Lane spoke for the tape, 'This interview is suspended at 11.24.' And she switched off the recorder.

*　　*　　*

On the other side of the wall the other interview had reached a similar point. Kersey said, 'All right, you admit removing your wife's body, but the question is, why did you do it?'

Roger sat, staring at the table top. When it seemed that he would not answer he ran a hand through his short, greying curls and, without looking up, said, 'My main reason was that I'm a coward. If I had let things take their course, when it came out that Julia was pregnant by another man, I would have been accused of murder, at least of manslaughter . . . I couldn't face it. Even if I was acquitted I wouldn't have wanted to go on living . . .'

Another interval before he added, 'I did not kill my wife. I did *not*! She slipped down as though she had fainted, and struck her head as she fell.'

'You said your main reason – there were others?'

The question seemed to trouble him even more deeply than the others. He played a little tattoo on the table top with his fingers. 'I am what I am, I can't help it. To me, Julia was a Kemp – only by marriage, it is true, but still a Kemp, and I wanted her in some private place where I could pray for her soul, especially in some place where that man, whoever he may be, could not approach her.'

'You have no idea who he was?'

'None and I don't wish to know.'

When the interview was resumed next door, and after the ritual announcement for the tape, Wycliffe said, 'You were about to tell us what happened on the morning after Julia's death.'

'Yes. It was about half-past four when I returned to the bedroom and found it empty. I was frantic, I couldn't imagine what had happened.

'Then, perhaps half an hour later, Roger turned up. It was strange, uncanny. I had never seen him so calm.

He said, "I've laid Julia to rest." And that was all I could get from him at first. I pointed out that he would have to tell somebody exactly what had happened, that there would be an inquiry, an inquest . . . But all he would say was, "Julia is at rest; she will never be seen again on this earth and I shall pray for her soul."

'I lost my temper but it got me nowhere. It was a nightmare.' She stopped speaking and seemed to be reliving those moments.

'Then, as though he were planning something ordinary and rational, he explained what he intended that we should do. Of course it was the boat trip, the accident, and all that followed . . .' Her voice trailed off.

'And how did you react?'

'I was horrified. It seemed inconceivable.'

'But you agreed.'

She nodded. 'In the end, yes. He said that if I didn't he would certainly be charged with murder . . . He went on about the disgrace, the scandal that would destroy the family. He even said that I owed it to the family after being brought up by them. I don't know how long we kept it up but at the finish I decided that in view of what he'd already done, to do as he wanted would be the lesser of two evils. After all, Julia was dead and nothing would bring her back . . .'

'Did you then, or at any time since until now, find out what he had done with his wife's body?'

She shivered. 'No! And I have never wanted to know.'

'Just one more question: Did you know that Julia Kemp was pregnant?'

A shrewd look. 'I guessed as much.'

'Was it ever mentioned between you?'

'No.'

'Had you any idea as to who the father might be?'

She hesitated, lips pursed. 'I had a suspicion that

there was something between Julia and Roger's brother, Francis. But that was all it was – a suspicion.'

It was some time later when Roger Kemp and Clare Jordan left the police station, having initialled their tapes. No charges were brought, but it was made clear that the investigation would continue.

Back at the Incident Room with Kersey and Lucy Lane, Wycliffe telephoned John Harvey at his surgery. 'I think we should talk; this afternoon if possible.'

Harvey sounded anxious. 'At your Incident Room?'

Wycliffe hesitated, he wanted the contact to be unofficial. 'I would prefer your cottage.'

Wycliffe lunched at the New Inn with Lucy Lane and Kersey. Mrs Sara gave them a small room to themselves at the back of the house.

'A bit more private, like.' She went on in the same breath, 'Today it's a fricassee of chicken, and a nice light almond sponge-pudding to follow with cream or custard . . .'

When they were served Kersey put down his bait. 'So the first Mrs Kemp had a heart attack during a fairly athletic quarrel with her husband. She fell, hit her head on the fender, and it was all over.' He paused to masticate the latest forkful. 'I suppose it could happen.'

Wycliffe refused to be drawn. After lunch he walked down through the village and along the cliff road to the cove. The sky was uniformly overcast with high cloud, colours were muted, and not a breath of air disturbed the glassy sea. Wycliffe found the brooding stillness oppressive.

No sign of Helen or of any life in the cove, but Harvey's Deux-Chevaux was parked by his cottage and Harvey met him at the door.

'This is building up for a storm.'

They sat by the open door. Wycliffe was facing

Julia's painting of the cove and Kellycoryk seen from the sea. Magical and sinister; they were the words which had come to his mind when he first saw the painting and they came back to him now. Harvey, looking tired and haggard, watched him, waiting for him to begin.

'First, I'm sorry that it fell to you to identify your sister; sorry too, for all the circumstances.'

Harvey was silent for a while, then he said, 'It's hard to realize that the boating accident, an event which one has accepted and lived with for several years, turns out to have been no more than a piece of fiction – a charade.' He sounded bitter.

Wycliffe did not rush his fences, he allowed time for the silences to work. Then, 'I'm wondering whether Franks has mentioned his findings to you?'

'No, Franks was strictly professional and I was, quite properly, treated like any other relative. You've had his report?'

Wycliffe gave him the substance of what Franks had said and Harvey listened until he had finished.

'So Julia was pregnant.'

'You had no suspicion?'

'None. She didn't tell me and I wasn't seeing enough of her to tumble to it for myself.' There was another break before he went on, 'This blow to the head – there's no indication of how it came about?'

'Before I answer that question, do you know anything of your sister's medical history? Did she, for example, suffer from hypertension or a heart condition? Was she subject to fits . . . ?'

Harvey looked at him in surprise. 'She never confided in me as a doctor. When she needed one she went to Tim Paul in St Mawes.' Wycliffe thought that he had finished but after a time he went on, 'Tim did mention to me once, in confidence, that there was evidence to suggest a degree of mitral stenosis and that he had recommended her to see a cardiologist but she had flatly refused. Tim assured me that he would monitor the situation and that he wasn't unduly concerned.' Harvey broke off abruptly. 'Why are you asking me this?'

Wycliffe said, 'Franks thinks that your sister might have struck her head in falling and the question arises how she came to fall.'

Harvey nodded and Wycliffe continued, 'From what you know of her medical condition, does that strike you as credible?'

Harvey hesitated. 'If, as you say, she was four months pregnant, having had no medical supervision, and given her heart condition, I have to say that it does.'

Chapter Ten

Thursday evening/Friday morning 13/14 May

'Here is a severe weather warning: southwesterly gales are expected to affect Cornwall and south Devon in the early hours of tomorrow morning. Winds are likely to reach storm force on exposed coasts and, in rain squalls, gusts may exceed ninety miles per hour with the possibility of structural damage. Gales with heavy rain will continue into the daylight hours and winds will remain strong until at least midday.'

Agnes always paid attention to the weather forecast and this one was the signal for a strategic placing of buckets in attics and roof spaces. She was not deterred by the stillness of the evening.

The Kemps, all four of them, ate their evening meal with scarcely a word exchanged and Roger did not refer to his interview with the police. When the meal was over he turned to Agnes and said, 'I'm expecting a visitor, so if you hear voices . . .'

'Doesn't this visitor have a name?'

Roger looked at her, his expression totally blank, and said nothing.

At about half-past ten Agnes went to bed.

The weather was still quiet but at a little after midnight the wind began to pick up and within an hour it was roaring around the old house, punctuated by explosive gusts and violent rain squalls which seemed to threaten the windows if not the walls themselves.

As usual Agnes's alarm clock went off at seven but she was already up. The wind was unabated and outside pandemonium reigned. Inside, windows rattled and from time to time the whole building seemed to shudder. She had discovered without surprise that the electricity was off.

Still in her dressing gown, she had made a quick check on her buckets and bowls: two fresh leaks, though nothing calamitous. Now, washed and dressed, she was in her kitchen, thanking God for the Aga.

At some time after eight she knocked on the library door. 'Breakfast, Roger!'

There was no response, but that was not unusual. When she returned to the kitchen Crispin was already in his place. His right hand was bandaged and blood had seeped through to stain the dressing.

A strange look passed between them. Complicity? 'How does it feel?'

'All right.'

'Not throbbing?'

'No.'

Roger did not come, and after ten or fifteen minutes Agnes went back to the library. In the hall she glanced up the stairs and saw Isobel in her dressing gown, apparently half-asleep, on her way to their only bathroom.

Agnes called to her, 'I'm trying to get your father in to breakfast.'

The Wycliffes, awakened in the small hours, were having their first experience of the front line during a real blow. When they finally convinced themselves that their cottage, having been there for a hundred and fifty years, would probably survive the night, they went back to bed and, improbable as it seemed, they slept.

It was broad daylight, or as near to it as conditions allowed, when Wycliffe drew back the curtains in the living room and looked out through a deposit of finest salt crystals on a grey waste of sea streaked with white. He had already discovered that there was no electricity. Out of curiosity he tried the telephone; it too, was off, but there was an RT in his car outside.

The pendulum wall clock struck eight on its tinny gong. He was late – very. So what? It was strange, though he had noticed before that the violence of nature, a gale, a thunderstorm, seemed to put him on a high, and to trivialize the concerns of everyday. 'What is man that thou art mindful of him?' And all that.

So he searched for a little Gaz stove that he remembered seeing in one of the cupboards and set about brewing coffee. Then, with a sense of achievement, he offered the result at the bedside of his wife.

· The house felt cold, and he kindled a fire in the open grate. Driftwood, which they had collected at a whim, came into its own and by the time Helen was down the place was almost cosy. She set about getting breakfast on the little stove.

It was only then that his thoughts returned to the case and to wondering where events were leading. The death of the first Mrs Kemp was unlikely to result in a charge more serious than conspiracy. Conviction on a conspiracy charge could mean anything from a suspended sentence to a long term of imprisonment but his gut feeling was that the scales would be weighted in favour of leniency. The shooting of Bridget Kemp was a very different matter; the only feasible charge was murder, but such a charge must be supported by evidence and so far there was none that would get past the CPS let alone the courts.

His broodings were interrupted by the sound of a car engine which was cut, followed by knocking on the front door.

Wycliffe opened the door to a miniature tornado of wind. John Harvey pale and agitated was on the doorstep. 'I'm sorry to burst in on you like this but I had to – the phone isn't working. I've just come from Kellycoryk . . . Roger has shot himself.'

'He's dead?'

'Yes. Crispin came over for me. I've got my car outside.'

Wycliffe said, 'We'll get over there as soon as I've been in touch with my people on the RT.'

'Wouldn't it be better if I went back there right away?'

Wycliffe had to spell it out. 'I'm sorry, but you would be putting yourself and me in an invidious position. We will stay together.'

It was obvious that Harvey was shaken by the implication.

A few minutes later they were out in the grey turbulent world. The rain had stopped, but the wind was carrying salt spray well inland. The stream had overflowed its banks but as far as he could see, the road and the bridge were clear.

To his relief he was able to speak to the Incident Room. Kersey was already there.

Wycliffe gave him the news. 'I want you to stay there for the moment; see that the coroner is notified, also SOCO and Forensic. I'll talk to Franks. We need a small team. Is Lucy with you . . . ? Then send her along. I think we have to look at this with an open mind.'

Harvey, sheltering in the car at his side and still coming to terms with his implied status, said, 'You're treating this as a suspicious death?'

'As you know, I haven't even seen him, but I can't afford to be wrong.'

A moment or two later they were in the drive on the way to the house. Twigs and small branches torn from the shrubs littered the track and were crunched under the car wheels. A fresh rain squall battered the car from the rear and, in front of the house, Wycliffe pulled in as close as he could to the steps. He got out, put his finger on the doorbell, and kept it there.

John Harvey joined him. 'I left them in the kitchen. It's the only room that's warm in the place and with no electricity you can hardly see to think.'

It was Agnes who answered the bell. She was white-faced but composed. They had to help her close the door against the force of the wind.

Wycliffe spoke to her sympathetically, but she merely said, 'You know where to go.'

Wycliffe turned to Harvey. 'All right, let's take a look and you can tell me what you know.'

He led the way down the short passage to the library and opened the door. As he did so he received a shock. Roger was seated at his table, leaning back in his chair in almost exactly the posture in which Wycliffe had found him two days earlier. As then, his eyes were wide open and they seemed to stare at the ceiling, though now the expression in those eyes was one of astonishment. And there was another difference: there was a small, neat entrance hole in his right temple. Wycliffe looked for an exit wound but there was none. Two thin trickles of blood had run down his right cheek and one had dripped on to the lapel of his jacket.

Wycliffe moved around the table. Kemp's arms hung straight down, and on the worn carpet not far from the fingers of his right hand there was a little pistol with an ivory butt.

'Who found him?'

Harvey seemed lost in his own thoughts.

'What . . . ? Oh, it wasn't quite like that. It seems that this morning, as usual, Agnes banged on the library door and told him that his breakfast was ready. He didn't answer, but he never does. When, after a little while, he didn't turn up she went back to the library and it was then that she found the door was locked. She called to him but got no reply. She then tried the door which opens from the back hall into the little room adjoining the library but that too was locked.

'In the end, Crispin went outside and saw his father through the window. He smashed a pane of glass and cut his hand doing it but he reached the catch and raised the sash. Of course he climbed in. The phone wasn't working so Agnes sent him to fetch me.'

The two sash-windows had small panes, and one of the panes, near the catch in the left-hand window, had been smashed, leaving a jagged hole through which rain now blew into the room.

Wycliffe turned his attention to the desk; the usual litter of books and papers, but immediately in front of Roger was a clean sheet of paper on which a message had been written in block capitals: 'THIS IS ONLY WHAT I DESERVED.' A felt-tipped pen lay beside the paper.

'Did the boy tell you exactly what had happened?'

'No. He said that his father had been taken ill and would I come over at once. He was obviously in shock and I didn't question him. It was only when I got here that I heard the full story from Agnes.'

'Presumably you made some sort of examination to confirm that life was extinct. How long, in your opinion, has he been dead?'

Harvey ran his fingers through his hair. 'Of course I was expecting to be asked that and I've thought about it. Rigor is by no means complete but, as I judge it without disturbing him, the body has not yet reached room temperature. In my opinion he's been

200

there a good part of the night. I'd say some time in the small hours.'

'Nobody's mentioned hearing anything that could have been a shot?'

'No.'

'By the way, what's happened to the cat?'

'The cat? I've no idea.'

'It wasn't here when you arrived with the boy?'

Harvey looked puzzled. 'No, is it important?' Then understanding dawned, and he seemed surprised at Wycliffe's interest. 'Oh, the Kemp moggies!'

Wycliffe did not reply, he was preoccupied, and his manner was abrupt. 'I'm going to take a look around. I'm not entirely satisfied that this is suicide. Perhaps you will join the family.'

Harvey looked doubtful but he said, 'Of course.'

Wycliffe went on, 'Obviously they will be distressed but we shall need to talk to them later.'

Left alone, Wycliffe stood for a minute or two looking down at the dead man. He could not shake off a feeling of unreality. It was corny; a 1930's thriller with the squire shot at his desk in a locked library. Wycliffe recalled a cavalcade of fictional, homicidal butlers.

And yet there was nothing inherently unlikely in what seemed to have happened. It would not be surprising if Roger had become suicidal. And if he had decided to kill himself he might well have chosen to do so in the place where he spent most of his waking hours. It might even be expected that he would lock the doors for fear of being disturbed during those agonizing moments when his resolve was faced with the ultimate test . . . All the same . . .

All very reasonable but Wycliffe did not believe a word of it. And at bottom he felt guilty; he had hesitated about what line to take with Roger. There had been enough circumstantial evidence to detain him for further questioning in connection with the death of his second wife. Kersey, left to himself, would certainly have done so and Roger might now still be alive.

From his car he phoned Franks and spoke to the pathologist's secretary.

'He's due in at any minute, Mr Wycliffe. I'll get him to contact you . . .'

Back in the library he was startled momentarily by a flicker, then the lamp on Roger's table lit up, its circle of light achieving a bizarre effect: the table top with its papers and Roger's torso, brightly lit but leaving the head in shadow.

The power was back on. He searched for and found a bank of switches which he flicked over. Half a dozen ceiling lights came alive; they were low-powered and grimy, but even so there was a dramatic transformation. The room with its elegant proportions, the towering bookcases with their orderly rows of dimly lit spines, the tall windows with their red velvet curtains, were replaced by peeling, cracked plaster, ubiquitous dust, a littered floor, and faded, threadbare hangings.

He had seen enough of suicides with a handgun to beware of attaching too much significance to the posture of the victim and to whether or not the weapon was retained in the hand that fired it. All the same, he had never before come across a suicide lolling back in his chair, staring at the ceiling.

Thoughtful, he moved about, looking at this and that but disturbing nothing. He came to the door which led, presumably, into the little room where Roger spent some of his nights. The door was partly open and he pushed it wide. A heavy curtain drawn across the window excluded most of what light there was. He felt for, and found, a light switch.

The room was little more than a passage. A massive

settee took up most of the space and on it was a grubby pillow with a couple of carriage rugs. The only other furniture was a kitchen chair and an electric fire with fireclay elements which should have been in the Science Museum. The floorboards were uncovered except for a thin mat beside the settee.

Another door at the far end of the little room was locked but there was a key in the lock. Wycliffe opened the door and found himself in a small, tiled hall with a passage leading off, presumably to the kitchen area. There was also a glass-panelled door to the outside. The key of this door too was in the lock and it opened into the alleyway between the house and the ruins.

Wycliffe stepped out into the alleyway. It was not raining but wind still whistled and roared around the building. A little to his right was the window of the passage room from which he had just come, the room where Roger had spent most of his nights recently. On the night that Bridget Kemp disappeared, her car must have stood outside that window for more than an hour. Above his head were two more windows, not far apart, one belonging to Isobel's room, the other to Crispin's. It was from one of those that Crispin claimed to have seen the car being driven away – by, as he said, a woman.

As Wycliffe returned to the library he was again troubled by the posture of the dead man, so reminiscent of how he had seen the man alive a couple of days earlier. Of course it was just possible that he had shot himself or even been shot while in that position, but Wycliffe was uneasy. He went closer, and now, with the lights on, he noticed something which had escaped him before; the top sheet of a little pile of manuscript on the table carried two spots of blood but they meant nothing to him at the time.

He was interrupted by the ringing of the doorbell and went to answer it himself.

Odd. A few days earlier Kellycoryk had been inaccessible, an intriguingly mysterious house and a
family on the fringe of history which he could only
read about. Now, here he was, on the inside, only to
discover that the house was no more than a shell
inhabited by the sad remnants of a family that had lost
its way.

Lucy Lane and WPC Rees were waiting on the
doorstep. There was a message to telephone Franks
at his office, so he left the newcomers in the hall while
he went outside to his car phone.

Franks said, 'Kersey told me that Kemp has shot
himself.'

'That is what I want to be sure of.'

'It must go a long way towards solving your
problems, Charles. Surely, you don't want me?'

'I'm afraid I do.'

They needed a room in the house which they could
use as a base. No point in involving Agnes, so Wycliffe
tried the door across the hall from the library. The
room was large, and still impressive, but entirely
devoid of furniture. He tried the room behind, and
fared better; it was the dining room, still with its
gate-table and a set of chairs, but little else. A bloom
of mould dulled every polished surface. It was there
that he briefed his troops, including Kersey who had
just joined them.

Wycliffe began with a review of the situation
as he now saw it and went on, 'We must officially
notify Roger's brother, Francis, and his cousin Clare
Jordan. Perhaps you will see to that right away,
Lucy. Later we shall want statements from all concerned. Clare Jordan and Kemp himself were at the
nick until three in the afternoon yesterday when
they were released without charge pending further
inquiries. So watch your step in dealing with the

Jordan woman or we may be tripped up by lawyers.

'Leave Agnes until I've had a chat with her. Reports and queries to Mr Kersey.'

He found Agnes alone in the kitchen, sitting at the big table, a teapot, a carton of milk and a mug in front of her, but there was a strong smell of spirits and her cheeks were lightly flushed. Not surprising in the circumstances but the bottle was hidden. He offered sympathy. 'I'll trouble you as little as possible.'

She looked at him without speaking. How old was Agnes? As far as he could remember she must be still short of fifty, yet in her appearance and attitudes she could have passed for the middle sixties.

'Has Dr Harvey left?'

'He had surgery and I told him there was no point in him hanging around here.'

'How about Isobel and Crispin?'

A slight shrug. 'They're probably up in their rooms. They never tell me where they're going.'

'Are they very upset?'

She grimaced. 'How would I know? There's no way of telling. Nobody says what they mean in this house, let alone what they feel. It's probably hit Crispy, but I wouldn't like to say about his sister.'

It sounded reasonable yet there was something which made him wary.

Agnes said, 'Do you want a cup of tea? It's not long made.'

He pulled out a chair and sat down. 'Thank you. I'd like one.'

She fetched a mug from a cupboard. 'Help yourself.' Her movements were listless, jerky and uncertain.

'Do you feel up to telling me exactly what happened this morning?'

She told her story and it squared with the account

he had had from Harvey. 'Just one point, was the cat in the library when Crispin broke in?'

She paused briefly, 'No, he wasn't. I've never thought of it until now . . . Odd that; always where you found Roger, you found the cat. And I haven't seen him since, either.'

Wycliffe said, 'Strange creatures!' and changed the subject. 'When did you last see your brother?'

'Last night when we had our meal – if you can call it that.'

'Did he mention what had happened at the police station?'

'Not a word.'

'And after the meal?'

'He went back to his books as usual. He said he was expecting a visitor.'

'Did he tell you who he was expecting?'

'No, but there was somebody. I happened to be outside the library at about ten and I heard him talking. I didn't hear whoever was with him.'

So Agnes had been eavesdropping, or trying to.

'Have you any idea who it was?'

'No idea.'

Didn't know or wouldn't say?

'And at no time during the evening or night did you hear a shot or a noise which could have been one?'

'No, but that's not surprising, there was enough noise from the wind. I thought the roof might come off.' She sipped her tea, watching him over the rim of her cup, and when she spoke again it was in a different, reminiscent vein. She said, 'A fortnight a year.'

He waited, and she went on, 'A fortnight a year was all the holiday I ever had from this place. I used to go to Torquay to stay with a girl I went to school with.' She put her cup down before continuing. 'Mavis Tate. She emigrated to Australia a couple of years back, so now I never leave this place.'

He sensed that she needed no prompting, that he would get more by listening. Agnes probably suffered from having no-one who would listen.

'And my fortnight away, five years ago, was what started it all. If I hadn't gone away . . . ' She made a movement of impatience. 'They were like children! Not safe to be left on their own.'

'You are speaking of your brother and his first wife?'

She did not bother to answer that. 'I mean, they should never have married. Julia's temper was liable to flare up without warning, and Roger exasperated her . . . God knows he would exasperate a saint.'

'They quarrelled a lot?'

She finished her tea and patted her lips with a grubby handkerchief. 'No, it didn't happen often, but when it did she could become hysterical . . . Violent sometimes. Roger had no idea of how to cope with her and that was when they needed me.' She stopped speaking for a moment or two before adding: 'And that last time . . . Well, I wasn't there.'

Wycliffe still did not speak; he felt sure that there was more to come.

Agnes raised her eyes to meet his. 'But whatever your post-mortem shows I don't believe that he killed her.'

Wycliffe allowed the silence to develop before breaking it with a remark that sounded almost casual. 'You've known all along that the boating accident was a fable.'

She did not answer at once, then, 'I suspected something but I didn't know the truth.' She made a gesture of impatience. 'I didn't want to know!'

'You had no idea that her body was concealed in Mayne's Closet?'

'No, I did not. That was a shock.'

Wycliffe handed her a print of one of Fox's photographs, taken in Mayne's Closet before the chest was disturbed. It showed the statue of the Virgin and the brass candlesticks with their candles in place. The inscription on the slate top was clearly readable.

Agnes studied the photograph. 'I can understand this; it doesn't really surprise me. It was as near as he could get to giving her a Christian burial.'

'You see that the date of her death is given as the thirteenth – the day before the supposed boating accident?'

She nodded. 'Yes. That doesn't surprise me either. Julia obviously died on the thirteenth and Roger could never have brought himself to lie to the Virgin.'

The way in which she said this was almost contemptuous.

For a little longer they sat in silence while the wind roared around the house. In the end it was again Wycliffe who spoke first. 'Your brother went to incredible lengths to cover up the way in which his first wife died.'

Agnes gave a small shrug. 'That was Roger; he could never face reality.'

'And his sescond wife? Do you think he might have tried something similar there?'

Agnes made an irritable movement. 'That is nonsense! What could he have done? In any case I've told you all I know about that, and Roger is dead.'

'I gather that relations between your brother and his second wife were quite different from those he had had with his first.'

She made an emphatic gesture. 'There was no comparison! He married that woman only because he thought she would help him to keep this place.' Agnes glanced around the barn-like kitchen and her expression was derisive.

Wycliffe persisted. 'Are you satisfied that your brother took his own life?'

She looked up sharply, then began fiddling with the frayed edge of the tablecloth. 'Who on earth do you think would want to kill him?' She stood up and reached across the table for his mug, dismissive. 'Anyway, you're the policeman.'

It was five minutes to eleven by the kitchen clock but to Wycliffe it seemed an age since he had made coffee on a Gaz stove in the cottage.

When Wycliffe left the kitchen he found Isobel waiting for him in the passage. She said, 'They've got Crispin in there now; I must talk to you before it's my turn.' Her manner was tense and urgent.

He followed her to the front hall and to a door beneath the stairs which looked like the door of a cupboard but actually opened into a little room where there was a window high in the wall. In the dimly lit hall he had not seen her clearly but here, where the light was better, he saw the dark-ringed eyes, the pale, drawn features, and was touched.

The room was furnished with a table and several kitchen chairs, one upside down on the other; books, looking like discards from a second-hand shop, were piled on the floor around the walls. And everywhere there was dust.

Isobel placed a couple of chairs and waited for him to sit down before launching into what she had to say. She looked straight into his eyes, holding his gaze. 'You won't understand, but I want you to know that I hate this place; I've grown up hating it, and the way we live . . . Our lives have always been dominated by Father's obsession. We are not like other people – we can't *mix*!'

Wycliffe said, 'But surely, you're of age, you've got a job, you could have broken away.'

She made an expressive little gesture of frustration. 'Don't you think I've thought of that? But wherever

209

I've been, wherever I go, I'm always "the Kemp girl". I stand out; I don't know how to behave!'

There was more of the same and though she spoke with vigour she paused now and then to choose her words. It was as if she were being driven to a commitment that she was scared of making.

Wycliffe sat motionless, wearing that cow-like expression which exasperated his wife but had served him well in the job.

Isobel relaxed and her manner became more reflective. 'Of course Crispy has always been different, he's never felt as I do.'

A long pause, then, 'While Mother was alive it was bearable, but when she died . . . I missed her desperately and, I know it sounds absurd, I also felt let down by her death – like a victim. And I suppose I became spiteful, I wanted somebody to blame and, of course, Father was the obvious one. He seemed to have been the cause of it all . . .'

Another long pause before she went on, 'But I never really believed the things I hinted about him.' There were tears in her eyes and in her voice; she turned away to hide her emotion.

Wycliffe waited, but no more came and in the end he said, 'I don't think you've told me all that you intended to say.'

She raised her eyes to meet his and spoke with a certain doggedness. 'I just want you to know that Father isn't – wasn't – a bad man. His trouble was that he could never face up to things. He dreaded change, or anything that forced him to look outside this place. He was like an ostrich . . . He couldn't face losing Kellycoryk and he couldn't face the changes that might have made it possible to keep it.'

She brought her pale hands together on the table top and stared down at them. 'Things that have happened recently have made me understand him better. I think I can understand now why he did what he did about Mother. He just couldn't face the suspicion, the questions, the meddling in his life that he would have had to put up with if they knew Mother had died in the middle of one of their quarrels.'

There was a break in her voice as she added, 'So, in a sort of charade, he hid her body, then made a little shrine out of the hiding place.' One might have thought she was speaking about the capricious behaviour of a child.

Wycliffe gave her time then, very quietly, he said, 'So you have never really believed that your father was responsible for the deaths of either your mother or your stepmother?'

Her response was emphatic and immediate. 'No!'

'And did he take his own life?'

She straightened up, facing him, worried, her manner less assured. She shook her head. 'All I can say is, I don't think so; I can't believe that he did. But who . . . ?' Her voice let her down.

Wycliffe was gentle. 'Thank you for talking to me. I'm afraid you will still be asked to make a statement about the events of last night but perhaps you will clear up one or two points for me now.'

She waited like a well-behaved schoolgirl.

'Apart from the noise of the storm, you heard nothing unusual in the night?'

'Nothing.'

'Nothing that might have been a shot?'

'No.'

'And what was the first thing you saw or heard this morning about what had happened?'

She stopped to think. 'I was on my way to the bathroom; Agnes was down in the hall and she called up something about trying to get Father in to breakfast. I didn't take much notice.'

'And after that?'

'When I came downstairs Agnes had decided there was something wrong and Crispy had broken a pane of glass in one of the library windows to get in.' She spoke with a curious detachment which puzzled him.

Crispin was being interviewed in the dining room by Kersey and Lanyon. Hollow-eyed and tense but lucid, he gave his account of the finding of his father's body, of breaking into the library, and of fetching Dr Harvey. He spoke slowly, with occasional breaks, but remained coherent and concise.

Kersey said, 'When you broke into the library the main door and the door from the passage room into the back hall were both locked. Is that correct?'

'Yes.'

'Were the keys in the locks?'

'Yes.'

'So, in your opinion, your father locked himself in the library and shot himself – is that what you think?'

'It seems that he must have done.'

'You are prepared to accept that as what actually happened?'

'Yes.'

'In your earlier evidence you said that you thought it was a woman who drove your stepmother's car away from Kellycoryk on the night she was killed. Do you still hold to that?'

'No, it was my father. I saw him.'

'You lied in order to protect him?'

The boy hesitated. 'I suppose so.'

Kersey said, 'You've hurt your hand.'

Crispin looked down at his bandaged hand. 'Yes. I cut it against the broken glass in trying to reach the window catch.'

Chapter Eleven

Friday late morning (continued)

Wycliffe let himself out of the house by the back door into the aftermath of the storm. The wind still blew but it was losing heart and there were even intervals of calm. Overhead the sky was still threatening but the rain had stopped. All that remained to mark the passage of the storm were battered shrubs, a few branches torn from the trees, and the swollen stream.

With no specific purpose in mind he wanted to renew contact with Chylathva, with Francis, and with Molly. Laughable as it seemed, even to him, he had come to think of that couple as representing some sort of norm, a species of yardstick against which he could measure the events in the big house.

As he walked he brooded on Roger Kemp; according to Miss Scott's little book, he was probably the forty-ninth Kemp to succeed to the tenure of Kellycoryk. A strange man! Wycliffe regretted that he lacked the facility to produce thumbnail character sketches of fellow human beings. He had to make his approach through vague approximations, odd phrases that occurred to him. A strange man . . . A semi-recluse, obsessed by his inheritance and his ancestry . . . A man who, lacking any apparent sense of pride, was burdened with an almost neurotic awareness of responsibility . . . A timid man – No! That wasn't right; no timid man could have done what he had done to cover up the death of his first wife . . . A fearful man – fearful of anything that threatened the continuity of life at Kellycoryk; that was better. But a man possessed of a certain courage . . . Above all, perhaps, a foolish man, who consistently refused to read the writing on the wall; a man ready to use all his energies and ingenuity to hold back the future . . .

A murderer? If Roger Kemp had ended up by killing himself with that little ivory-handled pistol then there could be little doubt that he had murdered his wife.

But Wycliffe shook his head as he walked, in total rejection of the idea.

Scarcely noticing what he was about he had negotiated a number of fresh obstacles in the path, mainly fallen branches, but in a couple of places the bank of the stream and the path itself had been washed away so that he had to pick his way around an expanse of black, glutinous mud.

However, Chylathva, when he reached it, looked the same as ever. There was no car outside, so one of the pair was probably away. But the front door was open as usual. He scraped and scuffed mud from his shoes as best he could and while he was at it Molly appeared, puffy eyed, looking as though she had just woken from sleep. She yawned and stretched without embarrassment. 'I must have dropped off. Francis is out. I haven't seen him since this morning. When he heard about Roger he pushed off.

'A couple of your lot came here looking for him about an hour ago. It's anybody's guess when he turns up now, and in what sort of state he'll be.' She added after a pause, 'I suppose it was him you came to see?'

Wycliffe hardly knew himself but as she moved away from the door he followed her into the living room.

'How did you and Francis hear the news? Who told you?'

'Crispin. It was this morning some time, I'm not sure when. That boy's in a bad way; at the end of his tether. If somebody doesn't take him in hand soon he'll do away with himself.'

Wycliffe sat in a rickety Windsor chair. The heat from a blazing wood fire disposed of any chill from the open door and he felt strangely at peace. The barn-like room with its wainscoted granite walls, open fireplace, sisal mats and basic furniture appealed to him. If the pathos of Francis's nudes disturbed him, there was no need to look that way.

And Molly, warm, loose and unshockable, went with it. Here there were no taboos, no pretences. Or so it seemed. In his present mood he could find it in his heart to envy Francis. But there must be a fly in Francis's ointment somewhere; the one that drove him to drink.

Molly said, 'They think Roger shot himself – is that right?'

'That's what it looked like.'

'You may as well know – he would tell you himself if he was here – Francis went to see Roger last night. Roger asked him to come.'

'What about?'

Molly reached for a packet of cigarettes from the table, lit one and drew on it like an addict. 'His lordship hasn't confided in me.'

Something in her manner convinced him that she was holding back. He said, 'I think you've got some idea. When did he go and when did he come back?'

She looked at him through the veil of cigarette smoke. 'You're pushing it a bit. Shouldn't you ask *him*? Anyway, I'm sure he'd tell you himself. He left about nine and he was back just after eleven. It was too rough to walk down through that bloody jungle so, as it was my night off from the pub, he took the car.'

Wycliffe was in a mood to listen rather than question so he said nothing and Molly was left to fill the silence. After a little while she said, 'He and his brother were a lot closer than you might think, and whatever Roger had to say to him last night, went deep. When he got back it was obvious that he'd had a shock.'

She smoked for a while, reflective; then, 'The Kemps are a funny lot; the three of them, Agnes, Roger and Francis . . . I get the impression that they never had parents like most people, they're more like if they'd been brought up in an institution . . . Anyway, this morning, when he heard that Roger was dead it pushed him over the top.'

'Did he say anything?'

'Not much. When Crispin told him Roger had shot himself, he became angry and shouted at Crispin as though it was the boy's fault, then he said, "This is bloody impossible!" I told him to calm down and he said, "I've got to think about this," and pushed off. I hope that doesn't mean what I think it does.'

Wycliffe, on his feet, wandered over to the famous picture which was almost a mural. As he got closer, so the composition and even the figures were lost in swathes and flurries of colour, like feathers on some exotic bird; the paint was almost structural, laid on with a palette knife – impasto.

For an instant he saw Isobel's pale face, intense and half-fearful. '. . . She was always referring to "Pasto" as she called him. I suppose it was her pet name for the man.'

It made sense; they were both painters and Julia had probably teased him about his lavish use of paint. She was a Gwen John painter.

Molly said, 'That sounds like him now.'

A moment or two later Francis's old banger pulled up outside the window and Francis came in; a leaner, older, grimmer Francis; or so it seemed. Even the Kemp features had become more pronounced. It was not the first time that Wycliffe had seen how stress can age people in a few days, and how those changes can be as promptly reversed when the tension is removed.

'Ah, the top brass!' Francis was worried, the banter was routine. 'I was thinking about coming to see you.' He pulled out a chair and sat astride it, arms resting on the back. He glanced across at Molly who was putting fresh wood on the fire. 'I expect she told you that last evening Roger phoned me – he asked me to come and see him at nine in his library. He said the side door would be unlocked so that I could get in without disturbing the others . . . Of course I went.'

He was staring at Wycliffe with his dark, brooding eyes and he seemed to find difficulty in deciding how to go on. He made a curious gesture with his hands, raising them from the chairback and letting them drop. 'I don't know whether I should be telling you this; I promised Rog I would leave the decision to him but now that he's gone . . .'

Suddenly Wycliffe saw in Francis a reflection of his brother; the same tendency to convoluted and ponderous reasoning, the same irrational hesitations and reservations, the same lack of judgement which had brought Roger to disaster. Now, imposed on all that was the slightly absurd image of Pasto, the secret lover.

He was irritated; he had had enough of the Kemps. When he spoke his manner was incisive, almost brutal. 'You were going to tell me that your brother did not kill his wife but that it was he who drove her car with her body in it to the headland, and that it was he who put her body into the sea . . . is that it?'

Francis looked bemused. 'Yes.'

'In other words it was an attempt at damage limitation of the same sort and of the same level of foolhardiness as the one he carried out five years earlier following the death of his first wife.'

Francis was stung. 'I think you should know that whatever Rog did he did it as much to protect others as himself—'

Wycliffe cut him short. 'But above all to sustain the Kemp myth. I want to make it clear that we have finished with these family charades. I want to know just two things: first, who killed Bridget Kemp, and second, whether your brother killed himself or was murdered? I have my own ideas on both questions but I need evidence, and I intend to get it.'

Molly had paused in the act of tending her fire, seemingly transfixed.

Wycliffe went on, 'If anything your brother told you last night or any other information you may have is relevant, then it is your obvious duty to tell me. And I want that message fully understood by the whole family.'

It took Francis a moment or two to collect his wits. In the end he said, his voice subdued, 'There was nothing. Roger was very careful not to involve anyone else in what he told me.'

Wycliffe stood up. 'Well, I hope that we understand each other better. I have only two more questions: first, did you see anyone other than your brother at Kellycoryk last night?'

'No-one.'

'My other question concerns the cat, Coryk. Was he with your brother as usual last night?'

'He was asleep on Roger's work table where he spends most of his time. Why?'

'Coryk seems to have disappeared.'

Wycliffe left Chylathva feeling anything but pleased

218

with himself; his treatment of Francis had served no tactical purpose and might be counter-productive; it had arisen from a sudden impatience with the whole Kemp ethos, with that entangling web of belief and superstition, convention and intrigue, which had scarred the lives of two generations.

On the spur of the moment he decided to take a break, to go back to the cottage and chance whether there would be any lunch. He found fish and chips from the shop in the village, a glass of lager, tea and sympathy.

It was afternoon, the wind had dropped, it no longer rained, and the sun struggled through thinning clouds. Seen from the library the surface of the lake was strewn with the detritus of the storm, while the wilderness of rhododendron and laurel looked as though a great broom had swept over it.

In the middle distance the roofs of the cottages seemed to stand out more starkly and, beyond the cove, the sea was grey, still troubled, still flecked with white.

Franks spent some time examining the body, dictating telegraphic comments to his secretary. Fox, looking like some giant stick-insect, hovered with his camera so that the pathologist's performance was recorded on film.

When Franks turned to Wycliffe he had dropped his usual bantering manner. 'I don't know what to say, Charles. You obviously have your own ideas about this but I can see nothing to suggest that he didn't shoot himself. What I've found in this preliminary is generally consistent with suicide.'

'Don't you see anything unusual in his posture?'

Franks considered. 'I admit that a seated body often slumps forward when shot as this man was, but that really depends on its posture when the shot was fired.

This is by no means the first case I've seen where the body has slumped backwards.'

Wycliffe's manner was dogged, almost sullen. 'That body was moved immediately after the shooting; I'm convinced of it. It was moved while blood was still trickling from the wound of entry. There are two little channels on his cheek at an angle to each other, one vertical in respect of its present posture, the other would be vertical if the body was in its original position – slumped over the table. If that doesn't convince you, there are two spots of blood on the top manuscript page of that little heap – just where they would have fallen had he slumped forward.'

Franks was unconvinced. 'It's pretty slim, Charles, but even if he was murdered what would be the point of shifting the body?'

Wycliffe had an opinion about that but not one that he was prepared to argue. He wanted to close the discussion. 'When we have the rhodizinate test on Kemp's hand, if it's positive I'll stop arguing.'

Franks held out. 'But even if it's negative it won't prove that he didn't fire the pistol.'

'No, but it will be a start. What about time of death?'

Franks looked at his watch (a confection mounted in gold which must have been capable of most things short of forecasting the weather). 'I'd say he's been dead for at least twelve, and not more than fifteen hours. That puts it between midnight and three in the morning. I may have more for you when I've had him on the table. Or Forensic may find something to cheer you up. Anyway, as far as I'm concerned, shift him when you want to.'

An hour after Franks had taken himself off, Wycliffe was still in the library. He was not short of company: Fox was there with his assistant, and so were the pair from Forensic – a man and a woman in white overalls looking like acolytes performing some arcane ritual. Wycliffe kept returning to the remains of Roger Kemp and his work table as though loath to tear himself away.

The last message of the dead man: 'This is only what I deserved.' Would a man about to shoot himself really write anything so trite and, at the same time, so objective and detached? Even if he did, why choose to do it in those clumsy block capitals dear to the mentally retarded writer of anonymous letters?

Fox had been working on fingerprints.

'Anything?'

Fox was never guilty of rapid response. After deliberation he said, 'The only prints on the pistol are the dead man's.'

'Anything strike you about them?'

Another interval while the appropriate circuits were engaged then, 'There is only one set, somewhat smeared, as would be made by grasping the weapon with intent to fire.'

'*No* other prints?'

'None, sir.'

'Any explanation?'

Fox considered. 'If Kemp shot himself one would expect to find his prints all over the pistol. I mean, how could it be otherwise?'

'So?'

'It's possible that he was shot by someone else and that the cleaned gun was pressed into his hand to take his prints.' Fox added after a pause, 'Not a very intelligent thing to do.'

For once Wycliffe warmed towards Fox. 'No, I agree. But we are not dealing with an experienced or a very intelligent killer.'

At a little after four Roger Kemp left his library for the last time and Wycliffe stood, watching idly, while the two earnest boffins from Forensic looked as though they might go on indefinitely.

He was mentally adrift, in a mood to grasp at straws. What he needed was time to think, at least to indulge in that capricious reverie which he regarded as a substitute for thought.

One of the boffins, the young woman, crouched on the floor, said, 'There's what looks like fairly fresh blood on the carpet here.'

She pointed to a patch perhaps the size of a twopenny piece and to several others that were smaller; they were grouped together, ten or twelve feet away from Roger's desk, in the middle of the room.

'How fresh?'

A mild shrug. 'I'd say it's been here ten to twelve hours.'

'You can type it?'

'Hadn't we better decide whether it's human first? These look like cat hairs on the carpet.'

She was young – twenty-five? Pretty; fair hair caught back in a protective hood; a career woman who had presumably found this esoteric profession to her liking. Was he being chauvinistic because he found that surprising? At any rate she wasn't intimidated by rank.

She had given him an idea and he called her over to the window where the missing pane of glass lay in jagged fragments on the floor. 'I would like you to check both the gap and the fragments of glass on the floor for blood.' He added, 'Human, of course.' And she grinned.

It was at that moment that Kersey joined them. He looked at Wycliffe. 'Something?'

'I think we've been led up the garden. There's no doubt that Roger Kemp was murdered and I'm pretty sure that the break-in this morning was staged.'

'Agnes and the boy?'

'Who else?' His manner changed abruptly. 'How long since you've seen Crispin?'

222

'Not since we questioned him before lunch.'

Without another word Wycliffe turned away and hurried from the room.

The girl looked at Kersey. 'Does he often get like that?'

Wycliffe tried the kitchen but it was empty, the dining room where the interrogations had been held that morning, but there was no-one there. He tried Agnes's room. A knock on the door was unanswered so he pushed it open and went in. The curtains were half-drawn and Agnes was sprawled on the unmade bed, asleep. She woke and looked at him uncomprehending. 'Is something . . . ?'

He snapped at her, 'I'm looking for Crispin.'

She sat up. 'I don't know—'

He dashed back to the hall, up the stairs and along the corridor to Crispin's room. The door was open and the room empty. Barely in his career had he been so near to panic. Isobel opened the door of her room looking scared. 'Has something happened?'

'I'm looking for Crispin.'

'I haven't seen him since—'

'Think! Where does he go when he wants to be on his own?'

The girl was becoming more agitated. 'Why, he goes up to his garden I suppose . . .'

Of course; it was obvious!

A couple of minutes later he was in his car; down the drive, across the bridge and up the steep slope of the cliff road. His car was fitted with a siren which he could not remember having used but he used it now, speeding along the waterfront and through the village. Then up the steep slope out of Porthendel with Kellycoryk woods on his left and the new houses on his right. St Endel Churchtown, the church tower, then a sharp left turn before he pulled up by the old farm gate mounted between the twin ornamental pillars of the northern drive.

How long was it since the evening when he and Helen had looked over that gate, deciding whether or not to trespass?

The lodge windows were shuttered but the door was slightly ajar and he threw it open. Inside the light was dim and it took a moment or two for his eyes to accommodate. It was a sizeable room; the floor consisted of slate slabs. He became aware of tools and what must be compost bins arranged against one of the walls; overall there was a rank smell of soil.

It was seconds later when he spotted Crispin seated on the floor in a far corner of the room, knees drawn up, hands clasped about them.

Wycliffe made an effort to speak calmly. 'I've been looking for you, Crispin.' The boy did not answer and Wycliffe went on, 'Do you think we could have some light?' He fiddled with the shutter of the nearest window and succeeded in releasing it.

Light flooded in. Crispin was seated on a little heap of plastic sacks. On the floor near him Coryk was asleep beside a couple of little earthenware bowls, one of which still held some milk. Also on the floor was an unwound, bloodstained bandage.

Wycliffe walked over to the boy; the cat, disturbed, looked up at him but showed no interest. Crispin's hand was unbandaged and Wycliffe saw small but ugly teeth marks in the fleshy part of the hand below the little finger. There was inflammation.

'You should have that attended to.'

It was as though Crispin's soft brown eyes seemed to become aware of him for the first time. 'He didn't mean to do it; he was very frightened.'

Wycliffe held out a hand, 'Let's get out of here.'

The boy came stiffly to his feet and as he did so a small pruning knife slid off the plastic sacks on to the floor. Wycliffe picked it up; the blade was razor sharp.

'What were you going to do with this?'

Crispin looked vague. 'I don't know.'

'How about Coryk?'

'He'll find his way back.'

In the car going back he asked one question. 'I'm not under arrest?'

Wycliffe said, 'Should you be?'

There was no reply.

Friday early evening

They were seated at the little table in an interview room at the police station. Wycliffe and Lucy Lane sat opposite the boy. Wycliffe had set his chair a little back from the table, nearer the door.

Crispin's hand had been freshly and professionally bandaged. His face seemed drained of whatever colour it had ever possessed but the dark eyes retained their serenity of expression making it impossible to guess at his thoughts.

Lucy Lane started the tape. 'This interview begins at 17.05 . . . You have been advised to have legal assistance but refused . . . Remember that you do not have to say anything but that what you do say will be recorded. You understand?'

'Yes.' The reply was firm but indifferent.

'I am going to ask you about the events of this morning.'

Wycliffe intervened. 'It has been explained to you that DI Kersey and DC Lanyon are interviewing your aunt next door?'

A curt affirmative and Lucy continued: 'At what time did you come downstairs and go into the library?'

'It must have been at about half-past three.'

'Was the door locked?'

'No.'

'Were there lights in the library?'

'Only the little lamp on my father's table. He was sitting there as though he had been working but I think he was asleep. Coryk was curled up amongst the papers as usual.'

'Did you expect to find your father there?'

'No, I thought he would have been asleep in the little side-room.'

'Think carefully before you answer this question: were you carrying a pistol?'

'Yes.'

'With what purpose?'

'To shoot my father.' The statement came in a level voice devoid of any emotion.

'Go on.'

'I walked over to his chair, his eyes were closed but he opened them as I bent over him. It was then that I shot him in the temple – the right temple. He slumped forward on to the table. Coryk was very frightened. He leapt off the table with a sort of howl. I grabbed him to take him to the little side-room until I could deal with him properly but I was still holding the pistol so I suppose I was clumsy, and he bit me.'

Crispin glanced down at his bandaged hand.

Although he had known, broadly, what to expect, Wycliffe still looked at the boy with incredulity. This mild-mannered young man had confessed to murdering his father in simple straightforward terms, not exactly as though it were a matter of no consequence but rather as though it had been the inevitable outcome of what had gone before.

'All right; what happened when Coryk bit you?'

The boy frowned as though in an effort of recollection. 'I think it was then that Agnes came in; she must have heard something.'

'Go on.'

'Well, first she said, "Give me the gun," and I did. Then she went and got a bandage to tie up my hand. After that she looked at Father.'

'And then?'

'She said, "I'll see to this. I'll call you when I want you." '

'So you left her there?'

'Yes.'

Lucy Lane turned to look at Wycliffe, her face expressive of helplessness and disbelief.

Wycliffe took over. 'What did you suppose your aunt was going to do?'

A small lift of the shoulders. 'She was going to try to cover things up like Father did when I shot Bridget and like he did when he killed Mother.'

'Did you want that?'

He looked vague, indifferent. 'It didn't matter; I knew that one day people would find out about me.'

'Does it matter to you now that they have?'

A momentary pause, then, 'I don't think so.'

'About the little pistol – you must have had it in your possession from the time you shot Bridget until you used it on your father. Where did you hide it?'

'In the Northern Garden, under a pile of sacks in the old lodge.'

'Right. Now, coming back to this morning; what happened when your aunt called you?'

For the first time he sounded irritated. 'You know what happened; she had tried to make it look as though Father killed himself and I had to pretend to break in and to cut my hand on the window . . . I'm not going over all that.'

Wycliffe looked at Lucy Lane and Lucy switched off the tape. 'This interview is suspended at 17.53.'

Wycliffe said, 'I think we could do with a break.'

Outside, Lucy Lane said, 'The shrinks are going to have a field day with him.'

Half an hour later they were back in the interview room, the arrangement as before. Lucy Lane performed the required rituals, Crispin, although he had been for refreshment, looked as though he had never moved from his chair.

Lucy Lane opened the questioning. 'Why did you want to kill your father?'

Crispin shifted uncomfortably then, with a deep sigh he said, 'I'd meant to do it for a long time.'

'But why?'

There was silence in the little room so that the traffic in the street below sounded louder and voices reached them from elsewhere in the building. For a long minute Crispin remained motionless, staring stright in front of him, trance-like; and when he spoke he could have been recounting a dream.

'It started the night my mother died . . . I woke up and heard sounds coming from my parents' room. Their door was open and their light was on. I went along the corridor and looked in. Clare was there and she and my father were lifting Mother on to the bed . . . There was nobody else in the house.'

Wycliffe could see in his mind's eye the boy creeping along the bleak unlit passage to peer uncomprehendingly at the scene being enacted in the brightly lit bedroom.

Only when it seemed that Crispin would not continue, he prompted, 'And then?'

The boy's eyes blinked rapidly and he turned to face Wycliffe. 'I went back to my room but I left the door open so that I could hear and look out if I heard anything . . . They were talking, and after a little I saw Clare go to her own room. Then everything was quiet . . .

'I waited a long time and then I decided to see for myself, but the door of my parents' room was shut and though there was a light under the door and I could hear low voices, I couldn't bring myself to go in or to knock . . .'

They gave him time before Lucy Lane asked, 'And in the morning?'

He seemed to be recovering from an experience which had been relived with great intensity, returning to the here and now.

'Clare got breakfast, as she always did when Agnes was away, and I asked her about Mother. She said that Mother had been poorly in the night but that she was all right again.'

'Did you believe that?'

'Yes.'

'And when, that evening, you heard about the boating accident?'

There was no change in the boy's expression but his hands, resting on the table top, shifted uneasily. 'I don't know . . . I suppose I began to wonder . . .'

There was another longish interval during which Crispin seemed about to speak but did not; then he said, 'It was almost two years later when I discovered what he had done in Mayne's Closet . . . Then I knew.'

'You knew what?'

'That he had murdered my mother and that I had almost seen it happen.'

It was some time before the boy added, simply, 'It was then that I decided to kill him.'

Wycliffe spent a good part of that evening alone in the DI's office at the police station, listening to the tapes. At intervals he heard the clocks chiming in the city centre but the passage of time meant little to him. At one point a timid constable brought him a mug of tea and a sandwich from the canteen.

The Crispin Kemp interview had lasted altogether for almost two hours and during that time his aunt had been questioned in another cubicle. Wycliffe juggled with the tapes to bring back passages which seemed to him of special significance.

'I couldn't think how to do it; I mean I had no weapon . . . I kept saying to myself, almost every night, "I'll kill him!" But time went on and I did nothing . . . I think that I might never have done it.'

Wycliffe recalled the sheepish, almost apologetic look which accompanied those words.

'But then he married that woman . . . And I said, "Now, I'll kill them both!" '

A little later in the tape he was explaining, 'I remembered my uncle Francis talking about a pistol that they had played with as children, thinking it was a toy. He said that they had found it in a box in the junk room . . . It was still there, and there was a little box of ammunition . . . I thought it had been kept specially for me.

'I knew nothing about pistols but I cleaned it and tried it out in the woods . . .'

There was extreme weariness in his voice when he added, 'You know the rest.'

Another question; Lucy Lane speaking. 'Why did you drive the car with your stepmother's body in the back to Kellycoryk? What did you expect to happen?'

An interval, then, 'I didn't care what happened but I wanted him to suffer before it was his turn . . . I suppose I thought that if he had known so well what to do with my mother's body—' The voice choked on an excess of bitterness.

Wycliffe sat motionless for some time. It occurred to him that Crispin was apparently unaware of the expert opinion that his mother's death had been accidental; unaware, or dared not accept?

It was after nine and he had not listened to the

230

Agnes Kemp tape. He ran through it as one might skim the pages of a novel. Only one question interested him: 'Did you shift your brother's body?'

'Yes.'

'Why?'

A brief pause then, 'He spent a lot of his time staring at the ceiling; I thought he might feel more at home that way than slumped on the table.'

Wycliffe thought he could detect the sneer behind her words.

Chapter Twelve

Saturday morning 15 May

A troubled night but Wycliffe fell asleep in the small hours and woke with the sun shining through the curtains. He felt confused, vaguely depressed; the morning-after.

With infinite care he extricated himself from the bed. Helen muttered something and turned over but did not wake.

Six-twenty. Ten minutes later, dressed but unwashed and unshaven, he was on the beach. Substantial waves, remnants of the storm, broke along the shore and a broad band of seaweed and marine jetsam marked the highest reaches of the tide. He admitted to himself that he was unreasonably anxious that John Harvey's door should open. And it did.

'Had a bloody night? Anyway, the coffee pot's gurgling nicely so come on in.'

They drank their coffee sitting not far from the open door. Julia's painting of the cove hung as usual on the whitewashed wall at the bottom of the stairs and, for reasons which he could not explain, Wycliffe began to feel more at ease with himself.

After a few exchanges he said, 'I suppose you are more or less up to date?'

Harvey nodded. 'Isobel was here last night.' He added after a pause, 'She's a strange girl and she was in a strange mood.'

But Wycliffe was preoccupied with the boy. 'We had two sessions with him yesterday evening and it was almost eight when we finished. He said he wanted to "get it over". He doesn't seem to realize that for him it's scarcely begun.'

There was an interval while they sipped their coffee and watched the waves breaking, then Wycliffe, with a total disregard for the rules, launched on a succinct summary of the tapes. It was an unloading, a catharsis. And he rounded it off. 'After nearly two hours of that I was asking myself – I am still asking myself – whether I listened to a young killer or the victim of a warped upbringing. Thank God it's no part of my job to decide.'

Harvey reached for the coffee pot and refilled their mugs. When they were settled again he said, 'After qualifying I did a year in psychiatry. It was more like a theological college, plenty of doctrine and not much substance. My guess is that when Crispin's case comes to court there will be no difficulty in finding experts to contradict each other all along the line.

'Not that it will make much difference; faced with a lad like Crispin, and the choice between prison and a secure hospital, the court will play safe and send him to the hospital.'

Harvey yawned. 'Our little Crispy will become a case for treatment. And it will all be played over again with a different cast when there's talk of letting him out.'

Wycliffe, feeling to some extent reassured, though guilty because he had used Harvey as a confidant, was anxious to change the subject. 'What do you think will happen at Kellycoryk?'

Harvey sat back in his chair. 'Yesterday I would have guessed that things might go on much the same for a while, until the place began to actually fall down.'

'But you've changed your mind?'

'As I told you, Isobel was here last night. She was uptight. It was obvious that she was distressed by all that had happened but there was more to it than that and in the end it came out. Agnes had been talking; with what motive, I don't know, but she pointed out to the girl that as her father had died intestate she and Crispin would inherit, but that almost certainly, Crispin would be debarred.'

Wycliffe said, 'Isobel, the new mistress of Kellycoryk.'

'Exactly, but I'm quite sure the idea had never entered her head until Agnes put it there.'

'How did she react?'

'She was very restrained but it was obvious that mixed in with her distress there was a sense of excitement, almost of elation, which she was doing her best to conceal.'

Harvey looked at him with a quirkish smile. 'An odd turn-up for the book, don't you think?'

Wycliffe was thinking that if Beasley, the lawyer, was right, the whole truth might prove to be even odder.

The lawyer had said, 'You are asking about Bridget's will. Unfortunately there is no will . . .'

'So who inherits?'

'As I see it the beneficiaries can only be Roger Kemp and his children.'

'But the children are not hers, they are his by a former marriage.'

'That doesn't affect the position . . .'

But these thoughts Wycliffe kept to himself. He had other things than the future of Kellycoryk to occupy his mind. The investigation would begin to wind down but the paperwork would increase.

When he arrived back at the cottage Helen was already downstairs. 'Can you manage another coffee?'

Over the ensuing months, involved sporadically, Wycliffe watched the case pursuing its tortuous path through the legal jungle. The papers did their best with stories that owed something to *The Fall of the House of Usher* and more to Agatha Christie. There was no indication that anybody at Kellycoryk had broken ranks to help them. In the end Harvey proved right, it was decided that Crispin was a case for treatment.

It was more than two years after their stay in the cove that Helen read him a couple of paragraphs from the *Western Gazette*:

'Coast and Country, the leisure company responsible for several major projects in recent years, has put forward plans for the development of Kellycoryk in Veryan Bay. The proposals include an hotel, a competition golf course, provision for fly-fishing in well-stocked waters, and facilities for water sports.

'Miss Isobel Kemp, chief executive of the company, and present owner of Kellycoryk, told our reporter that everything would be done to preserve the unique natural attractions of the area. At the same time the project would provide much-needed employment for local people.

'It may be recalled that two years ago Kellycoryk was tragically in the news in connection with the murders of Miss Kemp's father and step-mother.'

Wycliffe had in his mind a vivid picture of Isobel, staring straight into his eyes, holding his gaze. 'I want you to know that I hate this place; I've grown up hating it, and the way we

235

live . . . Our lives have been dominated by Father's obsession. We are not like other people – we can't mix.'

Times had changed.

THE END

WYCLIFFE AND THE THREE-TOED PUSSY

The peace of the village of Kergwyns has been shattered by a bizarre murder. A young woman has been shot. The only things taken from the scene are the shoe and stocking from her left leg . . . exposing her deformed foot.

Wycliffe uncovers evidence of an unhappy woman who routinely manipulated the men in her life. As half the men in the village have been known to visit her, and most have reason to lie about it, finding the murderer will not be easy.

Wycliffe's task is complicated by the discovery of some clues in the form of crossword puzzles left by the victim herself. If Pussy knew she was going to die why did she make no effort to save herself?

WYCLIFFE AND HOW TO KILL A CAT

The woman was young and slim, with auburn hair arranged on her pillow. When Superintendent Wycliffe saw her, he could almost believe she was asleep – that is, until he looked at her face. Although she had been killed by strangulation, someone had mutilated her face after she was dead.

As Wycliffe investigates, he finds more questions than answers. Why did a girl with expensive clothing and make-up end up in such a seedy hotel down by the docks? Why was there a thousand pounds hidden near her, beneath a pile of clothing? And why was someone apparently trying to hide her identity?

The more Wycliffe digs, the more he finds there are too many suspects, too many motives – and too many lies . . .

WYCLIFFE AND THE GUILT EDGED ALIBI

A river divides the little West Country town of Treen into East and West, with a ferry linking the two. But it isn't just the river which divides the community when a body is discovered by the ferryman . . .

Beautiful Carline Bryce came from the top of the social scale, so when her body is discovered the rumour mill goes into overdrive. Who would want to kill her? Was it a family feud or a lovers' quarrel? A long-hidden resentment or a moment of rage?

As Superintendent Wycliffe picks his way through the clues, he is soon on the trail of a psychotic killer . . . who will not hesitate to strike again.

WYCLIFFE AND DEATH IN A SALUBRIOUS PLACE

There was no doubt at all that the girl was dead. The front of her skull and her facial bones had been splintered like the cracked shell of an egg. What made it even more shocking was the setting of the murder – an idyllic corner of the Scilly Isles where violent crime was almost unknown.

Angry and distressed, the villagers instinctively turn against the only stranger in their midst, the famous pop star and teenage idol Vince Peters.

But Superintendent Wycliffe is not so sure. Slowly, methodically, he begins to dig beneath the calm surface of the community – and soon uncovers a violent undercurrent of fear and guilt . . .

WYCLIFFE AND DEATH IN STANLEY STREET

In a sprawling West Country port lies the insalubrious Stanley Steet, a dubious cul-de-sac just off the busy main road. And when a prostitute is found naked and strangled in her bed there, Chief Superintendent Wycliffe is called in to investigate.

But things aren't quite as straightforward as they seem. The victim, Lily Painter, is the kind of girl who likes Beethoven and has plenty of qualifications to her name – not the usual sort of prostitute at all.

The more Wycliffe investigates, the more surprises he uncovers. But it takes a dangerous arson attack and a second murder before the solution to this complex and fast-moving puzzle can be found.

WYCLIFFE AND THE PEA-GREEN BOAT

When Cedric Tremain is charged with murdering his father by booby-trapping his fishing boat, all the locals are agreed that he is an unlikely murderer. But the case against him is strong; he has the motive, the opportunity and the know-how; not to mention the fact that there is some hard circumstantial evidence against him. So Cedric is arrested.

But Chief Superintendent Wycliffe has a strong sense that something about the case just doesn't fit. As he quietly continues his investigations a confusing picture emerges. Twenty years ago Cedric's cousin was convicted of strangling his girlfriend and served fourteen years of a commuted death sentence.

As the wheels of justice begin to grind, Wycliffe searches for a link between past and present . . .

WYCLIFFE AND THE SCHOOL BULLIES

Two very different young women have been murdered within the same week. One was a singer in a nightclub, the other was a nurse, but both were strangled in their own homes in strangely efficient attacks that appear to be remarkably similar. The press are quick to assume there is a psychopath on the loose but Detective Chief Superintendent Wycliffe suspects the truth may be somewhat more complex than that . . .

When another attack is aborted halfway through for no apparent reason, Wycliffe becomes certain that this is no random spate of murders. But with his superiors and the media uninterested in his theories Wycliffe knows he will have to work alone to find the killer. as he searches for a link between the victims his investigations take him back in time – to a school trip, an isolated hotel and a cruel joke on a lonely student.

available from
THE ORION PUBLISHING GROUP

☐ **Wycliffe and Death in Stanley Street**
£5.99 W.J. Burley
9780752849690

☐ **Wycliffe and the Beales**
£5.99 W.J. Burley
9780752858722

☐ **Wycliffe and the Cycle of Death**
£5.99 W.J. Burley
9780752844459

☐ **Wycliffe and the Dead Flautist**
£5.99 W.J. Burley
9780752864907

☐ **Wycliffe and Death in a Salubrious Place**
£5.99 W.J. Burley
9780752865355

☐ **Wycliffe and the Dunes Mystery**
£5.99 W.J. Burley
9780752881850

☐ **Wycliffe and the Four Jacks**
£5.99 W.J. Burley
9780752849706

☐ **Wycliffe and the Guild of Nine**
£5.99 W.J. Burley
9780752843841

☐ **Wycliffe and the Guilt Edged Alibi**
£5.99 W.J. Burley
9780752880839

☐ **Wycliffe and the House of Fear**
£5.99 W.J. Burley
9780752881447

☐ **Wycliffe and How to Kill a Cat**
£5.99 W.J. Burley
9780752880822

☐ **Wycliffe and the Pea-Green Boat**
£5.99 W.J. Burley
9780752881867

☐ **Wycliffe and the Quiet Virgin**
£5.99 W.J. Burley
9780752849331

☐ **Wycliffe and the Redhead**
£5.99 W.J. Burley
9780752881430

☐ **Wycliffe and the Scapegoat**
£5.99 W.J. Burley
9780752849713

☐ **Wycliffe and the School Bullies**
£5.99 W.J. Burley
9780752880853

☐ **Wycliffe and the Tangled Web**
£5.99 W.J. Burley
9780752844466

☐ **Wycliffe and the Three-Toed Pussy**
£5.99 W.J. Burley
9780752880846

☐ **Wycliffe and the Winsor Blue**
£5.99 W.J. Burley
9780752858739

☐ **Wycliffe and the Last Rites**
£5.99 W.J. Burley
9780752849317

☐ **Wycliffe in Paul's Court**
£5.99 W.J. Burley
9780752849324

☐ **Wycliffe's Wild Goose Chase**
£5.99 W.J. Burley
9780752864914

All Orion/Phoenix titles are available at your local bookshop or from the following address:

Mail Order Department
Littlehampton Book Services
FREEPOST BR535
Worthing, West Sussex, BN13 3BR
telephone 01903 828503, *facsimile* 01903 828802
e-mail MailOrders@lbsltd.co.uk
(Please ensure that you include full postal address details)

Payment can be made either by credit/debit card (Visa, Mastercard, Access and Switch accepted) or by sending a £ Sterling cheque or postal order made payable to *Littlehampton Book Services*.
DO NOT SEND CASH OR CURRENCY.

Please add the following to cover postage and packing

UK and BFPO:
£1.50 for the first book, and 50p for each additional book to a maximum of £3.50

Overseas and Eire:
£2.50 for the first book plus £1.00 for the second book and 50p for each additional book ordered

---

BLOCK CAPITALS PLEASE

name of cardholder ....

address of cardholder ....

....

....

....

postcode ....

delivery address
(if different from cardholder)

....

....

....

....

postcode ....

☐ I enclose my remittance for £.................................

☐ please debit my Mastercard/Visa/Access/Switch (delete as appropriate)

card number ☐☐☐☐☐☐☐☐☐☐☐☐☐☐☐☐☐☐

expiry date ☐☐☐☐   Switch issue no. ☐☐

signature ....

prices and availability are subject to change without notice